e

Kate Thompson is an award-winning journalist, ghost-writer and novelist who has spent the last two decades in the UK mass market and book publishing industry. Over the past nine years Kate has written eleven fiction and non-fiction titles, three of which have made the *Sunday Times* top ten bestseller list. *The Little Wartime Library* is her twelfth book.

THE LITTLE WARTIME LIBRARY

KATE THOMPSON

HODDER &
STOUGHTON

First published in Great Britain in 2022 by Hodder & Stoughton
An Hachette UK company

1

A CIP catalogue record for this title is available from the British Library

Hardback ISBN 978 1 529 34871 2
Trade Paperback ISBN 978 1 529 39540 2
eBook ISBN 978 1 529 34872 9

Typeset in Plantin Light by Palimpsest Book Production Limited,
Falkirk, Stirlingshire

Printed and bound in Great Britain by Clays Ltd, Elcograf S.p.A.

Hodder & Stoughton policy is to use papers that are natural, renewable
and recyclable products and made from wood grown in sustainable
forests. The logging and manufacturing processes are expected to
conform to the environmental regulations of the country of origin.

For the East End friends who have passed on.
The splashes of sunshine in the shade.
Trish. Minksy. Dot. Jessie. Ann.

Thank you to all library workers, past and present,
whom I spent many an illuminating hour chatting with.
Not just bibliophiles, but people-lovers too.

And finally, my very own book club girls,
who transformed 2020 xx

'*Quantities of cheap fiction will be required. The soldier will carry a book in his kitbag; the civilian will keep books for his fireside. We are a nation of readers, and the war is only going to increase the demand for books.*'

Frederick J. Cowles, Chief Librarian of Swinton and Pendlebury Library Service.

PROLOGUE

7 September 2020

An old woman walks up the westbound platform of Bethnal Green Underground Station, moving painfully slowly on account of her arthritis.

'Mum, can we go?' asks her eldest daughter Miranda, trying to hide her irritation. She has an Ocado delivery due later and she's dying for a coffee. 'We shouldn't be on public transport, not in the middle of a pandemic.'

'Tsk.' Her mother waves her walking stick dismissively. 'You go if you like, but I'm not leaving.'

Miranda glances over at her younger sister Rosemary and rolls her eyes. God their mother could be tricky. 'All piss and vinegar,' as her ex-husband once memorably described her.

'At the very least Mum, pull your mask up over your nose,' Rosemary orders. But the older lady ignores them both, moving with a tortoise-like determination.

They reach the end of the platform and all pause, staring into the gaping black mouth of the tunnel.

'We clean our transport network regularly with antiviral disinfectant,' mutters the old lady, reading out loud from a poster pasted to the tunnel wall. 'That's nothing new. They did this nightly during the war.'

'You came here in the war?' asks Miranda, thoughts of her latte fast fading.

'We lived down here.' Their mother smiles, her face slightly crooked since the stroke. 'Your auntie Marie even took tap-dancing classes down here.'

Miranda presses her lips together, worried.

'You're getting confused, Mum. People only slept down here during the Blitz.'

'I might have snow on the roof, but I've still got all my marbles!' the old lady barks, her voice stiletto sharp. She loves her daughters desperately, but she wishes they didn't keep on doing this, fussing over her, checking her constantly for signs of senility.

She closes her eyes. Intrusive thoughts march through her brain like a brass band. *Heat. Blood. Smoke.*

Memories she had bolted down, assumed had turned to rust, only to resurface, sharp and slippery enough to get through the cracks. She stumbles, her stick clattering loudly up the platform. A few commuters glance up in alarm, then return like lemmings to their phones.

'Sit down, Mum.' Rosemary rushes forward, guides her to a bench under the Bethnal Green Underground sign. 'We need to get you home.'

'No!' she snaps. 'Not until we've found the library.'

She catches her daughters exchanging glances over their masks.

'Mum,' says Rosemary slowly, pointing upwards. 'The library's above ground, we're in the Tube, remember?'

'Technically it's not even a library at the moment,' says Miranda. 'It's a COVID-19 testing centre. I saw on the way down.'

A Central Line train comes rushing in with a hot exhale of air. Her brain is tired, her thoughts slow and muddy. What do they mean it's a testing centre, not a library? She doesn't understand this world anymore.

'Mrs Rodinski?'

Two men in TFL high-vis jackets, their faces covered with shining plastic, walk towards them.

'Yes, that's me.'

'I'm Peter Mayhew, the press officer, and this is Grant Marshall, station manager. Thanks for getting in touch.'

'Thank you, young man, for agreeing to return my belongings. They're very precious to me.'

'I can imagine,' says the press officer, sensing a good publicity angle.

'How old are you, Mrs Rodinski?' asks the station manager. 'If that's not too forward.'

'Not at all. I'm eighty-eight. I spent most of my formative years down this tunnel.'

'Gracious, you're holding up well,' he chuckles.

'I'm a woman, not a piece of scaffolding, sonny. Now, do you have my letters?'

'Mum, what's all this about?' Rosemary asks, but her mother isn't listening, for the press officer has lifted a bundle of letters and is handing them to her in a sealed plastic bag.

'We found them during the recent renovation, behind the tiles in this tunnel, tucked inside a book, in some sort of boxed-out unit.'

She nods. 'That was the back of the library.'

Her hands tremble slightly as she removes them from the bag and takes the letters bound in cream ribbon, raising them to her nose.

'They still smell of the library.'

'It would be wonderful if you would agree to be interviewed by the BBC about the return of your wartime letters.'

'Of course, but if you don't mind, I should like a quiet word with my daughters first.'

'Certainly, come and see me before you go.'

They leave and the old lady turns to a bemused Rosemary and Miranda.

'These' – she says, holding up her bundle of letters – 'are why we're here. I thought I'd lost them forever.'

Smell is evocative, the scent of old mildewy paper has opened up the pathways of her mind and memories crowd in. She hears the shriek of children's laughter rushing through the tunnels. The soft rustle of pages turning. *Thunk.* A metal fist stamping a library book. The creak of a book cart. She catches the scent of carbolic, the twentieth century equivalent of hand sanitiser. These are the smells of her personal history.

But deep down, deeper even than these tunnels, hide the *other* memories. One thought drums persistently: what if this virus gets her? Sometimes she feels it's not even a case of *if* but *when*. If she dies without telling her daughters the truth, then her story will end with her, and surely that would be a betrayal far more devastating than the secrets she has kept? What was it Clara told her?

You die twice. Once when your heart stops beating and again when your name is spoken for the last time.

It's time to blow the dust off her wartime secrets.

'I've been a coward not to tell you the whole truth,' she admits quietly, lowering her mask. 'I'm going to tell you everything. Let's start in the library.'

I

3 March 1944
Clara

I always felt that librarians should try to be encouraging, not judgemental, about reading. What you want to do is give people a great experience. Who are you to judge what that experience is?
Alison Wheeler, MBE. Former Chief Executive of Suffolk Libraries, library campaigner and a trustee of CILIP

'Is crying allowed in the library?'

'Heavens above! Where did you spring from?' Clara blinked back her tears. 'I thought I'd locked the door!'

It wasn't exactly seemly for a librarian to be seen blubbing, red-eyed and snotty over her returns trolley.

Clara peered over the counter. A small face peeked back behind a long fringe.

'Sorry sweetheart, shall we start again? I'm Clara Button, I'm the branch librarian.'

''Lo. I'm Marie.' The girl blew upwards and her fringe parted to reveal curious brown eyes.

'Want a boiled sweet, Marie?'

'Are sweets allowed?'

'I have a secret stash of sherbet lemons.' She winked. 'For emergencies.'

The eyes widened.

'I knew it, your favourite.'

Marie's hand shot out to take the sweet and crammed it in her mouth.

'How do you know?'

'I know everyone's favourite.'

'Bet you don't know my favourite book.'

'Bet I do! Now let me see. How old are you?'

She pressed eight fingers close to Clara's face.

'Eight, what a grand age to be!'

Clara walked to the children's section of the library and scuttled her fingers along the shelves like a spider. The girl grinned, amused by the game.

Her finger stopped at *Black Beauty* – too sad – then travelled on to *Cinderella* – too pink – before slowly coming to rest on *The Wind in the Willows*.

'Am I right?'

She nodded. 'I love the toad best.' Marie's eyes ran greedily over Clara's carefully stocked library.

'It's like Aladdin's cave in here.'

Clara felt a thunderclap of pride. It had taken her nearly three years to get her library as well stocked as this after the bombing.

'Can I borrow it? I had to leave my copy behind.'

'Are you an evacuee?'

Marie nodded. 'We left my dad in Jersey.'

'I'm sorry to hear that. Bet you miss him.'

She nodded and twisted her snot-encrusted sleeve over her fingers.

'My sister says I'm not to talk about it. Can I join then?'

'I'm sure we can get you enrolled,' Clara replied. 'If you can get your mum to come and see me and fill in the form. I only need to see her bunk ticket.'

'She can't come, my sister says to say she's very busy with war work.'

'Oh, righto, well maybe your sister could spare five minutes.'

'So why was you crying?' Marie mumbled, moving the sherbet lemon to the other side of her mouth, her cheek bulging like a hamster's.

'Because I was sad.'

'Why?'

'Because I miss someone special, well, three people actually.'

'Me too. I miss my dad . . . Can you keep a secret?' Her dew-bright eyes drew even wider. Perhaps it was the sweet that had softened her tongue, or the promise of *The Wind in the Willows*, but Clara felt this little girl desperately needed a confidante.

'Cross my heart,' she promised, licking her finger. 'Librarians are excellent at keeping secrets.'

'My m—'

'Marie Rose Kolsky!' interrupted a sharp little voice from the door. 'What do you think you're doing in here!'

Clara instinctively sized up the girl in the doorway, taking in the pale, serious face.

'I'm so sorry, miss, my sister oughtn't be in here bothering you. I told her to meet by our bunk.'

'I came to the bedtime story session,' Marie protested.

'Don't be such a silly goose Marie, they're shut.'

'Oh, no,' interrupted Clara, feeling the need to defend the little girl. 'Your sister's quite right. Every evening, we have a bedtime story session in the library at six p.m., only I've had to cancel it this evening on account of a function. But do come back tomorrow.'

'P'rhaps. Come on, Marie.'

She pulled her little sister's arm and wrenched her in the direction of the door.

'*N'en soûffl'ye un mot.*' Clara didn't speak French, but it was obvious Marie was getting a good ticking off.

'Do come back, I'll save that book for you.'

But they were already gone, their footsteps echoing down the westbound platform.

Clara walked to the door and stared after them, intrigued, as they walked past the shelter theatre. Marie skipped as she was half-dragged, in odd socks and plimsolls. Her older sister was tight and buttoned-up. Not a bit like most of the young adolescent girls who slept nightly down Bethnal Green Tube shelter in a great rabble of noise. The Minksy Agombars and Pat Spicers of this world were all mouth and swank. She saw them every evening huddled round their metal bunks when she locked up the library to go home, plotting or piercing each other's ears with their mothers' sewing needles. Not this one. Still, she saw all sorts in her little underground library. The sisters disappeared from Clara's sight into the acrid gloom of the Underground.

Up in the café in the booking hall above, Dot and Alice were frying up fish for the Jewish residents of the shelter in preparation for the Sabbath and the odour drifted down and curled through the carbolic. You could cut the smell down here in the tunnels.

With a heavy sigh, Clara realised she had even less time to repair her face and paint on a new one before the excruciating pantomime that lay ahead.

Her gaze fell heavily on the evening edition of the *Daily Express* that lay open on the library counter.

BLITZ CAUSES BOOK BOOM trumpeted the front-page headline over an awful photo of her captioned: *Library lovely goes underground.*

Library lovely?

The article hadn't stopped there either.

Young childless widow Clara Button is doing her bit for the war effort, running Britain's only Underground Shelter Library built over the westbound tracks of Bethnal Green Tube. When the Central Library in Bethnal Green was bombed in the first week of the Blitz, resulting in the tragic death of branch librarian Peter Hinton, Children's Librarian Mrs Button found herself propelled into the senior role. In the absence of male colleagues, she bravely stepped into the breach and arranged the transfer of 4,000 volumes underground, where she oversaw the construction of a temporary shelter library operating 78 feet below ground.

Our barbarous foes may be hell-bent on burning London to the ground, but beneath the city's surface, Mrs Button calmly carries on stamping books and ensuring everyone has a thumping good read to take their mind off the bombs.

It was the 'childless widow' bit that had brought on her tears. It was true, right enough, but did anyone need to have their status so bluntly announced to the nation?

Clara thought again of Duncan and her grief sliced deep, a hot knife to the heart. That was all it took. The thought of his face on the doorstep as he left to fight, boots buffed to a high shine, excited as a kid at a summer fair. Questions curled through her mind like weeds.

What had he been thinking in the moments before his death? Should she have given up work at the library? How much longer would the lies persist?

'No!' she scolded herself, pushing her knuckles into her eyes. 'We're not doing this now. Not today of all days.' One good cry a day and never in the library. Those were her rules and she'd already broken one. Besides, who here in Bethnal Green wasn't carrying an Atlas-load of grief. People needed to see a bright and jolly librarian, not this.

A rustle at the door tore Clara from the churn of her thoughts.

'Bleedin' hell, it might be March, but it's colder than a polar bear's cock out there . . .'

An enormous tray of sandwiches and sausage rolls was thumped onto the counter.

'Ham off the bone, real butter . . . What a touch. Dot from the café did me a deal . . . I promised her double the tickets next week. Hang about, you ain't even ready! The *Picture Post* photographer's parking.' A slim hand shot out to snatch up the copy of the *Daily Express* Clara had just been reading.

'Triffic, ain't it? Didn't capture your best side though,

did they? You look a right dog's dinner in this picture,' she remarked with eviscerating honesty. 'We better get you scrubbed up so you look better in the next ones.'

'Thanks Rubes!' Clara laughed.

Ruby Munroe was her best friend and, latterly, library assistant. 'Not qualified, unlike our Clara,' as she told anyone who enquired, and those that didn't. 'Thick as two short planks me.' Except she wasn't. She possessed more guts and guile than most men Clara had ever met. Her best pal since primary school breezed through life, Formica-coated and with more chutzpah than the average Bethnal Greener. Nothing was impossible in Ruby's world, no deal that couldn't be fixed or negotiated.

It was true that Clara selected the books, oversaw the cataloguing and Browne Issue System, answered the more complex enquiries and did bibliographic searches. But it was Ruby who had the social intelligence to be able to connect with the vast spectrum of life they saw in the library.

'Oh, doll, you've been crying.' Ruby unknotted her towering headscarf and pulled a face. 'Thinking about him?'

Clara nodded.

'Duncan or Peter?'

'Both really. Just this award, it's got me thinking about how much they'd have loved this evening.'

Ruby shook her head. 'This is your night, Clara Button. We're going to have a quick tickler, and yes, I know it's no smoking in the library, but you can make an exception for one night. Then, while you get changed into this' – she rummaged around in her string bag and pulled out something entirely unsuitable in fire-engine red – 'I'm going to mix us a quick heart-starter.'

Clara felt acid churn in her stomach. 'I don't think I can do this.'

'Nothing two aspirin and a gin won't fix, Cla!' Ruby grinned as she lit a black Sobranie and poured a generous splash of clear liquid from a flask into two jam jars. 'You've got half the East End Reading for Victory. All they want to do is say thanks.

'Bad times are good for books,' she went on, chucking back her drink in one gulp and shuddering. 'Hell's teeth, that's got some poke in it. You're an essential cog in the war machine, so enjoy your moment, girl.'

'But Rubes, don't you think this award, the timing of it, tonight of all nights, is a bit charry?'

'Course.' Ruby shrugged. 'It's called burying bad news. Accentuate the positives of the shelter to hide its past. Anyone can see through that.'

'But don't you mind?' Clara persisted. 'After everything you and your mum went though. To say nothing of half the people in this shelter. There's not a person down here unaffected by that night.'

Ruby smiled tightly as she reapplied her red lipstick. 'It happened. Who down this shelter ain't lost someone? Now come on, slowpoke, get changed.'

'I thought I'd just wear this,' Clara replied, looking down at her usual rig-out of blouse tucked into slacks.

'You're going to be on the front page of every newspaper tomorrow, you ain't looking like a spinster librarian.'

'I'm not far off it,' she laughed.

Ruby lifted one pencilled brow. 'Behave. You're only twenty-five.'

'Fair enough, but I draw the line at this!' Clara grimaced, pulling out the red dress.

'Let's talk about it while I zip you up.' Ruby winked, clamping her Sobranie between her teeth.

Half an hour later, poured into the dress and a pair of Ruby's vertiginous heels, Clara had never seen her little library so busy: officials from the Ministry of Information mingled with the press and regular library users. Due to the curved roof of the underground tunnel, the acoustics were such that the noise seemed to have reached a crescendo in her head. The shelter theatre next door was hosting a Russian opera singer that evening and as he warmed up for his evening performance, his rich voice rolled like a Tube train up the Central Line tunnel.

Mrs Chumbley, the officious deputy shelter manager, was doing her best to hold back the sea of inquisitive shelter kids all clamouring to get into the library and filch one of the sausage rolls.

Clara caught sight of Maggie May and her best pal Molly, along with Sparrow, Ronnie, Tubby and the rest of the Tube Rats as they called themselves, crawling in on their hands and knees.

Clara winked at them. She'd far rather be sitting cross-legged and shoeless on the floor reading aloud with the children, than trussed up in here like some sort of show pony. They were halfway through *The Family from One*

End Street by Eve Garnett, and a couple of chapters in, the antics of the Ruggles family were already proving irresistible.

'Out!' boomed Mrs Chumbley, catching sight of the group and grabbing Sparrow by the scruff of the neck.

A gentle tap at her shoulder and Clara turned to see one of her regular library users, Mr Pepper, an elderly gentleman, and his wife, who had been bombed out of their home two years ago and now lived down the Tube permanently.

'I shan't take up your time, my dear,' he said. 'It's a bit noisy in here for my wife so we're retiring to our bunks, but I just wanted to say jolly well done on this award. This library is the best thing to happen to this shelter.' He smiled, showing off a web of crinkles around his eyes.

'Thanks Mr Pepper. You're one of my most prolific readers.' She glanced at his wife. 'There's not many who can say they've got through *War and Peace* in two weeks.'

'He'd read the print off our entire collection at home, until we were bombed out,' said his wife in such a little voice, Clara had to lean in closer to listen to the elderly lady. She smelt of Yardley's Lavender and had the softest-looking skin.

'Losing his whole library was quite a blow, but finding your little wartime library has been a tonic, my dear.'

Mr Pepper gazed adoringly at his wife.

'Alas, my eyesight prevents me reading what I used to in my youth, but I'll admit, it's been my luxury and my escape these past few years. I can't tell you what you've done for me, Mrs Button.'

'Come now, Mr Pepper,' she teased, 'you've known me three years now, please call me Clara.'

'He's always been a stickler for formality, comes with being a headmaster all those years,' smiled Mrs Pepper. 'You shan't get him to change now, my dear. Before we go, I must just tell you, I've a cousin in Pinner who's giving away some books for the salvage drive, but we've persuaded her to give them to us instead, so we can donate them to your library.'

'Oh, how terrific!'

'She's a devil of a reader, particularly loves her thrillers and mysteries. She's built up quite the collection of Agatha Christie, Dorothy L. Sayers and Margery Allingham. Would you like them?'

'Can a duck swim? Thrillers, along with historical romance, are our most borrowed books; they fly off the shelves.'

'You'd think people would have had enough of violence in the real world,' Mr Pepper remarked.

'It's the intrigue, the whodunnit suspense. It's the perfect antidote to this war,' Clara mused.

'Downright queer!'

The figure of Mrs Chumbley loomed over them. Even in heels, Clara had to strain her neck to look up at her. Poor Mrs Chumbley. She'd never been married. She was only called Mrs as a courtesy. Her face was always fixed in one permanent expression, disapproval.

'More of a Mills and Boon reader, are you?' Mr Pepper smiled.

'Don't be absurd.'

'What do you like to read then, Mrs Chumbley?' Mrs Pepper politely enquired.

'Read?' she scoffed. 'And where would I find the time to read! Keeping this shelter running smoothly demands all my time. Tubby Amos, put that book down this instant!'

'I don't mind them pi—' Clara began.

'I know what bunk you sleep in and I shall be talking to your mother! Where was I? Oh yes, I shall take up reading when we've blitzed Hitlerism out of the world.'

'Come now, Mrs Chumbley, it's not self-indulgent to read,' Mr Pepper remarked. 'Mrs Button here could recommend something perfect for you. She seems to have something of a gift of matching people to their perfect book.'

Mrs Chumbley softened as she stared at Mr Pepper. The elderly gentleman was held in high esteem by the occupants of the underground shelter, and even Mrs C wasn't immune to his debonair charm.

'Perhaps,' she blustered. 'But only if it were educational. I recently read a technical book *War Wounds and Fractures: The Definitive Guide*. It was capital!'

'Sounds riveting,' said Ruby dryly, as she sidled up next to them, clutching the arms of not one but two men. 'Watch out Georgette Heyer.

'Now, Clara darlin', sorry to interrupt, but there are some people here you must meet. This is Minister Rupert Montague, Director of Home Publicity at the Ministry of Information. He's been trying to talk to you for the past half-hour.' She turned to the smaller of the men. In her heels, Clara found herself in the unfortunate position of standing two inches taller than him.

'And this is Mr Pink-Smythe.'

'Pinkerton-Smythe,' he corrected, taking out a handkerchief and wiping his head with it, which had the unfortunate effect of sticking up the last few strands of hair he had left like an antenna.

'He's the chair of the Library Committee. Which makes him our new boss,' said Ruby.

'It's lovely to meet you,' said Clara. 'I'm looking forward to working with you.' She turned to the man from the Ministry, wishing she hadn't let Ruby talk her into this dress. 'And welcome to our underground library, Minister.'

'So, *you're* the librarian everyone's talking about,' he beamed, shaking her hand enthusiastically. 'This place is quite the find. Never thought I'd see the day where I came down the Tube to find books instead of trains. What are we, sixty, seventy feet underground?'

'Seventy-eight feet, the only place in Bethnal Green you can't hear the bombs,' Clara replied proudly.

'And forgive my ignorance. What happened to the trains?'

'Bethnal Green was an unfinished stop on the Central Line, connecting Mile End with Liverpool Street Station,' she explained. 'At the outbreak of war, construction was suspended. It was locked up and left to the rats, until the bombings began.'

'So how did it get opened up to this' – he spread his arms wide in wonder – 'underground village? If that doesn't sound too daft.'

'Not at all. All of us who live and work down here in this other London often think of ourselves as inhabitants of a secret village.' Clara's eyes shone as she looked about. 'We are all very proud of our subterranean community. Not many Tube stations can boast triple bunks for five thousand, a library, a theatre for shows, plays and dancing lessons—'

'With a grand piano, if you please,' interrupted Ruby.

'Quite. Not to mention a nursery, café, first-aid post with nurses' and doctors' quarters, all below ground,' Clara continued.

'Even got our own Tube hairdresser.' Ruby winked, plumping the back of her wavy updo.

'Can you hear the opera singer warming up next door? They're putting on a performance this evening. Sadler's Wells are bringing a ballet here next week.'

'Good grief. Culture, books and a built-in community. I may have to move here myself if this is what life under-ground has to offer.'

Clara felt herself relax. If there was one thing she loved to talk about, it was shelter life and its people. They were a community, albeit it a strange one, living along the Central Line but going nowhere. The way Clara saw it, she had a captive audience. Her little library lay firmly at the heart of this underground neighbourhood, the cultural equivalent of the village pump.

'Astonishing what lies beneath one's feet, without one even really knowing,' the Minister mused. 'How did it begin?'

'It was the people who got this place opened,' Clara enthused. 'Everyone had their pride; the street shelters weren't fit for a dog. It was little Phoebe's dad who,' and here she inverted her fingers, '"acquired" the keys during the first week of the Blitz and in came the families, in their thousands, in search of safety.'

Ruby laughed. 'Old Harry's a terrible gambler, he'd bet on two flies crawling up a wall, but he weren't prepared to take a chance on his family's life.'

'I hardly think the Minister wants to hear about the lawlessness of the subversive elements of Bethnal Green,' said Mr Pinkerton-Smythe quickly.

'On the contrary,' he replied. 'I find it intriguing. I know in Whitehall there was a fear of deep-shelter mentality, that people would descend and never come back up again, but quite clearly that's not the case here.'

'Chance'd be a fine thing,' scoffed Ruby. 'In the day, people have jobs to go to. We're working people, not moles!'

The Minister roared with laughter, clearly very taken with Ruby.

'Do you have sun-lamps,' he continued, 'to counteract the lack of daylight?'

'No sir,' Clara replied. 'I suppose we've got used to working underground. We do suffer with catarrh, and the smells down the tunnels can be somewhat, how can I put this, earthy.'

'But the morning fumigation usually sorts that out,' Ruby added.

'And where are the latrines?' he enquired.

'Latrines!' Ruby screeched, and Clara braced.

'When we first came down we had to do our business in a bucket. Now at least we got Elsan lavs. Must be moving up in the world, eh Cla!' she hooted. Ruby had a dirty great dollop of a laugh; she was famous for it in Bethnal Green.

'To begin with, we all slept here in the westbound tunnels,' said Clara. 'But three months after the bombings began, the council officially leased the station from the London Passenger Transport Board.'

'Which is where I came in,' jumped in Mrs Chumbley. 'We scrubbed the tunnels, whitewashed the walls and formed a shelter committee. If you want anything to happen, one needs a committee, don't you think?'

'And you are?' he enquired.

'Mrs Chumbley, deputy shelter manager under Mr Miller. Besides us, there are twelve full-time wardens, plus the nursery, theatre, café and library staff.'

'But tell me, why do people sleep down here even now?'

'Housing,' Clara replied. 'There's a desperate shortage of habitable homes. Besides, people have got used to and like it down here. For some children, it's the only safe home they've ever known.'

She hesitated. 'That's not to say we haven't had our share of tragedies here. Did you hear—'

'Shall we press on?' Mr Pinkerton-Smythe said, interrupting Clara.

'Good idea,' the Minister remarked, clearing his throat and calling for silence.

'And now, without further ado, I should like to award you, Mrs Button, with your official Reading for Victory certification of excellence.'

Clara pushed down her anger. Why were they never allowed to discuss it? Why must their grief always be sacrificed in the name of morale?

Her mother-in-law's face flashed unnervingly into her

mind. The hasty funeral. The doctor's words. *Pull yourself together.*

'Clara . . .' Ruby hissed, digging her elbow into her side. 'You all right?'

'Sorry,' she mumbled, breathing out slowly and touching her throat.

Her new boss, Mr Pinkerton-Smythe, was staring at her curiously.

The Minister had hustled the photographer of the *Picture Post* to the library counter.

'Take a photograph of myself and Clara Button, branch librarian of Britain's only Underground Tube Station library, would you, Bert? She's the new poster girl for Reading for Victory.'

'Am I?' said Clara, blinking as the camera bulb flashed in her face.

'Absolutely. Everyone's talking about this library. Word has reached Whitehall . . .' He lowered his voice. 'Even Churchill knows about this little place. Quite the propaganda coup.'

'Thank you all for joining us underground today.' A silence finally fell over the library. Clara saw Mr Pepper and his wife slip out of the door and wished she could join them.

'The enemy is trying to infect our minds with the dry rot of doubt and discontent, in the hope that our morale will crumble. We must continue to inform ourselves upon the issues that underlie the conflict and upon what is at stake. To this end, books are indispensable. Bethnal Green Underground Shelter Library is rendering service to the

National Cause by providing the matter and the method of good reading.'

All eyes were on her and Clara wanted to fold herself away in a library book.

'When the library took a direct hit and its most senior member of staff was killed, there cannot have been many gals who would have the gumption to step into the breach.

'As book sales dip through paper rationing and with the scarcity of new books, the role of the publicly funded municipal library takes on great significance.'

More flash bulbs, reporters scribbled, and Clara prayed for the speech to be over. But the Minister was warming up for a Churchillian finish.

'Libraries are the engines of our education and our escape, never have they been more important in transforming our lives.

'Please accept this certificate with the grateful thanks of all at Whitehall.'

Clara took the framed certificate and knew she had to say something.

'We have been urged to fight for victory, to dig for victory and to save for victory. There can at least be no harm in suggesting that we read for victory,' she concluded, with a smile.

Applause burst throughout the library and Clara laughed as Ruby put her fingers between her lips and let rip an ear-shattering whistle that drowned out the opera singer next door. The Tube Rats whooped and stamped their feet from outside the door. Mrs Chumbley charged through the crowd in their direction.

'Gracious,' said the Minister. 'I thought libraries were supposed to be quiet spaces.'

'Not this one,' Ruby replied, pressing a glass into Clara's hand. 'It's always like this. Especially when we have the children's storytime in the evenings.'

'First class. Grab them when they're young and you've a reader for life.'

Clara nodded eagerly. 'Absolutely, but we don't just cater for the young. We offer a weekly mobile library service to local factory girls every Friday afternoon. If they can't come to you . . .'

'You take it to them,' he finished. 'And this must be on the—'

'Bibliobus.'

Clara was rather proud of the old 1935 Morris 25 HP saloon donated by Kearley and Tonge cake and biscuit factory on Bethnal Green Road. 'A Library to your Door' service had proved tremendously popular, especially with the local factory girls, who loved their weekly romance fix.

'I think it's marvellous and you are so in tune with Whitehall's thinking. Librarians must be dynamic in their encouragement of reading for victory.'

The Minister was getting excited now as he warmed to his theme. 'I'm going to put you forward to be interviewed for *The Times*. They're investigating the work of public libraries in impoverished areas.'

'Oh, well. I don't know,' Clara hesitated.

'Don't be bashful, my dear,' said the Minister.

Clara's feminine intuition sensed Mr Pinkerton-Smythe radiating resentment next to her.

'Our aim, Minister, should be to raise the borough's reading standards,' he chipped in with a thin smile.

'We have a moral duty, do we not Mrs Button, to educate? There is an awful lot of . . .' and here he cast an eye over Clara's bookshelves, '. . . mental opiates available now. Fluff. Whimsy. Dreadful tedious romances. Books written by the half-educated for the uneducated.'

Clara felt a strain of red flush over her chest.

'With respect, sir, I disagree. Peter . . . my colleague, believed that pleasure in reading is the true function of books.'

She thought wistfully of the man who had nurtured her love of reading, encouraged her parents to allow her to sit the entrance exam for the Central Foundation Girls' Grammar School in Spitalfields and encouraged her to study for the Diploma in Librarianship.

'Who are we to say what people ought or ought not to read?' she persisted.

'She has a fair point, does she not?' said the Minister, turning to Mr Pinkerton-Smythe. 'War has opened the public library door to many users who previously would only have used a tuppenny library, and we should hate to lose them.'

'Listen,' ordered Mr Pinkerton-Smythe. 'I admire your youthful energy, Mrs Button, but let us remember that, as librarians, it is our duty *not* to tamely accept and cater for lack of taste, but to rectify so sad a condition as speedily as we may and educate our patrons.'

Something inside her snapped.

'No!' She slammed her glass down on the library

counter. 'You're wrong! The women in this shelter are desperately seeking escape, not education.'

'If they don't have enough energy left to read anything but trash, we should be doing them a real service if we could prevent them from reading at all,' he shot back.

'Prevent them from reading!' she exclaimed. 'What would you have me do, build a romance book bonfire on the platform and burn them all? That way lies Hitler!'

Ruby and the Minister observed the heated exchange in growing disbelief.

'Well, well, well,' chuckled the Minster. 'As you can see, Mr Pinkerton-Smythe, there is nothing tame about your young librarian. She has fire in her belly.'

A terrible silence fell between them. The Minister flicked a look at his wristwatch.

'As much as I love a robust debate, I must be on my way; my motorcar is waiting.'

He shook everyone's hand.

'Mrs Button, once more, it's been a pleasure to meet you. Mr Pinkerton-Smythe, watch yourself. You've a fire-cracker on your hands here, what! My people shall be in touch about that *Times* interview.'

'I must be off too,' muttered Mr Pinkerton-Smythe. 'I'll be back soon and we can continue this.' His voice dripped poison as he stalked from Clara's library.

'Drink up,' Ruby muttered, topping up her glass, 'you're going to need it when you see who's just walked in.'

Clara turned and the glass froze halfway to her lips.

'Mum. You came.'

Her mother's lips were as thin as a paper cut.

'Please tell me you weren't photographed in that! You look like a floozy! Your mother-in-law's still in mourning dress you know.'

'Can't you be pleased for me Mum . . . ?' her voice trailed off as her mother's eyes filled with tears. How did she do that? Cry almost on command.

'Thank God your father's not here to see this,' she wept, pulling out a hankie.

Clara swallowed sharply, her mind muddied with images of her parents sobbing over Duncan's grave. No one had come right out and blamed her for what had happened, but the look of recrimination was thinly concealed.

How many times had she seen them since then? Three, maybe four times in four years? Plus that awful charade last Christmas.

'I just wanted you to come to the library and see what I've been doing. I thought it might help you to understand why I carried on working.'

'Well I don't understand. It was a mistake to come here. I had hoped you'd have thought better by now and packed it in.'

Clara lowered her voice as she noticed people around her staring.

'Mum, I need to work. Duncan's gone and I can't bring him back, but at least down here in the library I'm helping people.' She reached for her mother's hand. 'Besides, I'm on war work now. I can't leave even if I wanted to.'

Her mother shook her hand free.

'You won't be told, will you, madam. It was always the same with you, even as a child.' She moved to leave.

'Mum please stay . . .' Clara begged.

'I'm sorry dear, but no. You've made your choices. And now you must live with them. I wash my hands of you.'

She tightened her headscarf and left, the air behind her shimmering with condemnation.

Clara stared after her stunned and then looked down at the Reading for Victory certificate. Had she just sacrificed her family for the library?

2

Ruby

When bombs were raining down on Britain, all people wanted to do was shut themselves away from the horror and escape to a new world that offered excitement and fantasy. That new world could be found between the covers of a work of fiction.
Dr Robert James, Senior Lecturer in History at the University of Portsmouth

Ruby kicked the slat under the last trestle table and heaved it back into the adjoining reading room. Pulling her red lipstick from between her cleavage, she used the back of a knife as a mirror to reapply a thick coat of her favourite, Renegade Red.

'I think we can say that was a success,' she said, peering into the knife to check she hadn't got any on her teeth.

'Can we?' Clara groaned. 'My own mother's disowned me and our new boss hates me.'

'Oh Cla. You and your mum. You're very different people. She'll come round.'

Clara shook her head. 'Not this time. I really think she means it.'

Ruby looked at her beautiful, formidably intelligent, compassionate friend and wondered how someone so humane had ever come from the loins of Henrietta Buckley.

'And why did I call our new boss a mini-Hitler!' she sighed.

Ruby reached for the bottle of gin and realised in alarm it was empty.

''Cause he is. Imagine wanting to stop women reading! Pompous twit.'

'True, but I don't want to make an enemy of him.'

Ruby glanced at her watch and swallowed sharply. It was time. How could she do this? She hadn't had anywhere near enough to drink.

Her hand shook slightly as she lit another cigarette.

'Shall we go up now, Rubes?' Clara asked softly. 'It's quarter past eight. They'll be starting in a minute.'

'I . . . I don't think I can, Cla. I think I'll just wait down here.'

Clara squeezed her hand. 'I promise I won't let go. Come on. Let's do this. For Bella.'

Bella. Ruby hadn't spoken her name since she died one year ago this very evening, but there wasn't a single moment when her big sister wasn't in her thoughts. When Ruby didn't torture herself with thoughts of *if only.*

Clara locked up the library and, together, they walked along the platform, their heels clicking on the concrete floor, and clattered up the out-of-use escalators, which didn't escalate.

Up in the ticket hall, two men walking the other way looked admiringly at her undulating curves and Ruby tossed them a contemptuous look, before realising in alarm that she had ended up in bed with one of them over a month ago on a hazy gin-fuelled night.

'Those sarnies do you all right?' called a little aproned lady pouring tea behind the hatch of the café.

'Spot on, Dot,' Ruby called back.

'You're always welcome darlin', you know that. Clara, keep us somefin nice. I'll pop in tomorrow, ducks.'

'What you in the mood for?'

'Errol Flynn and a stiff gin,' she cackled, 'but in the absence of that, a book'll do.'

'Anything in particular?'

She twinkled behind the steam of her huge tea urn.

'If it's got the words passion or pant in, it'll do for me, love.'

'I think you might have an appetite for Denise Robins' *Gypsy Lover* . . .' said Clara.

'You choose, love, you ain't let me down yet.'

'Give her Denise's,' teased Ruby. 'How can any woman say no to a gypsy lover on a rainy afternoon?'

Dot hooted with laugher and Ruby realised that with her dirty jokes and reckless behaviour she was well on the way to becoming a caricature. Bethnal Green's bosomy blonde . . . the tart with the heart . . . all fur coat, no knickers! Funny how there was no shortage of sayings for women who didn't play by the rules. Even her nickname, Ruby Red Lips, made her sound more like a racy tabloid cartoon strip than a woman.

But what was the alternative? Go grey overnight and end up a drudge like her mum? No thanks. She'd take all the sexual freedom war had afforded her, because let's be honest, it wouldn't be tolerated once the war was over.

'Saucy piece,' Dot called. 'Ta-ta girls, be lucky. See you tomorrow, please God.'

'PG,' Ruby echoed, as they paused at the bottom of the notorious stairwell.

Clara held her arm to steady her.

'I've got you,' she murmured.

Ruby felt her breath grow shallow. *Not now, please.* It was no time for an episode.

She squeezed her eyes shut and slowly walked over her sister's grave. Bella's beautiful face slipped into her mind like the blade of a knife. In the sudden darkness, she couldn't escape the images that haunted her, taking her back to that rainy Wednesday evening.

Screams. Thuds. Grunts. Why had someone dumped hundreds of wet overcoats in the stairwell? Then she'd realised. The coats contained bodies. Hundreds of writhing, gasping bodies in a seething pit. Limbs tangled into impossible shapes, faces turning from pink to purple. A charnel house of such horrifying complexity it was impossible to see where one body began and another ended.

There was Mrs Chumbley leaning over the top of the bodies, desperately plucking children from the crush with such force their shoes were left behind.

'Bella! . . . Bella!' Ruby had screamed, wrenching at hands and legs in a frantic bid to free people, to find her sister.

But she hadn't found her. Not then. It had been another five days before she'd turned up in the morgue, her face covered in boot marks, her beautiful red hair fanned out like flames.

Ruby saw herself from above, holding her sister's body, trying to rub life back into those cold, cold hands. Weeping. Apologising.

'Rubes . . . ?' Clara's concerned voice wrenched her back to the present.

Tears flowed down her face as she leant back against the wall of the stairwell and nodded, speechless with exhaustion and pain. Her fear rose and sank, in great plunging waves.

'Did it happen again?'

She nodded. 'I know what you're going to say Cla,' she said finally, 'but please don't.'

'How long are you going to go on blaming yourself?' Clara whispered.

'Until I die probably.' Ruby drew in a shuddering breath, but it felt like she could never get enough air in her lungs. Was that how Bella had felt, in the moments before she died?

Ruby looked down at the dirty concrete step under her feet. What a place for a life to end. How quick the authorities had been to wash these steps once the bodies had been removed. Her anger should have eviscerated her guilt, but it didn't. It only seemed to make it all the more potent.

A small green weed had sprouted through a crack and was pushing up towards the light. She wondered how anything could grow where so much horror still reverberated.

'Rubes, look at me,' Clara begged. 'Even if you hadn't been late, she probably would still have got caught up in the crush.'

'I guess we'll never know, will we. Come on.' Ruby drew

in a shallow breath and tried to get a grip on herself. 'Let's get out of here.'

They emerged blinking into the bluish light of a still March evening. There wasn't a breath of wind.

A strange silence had descended over the station entrance, even the birds had fallen quiet, as if they had simply tumbled from the sky. It took a while for Ruby's eyes to adjust, as it always did when she stepped out from her subterranean world. In the gloaming, she realised there must be a hundred or more people gathered outside the station entrance.

Men in flat caps, women in black headscarves. Even the services had come, ARP and Heavy Rescue men, heads dipped in respect. Ambulance men in white tin hats had turned out in force, Ruby realised in surprise. Of course, they'd all been there that night, witnessed sights that would haunt their dreams for years to come.

Bethnal Green was the noisiest place on earth, so to see it so sombre and still was affecting.

She searched the crowds looking for her mum. So many faces, etched with grief. There was Maud, whose two girls, Ellen and Ivy, had walked down those stairs never to return. Maud had survived but seemed determined to kill herself more slowly by drinking herself senseless every night. There was scarcely a pub in Bethnal Green she hadn't been banned from. And there was Sarah, standing like a pale-faced spectre on the steps to the church. Rumour had it that it was Sarah who had caused the crush by tripping and falling over at the bottom of the stairwell, while carrying her baby. Her baby had died. Sarah had survived. She'd gone grey overnight, condemned to a living hell, and scarcely left St John Church these days.

Weeping silently next to her was Flo. Younger sister crushed down the Tube, eldest sister decapitated by a lorry in the blackout. The middle sister with nothing either side. You couldn't stretch out an arm in Bethnal Green without touching someone who was sitting on a powder keg.

But for Ruby, one year on from Bella's death, her grief was no longer white hot. In the weeks after, she had felt like a tightly screwed-up paper bag. One year on, she had gradually unfolded, but now she was full of creases.

'There's Mum,' she whispered, eventually spotting Netty in front of the bombed library opposite the station entrance. Ruby took in the lipstick and battered hat. Her heart ached.

'You look nice, Mum,' she said as they got close.

'Made an effort, for our Bella.'

Ruby bent down and kissed her gently on the cheek, wondering when it was her mum had got so thin.

'So, what's happening?' she asked.

'The priest's been and said a prayer. Now people are leaving notes and flowers and what have you. I've left that.' She pointed to a jam jar full of pretty daisies at the top of the steps to the shelter entrance.

'Not much for a life, is it?'

Ruby didn't know how long they all stood there, shoulder-to-shoulder, alone with their thoughts, but united in their grief. But it was enough time to remember.

It's not your fault. How many times had Clara told her that?

But whose fault was it that her sister and 172 other

people had plunged into the pit of hell that night, tripping and tumbling over each other down the stairs until the breath squeezed from their lungs? Not Sarah's, that's for sure. Rumour had it the council had written to central government requesting funds to make the entrance safer, insert a central stair-rail, level out the uneven steps. The request had been denied. The verdict of the investigation was still pending. Perhaps it was easier to let the people take the blame than look for the truth?

Ruby had long been of the opinion that when it came to war, the working classes were cannon fodder. What she hadn't realised until last year, was that the sacrifice extended to the home front as well as the battle front. For too bloody long now they'd be slapped around by representatives of wealth and privilege. They only had the comparative safety of the Tube shelter because they had taken matters into their own hands. She breathed deeply, trying to calm herself.

'Watch where you're going pal.'

Ruby turned round to see a thick-set man in a donkey jacket barrelling his way through the silent crowd towards them.

'Oh, that's all we need,' she sighed. 'I thought he was out with his pals tonight?'

Netty shrunk into herself. 'He was supposed to be at the unveiling of some statue down the docks, some merchant he's got it into his head he's related to.'

The man reached them and stood beside Netty with a territorial grunt.

'Hello, love,' Netty said, mustering a smile. 'I thought you'd be gone for the evening?'

'I can see that. Soon as my back's turned, it's over here making a show of itself.'

It?

'No one's making a show of themselves, Victor,' Ruby snapped. 'We're paying our respects.'

'Why you all dressed up?' he said, flicking his wife's hat. 'You can't make a whistle out of a pig's tail, you know.'

He laughed at his own joke.

'You're drunk,' Ruby said.

'Got any money?' he demanded, ignoring his step-daughter. Victor Walsh was her mum's second husband, married on the rebound after her father had died. It was a mystery to anyone why sweet-natured Netty had married him.

'Sorry, love, I'm all out.'

'But you got paid today,' he went on, raising his voice over the silent crowd.

'Sorry, love,' she repeated, looking embarrassed.

'Ain't you paying her?' he demanded, turning on Clara. Netty did some cleaning in the library once a week, as well as charring in the city and part-time work turning collars.

'Please, love, don't create a scene. Course Clara's paid me, but it's gone on rent, food and the tallyman.'

Without a word, Victor grabbed her handbag, pulled out her purse and started hunting through it.

'Leave her alone,' Ruby ordered, snatching the purse out of his hands. 'Even if she did have any money left, like she'd give it to you, you scrounging git.'

'Any trouble here, Netty?' The figure of Mrs Chumbley loomed over them. Victor might have been a lowlife, but he did seem to have a certain amount of grudging respect for the deputy shelter manager.

'Everything's fine, ain't it, love?'

Netty smiled tightly. 'Yes, yes, no bother here, Mrs Chumbley.'

'We're going home,' Victor said, clamping an arm round Netty's shoulders.

'I swear, one of these days . . .' Ruby muttered as she stared after them. 'I'd better go and help Mum. She won't half catch it when she gets home.'

Ruby leant over and kissed Clara on the cheek.

'You was smashing tonight, girl. I'm so proud of you.'

Clara brushed a gentle hand across her friend's cheek.

'Thanks Rubes. And remember: it's not your fault!'

Ruby caught up with her mum and Victor, and as they walked back to their buildings, she could see her stepfather was limbering up for a real slap-up row.

Sure enough, as soon as they let themselves into the flat, he started needling Netty.

'Where's my tea?'

'Going as fast as I can love,' she said, frantically peeling spuds. Ruby picked up a peeler.

'Here Mum, I'll help.'

'Thanks love.' Netty smiled gratefully.

Victor sat down with the paper.

'If you hadn't been out making a show of yourself, I wouldn't have to wait,' he said, rustling the paper. 'Make sure it don't happen again.'

'Course not, love. I only wanted to pay my respects to our Bella.'

He grunted.

Ignorant pig.

Ruby kept her thoughts to herself. They needed peace, tonight of all nights.

In no time at all, Netty had rustled up three plates of ham, egg and chips.

'No one makes chips quite like you, Mum,' Ruby said appreciatively, sprinkling a good glug of vinegar over hers. 'Do they Victor?'

'S'right,' he said, jamming a fork-load into his mouth as he carried on reading the paper.

'Look, they're talking about that merchant I'm related to,' he said.

'Who's that then?' Ruby asked.

'Count Walsh.'

'Drop the O and I reckon you might be related,' she said with an irreverent grin.

A bark of laughter escaped from Netty before she could stop it.

'Oh, you think that's funny, do you?' Victor said, his head snapping up.

Netty paled. 'No love, I weren't laughing at you, only at our Ruby . . . .' She started to shake as he scraped back his chair and stood up.

'You know, she's quick is all.'

'Let's see how funny you find this, shall we?' he said softly, standing behind her.

Ruby's heart started to thunder and she felt the blood rushing through her ears.

'Victor, leave it,' she pleaded. It was just a joke.'

'Is this funny?'

With that he grabbed the back of Netty's head and slowly lowered it into her plate.

Without taking his eyes off Ruby, he wiped her face one way, then the other. Netty's eyes bulged in shock as egg yolk dripped off her chin.

'I'm sorry,' she gasped.

'For God's sake Victor, stop, she can't breathe!' Ruby screamed.

Victor yanked back Netty's head and tipped the rest of the plate over it, scattering chips and bits of egg over the floor.

'Watch your mouth. Both of you. I'm going down the Camel.'

Grabbing his paper and coat, he stormed out of the kitchen. The door slammed shut and the sash windows rattled.

There was a moment's stunned silence before Netty reached for the cloth.

'Please love' – she trembled, holding up a hand – 'I don't want to hear it. He's my husband and that's that.'

'Mum, please . . . you've got to leave him.'

'Just put the kettle on, would you, and I'll make us a brew,' she muttered, scrubbing at the stains on the lino. 'We're out of milk though. Pop down to Mrs Smart and see if she can spare some, would you?'

Ruby wanted to scream. *I don't want a bloody cup of tea!*

I want to get you of here, away from that animal! She ran her hands despairingly through her hair. This . . . this was why she was bound to Bethnal Green. Why she sought escape in a bottle or a stranger's bed. Sometimes, she thought, if it weren't for Clara and the library, she wondered whether she'd exist at all.

She'd reached for her coat when her mum clutched her arm.

'You won't leave me, will you love?'

'Course not Mum.'

'Only, after Bella, I couldn't stand to lose you as well.' She smiled feverishly. 'It's just the two of us now ain't it.'

'Oh Mum.' Ruby hugged her as tight as she dared, rage spreading black through her belly.

How long could she keep on making piecrust promises? How long before something inside her snapped? Her love for her mother felt like a river with no bridges. Something she couldn't cross. Every slap, punch and unkind word just ground her mother further into the sodden ground.

That man was peeling away Netty's humanity layer by layer until soon, what would be left? Never mind *Beauty is Your Duty. Shut Up and Put Up* was a more realistic wartime slogan, at least for her people.

'I'm not going anywhere,' Ruby vowed, kissing the top of her head. 'I promise. You and me against the world.' She pulled back and smiled to reassure her mum. 'I'll go and get the milk, shall I? We'll have us a nice cup of tea.'

Ruby stepped over the congealed egg and left the airless flat, her smile slipping as soon as she was out of sight.

3

Clara

Librarians require infinite patience and politeness in the face of adversity. A love of people is as, if not more, important than a love of books.
Charlotte Clark, Manager of Southwold Library

After Ruby left, Clara sat on her own for a long time in Barmy Park, until darkness fell and she saw bats flitting from the roof of the old bombed library.

After the memorial gathering outside the Tube, she had no desire to go back to the four walls of her tiny flat down Sugar Loaf Walk. In her room, stripped of her librarian status, she was just plain old Clara, the widow.

For a long time after Duncan's death, she'd slept in the library, bathing in the warmth of that giant underground community. Their little wartime library, knocked together on fifty bob and a wing and a prayer, had saved her life. Quite possibly her sanity too. The hours were punishing, 8 a.m. until 9 p.m. every day, when the shelter dimmed its lights for the night, with only a half-day off on Wednesday and Sunday. But the work had stopped her buckling under her grief. After what she'd witnessed this evening, seeing so many of her patrons in the crowd, standing with their heads dipped, she knew the library was helping them just as much as it was her.

And that's why, no matter how painful her mother's rejection of her, she could not turn her back on the library . . . or Ruby. They clung to each other, two lost souls, struggling with their pasts.

A dog barked nearby and she turned quickly, but the moon had dipped behind a cloud and Clara found herself staring into a curtain of darkness. Her stomach tied into a queasy knot. No one wanted to get caught out after blackout. The Blackout Ripper, as the Soho murderer and rapist had been dubbed, had long since been caught, but it had been a warning to all women out alone after dark.

Clara wrapped her coat tightly and headed back to the park gates, feeling her way along the railings. At Sugar Loaf Walk she slipped through the shadows of the alley. The housing down here was a hugger mugger of rooms. Damp, leaky homes built in the last century, sub-divided and rented out to as many as could be piled inside. But out here she was quite alone.

She stopped at what she hoped was her door and fumbled inside her bag for her keys. 'Come on, where are you?' she muttered. Where was a bomber's moon when you needed it?

A dog barked again and she stopped. A prickle ran up her spine and in that moment, she knew with a certainty she was not alone.

'Who's there?' she called up the dark alley. Silence. The engulfing blackness made her ears ring.

Finally, she felt the cold steel of her key and in relief guided it towards the lock, but instead of a door, she felt a body.

She went to scream but a hand shot out and covered her mouth. Panic slammed down as she thrashed about, trying to free herself, but the figure was too strong and she could feel him dragging her back up the alley. The buttons of his coat dug into her back, his breath hot and heavy in her ear.

She heard a yell and his body bucked against hers. Suddenly his hand was released from her mouth.

'HELP!' Clara screamed, gasping for breath. In the darkness she could just about see a white helmet, two bodies fused together.

A muffled thud, a groan and then the sounds of running footsteps.

'It's all right,' panted a male voice, 'he's gone.'

'Oh my God,' she said, bursting into tears.

'You're safe . . . you're safe, I'm an ambulance man,' soothed the voice. Her rescuer flicked on a masked torch and a weak pinprick of light lit up the space between them.

'Are you injured?'

'No . . . no, I'm all right,' she said, feeling anything but.

In the pale light she recognised the man from the memorial gathering outside the Tube earlier.

'You're hurt,' she exclaimed, staring at his bruised and bloody lip.

'No, no, I'm fine. He just clipped me on the lip when I pulled him off you.'

'Thank goodness you came along when you did. I . . . I don't know what would have happened.'

'Did you see his face or recognise him?'

She shook her head.

'No. It all happened so fast.'

'Come on,' he said. 'I think we better get to the Tube shelter and we can report it and get you something for the shock.'

'I'm fine. I'm sure he was probably just after my bag; I don't want to make a fuss.'

'I really ought to check you over.'

Something wet snuffled at her hand and she jumped.

'Sorry, that's my mutt,' he said. 'Down girl.'

'Oh, that was your dog in the park?'

'Yes,' he said. 'I saw you leave the park and then the man followed you, so I thought I'd better check.'

She felt his eyes on her. 'Look here. I know you feel all right now, but shock's a queer thing. Do you have anyone at home to keep an eye on you?'

Her throat constricted. 'No,' she admitted. 'It's just me.'

'Come on. Half an hour can't hurt.' Something about the softness of his voice made her relent.

Down in the Tube, Clara unlocked the library and the man followed her in.

'Let me put something on that lip,' she said. 'You're dripping blood on the floor.'

'Terribly sorry!'

She laughed shakily, relief crashing through her as the adrenaline wore off.

'After what you've just done, I scarcely think you need to apologise. Sit down,' she ordered, grabbing a fold-up chair from the reading room.

She reached behind the counter for the first-aid kit and pressed a small piece of gauze soaked in disinfectant to the stranger's lip.

'Are you sure you're all right?' he asked concerned, as she hovered over him. 'I'm the ambulance man; I really ought to be looking after you.'

'Honestly, I'm fine. It was all over very quickly. Went through worse in the Blitz; besides, I'm sure he was only after my bag.'

Why was she making light of it? Was it because she hated to think of another reason why the man had followed her?

As she mopped him up, she took in her rescuer. He was tall. All elbows and knees. He had the palest blond hair and a face that would have been unremarkable but for the bluest eyes Clara had ever seen.

He gazed back at her curiously.

'You're not a bit like what I expected.'

She drew back, still clutching the blood-stained rag.

'Do I know you?'

She saw it straight away, his embarrassment, as he fumbled for an answer. His eyes fixed on the *Daily Express* that Ruby had mortifyingly insisted on pinning to a corkboard alongside the library rules.

'I-I read about you in the *Daily Express*. You don't look like that in real life.'

'Thank heavens for that.'

She dabbed some antiseptic on his lip and, still, he watched her.

'Are you sure we haven't met?' she asked.

'You've probably seen me around. I'm based at Somerford Street.'

The dog barked and rubbed against Clara's shin.

'You're honoured, means she likes you.'

'You're patched up,' Clara said, putting away the first-aid kit and crouching down to stroke the terrier.

'And what's your name?'

'She's called Beauty.'

Clara looked up at him and lifted one brow.

'Seriously?'

He crouched down on his haunches and covered Beauty's ears.

'Pay her no mind,' he chuckled.

Beauty had stubby little legs, snaggle teeth and a bushy beard.

'She's gorgeous,' Clara smiled, rubbing behind her ear. She immediately rolled over onto her back, all four paws stuck up in the air.

'She's shameless in her pursuit of a tummy tickle,' he chuckled. 'I came across her when we were called to an incident in Shipton Street. Whole family wiped out by a parachute bomb and only this old girl still standing.'

'How sad,' Clara mused.

'Yes, it was, but she's proved her worth since then. She's good at sniffing out bodies.'

'And what's your name? The beast?'

'Ha ha, no, Billy actually. Billy Clark,' he grinned, standing up and staggering slightly.

'Oh, I say, are you all right?'

'Sorry, yes, think he might have hit me harder than I realised.'

'Here, sit down, I'll get you a brandy. You've probably got a bit of concussion.'

She walked over to the non-fiction bookcase and pulled out *The Art of Homemaking*. Hidden behind it was a selection of bottles. She pulled out the brandy and poured a large slug into an enamel cup.

Billy drank then scrubbed wearily at his face.

'Do you always conceal hard liquor behind books on domesticity?'

'It's our least borrowed book, so I figured our secret stash would be safe there. No one has much of a heart to read how to frame pressed flowers when you mightn't have a wall to hang them from.'

She stared at the book before replacing it.

'It was a gift from my mother-in-law, funnily enough, when I married her son.'

'Subtle.'

'Subtlety isn't her strong point.' Clara grimaced, thinking back to when Maureen had pressed it into her hands with a warning. *This is the only book you should be reading, dear, now that you're married. But be careful not to read it when my son is present, otherwise he'll think you're not listening to him.*

'I take it she doesn't approve of you working here?'

'You could say that. Nothing I'm not used to.'

'How so?'

'People don't like it when girls are bookworms,' she

mused, deciding to join him in a brandy. His pale eyes raked over her curiously as she took a sip of the drink and shuddered.

'I learnt to live with the attitude, growing up, that if you read books a lot as a girl, you were a bit unnatural, subversive even.'

'Really?'

'Truly. Even my teacher chided me at school for always having my nose in a book.'

It's not healthy, you'll ruin your eyesight, had given way to *It's not feminine, you'll never catch a husband.* Aged thirteen, she'd rather have caught pneumonia than a husband, but the message was always the same, as if, for a working-class girl like her, the very act of reading was daring.

'You've got a terrific selection here,' Billy said, gazing round the library. 'What do people down here like reading?'

'Historical romance, thrillers and non-fiction on British military triumphs fly off the shelves . . .'

He looked puzzled.

'You know, how we faced a superior fighting force, like the Spanish Armada, and triumphed against all the odds.'

'Aah, I see. We conquered a small, unhinged continental dictator once before, we can do it again, you mean?'

'Exactly. People are looking to the past for hope and reassurance. History with a side order of pleasure, not pain.'

He laughed as he leaned over and topped up their glasses.

'I can see you love working here, surrounded by all these books.'

'Oh, I really do,' she replied, feeling suddenly light-headed. 'Sounds strange, but library work isn't all about books. It's the people who make it special; you never know who's going to walk in and what their story is.'

He smiled broadly and it transformed his whole face.

'Stories are the grease of life.'

'Now let me guess your favourite book,' she said, 'I don't mean to sound smug but it's a talent of mine.'

'Go on then.'

'You're a Yankophile. You love these new American authors. *The Grapes of Wrath*, John Steinbeck, that's your favourite book.'

She sipped her drink and smiled triumphantly.

'Very good guess and I admire him and Hemingway greatly, but keep guessing.'

'J. B. Priestley. I'm sure he's a man after your own heart. I bet you loved *Blackout in Gretley*.'

'Indeed, I did, but it's not my favourite.'

How annoying. She usually managed to pin someone down in two or three guesses.

Billy stood up and walked around the library, pausing every so often to pick up a book. In the distance they heard the faint rumble of trains, zig-zagging their way through the guts of London.

'Astonishing, to have a library built right over the tracks,' he marvelled.

'Don't look too closely. It's plasterboard mainly, stiffened with wooden slats.'

'No expense spared!'

'Ha, quite. We asked for one hundred pounds, but the

Powers That Be didn't see eye-to-eye with us, so we built it all on fifty bob and elbow grease.'

She smiled. 'Coming underground, being a part of this shelter community, has been the making of this library. Everyone is now invested in it, they feel it's *their* library.'

'Perhaps it's you they're invested in, Clara,' he said slowly.

She blushed. 'I don't know about that.'

'Do you have a book club?' he asked suddenly.

'No.'

'Why not?'

'Bit high-brow, isn't it? Can see that over in Hampstead, but I can't see it going down a storm in Bethnal Green.'

'What is it with the brows?' he grinned, wickedly raising both of his. 'Break the mould, Clara. Make book clubs about sharing a love of reading, not education. Clubs oughtn't be the preserve of the elite.'

'You're right. Would you join? I'd love to see you again.'

'I don't think I'll have time, sorry. My shifts are terrifically long.'

'Of course.' She looked down, feeling embarrassed. She'd been too bold. It was the relief of feeling safe, or the brandy.

The change in mood was like the flick of a switch.

'I'd better go,' Billy said, putting down his enamel cup and glancing at the door.

'Yes, course. I've kept you too long.'

'No, no, not at all. I've enjoyed your company, and I . . .' He broke off, and she could see his mind grappling with something.

The silence unspooled between them.

'I . . . I . . . oh never mind.'

He picked Beauty up. 'Please let me walk you home.'

'No don't worry, I'll sleep down here this evening. I'll feel safer. I've got an old camp bed behind the counter.'

They both made a move to clear up the cups at the same time, and their hands brushed. Billy pulled his hand back quickly.

'Sorry,' she mumbled, confused at the sudden change in him. Had she offended him?

Outside the library entrance, on the station platform, Billy shook his head in amazement. The curved walls were plastered in a plethora of orders. *Public Shelter Rules. Carry Your Gas Mask. Please Be in Your Bunks by 11 p.m., fumigation of platform takes place then.* So numerous, in fact, that no one gave them much heed any longer.

'It's so odd. When you're in the library, you forget you're in an Underground station, then you come out and feel all discombobulated,' he remarked. 'Not sure if I should be renewing a book or rushing for a train.'

'You better shake a leg before you end up being fumigated,' Clara grinned.

'Oh look, you even have a sign for the weather,' he said, noticing the small wooden sign fixed to the tunnel wall that Mrs Chumbley used to change depending on the weather up top. 'That must come in handy.'

'It did,' she replied, 'until some wag glued the "windy" sign on permanently during the Blitz.'

A cough startled them.

'Like your dog, mister.'

In the shadows, peeking round the interconnecting passage that led to the eastbound tunnels and the bunks, she saw two enormous brown eyes.

'Marie!'

It was the evacuee girl who had come into the library earlier.

She raised one finger to her lips. 'Sssh, don't tell me sister. She's asleep in her bunk. I like to dare myself and see how far I can go.'

She wriggled down into the pits. It was the only part of the tracks that hadn't been boarded over and led directly into the gaping mouth of the westbound tunnel.

'I'm going to make it to Tottenham Court Road one of these days.'

'You mustn't,' Clara urged. 'This track joins the live ones at some point.'

'S'right.' She winked. 'The end of this tunnel's sealed off.'

And then she was gone, scurrying into the darkness, her voice echoing behind her. 'Remember, librarians are excellent at keeping secrets!'

'Why you cheeky little . . .'

'And save me that book too,' her voice called back, already growing more distant as she vanished into the murky underbelly of London.

'Tube rat,' grinned Billy. 'This place is crawling with 'em. I'd have been just the same at their age.'

He stuck his hand out formally. 'Well, goodnight then.'

'Goodnight,' she said, shaking it. 'Not sure how I'll ever be able to thank you for what you did this evening.'

'You're safe Clara,' he said. 'That's all that matters.'

He smiled tersely, cutting a ribbon neatly between any further conversation.

'Goodbye then.'

'Bye.' She watched Billy stride up the platform, whispering something in the little dog's ear.

Back in the library, she spotted his white tin helmet sitting on the counter. She grabbed it and dashed back to the platform, but he had already gone, vanishing out of her life as quickly as he had come into it.

Clara wondered what it would feel like to kiss the tall ambulance man. Not because he was a dish, as Ruby might say, but because there was just something curiously comforting about him.

'Don't be ridiculous,' she muttered to herself, immediately feeling guilty. My God, if her mother and Duncan's could be this scandalised by her continuing to work in the library after his death, imagine what they'd have to say about her stepping out with another man!

Her parents had regarded children's librarianship as a respectable career, but only until the ring was on and her primary function as a woman could be fulfilled. As if, somehow, childbearing would turn her away from books and into the sort of woman who washed her aspidistra. Her education, they fancied, had been a passing phase that could be cured by a good husband.

Clara had qualified as a librarian a year before her marriage to Duncan and the outbreak of war, and though she had never dared to admit this out loud, the declaration of war had in one fell swoop nullified the married woman's regulation, allowing her to continue work. A fact that had appalled her mother and mother-in-law and secretly pleased her.

She shut the library door and on instinct locked it. As she pottered about tidying up, she wondered why guilt and grief were so entwined. What was the 'respectable' amount of time one ought to wait before entertaining love?

Not that it mattered much. Billy clearly wasn't remotely interested in her. Besides, falling for your rescuer was too clichéd for words.

'You'll never see him again,' she assured herself as she made up her camp bed and slid into it. And yet, as she lay there, cocooned by books deep below ground in the little wartime library, her mind kept dancing back to him. Those blue eyes were the last thing she saw as she finally fell into a deep sleep.

4

Ruby

When you close a library, bad things start to happen in the neighbourhood where the library used to be. The library is the glue that holds a community together and you only miss it after it has gone.
John Pateman, Chief Librarian in Thunder Bay, Canada

'Cooey . . . only me.' Mrs Smart from downstairs popped her head round the door. 'Old man kicked off?'

'What do you think?' Ruby replied.

'Reckoned as much, thought me ceiling was going to come down.'

Ruby cast her mind back to the events of the previous evening. Her stepfather had come home from the pub in a fearful mood, worse, if that were possible, than when he left, fuelled by black-market booze and bitterness. This time he'd smashed Netty's false teeth and three plates.

Ruby stared at her mother, sitting huddled in a chair by the window, pale and broken. Her knees were pulled up under her chin and she just sat there, scrutinising the rocky spurs of her arthritic knuckles, the pearls of her spine visible through her apron. Everything about her was bruised. Her face, her back . . . her soul.

'I really don't want to leave her,' Ruby whispered to Mrs Smart. 'She hasn't said a word all morning.'

A loud toot sounded outside and Ruby peered through the gaps in the anti-blast tape on the window. A Morris saloon idled by the kerb.

'It's my lift to work.'

'You get off, love,' Mrs Smart ordered. 'She'll be in safe hands with me. I'll make her a cuppa and a bit of breakfast. We'll have her fixed up in no time.'

'Thanks, Mrs S,' Ruby said gratefully, squeezing her shoulder. Mrs Smart was the matriarch of the buildings, always on hand to deal with any spot of bother that might emerge: lending money, birthing babies, laying out the dead and, more often than not, patching up women. Without Mrs Smart, the buildings would have crumbled long ago.

Ruby pulled a tube of vermilion red lipstick from the kitchen drawer and applied her armour.

'That's the ticket, girl,' said Mrs Smart, already taking charge and spooning tea into the pot. 'Put on your lippie, show 'em your flag's still flying.'

Ruby glanced at her mum.

'Bye, Mum,' she said softly, clicking shut her compact. Netty looked up and gave her a small, closed-lipped smile.

Ruby turned away. Clattering down the stairs of the buildings, she tied a silk headscarf covered in faded Spitfires over her blonde waves and strutted across the courtyard.

She jutted her chin out angrily. He was killing her. It was murder in slow motion and, worse, she felt absolutely powerless.

'Oi, Jean Harlow!' shouted a deep male voice. 'Come to the flicks with me tonight!'

Stanley Spratt from number 42 loitered by the gate to the buildings. Stan was as slippery as they come and had his finger in every black-market pie going.

'You and me, Ruby Red Lips, we'd make beautiful babies.'

'Fuck off, Stan,' she said with a sweet smile, opening the motorcar door then shutting it in his face.

'I'll take that as a maybe?' he grinned, running after the motorcar as Clara crunched the gears and they jerked away from the kerb belching black smoke.

'Your new chap?' Clara grinned.

'Stan? Behave. All he's got is high hopes and herrings. Tinned herrings at that.'

Clara laughed, casting her a sideways glance.

'How do you do it?'

'Do what?'

'Always look like you should be on the cover of *Vogue*. I look like I've been dug up.'

Clara was back to her usual ensemble of simple cotton blouse tucked into high-waisted slacks, and open-toed wedges. She was as slender as a candleflame and could make a sack look chic.

Ruby thought about telling Clara what had happened, but decided there and then to nail it down. By compartmentalising her pain, she at least had some spaces in her life in which she could breathe.

'Warpaint, darlin',' she said instead, smiling brightly. 'How comes we're in the bibliobus? It's Saturday.'

'I thought we'd visit the factories today, seeing how we missed it yesterday because of that do,' Clara said.

The motorcar rattled up Bethnal Green Road, past the Saturday-morning market stalls, all the costers shrieking their wares.

'What do you reckon to a book group?' Clara asked, changing gear with such a grinding shriek half the market turned to stare. Ruby smiled. Her best friend was one of the cleverest women she knew, qualified and everything, but she was a lousy driver.

'A good idea,' Ruby said, gripping the seat as Clara swerved round a man selling beigels on a bike and sent him wobbling into the gutter.

'Only, Billy reckoned—'

'Stop right there! Who's Billy when he's at home?'

She sighed. 'There's no easy way to say this. Some man followed me home last night and made a grab for me outside my door.'

'What!' Ruby screeched. 'Pull over now.'

'Calm down, it's all fine. He was just after my bag, I think. Anyway, this ambulance man Billy had noticed him following me and jumped to my rescue.'

'My God Clara, are you sure it was a mugging? Don't sound very likely to me, not round these parts.'

'Who knows. Thanks to Billy, I didn't have to find out.'

'I need to meet this Billy fellow and thank him.'

'I shouldn't think I'll ever see him again, to be honest.' Clara smiled sadly. 'He was nice though. Kind, with the bluest eyes you've ever seen.'

'You like him!' Ruby screeched.

'Stop it. I'm just very grateful he came to my rescue, is all.'

As they drew level with the factory, Ruby instinctively braced. There was only one thing worse that Clara's driving and that was her parking.

They hit the kerb, the motorcar backfired and shuddered to a halt. Ruby closed her eyes.

'I need someone to come to my rescue.'

'Cheeky minx,' laughed Clara, leaping out in front of Rego's garment factory.

'Come on. Can't keep the girls from their books.'

Groaning under the weight of two boxes full of paperbacks, they staggered up three flights of stairs and Ruby knocked the door open with her rump.

Pat Doggan, the oldest machinist on the floor, looked up from the mountain of khaki she was machining, with a gap-toothed grin.

'Aye aye, girls, the book fairy-godmothers are here. Or should I say, library lovelies?'

All the machinists started wolf-whistling.

'You saw the paper then,' Clara groaned.

'Course we did and we're proud of you. Getting our shelter in the news like that, it's smashing, so it is.'

She raised her voice.

'Boss, the library girls are here. Permission to pull out.'

Mr Rosenberg, the foreman, wandered out of his office wearing a curmudgeonly scowl.

'It weren't two minutes ago I switched the machines off so you could all get salt beef beigels. Is this a factory or a holiday camp?'

'Oh, go on with you.' Ruby smiled, putting an arm round him and kissing the top of his bald head, leaving a bright red lipstick mark.

'What does Mrs Rosenberg like?'

'A bloody good moan,' he grumbled, wiping his head with a hankie. 'She likes them Mills and Swoon.'

'Mills and Boon,' Clara interjected. 'All out of them, but I've got a few Georgette Heyer here. Tell her to try this, *The Spanish Bride*. Should take her out of herself for a while.'

While the foreman shuffled off to get his ticket, the rest of the factory girls fell upon the boxes of books like the blind who'd just been gifted their sight. It was lovely to see the infectious joy these women had for reading. Books were their escape into another, less punishing, world. Their eyes ran greedily along the spines as they picked them up, some turning straight to the back page, some reading the first few pages. It was like watching the hatching of a hundred different dreams.

Pat Doggan picked up a book and buried her face in it.

'Ooh, I do love the smell of a book, don't you?'

'What you in the mood for, Pat?' asked Ruby.

'A good saga.'

'How about *Gone with the Wind*?' Clara suggested.

Pat flicked through it and then put it back.

'I can't commit to nine hundred pages, love, I got nine kids, you know.'

'If you'd have committed to nine hundred pages, maybe you wouldn't have had all them kids,' teased the woman in the queue behind her.

'Shut your cake hole, Irene, you can't talk,' Pat laughed. 'Talking of nippers, all right if I send the boy up to your storytime whatnot?'

'Course, all your kids are welcome,' said Clara.

'You must want your head examining,' she remarked, picking up *Vein of Iron* by Ellen Glasgow. 'Set in Virginia, about four generations of strong women,' she said, reading the blurb. 'Now, this is right up my alley, I'll have this one.'

Ruby stamped the date label with a satisfying *thunk thunk* and the next woman shuffled forward. She had seen her down the Underground shelter and often wondered how she did it. Her husband was somewhere in the Far East. She had twelve kids, three jobs and a never-ending reserve of patience.

'You got that *No Orchids for Miss Blandish*?'

Clara's eyes opened wide and Ruby tried hard not to laugh.

'It's a bit risqué, Irene,' Clara explained. 'The *Bookseller* described it as drunk and disorderly reading.'

'All the more reason to read it.'

'Sorry,' Clara replied. 'I've not got a copy.'

Irene looked disappointed and settled, without any seeming trace of irony, for a Margaret Irwin historical novel, *Fire Down Below*.

Clara and Ruby had often discussed women's love for something with a bit of spice in it, and Ruby had noticed, as the war had groaned interminably on, women's appetites for something more risqué had increased. By 1944, with so many husbands and boyfriends away for years now, reading was the only way they could explore some of the feelings of loneliness.

'One of these days, I'm going to write a bodice-ripper, jam-packed full of sex,' Ruby said with a salacious wink.

'You write it, darlin', I'll read it,' said Irene, as she laid down her book to be stamped.

'I hate sex,' sniffed the next woman in the queue, with more rollers crammed under a turban than Ruby had ever seen. 'Terrible messy stuff. Gave it up a long time ago.' Queenie Jenkins spoke fast and always had a lot to say.

'Don't blame you, Queenie,' Ruby replied. 'How's your Brian take that?'

'Who cares! I only sleep down the Underground to keep his mucky paws off me.'

Queenie left happy with Dorothy Sayers' *Strong Poison*, and Ruby almost felt sorry for Brian.

Ruby looked up, bracing herself for the next factory motormouth, to find herself face-to-face with a new starter.

'Hello, sweetheart, what would you like?'

'Do you have *Rebecca* by Daphne du Maurier?'

Ruby couldn't place her accent.

'You new round here, darlin'?'

'I'm from Jersey.'

'You're a long way from home.'

'Hello again,' Clara smiled. 'You're Marie's sister. We met yesterday when your sister visited the library.'

'I'm so sorry if she was a nuisance.'

'Not at all, she's a delight. I'd really love her to come to the storytime session this evening.'

'Perhaps.'

'She's no bother and she'd make some friends too.'

'Hmm, perhaps.'

Ruby watched the one-sided exchange, intrigued.

'Sorry to be nosy, but what was the language you were talking in as you left yesterday? French?' Clara enquired.

'Jèrriais. It's a Normandy French patois. We use it in Jersey when we don't want outsiders to understand what we're saying.'

'Oh,' Clara replied, taken aback. 'Well, it's lovely.'

There was an awkward silence as the girl browsed the book selection before picking up a non-fiction, *Seven Pillars of Wisdom*, an autobiographical account of T. E. Lawrence.

'Are you sure you wouldn't like something a little lighter?' Clara asked.

'I'm not a child,' she snapped. 'I'm sixteen, you know. Clearly old enough to earn a wage.'

'I'm sorry. I didn't mean to offend you. Look here, we haven't got off to a very good start. You and Marie are welcome in my library to read *any* book you like, *any* time.'

'I thought you said my mother had to enrol us.'

'Usually you do have to be over sixteen to enrol in the library, but seeing as your mother's busy, I'll make an exception. Bring your sister to the storytime session at six p.m. with your shelter ticket, and I'll get you registered.'

'Thanks,' she said quietly. 'I'm Beatty.'

'Stop jawing!' yelled Mr Rosenberg, and Beatty jumped. 'This ain't a coffee morning. Any danger we could make some uniforms for the British Army sometime this century?'

'Keep your wig on!' yelled Pat Doggan, heaving her bulk back behind her sewing machine.

'Just one more thing, Mr Rosenberg, before you switch the machines back on,' Clara interjected. 'Ruby and I are thinking of starting a book club in a few weeks, The Bethnal Green Bookworm, on Friday nights in the library. Who's interested in joining up?'

A sea of blank faces stared back.

'I'll be making gin cocktails?' Ruby added.

'Why didn't you say?'

'What time do you want us?'

The chorus of approval came all at once.

'What's your first book?' asked Pat.

'Er . . .' Clara clearly hadn't though that far ahead.

'Go with a crowd-pleaser,' Ruby hissed.

'*Gone with the Wind*,' Clara blurted, her eyes settling on the book on the top of the pile.

Outside, they heaved the books back into the bibliobus before Clara turned to Ruby, hands on hips.

'And where exactly are you going to get enough gin to satisfy that lot?'

'Leave it with me, Cla.'

'Rubes! It's a library, not a speakeasy!'

'Books and gin, what's not to love? 'Sides, you adore me really.' She winked, slamming the back doors shut so hard that all the bracelets on her wrist jangled.

'You're a bloody liability at times, Ruby Munroe,' Clara laughed. 'But yes, I do.'

'Who was that girl?' Ruby asked as they got in. 'Right little madam.'

'I rather like her,' said Clara, gunning the engine. They sprang forward into the traffic with a lurch. 'She's intriguing.'

'Even you'll have your work cut out with that,' Ruby sniffed, lighting up a cigarette, and puffing it out slowly into three perfect smoke rings. 'Did you hear the way she described you as an outsider? She's hiding something.'

Back in the ticket hall, Dot whistled them over and gave them tea and cake on the house. 'You better open up that library soon, girls. Seems that article's done the trick. They'll be knocking down the door soon.'

At the bottom of the escalator, the shelter manager was waiting with a younger man.

'Aaah Mrs Button. There you are. This is Detective Constable Devonshire from Bethnal Green Police Station. Mrs Chumbley told me you had to sleep in the library last night after you were attacked outside your home.'

Ruby saw the unease on Clara's face.

'I think attack's a bit much. He was just after my bag.'

The detective spoke in a low voice.

'I rather think it may have been more than that, I'm afraid. A young woman was molested in Shoreditch last week and we are investigating a spate of other attempted rapes and abductions in the area.'

'Gracious,' Clara gasped.

'I'll need you to come in and make a statement.'

'Of course,' she nodded, paling. 'I'll come later after work if that's all right?'

They left and poor Clara looked totally stunned. Ruby felt an irrational rage. Was it not enough to be fighting a war, without some deranged man preying on women in the blackout?

'Thank goodness Billy was there,' Ruby said, hugging Clara tightly.

'Oi-oi, any danger of opening this library up?' hollered a voice. 'I only got ten minutes left of my dinner break.'

'Blimey,' Ruby murmured, pulling back from Clara and staring at the long queue which snaked down the platform. 'Dot weren't kidding.'

'Come on, back to work,' said Clara.

Ruby was nearly in the library when a man leaning against the curved tunnel wall stepped out in front of her.

'Say, Ruby Munroe, hey sugar.'

A tall GI stared at her expectantly. Down the tunnels, almost no one looked in such rude health. His height, combined with his good teeth and well-groomed appearance made him seem almost like a different species.

'So this is where you work?' he said, gazing curiously at the small door to the shelter library. 'Cute little library.'

He unwound a scarf, releasing the scent of Lucky Strikes and expensive woody cologne.

'Do I know you?'

He laughed.

'Jeez. You know how to deflate a man's ego.'

He took off his hat, raking his fingers through his blond hair.

'Eddie O'Riley. Dirty Dick's pub. Last October. You beat me in a drinking competition, then we went dancing and then . . .' He trailed off and raised one eyebrow. 'Boy oh boy, was that one hell of a night.'

A memory surfaced. *Oh God yes*. It had been Bella's birthday and Ruby had been so determined to forget, she'd ended up in the most notorious pub in East London. She did have vague recollections of an American, jitterbugging, swapping tops, then it got cloudy.

'Oh, well, lovely to see you and all, but I've got to press on.' She turned to the library.

'Whoa, not so fast Ruby Red Lips,' he said, grabbing her arm.

Out of nowhere, tears mustered. Unshaped thoughts flew through her mind. *False teeth skidding across the lino. Her mum on her hands and knees pleading. Nineteen steps.*

'Get your hands off me,' she said icily.

'Sorry . . . sorry.' He held his hands up. 'I didn't mean to scare you. Only, I had kind of hoped it might be a nice surprise. I've been training in Wales and this is my first furlough in five months.'

She stared at him suspiciously.

'I really am sorry,' he said. 'Boy, this isn't going the way I planned.'

He looked so mortified that Ruby almost felt sorry for him.

'You told me you worked in a library in East London, if you remember?'

She didn't.

'Said to look you up when I got back to London?' He frowned. 'I didn't realise how big East London is. Or how many libraries there are. Believe you me, I've met quite a few librarians lately, but now I've finally found you.'

'Well, sorry you've had a wasted trip pal, but I really have to get to work.' She could see Clara gesturing to her out of the corner of her eye.

'Is there anything I can say or do that might persuade you to come out with me again?' he asked hopefully. 'Only, you left quite the impression on me.'

She smiled sadly and shook her head.

'So long, Eddie.' She turned and was about to walk back into the library when a thought struck her.

'Actually. I will go out with you. On one condition.'

'Anything!' He grinned, his composure recovered.

'Bring me ten copies of *Gone with the Wind.*'

'Ten!'

She nodded. 'I need them for a book club.'

'Where will I find ten copies?'

She shrugged. 'London's full of book shops. I'm sure a resourceful man such as yourself won't have a problem.' She winked and walked into the library.

'Who was that?' Clara asked with a raised eyebrow as she lifted the counter hatch.

'Him? Oh nobody. I don't expect we'll be seeing him again.' Ruby tucked a stray curl back under her headscarf and forced a chipper smile on her face. 'Now, come on. These books won't lend themselves!'

5

Clara

I'm a gatekeeper to the past, sharing my knowledge of the riches of our books for others to discover. I'm a facilitator of joy.
            Mareike Doleschal, Librarian at the Shakespeare
                    Birthplace Trust in Stratford-upon-Avon

By 6 p.m., Clara had barely drawn breath. It had been the busiest Saturday on record. They'd worked flat out all afternoon, recommending and issuing books and shelving returns, sustained by nothing more than one cup of tea and a slice of Battenberg.

A sudden squawk at the door caught their attention.

'Oh no . . .' Clara said, backing up against a bookshelf. 'Not today, Rita, we really are terrifically busy . . . I . . .'

Blousy Rita Rawlins who worked somewhere 'up West' had taken to depositing her pet parrot at the library when she clocked on for her Saturday evening shift.

'Ta Cla, I owe you one. My bunk neighbour complained about little Petey to Mrs Chumbley and she's gunning for me. Reckons if I don't get rid of him, she'll stuff him herself.'

She waggled a talon at the mangy bird.

'Poor little Petey.'

'Really, Rita . . . I oughtn't—'

'He's a terrible potty mouth I'm afraid. He gets that from me. Chuck a tea towel over his cage if he starts up. Ta-ra.' She waved scarlet-tipped fingers in the air.

'Rita . . . We can't . . .'

Clara found herself talking to thin air. Rita had already left.

'This is a library, Clara darlin', not a petting zoo,' Ruby said, hooting with laughter.

'I suppose you'd like to join the library too, would you?' Clara sighed, holding up a cage containing a belligerent-looking green parrot.

'Saucy bugger!' screeched the parrot.

Clara looked at Ruby and hysteria kicked in.

'Oh, this is priceless!' Ruby howled. 'Oh, Mr Pepper, just the man. Are you any good at teaching parrots elocution?'

Mr Pepper stood hesitantly at the door, clutching a string bag full of books.

'Mr Pepper,' she said, 'are you all right?'

'Bit of a do really, my dear,' he puffed, pulling out a handkerchief and shakily mopping his brow.

'I'm so sorry for not dropping this off sooner . . . It's a long way to my wife's cousin in Pinner. There's a terrific crime selection.' He started to pull out the books and dropped the lot.

'Oh, dash it.'

'Mr Pepper. Are you sure you're all right? Should I fetch Mrs Pepper?'

'She . . . she died.'

'What! How? When?' Clara gibbered. 'You were only here with her last night!'

'W-we left the shelter very early this morning to collect the books and we got caught in a raid on the way home.'

Clara and Ruby stared at each other in disbelief.

'It was so sudden. One minute we were at Liverpool Street, waiting for a bus back to Bethnal Green and the next . . .'

He stared at them, utterly bewildered.

'I . . . I feel a bit peculiar.'

'Rubes, ask Dot or Alice to make Mr Pepper a strong cup of tea, with as much sugar as they can spare.'

'Right away,' she said, squeezing Mr Pepper's shoulder as she passed.

He turned to Clara, his rheumy blue eyes bewildered.

'I-I don't know what to do, Mrs Button. Apart from the Boer War, we haven't spent a day apart. Please forgive me for coming here and being a nuisance, only I didn't know where else to go.'

'Oh, Mr Pepper. I don't know what to say . . . I'm so very sorry for your loss. Do you have anyone you can stay with?' she asked.

'My wife's cousin offered to put me up, but I don't like to impose. Besides, I feel safer sleeping here, in the tunnels.'

Clara understood that.

He started to cry, and Clara folded the frail man in her arms.

'I'm so very sorry Mr Pepper. She was the most wonderful lady.'

'Whatever shall I do without her?'

Clara couldn't answer that. For she knew that grief was sharp and unpredictable. Losing Duncan had been the most frightening thing she had ever experienced. The sense of loss had crept into her bones and she felt it with every step she took.

'You'll not be on your own, Mr Pepper,' she said fiercely. 'I shan't allow it. Sleep in your usual bunk, but in the day, you're to come here.'

'Y-you're so kind,' he wept.

The sound of children's laugher echoed up the tunnels.

'It's going to get rather busy in here I'm afraid, Mr Pepper, but Ruby will be back soon with your tea, so stay put. Then later, when we're locked up, I'll walk you back to your bunk.'

'Thank you, my dear, I'm sorry to be such a bother.'

'Oh, Mr Pepper,' she said, hugging him. 'You couldn't be a bother if you tried.'

The children's storytime sessions underground at Bethnal Green were halfway between a riot and a reading group.

Ruby made it in with Mr Pepper's tea just before a great deluge of children swarmed the library. The noise rose like an enormous wave as in they came. The tall, the small, the snotty, the accident prone, the gigglers and the garrulous. Despite the sadness, Clara felt a great rush of pure, undiluted joy. The Tube Rats, as the kids of Bethnal Green Underground had named themselves, never failed to cheer her up.

'In you come,' she grinned, 'straight through to the

reading room. Oops-a-daisy, mind yourself,' she cautioned, as one little girl tripped over Mr Pepper's walking stick and sprawled flat out on the floor.

'Sorry mister,' she apologised immediately. She picked up a pair of broken glasses with the arms held on with chicken wire.

'No, no, my dear, it's my fault,' he apologised, helping her to her feet.

'Sorry about the noise,' Clara said.

'Please, no apologies,' Mr Pepper replied shakily. 'Why should they not chatter to their heart's content?'

Clara had just about had time to stack the trestle tables away and lay out blankets and cushions. Maggie May (Mrs Smart's granddaughter) and Molly (Dot from the café's daughter) were first in, already dressed snug as bugs in their nighties and trailing a rag-tag assortment of teddies behind them.

'Beatty!' Clara exclaimed, looking up. 'You came.' Beatty hovered by the library door. Marie showed no such restraint.

'Clara!' she yelled, hurling herself into her arms with a thump, sticky little fingers threaded behind her neck. 'You're my best friend.'

'Is that because I gave you a sherbet lemon yesterday?'

'No,' Marie whispered, her face inches from Clara's. She smelt of jam and pencil shavings. 'It's because you didn't tell on me.'

Clara winked and set her down.

'Ruby, would you mind registering Beatty? And Molly, would you make room for Marie?'

'Course,' said Molly, shuffling on her bum. 'Come and sit with us. We're tomboys.'

'Me too,' Marie said, as amazed as if they had just discovered they were long-lost sisters.

Clara laughed at the ease with which the intrepid little girl slotted into the group.

Beatty hovered by the door.

'I'd better go,' she muttered. 'I'll come and fetch her later.'

'Please stay, Beatty. You're so welcome here.'

She peered back at her, dark eyes questioning.

'Even after I was so rude to you earlier in the factory?'

Clara frowned, puzzled.

'You weren't rude.'

'I was and I'm sorry. You won't tell the shelter manager, will you?'

'There's nothing to tell. Besides, I'm in charge here, and I really would love you to stay.'

Beatty seemed to relax and Clara felt on safer ground.

'You're a long way from home and I expect you could use a friend.'

'Books are my friends,' she said quietly.

'I should like to be too,' Clara replied. 'If you'll let me.'

She wanted to spend more time with Beatty but Pat Doggan breezed in, kids hanging off every arm and leg.

'Go on then, you little bleeders, in yer go,' she said, shaking them off and pretending to boot them up the bum.

'You want me to stay, Cla?'

'No, you get off Pat and have an hour of peace and quiet on your bunk.'

'Sparrow,' she said, turning to her eldest boy. 'Make sure this lot mind their Ps and Qs and bring 'em back to the bunks after!'

Eleven-year-old Sparrow Doggan and his best friend, Ronnie Richards, were the oldest children in the reading group and usually felt they were past something as 'babyish' as reading time. Clara and Ruby saw them all the time round Bethnal Green. They called themselves the Schoolboy Gardeners of Russia Lane and had set about turning bombsites into allotments. When they weren't digging, they were racing their bikes round the debris or playing 'It' up the tunnels.

'For you, miss,' said Ronnie, plonking a muddy swede and a homemade Woolton pie onto the library counter. 'The pie's from Nan, the swede's from me. Oh, and me muvver wants a murder.'

Beatty watched the comings and goings and Clara was pleased to see an amused smile twitch at the corner of her mouth.

'Thanks, Ronnie. But I'm afraid she'll have to come in tomorrow and choose one herself.'

As the reading room filled up, Ronnie and Sparrow were joined by the third member of their group, Tubby Amos, who could always be heard coming up the tunnels as he had his leg in a brace after an early childhood bout of polio. Having his leg in irons didn't seem to slow him down much.

'Sorry I'm late,' he said cheerfully, rubbing the side of his head. 'I caught one from Mrs Chumbley for running through the station.'

'That's all right, Tubby,' Clara smiled, 'we haven't started yet.'

'I brought back *The Family from One End Street*,' he said, handing her the book. He used a piece of string weighed down with a half-sucked pineapple chunk covered in fluff as a bookmark.

'Oops, sorry miss. Smashing book that.'

'So glad you liked it, Tubby,' she said, peeling the sticky string off the page. That could be added to the chapter she one day planned for her memoirs: obscure items used as bookmarks, alongside rashers of bacon and stockings.

'You galloped through it.'

Tubby was the most voracious reader, drinking words and gobbling books.

She only wished Sparrow shared his appetite for reading.

As Ronnie and Tubby sat down, Sparrow sat stubbornly at the back of the room on a trestle table, arms crossed, all scabby knees and swaggery defiance. He had a catapult stuffed in one pocket and a *Dig for Victory* manual in the other.

'Do you want to come a little closer so you can hear, Sparrow?'

'Nah. I ain't interested in books. I'm just here to run me bruvvers home.'

'Saucy bugger!' screeched a voice, and Clara groaned.

The children's faces were a picture at the realisation that someone or something had sworn in the library.

'Rubes,' Clara called, 'put a tea towel over Petey's cage, would you?'

'Cheeky cow!' said the parrot, hopping up and down. 'Cheeky cow!'

It was too much. The kids fell about. Sparrow's studied look of indifference had melted and his face crinkled into pleasure. Even Beatty was openly laughing now.

'I know we're still reading *The Family from One End Street*,' Clara grinned, 'but seeing as we have Petey with us today, who'd like to read *Treasure Island*?'

'Yes!' came back a chorus of voices.

Every so often, Petey would interject and the kids clearly thought this was just about the best thing since pineapple chunks. You could have heard a pin drop as she recounted the tale of buccaneers and buried gold. But it was Sparrow and Beatty's faces that mesmerised her.

Jim Hawkins' story had them both gripped from the first thrilling scenes at the Admiral Benbow Inn. A light had come on in Sparrow's eyes. A leering, one-legged man with a tricorn hat, a scarlet coat and a raucous-looking parrot on his shoulder held him captive. Clara looked up and saw two men standing by the doors to the reading room, like a couple of bookends. They had snuck in silently while she was aboard the *Hispaniola*. On one side was Billy. On the other was Mr Pinkerton-Smythe wearing an expression as murderous as a mutineer. Her heart simultaneously leapt then plunged.

Clara returned to her book, but now she felt conspicuous and on show.

She closed the book and smiled brightly.

'That's enough for this evening, but tell me children, what do you think is the real treasure in this book?' she asked.

'Well, it's yer classic coming of age, miss, ain't it?' remarked Tubby sagely. 'The real treasure ain't gold coins, it's Jim discovering his own bravery.'

'I also reckon there's another lesson in there,' said Sparrow.

'Oh yes?'

'Never talk to old sailors at the bar.'

'Hello, sailor,' piped up Petey.

Everyone giggled. Marie giggled so hard, she let out a squeaky little fart, which of course set everyone off even more. Molly laughed so much, she rolled over and had to stuff her teddy into her mouth.

'Mrs Button, we are disturbing the tranquillity of the shelter,' Mr Pinkerton-Smythe said crisply. 'What a basinful of noise! I was under the impression that this storytelling session was to encourage the juvenile members of this library into a state of sleepiness. It rather looks to me like it's having the opposite effect.'

'Sorry. Come on now children, settle down. Time to go back to your bunks. And don't forget, I'm starting my spring/summer reading challenge tomorrow. Any child who reads ten books before the end of summer gets a free doughnut.'

The spell was broken and the room instantly filled with noise again as children scrabbled to their feet.

'Sparrow,' she called, as he gathered together his younger brothers. 'A quick word before you go. It was so lovely to see you enjoying that book.'

'Yeah, well, that one was good. It weren't written for babies, see.'

'I've had an idea. How would you, Tubby and Ronnie feel about being official library helpers? I'm afraid I can't pay you, but there'll be free doughnuts . . .'

'Mrs Button. Your time please,' Mr Pinkerton-Smythe interrupted, snapping his fingers.

'Yes, yes, I'll be right there. Just one moment . . . I'd also love for you to come in and read to the younger children. Be a reading pal.'

He shrugged.

'Ronnie and Tubby can, but I can't, miss.'

'That's a shame, Sparrow, do you mind me asking why?'

'Can't read.'

'Oh, oh I see.' Clara cursed herself. 'Well perhaps . . .'

'I'm on a tight schedule, Mrs Button . . .'

'I really shan't be long, I just wanted to talk to this young man . . .' But when Clara turned around, Sparrow was already gone, hustling his younger brothers out of the library door.

Damn it.

'Yes, Mr Pinkerton-Smythe. I'm all yours,' she said, unable to keep the irritation from her voice.

'While you were conducting the reading session with the juveniles, I had a good look around the library and I've made notes on where I feel we are going wrong.'

'Going wrong, sir?'

He pulled a notebook from his briefcase.

'Firstly, reading to children every night strikes me as indulgent. Once a week should do it.'

'Once a week?'

'Yes. I rather think we wish to discourage some of those children from setting foot in the library. Some of them look positively verminous.'

He sniffed disdainfully.

'The Froebelian approach might work in some libraries Mrs Button, but having children tumbling about the place simply will not do in an underground library. This library must run along more regimented lines.'

Clara barely had time to muster her outrage before he continued.

'Can you tell me why you've devoted such a prominent space towards books that have been adapted into motion pictures?'

'We can't ignore the influence of Hollywood,' Clara protested. 'I've found that whenever a novel is adapted into a film, there is a huge surge in borrowing requests.'

'But are these the *sort* of readers we want in our library, Mrs Button? It's like I was trying to explain yesterday. What you need to understand, my dear, is a lot of these women come from a lower mental stratum and their use of the printed word needs more encouragement and direction. We must raise their standards, point them towards more edifying fare.'

Clara couldn't speak.

'Look at this,' Mr Pinkerton-Smythe went on, waving a hand over the women's fiction bookcase. 'Light fiction from writers such as Ethel M. Dell and Denise Robins poses a grave danger to literature. You are doing the barest minimum to raise the intellectual standard by allowing women to read this.'

'*Allow* them to read it?' Clara exclaimed. 'You're talking as if my patrons don't know their own minds.'

She felt her heart beating faster, but his absolute opprobrium of her was like being struck with force.

'Now, calm down, my dear, you're getting excited again.' His smile was cold and contemptuous. 'I really must be off. We shall pick this up again, but one last thing. Your toes.'

'My toes?'

She looked down at her painted toenails peeking out from under her slacks.

'They're on show.'

'Well, yes, but my last pair of stockings have laddered.'

'Be that as it may, naked toes have no place in a library. I heard about what happened to you last night. How can I put this delicately my dear . . . we don't wish to give a man the wrong idea, do we? I shall raise the issue at our next library committee meeting, but in the meantime, please wear shoes that cover up your toes.'

For a moment, anger stole Clara's voice. How dare he imply what had happened was her fault!

'Very well, sir,' she said shakily. In that moment, she saw her reflection through his judgmental gaze, and she knew with a certainty, he didn't just dislike her, he loathed her.

He bent down to pick up his briefcase.

'Oh, and Mrs Button? Please get this library cleaned up, the children out and the parrot removed.'

She didn't watch him go but turned to the bookcase and stuffed her knuckles in her mouth.

'For what it's worth, I don't find your toes in the least bit offensive. In fact, they're rather nice.'

'Billy.'

She turned round to find him looking down at her with an amused smile on his face.

'How much of that conversation did you hear?'

'More than I wish I had. Who was that funny old stick?'

'My new boss.'

'Hello, you must be the mysterious Billy,' said Ruby, joining them with a sly smile on her face. 'I'm not sure what I can ever say or do to thank you for stopping that man last night.'

He reddened slightly.

'I didn't really do anything. Right place, right time.'

He turned to Clara. 'Did I leave my helmet here last night?'

'Oh yes, I'll just get it.'

By the time she came back, Clara could see Ruby had come over all twinkly and Billy looked like a hare in head-lights.

Ruby's usual 'look' could best be described as smouldering. No one could accuse her of ignoring the *Beauty is your Duty* call to arms and it was a rare day that her lips weren't redder than a pillar box. Even her shapely legs always had a liberal coating of Cyclax Stockingless Cream. Clara knew the version she presented to the world was bravado, as fake as the beauty spot she applied. The real Ruby was nuanced and with more layers than an onion, but weren't they all hiding behind a character?

'How's your lip?' Clara asked Billy.

'I'll live. I feel much better for listening to *Treasure Island*. It was one of my favourites growing up.'

'But not your favourite book now?'

'Nope.' He smiled, his eyes ever so slightly teasing.

She gave him his helmet.

'Did you hear there's been a spate of other attacks in the area?'

Billy dropped his helmet.

'No!' He looked absolutely horrified.

'Yes, I'm afraid so. A detective came by to see me earlier. He'll probably want to take a statement from you this week.'

'Clara, that's awful,' he said, stooping to pick it up. 'You mustn't walk home by yourself. Or you, Ruby. Ever.'

'Don't worry, I shan't.'

He frowned. 'I could come and see you home after work, if my shift patterns allow.'

'Billy, there's really no need,' she replied. 'You've done more than enough.'

'But of course there is. I . . . it's just beyond imagining. You're not safe on your own.'

She stared at him curiously.

'But I'm not on my own. I've got Ruby here. Besides, we're perfectly fine down here in the library.'

He twisted the helmet between his fingers and then tapped it nervously, clearly thinking to himself.

'Please don't take any risks, Clara.' He gazed at her searchingly then looked down at his watch.

'Damn. I've got to go. You must promise me to take care, Clara.'

She nodded. 'I promise.'

They watched as he left the library, ducking his head under the low door as he emerged onto the platform.

'He's sweet on you,' Ruby said, clicking her tongue against the roof of her mouth.

'Don't be daft you nit.'

Ruby arched one perfectly pencilled eyebrow. 'Trust me, he likes you.'

'Rubes. I'm married . . . was married.'

'I know darlin' and I don't mean to be disrespectful to Duncan's memory, but it has been nearly four years now. You are allowed to fall in love.'

Clara stared at the door, intrigued, confused and, maybe, just a little hopeful. *Was that what she was doing?*

She shook away the ridiculous thought. Her attraction felt like a betrayal to Duncan's memory. Besides, she knew next to nothing about Billy Clark, save for the fact that he had an uncanny knack of being in the right place, worked long hours and had a ridiculously cute dog. She didn't even know his favourite author!

By now, the only people left in the library were Marie, Beatty and Mr Pepper. Clara decided to close early and walk all three of them back to their bunks.

Together, they formed a group and made their way down the platform, cutting through the small, dark corridor that linked the westbound tunnel to the sleeping quarters of the Tube in the out-of-use eastbound tunnels.

It was 7.45 p.m. and the occupants of the sleeping tunnels were settling themselves down for the night. Three-tier metal bunks (less hospitable to lice) had been assembled by the Scouts stretching east along the tunnels for three quarters of a mile.

It took Clara's breath away every time. It looked like the interior of a giant sleeper train. Compartments labelled A through to D could sleep up to 5,000 people, though 8,000 had crammed down here one fiery Blitz night in 1940.

'What bunk number are you, Mr Pepper?' Clara asked, pulling out her smelling salts and discreetly having a quick sniff. These tunnels saved lives, but the fetid air from so many unwashed bodies pressed together night after night had to be smelt to be believed.

'I'm afraid I'm all the way at the end of D.'

'And where are you, girls?'

'Number 2,023 in B,' said Beatty.

Marie clung on to Clara's hand, skipping and waving to friends.

'I love sleeping underground,' she remarked. 'One day, Bea said I can have the top bunk.'

'*N'oublyie pon chein qué j'té dis*,' Beatty muttered.

Marie immediately fell silent.

'This is us,' said Beatty awkwardly.

'Where's your mum, sweetie?' Ruby asked.

'She works nights,' Beatty replied, 'at the Plessey aircraft factory in Ilford.'

'When does she get back?' Clara asked.

'Not sure, sometimes she goes straight into a double shift.'

'So who looks after Marie?' Ruby asked.

'I do,' Beatty said defensively, 'I'm old enough. I take her to the nursery before clocking on at Rego's.'

'Could you read to me, Clara?' Marie asked as she snuggled down under a scratchy blanket. 'Please!'

'No, she can't,' Beatty said. 'She's busy.'

'Another time, I promise,' Clara said. 'But you be sure to come to the library tomorrow evening.'

'But that man said you're only to do bedtime stories once a week.'

'You heard that, did you? Don't worry, I'll be reading every night, poppet. Night night, don't let the bedbugs bite.'

'Night, Mrs Button,' Beatty replied.

'Clara, please. We're friends now, remember?'

She smiled shyly. 'Thanks Clara.'

Beatty picked up the torch from her bunk and hunkered down in her blanket with her book, just like Clara herself used to when she was younger.

'Bloody irresponsible if you ask me,' Ruby muttered once they were out of earshot. 'Beatty's only sixteen; her mum oughtn't be leaving her to look after an eight-year-old all night.'

'What can she do?' Clara replied.

'Still. Girls that age need their mum. I'm going to give her a piece of my mind when I see her.'

After seeing Mr Pepper back to his bunk, they continued their way along the echoey tunnel, up the escalator and out of the Tube entrance.

'Told you so.' Ruby dug her elbow into Clara's side. 'It's old Billy Blue Eyes himself.'

'Billy!' she exclaimed. He was standing against the railings next to the Tube.

'You can't keep away, can you!' Ruby teased.

'I managed to swap shifts tonight. I just wanted to see you both home safely,' he said, a lock of his sandy blond hair falling over his face.

Clara felt a warmth snake through her tummy. The attraction she felt towards this kind and conscientious man was undeniable.

He held out his arm and she linked hers through it.

Ruby insisted they go via her buildings first and gave Clara a not-so-subtle wink as they left. Five minutes later they were back down Sugar Loaf Walk.

They paused on the doorstep and Billy seemed reluctant to leave.

'That was rather nice being walked home,' she said. 'I've got so used to living on my own and being independent.'

'I read you had been widowed,' he said softly. 'I'm so sorry for your loss.'

'Thank you. My husband . . . well he was killed in action in France. My losses are no worse than anyone else's, that's what I have to keep reminding myself . . . Sorry, I'm talking too much.'

'Not at all!'

'What about you?' she asked. 'You must see some awful things in your job.'

'Yes, but I have a strong stomach, and besides, I love what I do.'

'Were you exempt from the army?' she asked, curiosity overcoming her.

'I'm a conchie. You know, conscientious objector.'

'Oh I see. That must have taken guts.'

'You're one of the few people to think that way, Clara, believe me.'

'Why?'

'Same reason I suppose people don't like to see young girls reading non-stop. It's not the done thing . . . Besides, it's not very heroic, is it? Being a conscientious objector.'

'But you're doing your bit on the Home Front, aren't you? I don't expect it's a piece of cake being an ambulance worker.'

He sighed wearily.

'No, it certainly isn't. I worked seventy-five hours last week, but people form opinions, don't they? Oh, I don't know. If they could see what I saw when I was over in Dunkirk as a stretcher-bearer.'

A long silence unspooled between them. *Dunkirk*. Her throat tightened.

'I'd invite you in but you know how people talk.'

'Oh please, I understand. I best be pushing off anyhow.'

'Thanks again Billy,' she said, pushing her key into the lock.

'Just doing my civic duty.' He smiled, stepping back abruptly.

In that moment she had the most terrific desire to reach up and kiss him, to be held in his arms, to feel the warmth of a body in her bed, to feel hope again. *Anything* other than step into her lonely flat, where reminders of her failure as a wife sung from the walls. The absolute silence. That was the worst thing about being on her own. It's not as if she and Duncan had a terrific amount in common. Most evenings before the war, they'd sit by the fire, she with a novel, Duncan with the racing pages, but it was the quiet companionship she missed most. If it hadn't been for books, she was quite sure she'd be talking to herself by now.

'Oh, hang it all,' she blurted. 'Do come in for a cup of tea, it's hardly scandalous to drink tea is it?' She laughed uneasily.

'Thanks all the same Clara, but I'd better not.' He turned and strode back up Sugar Loaf Walk, Beauty trotting behind him. Clara groaned and leant her forehead against the front door.

You absolute ninny.

This wasn't one of Dot's bodice-rippers. Billy wasn't going to sweep her into his arms and kiss her hungrily on the doorstep. Curiosity tugged as she watched him disappear into the blackout. Who was this man, who deplored the war, yet dealt with its grisly consequences daily? Billy Blue Eyes was a paradox all right. He couldn't wait to leave, and yet what was it Ruby had said to him earlier? *You can't keep away.* She tapped the doorframe, then with a big sigh reluctantly walked into the yawning emptiness of her flat.

6

Ruby

If you have a book, you have a friend. As an only child, reading gave me a friend ALL the time.
Andrea Homer, former Saturday Girl at Cradley Library in Halesowen

Summer spilt through Bethnal Green, sticky and smothering. Bombsites all through the district were already sprouting great blousy drifts of willowherb, the hot air prickling with the scent of melting asphalt and coal dust.

The Baby Blitz, as the short spell of bombing raids that killed Mrs Pepper had been named, had passed, and something more ominous rumbled like an incoming storm on the horizon. Thirteen weeks had passed since Clara had been grabbed on her doorstep, and since then, two more women had been attacked. One in Hoxton where the woman had fought him off and another in Whitechapel who sadly had not been able to. Police were warning all women in the East End to be on their guard. Ruby had slipped a knuckle-duster into her handbag and wouldn't hesitate to use it should the occasion arise. Not that she ever found herself out after dark alone much. Not now Billy was on the scene.

Ruby pondered the enigma that was Billy Clark as she walked up the stairs to her buildings after work, having waved him and Clara goodbye. He seemed to have taken it upon himself to be Clara's protector and walked her and Ruby home whenever his shift pattern allowed it, always accompanied by his little dog.

Billy was the perfect gentleman, always making sure to walk closest to the road, seeing them right to their doorsteps. And yet this curious chivalry seemed to mask something else. There was something about the ambulance man she couldn't quite fathom. He was obviously sweet on Clara and yet seemed determined to keep their relationship on a formal footing, refusing all offers to join them for a drink in the library.

A nasty thought wormed into her mind. He better not be married. She'd come across more than her share of adulterers, especially during the Blitz. Men who ought to know better, packing their wives off to the countryside, liberating themselves to indulge in affairs. Every dark alley was a soft bed these days!

Bloody men. If you asked her, most of them wanted their dingle-dangles chopping off. Especially her stepfather. Useless toe rag. Not a whiff from that GI Eddie either, but then Ruby wasn't surprised. She had set him an impossible task. What with paper rationing, popular novels like that were hard to find. Tonight was their first proper book club meet up and they only had two tatty copies of *Gone with the Wind* between them!

Sighing, she pushed open her front door.

'I'm home.'

'In here, love. Put the wood in the hole.'

Ruby slammed the door and went to find her mum.

Netty was in the kitchen – where else – frantically blackleading the stove, arm going up and down like a fiddler's elbow. The potatoes were peeled and sitting in salted water in a pan ready to be made into chips.

'I'm not stopping long. Just changing before I go back to the library.'

'What about your tea?'

Ruby sliced off a chunk from the loaf on the side and spread it thinly with marg.

'This is it.'

'That won't keep body and soul together,' Netty worried.

Ruby shrugged as she chewed. 'It'll sop up the gin.'

'You're drinking too much my girl,' said Netty, washing the grime off her hands before drying them on her apron. 'That's what Victor reckons.'

'And he ought to know,' she murmured under her breath, 'drunken lout.'

'What's that, love?'

'I said, it's our first book club this evening. Should be a good turn out.'

She wiped the crumbs off her plate into the bin, before reapplying her lipstick.

'Say, why don't you come, Mum?'

'To the library? And leave Victor to cook his own tea?'

Ruby rolled her eyes. 'Imagine.' She rotated a stiff shoulder and sighed.

'Tired, love?'

'Librarian's elbow.' Ruby grimaced. 'We must have

lugged boxes of books in and out of a dozen factories. Oh, please come tonight, Mum. You might enjoy yourself.'

'You know me, love. I'm not much of a reader. Too stupid. *Woman's Own* for the knitting patterns is about my lot.'

'Oh Mum, don't run yourself down . . .'

A heavy bang sounded downstairs.

'Oh gawd, Victor's back already. Christ alive, I ain't started his liver and onions. He'll cut up rough.'

'Mum, calm down.'

A noise rose from the courtyard.

Ruby went to the balcony. Staggering around the central courtyard of the buildings was Victor, bouncing off walls.

'I had a little back room to let, the cost was half a crawnnnnn . . . Wotcha all looking at? Gawn on, fack off! Get back to your kitchens, you nosy old cows!'

The women of the square were watching from the landings, laughing their heads off as he took two steps forward and three back.

'Oi, Victor! Is that the do-si-do you're doing . . . or the do-si-don't?'

'Oi, Netty love!' shouted Nell from number 10. 'You better come and fetch your old man. He's been on the sauce. Old Bill's here.'

Netty joined Ruby on the balcony.

'Hello, sir,' said the officer to Victor. 'Looks like you've mislaid your feet.'

He gestured upwards and the two policemen looked up.

'He belong to you does he, madam?'

'Sorry . . .' Netty began.

'Never seen him before in our life, officer,' Ruby shot back.

'I recognise you, you work down the underground library, don't you?'

'That's right, officer,' Ruby said, dazzling him with one of her smiles. 'Ruby Munroe.'

'I'm a bit overdue on my latest loan I'm afraid.'

'Leave it with me, officer. I'm sure you'll find the fine will vanish.' She winked.

'Much obliged to you, Miss Munroe.'

He looked back down at the crumpled mess on the floor.

'Oh well, a night in the cells should sober him up. I'm sure someone'll claim him in the morning.'

The pair dragged Victor to his feet.

'Or you could leave him in lost property?' she remarked with a wink. 'In all seriousness though, I'd be looking to charge him with a disturbance of the peace. There's a lot of nippers in this square who shouldn't have to listen to his language.'

'You're right, Miss Munroe.' He cast a last appreciative look at her before he and his colleague dragged Victor off to Bethnal Green Police Station.

'Oh, love,' said Netty. 'You oughtn't to have done that.'

'Oh, Mum, he was so drunk, he won't remember a thing about coming here in the morning. Serves him right. Now you've twelve hours off. And you're coming to the book group.'

'Victor won't approve. He don't like me reading books.'

Of course, he prefers you uneducated, is what Ruby wanted to say. Instead, she smiled sweetly.

'Mum, it's a book group, where's the harm?'

Ruby took the tea towel slung over her shoulder and tossed it down into the square. 'You're coming to the library.'

Ruby knew something was wrong the minute they set foot in the Underground.

Clara was rushing across the ticket hall.

'Who's manning the library?' Ruby asked.

'Mr Pepper. It's little Marie Kolsky.'

'What about her?'

'She's missing. She didn't show up to storytime and Beatty can't find her anywhere. Mrs Chumbley's leading a search party up the tunnels and I'm off to find Billy, see if he can spare any ambulance crew to help hunt.'

Sparrow, Ronnie and Tubby charged into the ticket hall.

'Right, you lot, come with me,' Ruby ordered. 'You Tube Rats can show me all your hiding places.'

Ruby, Netty and the boys clattered down the escalators and could hear the commotion rising to meet them.

'No, no, don't call her.'

Beatty was hysterical, and the shelter nurse was trying to calm her.

'I asked where her mum worked so I could call her and let her know about Marie, but she's adamant she doesn't want me to contact her at work,' the nurse explained.

'Please, you mustn't call her.'

'Let me take her to the library, give her a glass of water

and sit calmly for a bit,' Ruby suggested and the nurse nodded.

'All right. Call me if you need my help.'

'Thanks, nurse. Now, boys,' Ruby said turning to Sparrow, Tubby and Ronnie, 'comb every inch of these tunnels. Find Marie.'

They turned in a great tangle of limbs.

'Let's check the horror room!' Sparrow yelled.

'The horror room?' Beatty cried.

'It's just what they call the ventilation room,' Ruby muttered, 'it makes some funny noises.' Least, she hoped that's why they called it that.

In the library, Ruby poured Beatty a glass of water and guided her to a quiet corner of the reading room.

'Sit down, sweetie, and drink this. Your sister'll turn up, you'll see.'

Beatty sat down reluctantly.

'Must've been hard for you both leaving Jersey to come here, leaving your dad behind.'

Beatty sipped her drink and nodded.

'Tell me about Jersey,' she coaxed. 'I've always wanted to go. They were still advertising the Channel Islands as a bomb-free holiday even after the war broke out.'

'That was half the problem,' Beatty replied. 'We weren't prepared. After France fell, it was chaos.'

'What did your mum do?' Ruby asked.

Beatty squeezed back tears.

'She queued for hours to get us a ticket on the boat out and when the day came . . . oh, it was awful. Crowds of people fighting to get onto the boats at the quayside.

I never even got a proper chance to say goodbye to Dad.'

'How frightening. Why did your dad not come?'

'He wanted to stay behind and look after his business. I-I don't think he believed that the Germans would actually invade.'

Ruby nodded. She had read the chilling news when the Channel Islands had been bombed, then invaded. It seemed hard to believe that the Crown's oldest possession was now under Nazi occupation.

'Why come to the East End?'

'Mum had an auntie in Whitechapel, but when we got here, we discovered she'd evacuated as well.'

'War throws up many surprises,' Ruby said. 'Mostly unpleasant. So, what did your mum do?'

'What could she do? Mum got a job and lodgings, then we got bombed out and here we are.'

Ruby fell silent, intrigued by the strange odyssey that had wrenched this sixteen-year-old from her idyllic island home.

'Bethnal Green must be very different to Jersey,' Ruby remarked.

'You could say that,' she sighed. 'I miss diving in the saltwater pool at Havre des Pas. Helping to harvest potatoes, the smell of vraic seaweed drying in the fields.'

'Sounds heavenly,' Ruby replied.

'It was. But it isn't now. How can it be, now that our island is draped in swastika flags?'

'Maybe your father will be all right? It seems to be a less strict occupation than France,' Ruby replied.

'How exactly?' she replied scornfully. 'Please don't tell me you believe that outlandish propaganda? There is no good life under the heel of the Nazi jackboot. Especially not if you're Jewish, Miss Munroe.'

'I'm sorry, that was crass. Have you heard from your father?'

'The cables from the Channel Islands to Britain were cut as soon as they invaded and the mail boat stopped sailing, so my mother took us all to the Red Cross offices in London. They gave us a Red Cross letter.'

'And?'

'We've sent many, but we haven't had one response.'

The solemnity of her gaze told a thousand stories of loss and separation.

'I'll let you into a secret. I'm scared too.'

'You? But you seem so jolly.'

'Trust me sweetheart,' she sighed, thinking back to Victor, 'it's all a front.'

All through this conversation two things stood out for Ruby. First, that Beatty was fiercely bright. Second, her mother didn't seem to feature highly in her life down the tunnels. A clumsy suspicion began to form in her mind.

'Does your mum often work nights?'

'Every night.'

'That puts a lot on you.'

'I'm sixteen, I'm not a child anymore.'

Ruby nodded. Beatty and Marie's mum wouldn't be the first woman to have her head turned by a foreign soldier. London was a boomtown at the moment, and the Yanks and their free-spending ways had turned the head of even the most reserved of women. The GIs had brought glamour and colour, to say nothing of contraception. She ought to know. Turned out better uniforms and pay weren't the only extra perks the American forces enjoyed over their British allies. Perhaps Mrs Kolsky was enjoying her newfound freedom, leaving the Underground shelter as a nocturnal nursery?

'Still. Looking after Marie isn't just your job.'

'You don't know my mother, or me, so please spare me your judgement.'

'I'm only trying to help, Beatty.' An idea came to her.

'Look here. What do you need? I've got a friend who can source some stuff under the counter.'

'There's only one thing I need most right now and even you can't help with that, Miss Munroe.'

'Try me.'

'Space. Somewhere to put my thoughts.' She gestured around her. 'There's no privacy anywhere. I write letters to my dad every week and I keep them in my bag, but they do bag searches at work, and every time, Pat or Queenie makes some lewd comment about me having a sweetheart. The first time it was funny, now it's just, well, tiring, to be frank.'

Ruby laughed.

'I can imagine. Neither of them are known for their subtlety. I have an idea.'

She stood up and went to the non-fiction bookcase and pulled out *The Art of Homemaking*.

Beatty's dark eyes followed her inquisitively as she pulled out bottles of liquor that were stashed behind it.

'When they were building this library, they must have run out of timber, as this section here behind this bookcase was only plywood and it fell out. It's only supposed to be temporary, after all, and will all come down when the war's over.'

She reached into the dark cavity.

'It butts up against the side of the tunnel wall and right here is an alcove.' She pushed her hand deeper into the bookcase until her entire arm was swallowed up. 'I think it must have been built to store cable ties or such like, but now it's empty. You can store your letters there if you like.'

'You promise not to open them?'

'Promise.'

Beatty pulled out the letters from her bag and handed them to Ruby.

'Nothing in this library's what it seems,' Beatty said, gazing with curiosity at Ruby.

In that moment, she had a feeling she'd earned the trust of this strangely adult girl. Libraries are places that seem to invite confidences. All those books whispering from shelves, loosening tongues. Perhaps it was true. When you are surrounded by stories, maybe you can't help but share your own? Ruby often had the sensation that being beneath the ground in the labyrinth gloom of the underworld stripped away your everyday facade. People came into the underground library, breathed in the aroma of books and let down their guard. Right now, she saw a girl teeming with stories. Beatty was holding back the ending, but at least she had shared her beginning.

Beatty gazed around the little library, as if seeing it for the first time.

'Is that Marie's?'

She was looking at the wall Clara had devoted to the children's book reviews for the reading challenge.

One entire wall of the reading room was a colourful mosaic of words and pictures from the shelter kids who were taking part in the challenge to read ten books by the end of summer.

'Triffic, I love *Black Beauty* the hole world,' Beatty read her sister's review out loud. 'Dreadful spelling.'

'Don't be too hard on her, Beatty. It's not her fault the schools are closed at the moment, and you'd be surprised how much she's learning from life down here in the shelter.'

'What's she reading now?' Beatty asked.

Ruby looked down at the folder. '*The Princess and the Goblin.*'

'Miss Munroe.' Mr Pepper poked his head around the door. 'I think you better come . . .'

His words were drowned out by a commotion from outside the entrance to the library.

'Marie!' Beatty cried.

Outside, on the station concourse between the east and westbound tunnels, a group had gathered, in the middle of which stood Sparrow, Tubby and Ronnie.

'We found her,' gibbered Ronnie.

'You want to find a child, you gotta think like one,' added Tubby, tapping his head.

'What are you blithering on about, boy?' exclaimed Mrs

Chumbley, elbowing her way to the front of the crowd, followed by Mr Pinkerton-Smythe.

'Go on, tell 'em, Sparrow,' Ronnie said, nudging him.

'Girls,' he sniffed. 'You can't trust 'em.'

'Sparrow,' said Billy gently. 'Why don't you tell us where Marie is?'

'She's only gone and got herself stuck halfway down the fire escape. Girls can't handle the horror room.'

'Why in the devil is it called the horror room?' blazed Mr Pinkerton-Smythe.

'It's the ventilation room off the eastern tunnel,' explained the shelter nurse. 'It's a small room that connects to a shaft that leads up to Carlton Square. It's a designated fire escape route with a narrow stairwell up, I believe.

'It makes an unholy moaning noise through the door grille when it's windy up top,' she went on. 'It is rather creepy.'

'And something of a magnet to small boys and girls who ought to know better,' said Mrs Chumbley.

'Well, don't just stand there!' shrieked Mr Pinkerton-Smythe, but Billy was already buckling up his tin helmet and racing towards the eastern platform, followed by the rest of the group.

They plunged further into the eastbound tunnel, ringed on both sides by bunks, their footsteps echoing as they ran into the cylinder of darkness.

Finally, they reached the last bunk and the tunnel ran out, the hardboard partition a full stop in the darkness.

In the gloom, Ruby made out a soot-crusted little door cut into the tunnel wall, covered with a metal grille.

Billy opened the door and turned to Sparrow.

'Did she go up or down, son?'

'Down, sir.'

The metal grille covering the door clattered shut ominously behind him.

A tense silence fell over the group.

'I hope she ain't gone too far down,' whispered Tubby. 'They say there's a whole network of passages beneath the tunnels that stretch all the way under the Tower of London. A maze that can trap a person for all eternity.'

The assembled crowd inhaled.

'The child has a many-hued imagination,' Clara said lightly.

Just then Sparrow's mum Pat Doggan bowled up the tunnel.

'Right, you!' she yelled at Sparrow. 'You're for it now.'

'Does he belong to you, madam?' Mr Pinkerton-Smythe demanded.

'What's the little bleeder done now?'

'He and his little gang have been trespassing on London Passenger Transport property.'

'We weren't trespassing,' Sparrow protested, but his cries were silenced by a swift clout round the back of the head by his mother.

'He shan't be doing it again, you have my word, sir,' said Pat angrily.

'You're gonna stay at your auntie's above ground for a month.'

They disappeared, Sparrow being dragged up the platform with Pat muttering about flogging and no tea.

'I do not wish to see that delinquent in the library again,' Mr Pinkerton-Smythe said under his breath to Clara.

'He's not a delinquent. He's a decent kid.'

The whole platform stared curiously at the exchange until a noise rustled from behind the door.

Billy emerged, holding a very grubby little Marie Kolsky in his arms. A great wave of relief went round the group.

'Fetch a stretcher, would you please, nurse?' said Billy, gently setting Marie down on the ground. 'She's got a nasty sprain on her ankle.'

'What were you thinking?' Beatty cried.

Marie's hair was tangled in dirty clumps and an icicle of snot hung from her left nostril.

'I'm sorry,' she cried. 'But I wanted to see if there were goblins down there.'

'Goblins?' demanded Mrs Chumbley.

'The evil goblins who live underground. I thought it was them what was making the noise, miss. And I thought they was getting closer 'n' coming to abduct all the children.'

'*The Princess and the Goblin*,' Ruby said, clapping her hands together. 'That's where she got the idea for that.'

'Aaah,' said Clara, chuckling as the penny dropped. 'Did you find any goblins?'

'No. Only rat poo.'

Seeing all was well, the group dispersed.

'Billy, thank you so much,' Clara said. 'Again.'

'Just doing my job,' he blushed. 'I need a quick word with the nurse. I'll pop into the library afterwards.'

'Just another day in our little wartime library,' Ruby

sighed. 'I don't know about you, but I could murder a stiff drink.'

'Yes, and we have the book group starting soon,' Clara reminded her.

'Before that, a word, Mrs Button,' said Mr Pinkerton-Smythe. 'In the library.'

Clara followed him, shooting a grim look at Ruby as she passed.

Ruby needed a good thick lungful of nicotine. She made her way towards the escalators up to the ticket hall.

'Miss Munroe . . .'

She turned to see Beatty standing at the bottom of the escalators.

'Thank you.'

'What for?'

'For not telling my mum. And for the secret place,' she said softly.

'Told you she'd be all right,' she replied. 'Write that down in one of your letters to your dad.'

Beatty smiled and then darted back to join her sister.

Up in the ticket hall, it suddenly occurred to Ruby. *My mum!* In all the disturbance, Netty had slipped away.

'What's up?' called Dot from behind the café counter. 'You look like you found a penny and lost a shilling.'

'You didn't see Mum earlier, did you, Dot?'

'Netty? Yes, darlin',' she said she was going up the nick. Summit about the old man needing bailing out. Oh, before you go' – Dot reached under the counter, her eyes twinkling –'looks like you've got an admirer, ducks.'

'Oh, leave off. Who?'

Dot slammed down a pile of books on the café counter.

'Some Yank. Eddie, he called himself, come looking for you, but he says the library was locked. He was jibbed to have to missed you.'

'Oh,' Ruby breathed. 'Yes, we had an emergency and I had to lock up for a bit.'

'Shame. He's a right handsome bugger. He left you nine copies of *Gone with the Wind*. And this –'

She handed Ruby a scrawled note on the back of a Lucky Strike packet.

You're breaking my heart. Nine down. One to go. I'll be back. Yours in hope. Eddie x

Ruby started to laugh and, picking up the top copy, she fanned the pages open. It was brand-new too by the looks of it.

'Wherever did he get these?'

'I don't know, love.' Dot winked. 'But he seems awful keen to please you.'

'Oh, behave, Dot,' Ruby scoffed, scooping the books up. 'The only thing that man's after is a happy ending.'

Outside the Tube, Ruby lit a cigarette. She had to hand it to Eddie. He was certainly tenacious, but his motives were pretty transparent. *Men.* She tipped her head back and blew a long plume of blue smoke up to the heavens. She wouldn't give tuppence for any of them.

Frustration drummed in her chest. She had come so close this evening to getting her mum into the library. She could have let her hair down for a change, reminded herself of the sort of woman she used to be before she married Victor. Before he'd knocked the stuffing out of her.

Was there a library in the world that contained a book that could teach her mum the value of her own self-worth? If the previous four years of library loans had taught her anything, it's that history provides the answers.

Queerly, she remembered how, during the Blitz when London felt like it was burning to the ground, Mr Pepper had read extracts of Samuel Pepys' diary. Reckoned the bits about the Great Fire of London comforted him to know that the metropolis had been rebuilt and new civilisations formed in the ashes of the old.

Ruby had found it macabre at the time, but now she got it.

Her stepfather wasn't just a drunk bully. Victor was a home-front dictator. A man so twisted, he could smash his own wife's teeth to gain control over her. But their war wasn't being fought with bullets and tanks. Theirs was a silent war, waged behind closed doors.

She watched a gaggle of Rego's girls tripping by, three thrillers and two historical romances between them, off home to get stuck into a thumping good read. A precious hour or two before bed to forget their aching backs and powdered egg tea.

The solution was reading. On a shelf somewhere there was a book whose pages offered escape and emancipation. She just had to find it. Ruby ground out her cigarette and headed back into the underground library, clutching nine copies of *Gone with the Wind*.

7

Clara

That moment, where something clicks, and you know you've made a reader of a child. Pure magic.
Donna Byrne, Reader Development Librarian for
Havering Libraries

'Tell me, Mrs Button, when you took your library examination, did it include encouraging delinquents?'

Clara was staring down the barrel of an angry Pinkerton-Smythe.

'You were drilled in the importance of cataloguing, library administration and the merits of fine literature in order to discharge your functions effectively. I presume you did pass. You are a qualified librarian, aren't you?'

'Yes, of course I am. I studied for my diploma at the School of Librarianship at the University of London. I also had additional training in children's librarianship under Berwick Sayers, President of the Library Association.'

He sniffed, unimpressed.

'Then you of all people should realise that the majority of children who attend this library are either delinquents or weak in the head.'

'That's not f—'

'Don't interrupt me when I'm talking! These children should be in education, not here.'

'But the schools are closed. Where else are they to go?' she asked despairingly.

'It is not the job of a public library to help entertain juveniles. Do you have children yourself, Mrs Button?'

He snapped his fingers. 'No, of course not, otherwise you wouldn't be working here.'

'I don't see whether my being a mother has anything at all to do with my fitness to perform my duties as a librarian,' she whispered, hot tears gathering behind her eyelids.

'Look here. Now you're getting emotional. I understand your husband died at Dunkirk. I'm sorry for your loss, but this library cannot continue in its present form.'

'Why don't we consult the Director of Home Publicity at the Ministry of Information?' Clara said loudly. 'Because, as I recall, he seemed rather pleased with what I'm doing here.'

Mr Pinkerton-Smythe's face twisted from righteousness into anger and he leaned in closer to her.

'One day soon this war will be over and the Ministry of Information will be disbanded. Women will return to their homes, the rightful social order will return, and I will still be here, Mrs Button, as chair of the Library Committee. Where will you be?'

Clara went to open her mouth, but he beat her to it.

'You are a placeholder, filling in as branch librarian until our male librarians return from war. And when they do, you will go back to just being the children's librarian.'

Just the children's librarian?

He picked up his briefcase and left, the air in the space he'd occupied stale.

In a sudden rush, Clara's adrenaline drained out of her and she burst into tears.

Ruby breezed into the library carrying a stack of books, at the same time as Billy and Beauty.

'Wotcha Billy. Look at this Cla, nine copies of *Gone with the* . . .' Ruby trailed off.

'Oh that bloody man! What's he done now?'

Ruby put down the books and went to hug her, but was beaten to it by Billy.

'The man's a patronising snob,' he said, his long legs crossing the library in a few easy strides and scooping her into a hug.

For a moment, she stood with her head rested against his chest.

Reluctantly he pulled back. 'Sorry, Clara. I only popped in to say goodbye. I ought to be pushing off.'

Maybe it was the drama of the afternoon, but she felt reckless.

'Oh, please stay,' she urged. 'The book club was *your* idea after all.'

'I-I'd love to, but I really have to go.'

Behind him Ruby rolled her eyes.

'Oh, shut up and sit down, would you Billy, you ain't bleedin' Cinderella.'

Beauty barked, her paws skittering on the floor. 'See,' Ruby said. 'She agrees.'

'Rubes!' Clara exclaimed.

'It's all right,' Billy laughed. 'I suppose I had better stay now, prove to Ruby and Beauty I'm not going to turn into a pumpkin.'

'Good decision,' Ruby said with a mischievous grin. 'I'll leave you two in peace while I clear away the newspapers before book club. Come on, girl.' Beauty trotted after her.

'Subtle,' Clara mouthed.

And then they were alone. And something about Billy seemed even more attractive this evening. His face had tanned in the summer sun, making his blue eyes seem all the brighter.

'I wanted to give you something actually, Clara,' Billy said nervously, reaching for his bag and pulling out a package. 'I've been carrying these round all week.'

Intrigued, she unwrapped the brown paper parcel, bound with string.

'B-but you can't give me all these,' she protested as the wrapping fell away.

It was the complete set of Beatrix Potter, first edition.

'They belonged to my younger sister.'

'But they're valuable.'

'Felicity has no desire to have her own family. She's working somewhere hush-hush in the countryside. She's got brains the size of Bulgaria and the War Office has found a use for them. I told her about your library, and she wanted you to have them.'

Gently, Clara wiped away the fine layer of dust on the spine, the dust of generations.

'Thank you. This will bring so much pleasure.'

She glanced up and he was smiling down at her, enjoying her pleasure at the gift.

'Oh look, *The Tale of Mrs Tiggy-Winkle*,' she cried. 'I loved that one.'

'Me too,' he laughed.

'And look here, *The Tale of Jemima Puddle-Duck*. This was my favourite, used to send me into a nervous spasm waiting for the arrival of the foxy-whiskered gentleman and, do you know, even as a child it used to make me so cross that she couldn't see through him. Fancy falling for eating herbs to stuff herself, silly bird.'

Billy was really laughing now.

'I was more of a Peter Rabbit fan. I loved the way he outwitted Mr McGregor.'

Soon, they were absorbed in their favourite Beatrix Potter characters and a doorway opened into the past. Clara wondered whether Mr Pinkerton-Smythe had ever been read to as a child? Perhaps that was why he was so brittle? The spaces and cavities of his brain that reading filled up with empathy had calcified and hardened, turning his imagination to cement.

'Do you think I should offer to teach Sparrow to read?' she asked.

'What do you think?' he replied.

'I think every child deserves a champion. If I hadn't had Peter, I'd be . . . well, I'm not sure where I'd be, but I wouldn't be here.'

'Course you would,' he chided.

'No, really. My parents weren't readers. Growing up, we only had two books in our house, an encyclopaedia and the Bible. 'I used to go to Bethnal Green Library every Saturday with my three tickets.'

She smiled nostalgically.

'I still remember when Peter gave me *The Secret Garden* to read when I was thirteen. The idea of a forgotten garden on the other side of a secret door was intriguing. I used to go around checking all the doors in my house, just in case. That sounds terrifically silly, doesn't it?'

'Not at all.' He smiled back tenderly. 'Sounds like the book did open a door, at least in your mind.'

'It was magic. That book changed everything for me. Libraries are . . .' Her slender fingers traced the spines of the books. 'Tactile places.'

Clara had been three years old when the long-awaited Carnegie funded library had opened. Growing up, it been her very own book-lined palace of dreams. Not just hers either. She couldn't imagine how many lives the red brick library had transformed in Bethnal Green.

She stared down at the book. 'Sometimes, you just need someone to care.'

'Would you like to come out with me sometime? As a friend I mean . . .' he added hurriedly.

'Like where?' she asked, looking up in surprise. The question seemed to have come out of nowhere.

'I've been dying to see the Summer Exhibition at the Royal Academy and I always feel like a bit of a goose going to exhibitions on my own.'

'Well, in that case,' she laughed, 'I'd better go. But I ought to warn you that I only get Wednesday and Sunday afternoons off.'

'That's all right, I'll wait.'

Inside, her heart was doing triumphant somersaults. Had she ever felt this attracted to Duncan? Theirs had been a comfortable, convenient courtship. Duncan had worked in her father's cabinet-making firm from the age of fourteen, was virtually 'one of the family' anyway, so the marriage had felt like a foregone conclusion. They hadn't a thing in common, but there had been love of a kind. Duncan and her father had gone everywhere together, from work to the dogs, to the Speedway, not forgetting the Saturday pilgrimage to see West Ham play.

He had been the perfect husband. Kind and so loyal, the kind of man you could hang your hat on. She closed her eyes, feeling torn. Surely going to an exhibition with a man as a friend wasn't a betrayal of his memory, was it? The grubby voice sounded again. *If you'd been a better wife . . . if you'd given up work . . .*

'Are you all right?' Billy's voice tugged her back to the present. 'We don't have to go out . . . it's a bad idea isn't it. Forget I said anything.'

'It's all right,' she said softly. 'I'd love to go.'

'Mrs Button, may I borrow you?' called Mr Pepper from the reading room.

'Excuse me, Billy.'

Reluctantly, she walked into the reading room where he and Ruby stood in front of the *Daily Herald*.

'Someone's cut out the racing column,' Ruby said.

'Who?' Clara demanded.

Mr Pepper shrugged.

'We were hoping you might know?'

'I haven't a clue. How strange.'

'No time to start doing a Miss Marple now,' said Ruby. 'It's book club time.'

'It's sex I want,' Irene announced.

'No! Murder!' Queenie retorted.

'No, something nice and racy,' said Dot from the café. 'Makes me knit faster when I get to a juicy part.'

A cackle of laughter rose.

'Anyone for a top-up?' asked Ruby.

'Not many,' said Pat, sticking her glass out.

'Any more of these and I'll be on the floor,' laughed Alice. 'It's delicious; what's in it, Ruby Red Lips?'

'Well, the book club belter, as I've called it, is made up of three key ingredients. Gin, gin and gin. I'm joking. There is a bit of orange cordial in it,' she said, winking as she topped Pat up. 'But I don't like to go too heavy handed on the cordial.'

'Just as well it's a short stagger back to me bunk then,' Pat laughed.

The inaugural meeting of the Bethnal Green Bookworm club had got off to a lively start. Ruby's cocktail had made the women even more loquacious than usual.

Clara was drawing up a list of books to put on their reading list and, as per usual, the women of Bethnal Green weren't shy in putting forward their opinions.

'Back to the books,' Clara said.

'I'm very charry about the authors I read,' sniffed Pat. 'When I find an author I like, I stick with her.'

'Well, I only read Agatha Christie or Dorothy Sayers;

they ain't let me down yet,' interrupted Queenie. 'Not a dopey read among 'em.'

'But I hate murder,' protested the young shelter nurse. 'I see enough blood in the day job.'

'Yes,' agreed Dot. 'I need something light and easy. I could read a yard of romance a week if you let me.'

'Flimsy froth,' snapped Queenie.

'Let Mrs Button talk!' boomed Mrs Chumbley. It had the desired effect.

'Yes, well thank you, Mrs C,' Clara said. 'What I was trying to say is that the purpose of this club is to share our love of reading and to encourage you to try something new. I had a lady in yesterday who closes her eyes, runs her fingers over the spines and chooses one at random.'

'Why?' asked Queenie.

'She says she'd rather let the book choose her.'

No one moved as they digested this, apart from a lady who'd been sitting unobtrusively at the back, knitting.

'Sorry, love,' she said, getting to her feet and packing her needles away. 'But I hate books.'

'Why did you come?' Ruby asked.

'Somewhere warm to sit.'

She left, and Clara felt like putting her head in her hands.

'Why don't we start by sharing something we've read recently that has inspired us?' suggested Mr Pepper and everyone nodded. 'What about you, Billy, what do you like reading?'

'I like fiction that reflects real life. I like to escape but I want to feel I'm learning something about the war at the same time.'

'Aincha a conchie?' Pat demanded flintily. 'With respect, son, the only way to learn about the war is to fight in it!'

'This isn't the place for political discussion,' Clara jumped in, feeling the need to defend Billy.

'It's all right,' Billy replied, his long fingers raking through Beauty's fur as she slept curled up on his lap. 'Pat has a right to her opinion. Before May 1940, I'd have agreed with you.'

Clara shifted uncomfortably.

'But working as an ambulance man in Dunkirk during the evacuations changed my slant on things. It's impossible to explain.'

He stood up, placing a sleepy Beauty into Clara's arms.

'This book does a far better job of it than I ever could,' he said, pulling out *This Above All* by Eric Knight.

Clara felt the slow simmer of panic rise inside her. *Dunkirk. Duncan.* The two were inextricably woven in her mind.

'The lucidity, the fluency, the sheer realness of it will live in my memory for a very long time.'

A silence fell over the group.

'Sorry, it's the gin, it makes me talk too much.'

'Don't apologise, Billy,' said Mr Pepper. 'That's war, son. It never leaves you. It shapes you.'

'It's true,' said Pat slowly, 'When a man goes to war, he doesn't come back the same.'

Clara felt her face heat up.

'Oh, duckie, I'm so sorry, I didn't mean to upset you,' Pat said.

'It's all right,' said Dot sweetly. 'Least your Duncan

died a hero and you should always remember him that way.'

Clara smiled weakly.

'Well, I love *Rebecca* by Daphne Du Maurier,' said Alice, kindly changing the subject. This was met with universal approval.

'Any more suggestions?' Clara asked.

'I love a detective novel,' said a small voice.

Clara and the whole group swivelled round in surprise. Almost no one had spotted the lady who'd snuck in.

She was a tiny little thing, bundled up in a big scratchy coat. Clara recognised her from the down the tunnels. Mrs Caley permanently seemed to be either expecting or nursing a new baby.

'My husband hates me reading, unless it's a ration book.'

She fidgeted, uncomfortable with the scrutiny of the group.

'I miss it.'

'Why deprive yourself?' Clara asked.

She shrugged.

'I used to love a good mystery, but I can't now.'

'Why?'

'There's nowhere for me to read.'

'So, come in here and read,' Clara said.

A slow light dawned on her face.

'I usually attend a meeting at the Women's Institute on a Monday, but I could cry off with a headache, I suppose. What he don't see . . .'

'Won't hurt him,' added Ruby.

'Oh, I don't know what to say.'

'Who's your favourite author, love?' Queenie asked.

'I love Margery Allingham for mystery.'

She picked a book off the shelf, looking as if she wanted to disappear into its pages.

'Don't get me wrong, I love my husband, but books . . . Well, they've always been there for me.'

'I understand,' said Clara.

'Sounds like you'd be better off with *Who Killed the Husband*, dearie,' said Pat sagely and, to their surprise, Mrs Caley burst out laughing.

'We've got off to a smashing start,' said Clara. 'So, we're starting off with *Gone with the Wind*, and we can reconvene when we've all read it. We've got nine new copies, thanks to Ruby.'

A sudden thought came to her.

'Rubes, they're not black-market, are they?'

'As if,' she said huffily. 'I had a bit of a tangle with a GI. That bloke who was here recently, if you must know. He donated them.'

'In return for what?' Pat asked.

'Yeah, you want to hold on to your drawers, Ruby Red Lips,' said Irene knowingly. 'One Yank . . .'

'And they're off,' finished Queenie. The group fell about and Clara found herself looking over at Billy nervously, but if he seemed at all offended he hid it well.

On the subject of men, the book club quickly dissolved into raucous chat as the women fell back on their three favourite topics – births, deaths and bad husbands!

'Right,' said Mrs Chumbley, 'I hate to break up the party but the library needs to close. I'm doing a shelter patrol if anyone needs walking back to their bunk. Mr Pepper? May I accompany you?'

'That would be kind. My eyesight's not what it was.'

She held out her arm, and off they went down the westbound tunnel, the frail and the formidable.

Everyone helped stack the chairs and soon were gone in a cloud of laughter, their chattering voices echoing up the darkened tunnels.

Only Mrs Caley loitered behind, looking hesitant.

'Mrs Button. I hear you're an open-minded sort of librarian.'

'That rather depends on what you mean?'

'I need something to help me stop falling.'

She tapped her tummy. 'You know.'

'Ah, I see.'

'Only I can't have my husband find out.'

'I've just the thing,' Clara said, lowering her voice. *Birth Control for the Married Woman*. It's a pamphlet. Come back tomorrow for a Margery Allingham and I'll pop it inside. It's more discreet that way.'

'Thanks,' she said gratefully. 'You won't tell my husband, will you?'

'I wouldn't dream of it.'

She watched intrigued as Mrs Caley scurried off to her bunk.

'You heard that?' Clara asked Ruby as she cleared away glasses. Ruby nodded.

'Poor woman. She's got the luck of nine blind bastards to be married to the likes of him. He's cut from the same cloth as Victor.'

'Talking of which, I thought your mum was coming this evening?'

'Too busy bailing *him* out of the nick.'

Ruby paused.

'Cla, seeing how you helped Mrs Caley's given me an idea. Are there any novels about a woman who escaped from a bad marriage?'

'Let me think . . . Oh yes, I remember reading years ago *The Tenant of Wildfell Hall* by Anne Brontë. The protagonist left her brutal, drunk husband.'

'Go on.'

'In Victorian days, women were banned from reading this book – it was considered too controversial.'

'Will you put it on the book club list?'

'I'll try. But how'll you get your mum to the book club?'

'Don't worry about that. Just get the book and I'll get Mum into the library.'

Billy walked through from the reading room.

'I've put the tables back out. Can I escort you both home?'

'No need,' Ruby said, shrugging on her coat. 'I can walk myself.'

She was gone before Clara could protest.

'So, just you and me then,' Clara said.

'Just you and me,' Billy replied with a smile.

'I'm so sorry about the chat earlier. When they get together the girls can be a little lascivious.'

'Trust me, it's nothing I don't hear at the ambulance station.'

'I'm sorry too about what Pat said.'

He shrugged. 'I told you. I'm used to it.'

'Billy, can I ask a personal question? What did happen to you in Dunkirk?'

There it was again, like shutters drawing over a window. His blue eyes flickered downwards.

'I . . . I can't talk about it Clara. I've done something I'm not proud of.'

'You can tell me anything . . .' she said softly. 'We all make mistakes.'

He dipped his head and stepped back, the bookcase casting his whole face into shadow.

'Not like this one.'

He bent down and clipped on Beauty's lead and when he stood up, the moment had gone.

'Come on,' he said stiffly. 'We really ought to get going. I've got an early shift tomorrow and something tells me I'm going to regret that book club belter.'

In silence she followed him from the library, desperate to shake free his secrets. Billy Clark was determined to remain a closed book.

8

Ruby

Librarians are facilitators, entertainers, empathisers, listeners, educators and friends. Libraries are about more than their buildings.
    Carol Stump, President of Libraries Connected and
                Chief Librarian of Kirklees Council

One week after troops landed in Normandy, it was all anyone could talk of in the library. The reading room was stuffed with people poring over newspapers and the queue for library loans stretched along the platform.

Headlines were full of the Allied advance and the heroic push eastwards through Nazi occupied territory. A fragile hope had rippled through the tunnels.

Ruby's thoughts went fleetingly to Eddie. He must have been shipped out to France soon after he'd delivered those books to the library. She felt a rush of guilt that he'd used up his last precious furlough scouring London's bookshops for her, but she squashed it. Right now, looking after her mum was using up every last drop of her emotional energy.

'Next,' Ruby called. A middle-aged couple shuffled forward looking furtive.

'Hello. How can I help?'

The woman lowered her voice to an almost comic whisper. 'Do you have a book that might help a couple in the . . .' Here she mouthed the words, 'bedroom department.'

Ruby smiled and reached under the counter. When the library was above ground, they kept all their more inflammatory books locked in a cupboard, but here lack of space dictated they be kept under the counter.

'How about this?' Ruby said, sliding out *The Sex Factor in Marriage.*

Ruby barely had time to stamp it before the woman bundled it into her string bag and they hurried out.

A factory girl shuffled forward.

'I hear you've got a book that teaches you things,' she mumbled.

Ruby and Clara had long since learned that a careful process of deduction was often required in the library.

'Could you be a little more specific?'

'You know . . . bedroom things. You loaned it to my pal's mum.'

Ruby glanced at Clara. Word had clearly spread. It had been eleven days since they'd loaned the birth control pamphlet out. Mrs Caley had read it cover-to-cover in two days and since then it had gone out on loan to her friend and come back. Ruby glanced at the girl's ring finger.

'The only problem is, we aren't supposed to loan it to unmarried women—'

'It's all right Rubes,' Clara interrupted quietly, reaching for the pamphlet. 'Let her have it.'

She turned to the factory girl.

'But please be discreet.'

'Thanks,' she said gratefully, sliding it into her handbag. 'You've done me ever such a favour.'

She left and Clara shot Ruby a look.

'I hope I don't live to regret that,' she said.

'It was the right thing to do,' Ruby asserted. She herself had read it on more than one occasion and was pleased to see she wasn't the only young woman in Bethnal Green educating herself. Anything had to be better than soap pessaries and chance. By and large, her generation had been clueless up until the war. "Avin his way' before the ring was on had consequences, which, as far as Ruby could tell, were the woman's responsibility alone to bear.

Finally, by 4 p.m., they reached the end of the long queue. Mr Pepper went in search of refreshment, and a local dosser, who came in every afternoon for somewhere warm to doze, had wandered in, trailing a smell you could cut with a knife. The Major, as he was known down the tunnels, was a harmless soul.

Apart from him, the only two people left in the reading room were a local dentist and a woman who worked at the town hall. Ruby had long ago worked out they were having an affair.

Today, she was pretending to read an instruction leaflet, while his copy of *Diseases of the Gums and Oral Mucous Membranes* remained untouched. Instead, they talked in hot, furtive whispers.

'Don't you mind them two using your reading room to conduct their affair?' Ruby asked under her breath.

'Not really, no,' Clara whispered back. 'Least they're in the library. She must have more stamps on her ticket than anyone in Bethnal Green.'

'What's she reading?'

'An ARP pamphlet – handling incendiaries.'

'She'll need that if her old man finds out,' Ruby murmured.

They both burst into laughter.

The woman returned her pamphlet and left, shooting the man a lingering look. *Diseases of the Gums and Oral Mucous Membranes* didn't stand a chance. One minute later, he made a hasty exit, nearly colliding with Mr Pepper as he came back with the teas.

'Gosh, where's the fire?' he murmured.

'What is it with everyone today?' Clara asked, blowing the steam off her tea. 'They're all obsessed with sex.'

'It's the D-Day effect, ain't it?' Ruby reasoned. 'Danger, the nearness of death. No greater aphrodisiac.'

Mr Pepper chuckled.

'I think you might be right.'

'Helping out here, I've realised that they ought to expand your job titles,' he went on. 'Strikes me you're not just librarians, but social workers, Citizens Advice Bureau advisers, nurses, entertainers, listeners, teachers . . .' He broke off, his voice wavering.

'And friends.' His eyes misted over and he dug around in his suit pocket for a hankie. 'Goodness I'm getting emotional in my old age.'

'Don't be silly, Mr Pepper,' Clara said. 'You lost your wife not long ago. You're entitled to forget the stiff upper lip.'

'Fourteen weeks and four days,' he replied, removing his spectacles and mopping his eyes.

'You must miss her so much,' Ruby said, sliding her arm around him.

'I do, my dear. It's the little things one misses. The quiet companionship, the ticking off.' He glanced down and grimaced. 'The removal of unsightly stains from one's tie.'

Gently, Clara took the hankie from him and wiped a little mark from his old headmaster's tie.

'I don't know what I'd do without you both and this funny little library.'

Clara pulled them all into an embrace.

'Here's to our funny little library.'

It occurred to Ruby as they hugged what a disparate group of library workers they were. A twenty-five-year-old widow, an eighty-year-old widower and a confirmed twenty-six-year-old bachelorette.

'Does this mean you might call us by our Christian names now, Mr P?' Clara asked, drawing back with a smile.

'I'll try . . . Clara,' he said, sounding the word out on his tongue.

'That's the ticket,' Ruby remarked. 'All that formality makes me uncomfortable. Oh, and you forgot one thing from that list, Mr P.'

'Oh yes?'

'Parrot babysitters!'

'And to think, most people believe librarians are introverts,' Clara laughed.

'You'll never catch me in a cardie,' Ruby flashed back.

'A word of warning though,' Mr Pepper added. 'Don't let Pinkerton-Smythe find out you're dispensing the birth control pamphlet.'

'He's right there Cla,' Ruby agreed. 'He'd go loopy.'

Clara nodded.

'Don't worry. I can handle him. Ooh, I nearly forgot. Look what came in. Brand-new as well.'

She slid *The Tenant of Wildfell Hall* across the counter.

Being a wartime book, the paper was thin, the type tiny, the margins narrow, and it was hard to see where one chapter ended and another began, changes that had become compulsory to comply with the now-ubiquitous Book Production War Economy Standard. Newly published books might have been stripped of their finery, but they were still a tantalising prospect.

'Thank you, Cla,' she whispered. She only hoped this book would be half as liberating as the birth control pamphlet was so obviously proving to be. If her mother could find the strength to break free of Victor's control, then maybe they could all have a chance to heal.

Ruby tucked the book in her bag and glanced up to see Beatty and Marie walk in.

'You here for storytime girls?'

Beatty nodded. 'We're a bit early. Clara, I wondered whether you'd help me write a letter to the Red Cross about my dad? Now the Allies have landed in France, I wondered if they'd have any news on the Channel Islands.'

She chewed her lip.

'Mum's too busy to help, you see.'

Clara's face fell. 'Oh, sweetheart, I'm just about to do storytime, otherwise I'd love to have helped.'

'I'll do storytime,' Ruby insisted. 'You help Beatty.'

'Are you sure?' Clara replied. 'I thought you wanted to get that book to your mum?'

'Quite sure. Beatty needs you.' She looked at her pointedly. They'd both discussed ways in which they could help the Jersey girls. Beatty especially seemed to be shouldering so much of the burden of caring for her sister and she knew Clara had a soft spot for her.

'Come on then.' Clara grinned, guiding her to a table.

Ruby watched them go sadly. Clara would have made such a terrific mother. Too much had been taken from her; how she hoped motherhood wasn't another wartime sacrifice.

Twenty minutes later Ruby was ready as the children cascaded in for storytime, their energy filling the room like an uncorked bottle of fizzy pop.

'I finished the reading challenge, miss. Can I get me doughnut now?' piped up a fidgety girl with amber hair.

'Me too!' said Mrs Smart's granddaughter, Maggie May, holding her arm up so high she was in danger of a dislocation.

To Ruby's delight she realised that all bar one of their regulars had now completed the challenge and one wall of the reading room was a riot of colourful pictures and reviews. Clever Tubby had finished his challenge within three weeks, and she was so pleased to see most of the boys – tempted by the Just William series and classic adventure tales like *Adventures of Huckleberry Finn* – had followed in his impressive footsteps.

'How are you getting on, Joannie?' she asked a ten-year-old with a tangle of red curls.

'Rotten,' Joannie said sulkily. 'I don't like girls' books.'

'Who said you have to read girls' books?'

'Me mum. She says I'm to choose a nice book like *Little Women*.'

'What do you want to read about?' Ruby asked.

''Bout criminals and spies and that.'

'You should hang out at Westminster then,' remarked Tubby. 'My dad reckons it's full of criminals.'

'I liked that *Treasure Island* book we read, that was good that was, 'cept that's a boy book, ain't it?'

'No it's not,' Ruby protested hotly. 'There should be no such thing as a boys' book or a girls' book.'

She stood up and ran her fingers along the shelves, her mind crackling.

'Here. Try this. *Emil and the Detectives* by Erich Kästner. It's a brilliant book about a boy and his friends who catch a group of bank robbers.'

'Sounds good, miss, only me mum won't let me read a book by a Nazi.'

'Erich Kästner's no Nazi,' she said.

'Not all Germans are Nazis,' intercepted Tubby.

'Far from it,' Ruby agreed. 'Kästner's books are forbidden in Germany and some of his books have been burnt by the Nazis. *Emil and the Detectives* is the only one to have escaped Nazi censorship.'

'Why do Nazis burn books?' asked Maggie May. 'Haven't they got any coal?'

Ruby sighed. Every day, she and Clara faced a barrage

of questions from the shelter kids. What time do birds go to sleep? Do you have a book with photos of dragons? Why do we have tiny punchbags at the back of our throats (it took Ruby a while to work out the punchbags were tonsils).

But this one took some consideration.

'Because they want to stop people from thinking for themselves,' she said eventually, the thought occurring to her that there wasn't much between a Nazi and her stepdad.

'And now, as most of you know, Tubby is a reading pal – he's agreed to read for us.'

Tubby proudly showed everyone his copy of *The Wind in the Willows* then leapt to his feet, his iron leg brace clanking.

'Wonderful! Spellbinding! Outrageously magnificent! Was there ever such a master of motorcars as Toad of Toad Hall?' he mimicked in his best upper-class voice.

The library rang with laughter as Tubby did a brilliantly energetic impression of Toad escaping from prison dressed as a washerwoman and driving his automobile like a maniac to rescue his home from the clutches of the weasels.

'And the moral of that story is,' Tubby puffed as he slammed the book shut, 'never trust a toad.'

'Wise words, kid.'

All eyes swivelled to the back of the room to where a tall, almost ridiculously handsome GI stood, clutching a brown paper bag.

'Who wants some candy?'

Storytime came to an abrupt end.

'Ok, I got bulls eyes, I got toffee, I got those horrible sticky things that weld themselves to the roof of your mouth . . . '

'Me! Me!' screamed a chorus of voices.

'Eddie . . . what are you doing here?' Ruby murmured in disbelief.

'Delivering this.' He grinned and pulled a copy of *Gone with the Wind* from behind his back.

'I make that ten copies. I doubt there's a doughboy in all of Blighty who's visited more bookshops than me,' he said, laughing. 'So now you have to go on that date with me, right?'

'I assumed you were over in France.'

'I'm shipping out tomorrow.'

Clara wandered through to see what all the commotion was about.

'It's Eddie,' Ruby said.

'Eddie?' Clara said blankly.

'You know, *Gone with the Wind* Eddie.'

He laughed. 'She had me hunting round every bookshop in London to buy up copies. She's worth it though.'

'Oh, so *you're* Eddie,' said Clara.

'Couldn't leave without coming to say goodbye.' His eyes lingered appreciatively over Ruby's body.

A frisson ran round the room.

'Are you gonna kiss her then, mister?' asked Maggie May boldly and the girls all giggled.

'He better,' declared Ruby.

Eddie swept her back and kissed her theatrically, and

the kids went mad, all apart from Tubby and Ronnie, who pretended to vomit.

'Whaddya say then, Ruby?' he said, when he finally released her. 'Let's you and me hit the West End, The Windmill, then dinner and dancing.'

As offers went it was pretty tempting. She thought of her mum, tiptoeing round Victor, trying to keep the peace. Another night restlessly stirring in bed, replaying that awful moment she found Bella's body in the morgue. Sometimes it felt as if every moment of her life was spent trying to escape what happened on that stairwell.

'I got whiskey . . .' he added, lifting his jacket to reveal a silver hip flask. 'American too. The proper stuff.'

'Oh well why didn't you say,' she joked. 'I'll get my coat.'

Behind the counter, she dug around in her handbag and reapplied her lipstick, the good stuff for tonight, Renegade Red, her hands shaking slightly as she held the compact.

Clara lifted the countertop and joined her.

'Are you sure about this, Rubes?' she whispered. 'You know he's going to expect something in return for all those books.'

'I certainly hope so.' She snapped the compact shut and smiled a little too brightly as she shook her hair free from her headscarf.

'Please be careful,' Clara urged.

'I ain't stupid,' she replied, raking her fingers through her blonde curls before dabbing a little Evening in Paris along her collarbone. 'I'll make sure he wears a johnny.'

Clara looked hurt. 'You know I didn't mean that. I worry

about you, is all. I don't believe you enjoy this as much as you pretend you do.'

'Oh Clara,' she sighed. 'It's not about enjoying, it's about forgetting.'

Ruby nailed a smile on her face and went in search of oblivion.

9

Clara

All children need is kindness, patience and books.
Nanny Maureen, 'reading buddy' volunteer at
Havering Libraries

Clara watched Ruby and her GI leave in a perfume and
tobacco-scented cloud, trailed up the platform by the Tube
Rats. To the outside world they looked every inch the
glamorous wartime couple. Only she knew Ruby's licen-
tious behaviour was a front and she worried for her friend.
London was such a transient city right now. Here today,
gone tomorrow. Literally, in Eddie's case. Ruby didn't
know a thing about him.

A bolt of alarm shot through her. What if he was the
man terrorising East London right now? After all, the
Blackout Ripper had been unmasked as a respectable
airman in the RAF. It would make sense that the man
behind these new attacks wasn't from round these parts.
She steadied her thoughts as she returned to her shelving
duties.

Calm down Clara, she scolded herself as she gently
wiped down their only copy of *The Wind in the Willows*
and pushed it carefully back on the shelf. Ruby could look

after herself. At least she was pursuing love, of a kind. Eleven days on, she and Billy still hadn't managed to settle on a date to visit an art gallery – even as friends. Every time she thought they were getting close, he pulled back. She knew she had overstepped an invisible line when she had asked him about Dunkirk and though she was desperate to find out what he meant by doing something he wasn't proud of, she dared not push him.

Sometimes she wasn't sure if he liked her at all, and yet, the way he looked at her . . . it was all so confusing. His emotions were as fleeting as sunlight on water, but wasn't it the light and the shade which made him so intriguing?

'You look deep in thought.' Beatty was looking at her with a perceptive smile.

'Oh no, just thinking about what book to read next for storytime.'

'How about *We Couldn't Leave Dinah*?'

'By Mary Treadgold! Why yes, that's a marvellous book.'

'You've heard of it?' Beatty said, looking more alive than Clara had ever see her.

'Of course I have. It won the Carnegie Medal three years ago. It's about children in the Channel Islands after the occupation isn't it?'

Beatty nodded. 'I'd love it if you could read that. It'll remind me of home, or a version of it, at any rate.'

Clara smiled and realised what a rare and precious moment this was.

'I'll find it for you,' she promised.

'Thanks Clara and for helping me write that letter earlier.'

'You're so welcome. I just hope you hear some news soon.'

'Now the Allies are in France they'll help to liberate Jersey, it's so close after all, and then we'll get news of my dad. Don't you think?'

Clara grappled with the question. She had her doubts, but she didn't want to kill the girl's hope, not when Beatty was beginning to trust her.

'It can't be long. Come on, I'll walk you and Marie back to your bunks. Mr Pepper would you mind locking up?'

'Of course my dear, you go on.'

Clara scooped back her dark, wavy hair and knotted a yellow silk headscarf loosely into a turban. She loved this scarf because Duncan had once told her that the colour highlighted the threads of gold in her own amber eyes.

'You're very pretty,' said Marie, slipping her hand through Clara's as they left the library. 'Why don't you go dancing with GIs like Ruby?'

'Marie,' Beatty scolded. 'Don't be so rude.'

'It's all right,' Clara laughed. 'I'm far too boring.'

They reached their bunks and Beatty pulled out *The Secret Garden* from behind the cable tie on the tunnel wall.

'I don't think you're boring at all, Clara,' she said, pulling out her bookmark and snuggling down in her bunk. 'I think you're lovely.'

Clara felt her throat tighten. Beatty and Marie were such terrific girls, so clever and funny. What she wouldn't have given to be their mother. She'd be reading to them every night, smothering them with love and cuddles, not leaving them alone all night in a cold Underground tunnel.

She thought back to that first kick, as delicate as the fluttering of a butterfly's wing, but life all the same. The ache seemed to seep into her bones and she held on to the bunk for support.

'Are you all right, Clara?' Marie peeked out from the top of her book, large eyes full of curiosity.

'Yes sweetheart, I'm fine, just a little tired.'

The energy had changed to that sleepy feeling that preceded the dimming of the lights, and all along the eastbound tunnel people were settling down with books or knitting by the light of a guttering candle. A few were already asleep, their faces covered in homemade masks made from strips of muslin and sprinkled with a few drops of eucalyptus to ward off the smell and the dreaded shelter throat.

'I'd best be off. Night night, girls. Enjoy *The Secret Garden.*'

Beatty looked up, her eyes shining with excitement in the dim light.

'Oh I will. She's so close to finding the door.'

Clara had never seen anyone read with such hunger and intensity. Beatty reminded her of herself when she was younger and she felt glad at their growing closeness.

Librarians, like teachers, shouldn't admit to favourites, but Beatty was special. Books were Beatty's unquestioning friends, in the way they were to Clara. Little wonder.

Like Mary in *The Secret Garden*, Beatty had been uprooted from all she knew into a strange world. Granted the Tube wasn't a rambling manor house, but the noxious, complex world of the Underground shelter was just as alien to Beatty as Misselthwaite Manor had been to Mary.

It was up to Clara to provide her with books. Books with doorways to open into magical lands. A little smile touched Beatty's mouth as she turned the page, her eyes flickering left to right. Occasionally her mouth murmured the words.

Was there something unique about the fact that her library was deep underground? In a world obscured from natural light and noise, did it make the act of reading more intimate, sharpen the imagination?

Outside the Tube, double summertime was in full force and Clara was relieved to see the streets and Barmy Park bustling with people. She glanced left and right hoping to see a tall lanky figure but to her disappointment, Billy wasn't there.

'Stop thinking about him,' she scolded, as she set off to Russia Lane. Try as she might, she couldn't shake the horrible, sinking feeling she'd ruined it all, whatever 'it' even was.

She found Sparrow in his allotment, frying a fish over a small Primus stove.

'May I?' She gestured to an upturned wooden pallet.

He nodded.

'We miss you in the library.'

'It weren't my fault that stupid girl got stuck.'

'I know it wasn't, no one blames you for that.'

'Me mum does.'

'I should like to help you to learn to read.'

'Nuffin' to me if you do, nuffin' to me if you don't.'

He looked up suddenly, his eyes glittering.

'You'd be wasting your time though. I'm backward, ain't I? Leastwise that's what my teacher said.'

'Why would she say that?'

'He. Mr Benwell. He called me a dead-end kid.'

'That's not true,' she said softly.

'He had it in for me. Used to make me stand up in front of the whole class and point out all the holes in my clothes and shoes. Even made me stand in the waste-paper bin, 'cause I looked like a bit of rubbish.'

Clara felt anger rise inside her like a sharp punch.

'Did you tell anyone?'

'Yeah, and I got the cane for telling.'

'He's not a teacher, he's a sadist,' she murmured.

'Used to give me more if I flinched. Ain't as bad as my left though.'

He pulled his left hand out, turned the palm over, and Clara felt her anger solidify into something darker.

'This is why I can't read.'

'Why?'

''Cause I'm left-handed.'

'What do you mean?'

'Sir used to cane me when I wrote with my left hand. He said left-handers were weak in the head.'

'Just because you're left-handed does *not* mean you're weak in the head. All the really creative people I studied with at library school were left-handed.'

'Oh,' he replied, looking confused.

'I really want to help you, Sparrow.'

He lifted his chin. 'I don't need charity.'

'How about you teach me to grow some veg, and I can teach you to read? Would that be a fair exchange of skills?'

He scrunched his face up.

'All right, but don't tell no one.'

'It'll be our secret. We could make a start right now, if you like?'

'Not here. We could go to my auntie's s'pose.'

'Finish your tea first.'

As he ate, he talked her through his allotment, and Clara was impressed at what he and the Schoolboy Gardeners of Russia Lane had created with no money.

It had been his idea, he told her proudly, to use dustbin lids pierced with holes to sift through the earth of the old bombsite and get rid of all the glass and shrapnel.

'Double digging's key, miss,' he said. 'And manure is king.'

'Talking of kings, I hear you had a royal visit last year.'

His face lit up.

'Yeah. I gave Her Majesty some tips on how to stop blight in her spuds.'

Clara laughed out loud.

Backward? If this boy could learn to read, there would be no end to his ingenuity.

At Sparrow's, Clara quickly realised that his auntie Maisie was a lovely woman, but clearly overstretched as she juggled a swaddled infant on one hip while stirring a pot on the stove. Two small boys were tangled in a heap on the rag rug and Sparrow looked embarrassed.

'This is Mrs Button from the underground library. She's helping me with me reading.'

'Ooh, hello. Reggie and Albert, pipe down, I can't hear myself bleedin' think.'

She turned back to Clara with an apologetic smile and patted the front of her apron. 'Another one on the way for my sins.'

The baby stirred and yawned, eyelashes fluttering in a dream. The ache she'd felt earlier seemed to expand and fill every part of her with a tangible pain.

The baby's yawn turned to a low grizzle.

'Why don't we take him out for a walk in his pram?' Clara suggested, desperate to escape Maisie's obvious fecundity.

'Oh, would you?'

''Course, come on Sparrow.'

Together, they tucked the baby into a large coach pram that was parked outside the house and began walking. The jigging motion of the pram on the cobbles quickly lulled the fractious baby back to sleep.

What a world to bring a child into, Clara mused as they passed a bomb-shattered house with Rosebay willowherb bursting out of the window frames. At the end of the street, a huge team of kids played a complex skipping game, lost in their imaginations. 'Sorry, miss,' Sparrow sighed, kicking a stone. 'It's always like that at me auntie's. S'pose we won't be able to do lessons after all.'

''Course we can,' Clara replied. 'Words are all around; we don't just have to learn from the pages of a book.'

She glanced up at a giant hoarding on the side of the railway bridge.

'Have a go at reading that.'

'Easy, Dig for Victory.'

'Bravo,' she laughed. They passed under the shadow of the bridge and emerged the other side.

'I cheated. I guessed 'cause of the boot and the spade.'

'It was an educated guess, so that's not cheating. Now try that.' She gestured to a huge sign on the side of a pub.

'Guinness . . . ke . . .' he faltered.

'Keeps your strength up,' she finished.

She spied the edge of a *Dig for Victory* pamphlet sticking out the corner of his pocket.

'Let's read together from that. How do you use it?'

'Guesswork mainly, or else Tubby reads it while I do the grunt work.'

He pulled out the pamphlet and Clara guided him through it, reading some sentences and encouraging him to try out the simpler words. By building words into sentences and getting him to constantly read out loud she had a hunch it would be no time before he'd grasped it. He was smart as a fox. He just needed to believe it.

'What's your favourite word, Mrs Button?' he asked.

'Serendipity.'

'What's that mean?'

'The occurrence of events by chance in a happy way. As in, my meeting you in the library was a stroke of serendipity.'

'What's your worst word?' he asked as they passed back under the railway bridge. The train clattering overhead nearly drowned out his voice.

She thought. 'Moist.'

'How comes?'

'I don't know really. It just makes me feel all shivery.'

'What's your favourite?' she asked.

'Loamy.'

She stopped the pram and stared at him in surprise.

'I love that word. Where did you learn that?'

'Tubby told it me. Reckons London soil is loamy, 'cause it's full of sand and clay.' He winked. 'Lovely and moist.'

'Gracious, that train is terrifically loud.'

He squinted up at the sky. 'I don't think it's a train.'

She followed his gaze.

A black streak was moving fast over the rooftops in their direction.

The noise suddenly became tremendous. *Phut. Phut. Phut.* It bore through Clara's brain. Her palms, clammy with sweat, gripped the pram handle.

'Mrs Button . . .' Sparrow's hand on her arm tugged her back to herself. 'We need to run.'

To her eternal shame, Clara was rooted to the ground. She pictured Peter's face, pale and waxy, falling away from her into the dust, books exploding up into the air.

'I . . . I can't.' She swallowed. The object in the sky was moving closer now, roaring towards them, a fire coming out of its tail end. All of sudden, the noise stopped. She held her breath as it glided towards them, like an owl with outstretched wings.

Sparrow wrenched the pram from her hands and began pushing with one hand; with the other, he grabbed her by the sleeve.

'Run!'

Clara was shaken out of her terror and together they stumbled down Grove Road as fast as they could run, the pram wheels ricocheting crazily off the cobbles.

'In here.' Sparrow yanked her into a doorway and pushed her down. Grabbing his baby cousin from the pram, he hunkered down next to her. Instinctively, they covered their heads.

The air seemed to shudder and break apart at the impact of the explosion.

Darkness fell, followed by the soft pitter-patter of acrid debris raining down on their heads.

Clara couldn't breathe. She felt as if she was clinging to the kerb as the pavement rolled and tilted.

'Mrs Button . . .' Sparrow was pulling her to her feet.

The baby started to cry as the pair of them gazed back in astonishment at the road from where they had just run.

The stout Victorian railway bridge they'd walked under was gone. Houses had toppled in on themselves. Bodies littered the street like rag dolls. Houses and shops burnt fiercely and, out of the sky, sanitary towels from the chemist's shop spiralled like sycamore leaves, settling round their feet.

'My auntie!' Sparrow cried.

Buried in the side of the building was the tail end of the plane.

He began to move and she pulled him back. The clanging of ambulance and fire engine bells filled the air.

'No! You mustn't, Sparrow, it's too dangerous.'

Sparrow thrust the baby at her and ran in the direction of the burning buildings.

Clara couldn't bear to watch and sank down onto the kerb clutching the baby.

'Clara, is that you?' She looked up. Billy was holding one end of a stretcher as he headed towards the site of the explosion.

'Billy.' She began to cry as he crouched down next her in astonishment, his eyes full of concern.

'Are you hurt?'

'I'm fine. But Sparrow, he's gone back to find his auntie, please stop him, Billy.'

'Of course I will, but you must go to my ambulance station and get looked at.'

'I'm all right, I'll wait here.'

He put down the stretcher and held her tightly by both arms.

'No Clara, you won't. I would never forgive myself if anything happened to you. Go now!'

Without another word, he turned and ran into the thick curtain of smoke.

The milky light of dawn was spreading under the blackouts before Billy finally trudged, grey-faced with exhaustion, back into Station 98.

'Sparrow?' she asked. After the baby had been checked over and then safely delivered to Pat down the Underground, she hadn't slept a wink for worrying about him.

Billy pressed a hot cup of Bovril into her hands.

'He's absolutely fine. He and two of his cousins are with his mum down the Underground with the baby. They're all safe.' He drew the blanket around her shoulders and looked at her with concern.

'And you?'

She sipped the hot salty drink and shuddered.

'I'm fine, well, a perforated ear drum but if Sparrow hadn't forced me to run . . .' She trailed off.

'Sparrow's auntie?'

'I'm sorry. She didn't stand a chance.'

Clara shook her head, remembering the cheerful mum juggling kids and a pan of stew, blissfully ignorant that she was counting down the minutes to her own death.

'Anyone else?'

'Two of his cousins, young boys.' He swallowed sharply. 'Six casualties in all; there was nothing we could do.'

'Seven really. She was expecting.'

He scrubbed despairingly at his face and a cold fist clenched her heart.

'I'm so sorry.'

He nodded and turned to her, his eyes haunted by what he'd seen in those crumpled houses.

'You never get used to pulling children's bodies out.'

A silence stretched out between them.

'I'm sorry,' he sighed, rubbing his eyes, 'I really ought to work on my conversational gambits.'

He turned to face her.

'That thing that exploded, it wasn't a Messerschmitt or any kind of aeroplane.'

'What was it then?'

'Some sort of rocket, I don't know. But I do know there was no German pilot there, and believe me, the local men got together a posse. They'd have hunted him down if there was one.'

Clara remembered the awful clattering noise it had made before the engine cut out.

Hitler's secret weapon had been all anyone could talk of these past months. She had laughed it off as wild rumour.

'Well, let's hope it's the first and last,' she sighed, knowing that nothing in war was ever that straightforward.

He took her hands and she suddenly became aware of how close they were sitting.

'I know we haven't set a date yet for our trip to the exhibition, but let's do it,' he urged. 'Now.'

His eyes scanned hers.

'I'm sorry I-I've procrastinated.' His words were tripping over themselves. 'It's hard to explain why, but what I do know is that all we have is the moment. If last night proved anything, it's that.'

Clara's heart thumped as he finally said the words she'd been longing to hear.

'Yes . . . yes . . . I'd like that. But surely not now? Look at the state of me.'

Her hair was a bird's nest after all night on a camp bed and she was fairly sure there was crusted blood round her ears.

'You're beautiful, Clara.' He touched her cheek. 'All the more so for being alive. You . . .' he stumbled and she reached her fingers up to brush his. 'You can't imagine what you mean to me.'

Something intangible had been let out of the box. There was no going back now.

He smiled and it broke the solemnity of the moment. 'But yes, we can wait until we've had a chance to wash. But please, not much longer; I don't want to waste any more time.'

Clara longed to unload all the secret shame of her past, to dismantle the tissue of lies and deceptions. She felt she might have broken her silence – she was just vulnerable enough in that moment – had it not been for the sudden appearance of a well-upholstered woman banging a wooden spoon against a pot.

'Grub's up.'

Clara jumped.

'Mavis Byrne,' Billy grinned. 'Daughter of a Baltic Sea captain and our station cook. Rustles up the best steak and kidney pudding in East London.'

'Don't worry, you've enough mouths to feed,' said Clara, 'I'll get off.'

'You'll do no such thing,' said Mavis, taking her by the arm. 'Our Billy never stops talking about his librarian friend.'

Billy rolled his eyes at her. 'Sorry,' he whispered. 'Please stay and eat.'

Mavis led her, blinking, out into the station yard, where at least a dozen pairs of female eyes swivelled to stare at her. The sun had risen and the nightshift staff were sitting about in deck chairs tucking into plates of steak and kidney or smoking.

'I've got to accompany the new shift officer on his inspection of the vehicles,' Billy said. 'We can't leave until he's signed everything off. Shan't be long.'

He whistled to a girl with the longest legs she'd ever seen, polishing the door of a nearby ambulance.

'Blackie, look after my friend, would you?'

The woman walked over, fag welded to the side of her red-painted mouth.

'Alberta Black.' She extended a hand without removing her cigarette and surveyed Clara through the smoke. 'So, you're the mysterious girl who has our station officer in a tailspin.'

She had him in a spin? This was more information than she had gleaned from Billy.

'I didn't know Billy was station officer,' Clara said.

'Oh, yes, he's the boss all right,' remarked a redhead. 'I'm Angela Darlow, by the way. Everyone calls me Darling. Didn't you notice the three stripes on his uniform?'

Clara shook her head.

'Don't suppose he told you about his jewellery either?' added Blackie, reaching down and picking up Beauty, who'd wandered into the yard on the scrounge for steak and kidney titbits.

'Jewellery?'

'Oh yes, he won the British Empire Medal for bravery last year.'

'Did he? What for?'

'During the Blitz, he drove an ambulance through a solid sheet of flame to attend to a family trapped in the basement of their home. He slipped through a tunnel I doubt a whippet could get through to get to two children entombed in the basement. Administered morphine, got them both out alive.'

Clara was flabbergasted. The way Billy talked, referring to things he wasn't proud of, his conscientious status could hardly be reconciled with the fearless man they knew.

Angela removed her sunglasses and fixed her with penetrating gaze.

'We're a funny crew here, but we're all as close as family.'

Clara knew she was getting a friendly warning and felt relieved when Billy walked back into the yard.

'Right folks, inspection passed, you're all free to go.'

He put his hand on the small of Clara's back and guided her to the street outside.

'I'll come to the storytime later, if that's all right, and let's fix a date then?'

'Please do,' she said with relief. 'Thank you, Billy, for looking after me.'

He pulled her into his arms and she rested her cheek against the rough fabric of his boiler suit. Clara felt all her anguish slide away like wax off a hot candle.

'I feel I ought to be honest with you before our date . . .' he began.

'Yes,' she urged, relieved. 'I want to know everything there is to know about you. You can trust me, Billy.'

'Clara!'

The woman's shrill voice cut over hers.

Billy followed her gaze up the street to where a woman in an extravagant hat was advancing on them.

'Who's that?'

'*The Art of Homemaking*,' Clara sighed, pushing down her agitation.

Clara's mother-in-law advanced and she arranged a smile on her face.

'Hallo. This is a surprise. What are you doing here?'

'Clara, darling . . . You can't believe how worried I've been. There's talk of an invasion. I came as soon as I heard there was an incident at Bethnal Green. ARP man at Grove Road mentioned a woman fitting your description had been brought here.'

'Please don't alarm yourself,' Billy said. 'I was on the site and I can assure you there were no German pilots there. Talk of an invasion is just a rumour.'

She glared suspiciously at Billy.

'Do I know you?'

He shook his head. 'I don't think so.'

She pursed her lips.

'I do. I'm sure I've met you before.'

'I have one of those common faces I expect,' he said, laughing uneasily. 'I'll leave you two in peace. Clara, I'll see you at the library later.'

He turned and Maureen stared after him.

'He seems awfully familiar,' she remarked once he was out of earshot. 'Shifty eyes.'

'He's just a friend, and honestly, you really needn't have troubled yourself to come all the way here from Boreham Wood.'

'Clara, we're still family! Even if you have turned your back on your own mother.'

Clara sighed. Her mother and mother-in-law had clearly been talking.

'I haven't turned my back on her,' she protested. 'I love

her but she can't ask me to choose between her and the library. It's not fair.'

'Your mother and I are in agreement. You're not thinking straight. You haven't been for a while now, since . . .'

'Duncan's death? Well, is it a surprise! I'm sorry, I don't mean to be rude, I'm just so tired.'

'I can see and that's why you must come and live with us.' Maureen touched Clara's shoulder with a gloved hand, baring her teeth into a smile. 'It's not safe here. It's what Duncan would've wanted.'

Clara stared at a blackbird tugging a helpless worm out of a small allotment in the grounds of the ambulance station.

'We've been over this, Maureen. I-I have a job and friends, a life here in Bethnal Green.'

Maureen's face hardened, her little pink mouth puckering. How quickly the veneer of concern wore off. 'Which is more than my son has,' she hissed. 'Do you even miss him?'

'W-what? How could you say such a thing?'

'Well, why are you still working in that public library?'

'That library is my life!' Clara exclaimed.

A bitter laugh burst out of Maureen.

'Your husband ought to have been your life. Perhaps if you hadn't put your job before all else, it all would have ended differently.'

Clara stared at her, gobsmacked. The feathers were quivering on top of Maureen's ridiculous hat.

'Oh yes, you're probably pleased how it's all turned out. It means you get to stay on at the library. You'd have had to leave your position when war ends, but now he's dead you'll get to stay on; oh yes, it suits you very well doesn't it, madam.'

Clara couldn't breathe. The heat snaking round her throat was like invisible fingers.

'I miss him every day,' she managed at last. 'The library is my solace, but it's not the reason Duncan's dead.'

'Possibly not, but it is the reason my grandchild is dead. If you'd been at home resting, like we all told you, instead of working late in that library, you wouldn't have got caught up in the bombing.'

Her face was full of angry triumph as she thrust the knife in deeper. 'You wouldn't have lost the baby.'

Clara felt a small twist of relief. There now. She'd said it. They'd always skirted round the edges of this, both Maureen and her own mother, but they'd never come right out and said it.

'I think you'd better go,' she said quietly. The blackbird gave up on the worm and took flight, the black of its wings scratching the eggshell blue of the sky.

'He was my son, he had a right to be a father and have a happy life.'

'Don't you think that a single day passes when I don't imagine "What if?". I lie awake at night trying to imagine what our baby would have looked like.'

Clara closed her eyes. Saw again the charred and sodden piles of books, Peter's body pinned under the bookcase, and in the harrowing days that followed, the never-ending bleeding.

'The library is the *only* thing keeping me alive.'

Maureen seemed to deflate.

'I'm sorry. Please, just come and live with us, where you'll be safe.'

Clara thought of her mother-in-law's suffocating home, its privet hedges, its quiet respectability. To Maureen, books were ornaments to show her neighbours she'd made it. Books she felt one ought to have on display, sealed off behind glass doors in a cabinet. Duncan had told her once that she never read them, but dusted them copiously, scolding his father if he dared to get one out and read it.

Clara would always be at odds in a home like that. She shook her head.

Maureen sighed.

'Think it over, dear. I'll be back soon and see if you haven't changed your mind. And remember, Clara . . .'

'Yes, I know. Dignity in silence.'

10

Ruby

*My old manager Pat was an irreverent, anarchic man in a
tank top. 'You're never alone with a good book,' he used to say.
I've never forgotten him. He shaped me into the library worker
I am today.*

Deborah Peck, Library Development Officer,
Newham Libraries, East London

Ruby woke in a strange hotel room with the mother of all
headaches.

'Eugh,' she groaned, peeling her head off the pillow.

Her dirty blonde curls fell over the sheets. Her bra and
blouse were draped over a pair of shoes in the corner of
the room, as if they'd been fired there by a cannon.

'You know how to paint the town red,' drawled a voice.

She turned over and opened one eye. Eddie lay with
his arm behind his head, languidly smoking a cigarette.

'Time?'

'A little after five a.m. I have to haul ass if I'm gonna
make my train.'

He leant over and kissed her slowly on her naked
shoulder, trailing kisses down her arm, and groaned.

'Boy, do I not want to leave you. I want to stay here all day making love to you.'

'Why don't you then?' she said, smiling provocatively and pulling him towards her by his dog tag.

''Cause I don't want to get court-martialled.' He gently lifted a curl of her blonde hair and ran it between his fingers.

'In another life, in another world, oh baby . . . You are something else, Ruby Munroe.'

She looked at him. God he was young. Surely only twenty-one at most. Reluctantly, he swung his long legs over the side of the bed and pulled back the blackout blinds. A lacy dawn light filtered in and washed his body with pearlised light. She watched him pad round the room naked, retrieving items of his clothes, peeling her bra off his shoe with a wry smile. His body was a thing of glory, so smooth and strong, and she watched him unashamedly.

She thought back to last night or what she could remember of it. Gin and It cocktails, the beautiful bare-breasted tableaux at The Windmill theatre, hot sweaty jitterbugging at the Lyceum, then tumbling back into this hotel room and ripping each other's clothes off. Utterly shameless indulgence. She pictured Clara's shocked expression as she left the library yesterday on Eddie's arm and tried to see herself as others viewed her. She knew it'd be half the way round the shelter by now, but she didn't care. Let others judge. She'd take hussy over housewife any day.

Clara would say she was a woman of the times, but in truth, this is who she had always been, the times just happened to suit her.

'That was worth eight hundred *Gone with the Wind*s,' Eddie said, as he finished buttoning up his shirt.

Ruby swung her legs out of bed and, wrapping the bedsheet around herself, peeked her head out of the doorway to check no one was using the shared toilet next door.

'I just need to spend a penny. Wait a minute.'

'I don't even know what that means,' he laughed. 'But just one quick kiss before you spend it!'

Grinning, he made a grab for the sheet, but she ducked out of the way and teasingly blew him a kiss before she ran to the lav. Afterwards, she washed her hands, and tried to open the door, but it was jammed shut.

'Come on,' she muttered, rattling the doorknob. Bloody Blitz. There wasn't a door in all of London that opened properly after the nightly pounding. Suddenly the tiled walls seemed to press in on her and she was aware of the confined space she was trapped in. There wasn't even a window. Fear trickled down her throat.

'Calm down,' she told herself, trying the handle again, but the panic was taking hold, swelling in her chest, hot and greasy. Everything was too small . . . too cramped. Even her own skin suddenly felt tight. She stretched her arms out as if to somehow push the walls apart, but the toilet was tiny; there wasn't room to swing the proverbial cat. She rattled, then banged her fist over and over on the door. 'Help!' she screamed, her face inches from the door. 'Can anyone hear me?'

Silence. The walls seemed to be closing in; she imagined them crushing her skull.

She closed her eyes, saw bodies tumbling, tangled limbs,

people piling up one on top of the other. Logic told her that was the Tube, not here, not now, and yet . . .

'Let me out!' she bellowed. With a superhuman strength, Ruby yanked the door handle and it came clean off in her hand. She looked down at the handle in her hand and claustrophobia exploded, squeezing the breath from her lungs, sending black stars bursting through her head.

'Help me,' she whimpered. The floor rushed up as she sank down onto the tiles.

Suddenly, a blast of cool air. In one fluid movement, Eddie scooped her into his arms.

'It's all right, you're safe,' he soothed, as he carried her up the corridor and laid her down gently on the hotel bed. 'You're safe.' He kept up his mantra as he reached over to the bedside table for a glass of water.

Shakily she drank and as she recovered herself, Ruby felt more exposed than she had ever felt in her life.

'I'm fine,' she muttered, drawing back from him.

'No you're not,' he said bluntly, but his kind eyes seemed to be filled with concern. 'What in the hell just happened?'

Ruby pulled her knees into her chest and stared out of the window. Pink and orange ribbons of light began to streak over the rooftops.

'You better get going, don't want you getting court-martialled on my account.'

'Not until you talk to me.'

Something inside Ruby buckled. It was all just so bloody exhausting holding it together. Trying to be strong all the time.

'I get these . . .' Her voice fell to a whisper. 'Episodes.'

He said nothing, just kept on stroking her head.

'It started after my sister died down the Tube last year.'

'I'm sorry, Ruby, I had no idea.'

'Yes, it was an accident.' Bitterness laced her voice. 'Well, I say an accident, but actually it could have been prevented.'

'Tell me,' he persisted.

'One night folk were queuing up to come down after the sirens went. My sister Bella included . . .' She tailed off, tightened the sheet around her.

'Go on,' he said gently.

'Then there was an explosion. It made the most fearful noise. Course everyone pressed forward, thinking they was under fire from some new form of warfare, desperate to get underground.'

'And?'

She shook her head. 'I shouldn't even really be telling you this, we were warned not to speak about it.'

'Ruby sweetheart, where I'm going, do you really think that matters?'

'S'pose not.' She sipped her water, drew in a shaky breath. It felt strange speaking openly of this, like she was betraying someone, though who she didn't know.

'The crowd started filing down the steps. A woman carrying her baby tripped and before she could get up other people fell over her. One after one, they piled up on top of her. The steps were wet, uneven and slippery; just one tiny lightbulb lit the stairwell. They went down like dominoes.'

A shadow fell over Eddie's face.

'Soon hundreds of people were trapped on the stairwell.

I could hear the screams from the escalators as I ran up from the library.' She covered her eyes against the image and choked back a sob. 'It was chaos. Bodies all tangled up, crushing the life out of each other.'

Tears slid down her pale cheeks.

'I tried to get her out Eddie, I tried to find her, but I couldn't.'

She stared down at her useless hands.

'Every leg or arm I tried to pull free was stuck fast. People suffocated to death in front of me. Can you imagine? I watched the life trickle out of them . . .' she broke off sobbing and he pulled her into his chest. 'And I knew that somewhere in that ghastly mass of bodies, gasping for breath, was my big sister.'

'Oh Ruby . . .'

'I failed her,' Ruby sobbed. 'I think these . . . episodes, if that's what you call them, are my punishment.'

'No . . .' He pulled back bewildered. 'How can you possibly think that?'

Ruby dried her eyes. 'Because it's true.'

For a long time, Eddie held her in silence.

Eventually outside they heard the clanking of a bucket.

'The chambermaid's here. Eddie, you really have to go.'

He pulled back, his face etched with despair.

'How can I leave you now, Ruby? After what you've just told me.'

She smiled sadly. 'Because you have no choice.'

He gave her a last long, lingering kiss before sighing and resting his forehead against hers. 'I . . . I don't know what to say.'

They both knew where he was going. There seemed little point wishing him good luck. Nothing she could say would come close to touching the surface of what fear and adrenaline must already be starting to galvanise inside him.

'I'll write, baby. Then when I get—'

She silenced him by pressing her finger to his lips and shaking her head.

'Let's remember this for what it was, Eddie.' She kissed him again softly on the forehead. 'A glorious night. And I'm sorry if I brought you down.'

He cradled her face in his hands. 'Hell Ruby, you have *nothing* to apologise for. You are astonishing. Brave, funny, beautiful . . .'

He trailed off and stared hard at her, as if trying to imprint the memory of her into his mind.

'So long, Ruby Munroe.'

'So long, Eddie . . .' To her shame, she realised she didn't even remember his surname. He would always just be Eddie. *Gone with the Wind* Eddie.

After he'd left, the hotel room suddenly seemed stripped of its glamour and revealed itself for what it was. A cold, down-at-heel Piccadilly hotel room. Ruby dressed, tried her best to clean her teeth with her finger and checked out, smiling brazenly at the night receptionist who, by 1944, had seen too much to be shocked any longer. She walked slowly to Piccadilly Circus and glanced up to where the statute of Eros usually stood. The god of sensual love had been evacuated to Egham and now the plinth was sandbagged and empty. Seemed an appropriate metaphor for wartime love.

Ruby joined the queue at a WVS mobile canteen. She pushed her hand through her tangled curls and caught a glimpse of her reflection in the canteen window. Eyes smudged with last night's eye black, lips stained with residue of Renegade Red. Her vulnerability of earlier had gone, bolted back in its usual place.

The expression on the WVS lady's face said it all.

Ruby knew her kind. Haughty. Judgemental. *Lipstick and paint make a girl what she ain't*. How many times had she heard that? Well, bugger the lot of them.

'What can I get for you?' Predictably her voice was laced with a chill. God, who needed men when women could be such harsh critics?

'Tea, ta. Strong and sweet.' She knew it was naughty, but she couldn't resist. 'Like the Yank I had in my bed last night.'

Grinning, she took her tea and sauntered off. She took a sip and winced as its scalded the back of her throat. It was dishwater but it would take the edge off her headache. Was she drinking too much? Possibly, but who wasn't these days! Everyone drank to soften the edges. It was virtually de rigueur in wartime. The only problem with having a drop was that the next morning, it was harder than ever to silence her demons.

As she neared the Underground, a newspaper vendor was hollering the day's news. 'Incident in Bethnal Green. Witness reported unmanned missile.' Ruby dropped the tea and ran down to the trains.

She found Clara in the library and knew straightaway she had been caught up in the bombing.

'Hell's teeth, Cla, you look awful.'

'Oh thanks, you don't look so clever yourself.'

Ruby hugged her fiercely before pulling back.

'What happened?'

Clara shook her head. 'I wish I could tell you, it all happened so fast. I know one thing, I wouldn't be standing here if it weren't for Sparrow.'

Ruby stared at her best friend. 'My God,' she breathed. To her embarrassment, she burst into tears. 'I couldn't bear it if anything happened to you.'

'Come on now Rubes, this isn't like you. *You're* the strong one.'

'I know . . . ' She thought of her mum's battered face, her confession to Eddie earlier. 'Promise me you ain't going nowhere, Clara.'

'I'm staying right here, I promise. Now go and put your face back on and fetch us a cup of tea while you're at it. Me and Mr P are gasping.'

'You're the boss,' Ruby replied.

'Oh,' Clara grinned, 'And I guess there's no need to ask whether you had a good time last night?'

'Saucy mare,' she laughed throatily, flicking a stray paperclip at her.

Ruby nipped to the lav, repaired her lippie, cleaned up her smudged eye makeup and felt restored enough to engage in some mild flirtation with some ARP men queuing at the station café. By the time she returned to the library, she felt more like her old self.

Beatty was standing at the library counter, five books in front of her ready to be stamped as Clara plucked her ticket from the wooden tray.

'Didn't you only get *The Secret Garden* out a couple of days ago?'

Beatty smiled radiantly, touching a red, white and blue Union Jack silk scarf tried round her head.

'Finished it last night. Clara's agreed I could take five this week, instead of three.'

'Shh,' said Clara, raising a finger to her lips. 'Our secret, remember.'

'Ooh yes, sorry,' she said, smiling apologetically.

'Lovely to see you smiling, sweetheart,' Ruby said. 'And what a pretty scarf; suits you.'

'Thanks. My mum gave it to me.'

'She still stuck with the night shift at Compton's?' Ruby asked casually.

'Yes, that's right.'

Now Ruby knew she was spinning a yarn. The last time she'd asked, she'd told her her mum was working over at Plessey's aircraft factory. Just where was the absent Mrs Kolsky working in order to keep her daughters in silk scarves?

'Have you any new letters for your dad you want me to keep in our secret cubby hole?'

'No, I haven't written any and I shan't think I'll need to either; we'll be going home soon.'

'Really, how's that?' Ruby asked cautiously.

'Well, it stands to reason, doesn't it? Now the Allies have invaded France, it shan't be at all long before Jersey is liberated.' Her face lit up. 'Oh, I can't wait to go home.'

She was bursting with hope, and Ruby opened her mouth to point out that, surely, if the Allies had plans to liberate the Channel Islands, eight days on from D-Day, they would have done so by now. They were pushing on eastwards, in the direction of Berlin.

'I wouldn't get your hopes up too much just yet, my love,' she cautioned. She went to say more, but Clara shot her a warning look.

'Well, we'll all be very sorry to see you and Marie leave us,' Clara said.

'Thank you to you all. Marie and I will never be able to repay your kindness.'

'Just keep reading.' Clara grinned. 'That's thanks enough for me.'

'Oh, I will,' she said, picking up the newly stamped books.

The encounter had put a smile back on the faces of all the underground library staff, but they were wiped off approximately one minute later by the arrival of Pinkerton-Smythe.

He ran his hard-boiled gaze over the library counter before picking up the paperclip Ruby had flicked at Clara earlier.

'This ought to be with the rest of the stationery,' he said crisply. 'I can't abide squandered stationery.'

'Sorry, Mr Pinkerton-Smythe,' Clara replied.

'I've had a complaint.'

He pulled out a notebook.

'I had a visit from a Mrs Marshall.'

Clara looked baffled.

'Miss Munroe recommended a boys' book to her daughter, Joannie. *Emil and the Detectives* by Erich Kästner. A German writer.'

'Actually, that was me,' she said, shooting Ruby a look.

'Surely we can't object to the loaning of German authors,' said Mr Pepper bravely.

'Of course not, but her mother does object to her daughter being loaned books that are clearly aimed at boys. It's most unsavoury.'

'Yes, but—'

'Sssh. I'm talking, don't interrupt. As I was saying, it's called into question once more the appropriateness of your children's storytime sessions, Mrs Button.

'And I also saw a young girl leaving here just now with five books. Have you increased loan rates, Mrs Button?'

'No . . . it . . . it was a mistake,' she stuttered.

'And my colleague overheard a policeman saying how you had waived his fine.'

'Well, there was one time—'

'The fine is a penny a week! Really, it's just not good enough, Mrs Button. Rules are there to be implemented, otherwise we shall descend into squalor and chaos. It starts with paperclips and leads to anarchy.'

At that moment, the Major drifted in.

'I'll just be having a snooze before the Sally Army opens its doors, Clara my dear,' he called out. 'I'll be in my usual spot.'

He shuffled into the reading room, trailing a ripe stench.

Mr Pinkerton-Smythe looked like he might implode as he reached inside his briefcase.

'This is an official warning against your conduct.' He slid the envelope across the counter. 'Any more mistakes and I shall be tabling a motion for your instant dismissal and the closure of this library until the Central Library is refurbished.'

He clicked his tongue on the roof of his mouth.

'And get rid of the undesirable. We're not a community centre for vagrants. It is not your job to be an interventionist social engineer.'

And with that, he left.

'But it *is* my job to be human,' Clara hissed despairingly, once he was out of earshot.

'Cla,' Ruby said carefully. 'Why did you take the blame for me?'

'Because it's *me* he's gunning for. Don't you see? He's determined to catch me out. Well, he shan't.'

She looked from Ruby to Mr Pepper.

'It's a public library, isn't it, paid for by the local residents' rates? Which means it's there for the use of *all* the public in Bethnal Green.'

At 6 p.m., something extraordinary happened. The door swung open for storytime and Ruby had never seen so many children clustered in the library.

Word had spread of Clara's brush with death, and mothers had sent their children in with food parcels. Faces everywhere, and not just kids there for storytime either, but most of their regulars seemed to be pressed into the library, like so many well-loved books squeezed onto a shelf. There was Rita Rawlins with her foul-mouthed parrot, chatting animatedly with the Major. Sex-mad Irene debating with Queenie and put-upon wife Mrs Caley about crime versus romance. Even the middle-aged couple who'd come in to borrow *The Sex Factor in Marriage* had made it out of the bedroom and were standing arm-in-arm, a honeymooner's flush on their faces. Clara had made this library not just a space filled with books, but the shelter living room.

Soon, you could scarcely see a spare patch of space on the counter. It was an outpouring of love for Bethnal Green's favourite librarian.

'Three cheers for Clara!' boomed Mrs Chumbley, and the roof nearly came off.

'Bit louder kids, think there's a woman in Reading who didn't hear that,' Ruby called.

It was the arrival of Sparrow, his hand clamped firmly through his mum's that finally toppled Clara's composure.

'I don't know how to thank you, Clara,' Pat said. 'If he hadn't been with you out walking, I'd have lost my boy.'

'No, no, it's me who should be thanking your son,' Clara protested. 'He was tremendously brave.'

Sparrow shrugged, scuffing his shoe on the floor.

'Well, he's staying by my side and sleeping down here from now on, I can assure you.'

'I'm so sorry for your loss, Pat,' Clara said, resting her hand on the older woman's arm.

Pat nodded, pale-faced with exhaustion and grief at the loss of her sister and nephews. In her arms, she cradled her baby nephew, clearly wondering how on earth she would cope with an infant to care for and another mouth to feed.

'We just need to get the job done. Stop this bloody war, stop losing the people we love.'

Ruby nodded. 'Amen to that.'

In that moment, she saw with clarity just why her friend seemed to exhaust every last drop of her energy in keeping this little wartime library going.

'Can I stay for storytime?' Sparrow mumbled.

Clara held out her hand to him.

'Come on.'

He took her hand and Ruby heard her whisper, 'Thank you for what you did. You're braver than Jim Hawkins'.

He looked up at her, wiped his nose on the back of a sleeve.

'Nah. Right place, right time. Serendipity.'

Ruby started to tidy up and realised that in the midst of this dreadful war, being fought on so many fronts, only their little unconventional library family made any sense at all. She smoothed beeswax over the wooden counter and thought of Eddie, her skin still tingling from his expert kisses. He was a good man, after all. At least he'd delivered on his promise. He had been tender and kind and surprisingly attentive. He had listened to her without judgement; he was the only man she had confided in about Bella. He had seen her at her most vulnerable.

Regret whispered in her ear. Should she have agreed to write to him, offered him some hope of a shared future?

A vision of Bella crept into her mind, standing at the top of those nineteen steps, red hair shimmering in the dim light. *See you later, don't be late.*

The month before her death, Bella had confided she had finally saved up enough money from sewing army uniforms and cleaning toilets, to open a coffee stall outside the Tube, her own business. 'I'm on my way Rubes,' she'd told her. She had been clever and determined enough to do it too.

The guilt grew black in Ruby's chest and spread like a stain. She *had* been late. She'd omitted that part of the story when she'd recounted it to Eddie. Fifteen minutes and it had cost Bella her life.

If she had been prompt and been outside the Tube entrance at the top of the steps at precisely 8.15 p.m., like she had promised Bella, they would have been safely away before the sirens started wailing at 8.17 p.m. But she hadn't been, had she! The terrible, unavoidable fact of it was that while Ruby had been gossiping with a pal at the bottom of the escalator, her sister was getting jostled in the growing crowd above ground. Shortly after the siren sounded, three buses had stopped at once outside the Tube, disgorging more people onto the street. Cinemas and pubs had emptied, adding to the hundreds of people clamouring to get underground down those dark and narrow steps.

Oblivious, she had kept Bella waiting in a tense crowd. Sure Bella could have turned, attempted to push her way out, maybe she had tried? But Ruby also knew Bella. Her sister was as loyal as the day was long. There was no way she would have left the spot where they were supposed to meet, not with the sirens screaming. And so it was that she had been stuck there when another unearthly sound had ripped over the crowd's heads at 8.27 p.m. Not enemy bombs, but an anti-aircraft rocket as it later transpired, but no one queuing up that day in the dark knew that.

Bella had been wedged solid when the crowd surged forward down the Tube steps, thinking they were under fire. *When the mother with the baby tripped on the bottom step. When the bodies began to pile up . . .*

It had all happened in a matter of moments. Precious moments she had stolen. By the time Ruby heard the screams and shouts echo down the escalators, it was already too late. Her tardiness had cost Bella her life. Her beautiful big sister had tumbled headlong into hell and it was all her fault. She may as well have pushed her.

Ruby folded her cloth, her hands shaking, her head starting to fill with pins and needles as the old familiar panic galvanised inside her.

Oh, please God, no. Not again. Two in one day. Sometimes she could breathe through it, not this evening. The foul winged serpents were gathering in her mind, whispering their truths, only this time there was no Eddie to scoop her up.

She swallowed uneasily and looked about. Storytime was over. The kids were returning to their bunks. Clara stood at the door, waving them off.

'You look worn out Cla. You get off. I'll clear up here,' she offered.

'Oh would you, Rubes? Thanks. I am pretty tired.' She smothered a yawn. 'I didn't get much sleep at the ambulance station last night.'

''Course, now go on, be off with you, shoo,' Ruby laughed, flicking her duster at her and she kept on grinning right until Clara had left and she locked the library door.

She ran to the bookshelf, her vision growing blurry, her heart punching in her chest and with a shuddering relief, pulled out *The Art of Domesticity*. Just the one, she vowed as she reached for the bottle.

11

Clara

People without books are like houses without windows.
The Mayor of St Pancras, London, at the opening ceremony of London's first mobile library in 1941

August sent blue skies and soaring Sarsaparilla sales. Not
that the little wartime library saw much of the syrupy
summer sunshine, but they felt its muggy air down the
tunnels.

'Gracious it's close today,' Clara said, fanning herself
with a book catalogue as little rivers of sweat trickled down
her back. 'Is the sun out up there?' she asked a wiry looking
man who approached the counter.

'It's cracking the cobblestones, love,' he replied. He
glanced about feverishly and Clara could already predict
what he was about to ask.

'Got one of them mucky books?'

'I think you're in the wrong place,' Clara said smoothly.
'Try Charing Cross, there's many bookshops there who
could cater for your needs.' Since war had begun, plenty
of smaller publishers had opened, printing salacious
'novels' if you could call them that, on whatever paper
they could lay their hands on, even margarine wrappers,

to cater for the millions of foreign troops who passed through London. Five shillings could buy you one sealed in a brown paper bag, so Ruby had told her.

'Can you recommend one?' he persisted, absent-mindedly scratching his crotch.

'No,' she snapped, finally losing her cool. 'Please leave, I'm terribly busy.'

'All right, don't get your knickers in a twist, love.' He turned, but almost as an afterthought, stopped. 'Wish the blonde with the dirty laugh was serving today. You are one damn ugly woman.'

'I don't find you all that appealing either,' Clara said crisply. 'Goodbye.'

Mucky Books collided with Billy on his way out.

'Did that man just say what I thought he said?'

'Goes with the territory,' Clara said with a shrug.

'But he was so rude. Do you want me to go after him, make him apologise?'

'No need. Trust me, librarians see and hear it all.'

Billy shook his head, dimples creasing his cheeks as he laughed.

'I need to take you out of here.' He grimaced. 'Is it me or is the smell riper than usual down the tunnels?'

'Someone left a wet fish on top of *Mein Kampf* – must have been a protest. The stench was unbearable. We've had to send a whole stack of books off to be baked.' She blew her nose. 'My sinuses are still recovering. The air's so thick you could almost bump into it.'

'Is it worth stocking if that's the reaction?'

'Believe it or not, it's almost permanently on the reserve

list. People want to understand their enemy, inform themselves of the threat of his ideology.'

He nodded. 'Makes sense. Come on then, let's get you
into the fresh air.'

'Let me just shelve this lot, then I'll be with you.'

It had been eleven weeks since she'd been caught up in
the rocket attack, and in that time, she and Billy had grown
closer, feeling their way round the edges of their emotions.
Seeing Billy at work had cast him in an entirely new light.
She was desperate to understand him better, root out the
source of his shame, but knew she had to tread gently.
The most important thing was she meant something to
him. It was enough. For now.

Every time he came in, he was clutching a new book
to donate to the library. Ruby reckoned he was like a cat
bringing in mice to please its master. Clara had scoffed,
insisting they were just friends, but whenever she heard
Beauty's paws pattering up the platform outside, her heart
leapt right into her throat.

The government had finally admitted the existence of
the new pilotless 'revenge' weapon. Billy had worked every
single day for the past eleven weeks with his crew, often
turning up after a fifteen-hour shift haunted by the acts
of atrocity he had witnessed, the horrors of the rocket
sites clinging to him like a muddy blanket.

For her part, she had been busier than the Blitz and book
loans were at record levels as folk flocked to the library,
desperate for the diversion a good story could bring.

She picked up the pile of books and opened the wooden
counter, but Ruby barred her way.

'Put them down and get out of here.'

'What if Mr Pinkerton-Smythe comes in? I'm still on a warning, remember!'

'Then I'll tell him you're having your first day off in eleven weeks.'

'Oh, and one more thing. I found another defaced *Daily Herald* earlier with the racing pages cut out again. Seems our phantom paper snipper is back. You will keep an eye out won't you?'

''Course I will. Now scram!'

'You think you can tear yourself away from Bethnal Green Underground?' Billy laughed as they stepped out into the sunshine. After the dim lighting, the glare of daylight was almost blinding, causing her to squint.

'Sorry. I think I've developed troglodyte mentality after all!'

It was true. Any spare time she had was spent teaching Sparrow to read or reading to Marie and Beatty in their bunks.

'Thinking about Sparrow? Or the Jersey girls?' Billy grinned as they headed to the bus stop and hopped on the back of the number 8.

'That obvious?' she laughed. 'Sparrow will be catching Beatty up at this rate. I've given him his own special ladder ticket, so every time he reads a book, he moves up a rung and when he gets to the top, he gets a gold star . . .' She tailed off.

'Sorry, I'm talking too much, aren't I? Next I'll be telling you the finer points of cataloguing.'

'Not at all. I love listening to you talk about children and books. You used to be the children's librarian, didn't you, before the war?'

She stared out of the window as the scruffy, bashed-up streets flashed past.

'That's right, and when the war's over and I go back to my old job, provided Pinkerton-Smythe hasn't got rid of me, I have so many plans for reform.' She shook her head as she tried to articulate what 'after the war' looked like.

'The Underground library has proved to me how valuable reading is to children. I mean, I knew that anyway, but this war has crystalised my belief that books are their gateway to other worlds.'

Clara sighed and drew the outline of a book across the sooty window.

'Not only that but I'd like to expand the bibliobus service. People without books are like houses without windows, don't you think?'

She turned back to look at Billy. He was smiling at her so brilliantly, she felt the quickening of her own heart.

He hesitated, and then held her hand. She felt the rough calluses on his fingers, the warmth of his skin against hers. It felt more intimate than if he'd kissed her and Clara felt a bright dizzying flare of happiness.

In the West End, the bus belched to a stop.

'Come on!' he said.

The rest of the morning passed as if in a dream. They bought lemon ices and walked down by the grey ribbon of the Thames, savouring the unaccustomed fizz of sugar on their tongues as they gazed up at the clouds scudding over St Paul's cathedral.

Beautiful young women passed them by, a masterclass in elegance on a shoestring, unwashed hair hidden under stylish turbans, tiny waists emphasised with nipped in jackets. They wore their *Make Do and Mend* outfits with defiant aplomb. Clara looked down at her rather sorry stockings and patched up skirt, worn in place of her usual slacks in a vague stab at femininity. She heard her mother-in-law's voice. *What a shabby show.*

Unlike Ruby, the *Beauty is Your Duty* campaign was a call to arms that seemed to have passed Clara by. Would it be unseemly for a war widow to paint her lips red? Was it risqué or patriotic? Clara felt confused. Morality was a nuanced concept right now, though it was pretty black and white to her family.

She hadn't seen her mother since that dreadful night in the library when she had been awarded the certificate, or her mother-in-law since she saw her outside the ambulance station the morning after the rocket. They both worked so hard to protect Duncan's memory that sometimes it felt as if there were no room for her own grief. And yet she did miss him so very much.

Duncan would have hated going to an art exhibition, but he had loved her so greatly she knew he would have gone anyway, just to keep her happy. The ever-present guilt ratcheted up. And yet being here now, with this sensitive and thoughtful man, felt so very right.

At the Royal Academy they bought two tickets for the Summer Exhibition and wandered in a breathless hush through the rooms until they came to a painting entitled *Dunkirk Beaches*.

A column of men was queuing up for ships, and over them all was an ominous greasy pall of black smoke.

'It's very lifelike,' Billy said quietly.

Her mind teemed with questions that never seemed to make their way to her tongue.

What had he done, or not done? Had he taken a life, instead of saving it, is that why he was a conscientious objector? That had to be it and yet . . .

'Billy?' Her voice echoed in the gallery then seemed to die. She felt his hand grow tense in hers, then he pulled it away.

'Shall we go?' he muttered, staring at the door. Their intimacy of moments earlier evaporated.

'Yes, perhaps it's for the best,' she replied, her chest tight with frustration.

They got the bus back to Bethnal Green in subdued silence.

They hopped off the bus and stood in Barmy Park, both summoning up the courage to ask, 'What now?'. It was only 4.30 p.m. She couldn't bear the thought of turning the key in the lock and stepping into the void of loneliness, every minute ticking by like hours. Despite the sunshine she shivered as a breeze ballooned her skirt.

'Look,' he said suddenly. 'The window's open at the side of the derelict library.'

Clara frowned. 'I hope no one's broken in.'

'We better take a look,' he said, and before she could stop him, he was off.

'I really don't think we ought to—' she began, but he was already squeezing his slim body through the partially open window.

'I don't think it's a good idea,' she called to him, looking nervously about.

'I'll just take a look around,' he called back. 'Check everything's all right.'

Clara hesitated. She was the branch librarian for pity's sake.

'Wait a moment,' she called as she hoisted one leg up onto the window ledge.

She dropped down the other side into the gloom of the deserted library.

Her feet landed with a crunch on the glass-scattered floor. The noise disturbed a flock of roosting pigeons who rose in a dirty scrawl.

As their eyes adjusted to the darkness, they gazed around in dismay.

'Can't see anyone about,' she said. 'There's nothing really to loot in any case.'

'When was the last time you were in here?' he asked.

'The night it was bombed. I'm afraid I wimped out of coming back to salvage the books, so Ruby and a team of volunteers did it, while I set up the library below ground.'

'Too many memories?'

She nodded and looked about in more detail. She didn't know what she was expecting, but it was a bombsite. Chickweed and purple buddleia had grown up in the cracks in the floor where the stacks once stood. The interior furniture and shelves that hadn't been destroyed had been removed to furnish the underground library or sent for salvage, so it was hard to orientate herself.

Where had she and Peter been when the bomb had dropped? The adult lending library, at the back of the building, but all she saw in the Stygian gloom was water-logged pillars and flaking plaster.

'Burning books is beyond belief, isn't it?' Billy murmured as he looked about. 'Libraries hold no military value, do they?'

'Before all this, I used to think of this as the safest place in Bethnal Green . . .' She stared at the burnt-out reading room. 'I thought that no harm could come to anyone in a library.'

'What was Peter like?' he asked softly.

'So kind. He went out of his way to help anyone.'

Suddenly it hit her how extraordinarily alike Billy and Peter were.

'Hundreds of people attended his funeral, you know,' she continued. 'He used to say, "Good books provided through libraries fill up our soul".'

She looked up at the shattered remains of a large, glass domed roof that used to pour light into the library.

'He could be a little eccentric at times mind you. A year before war broke out, we had a spate of books go missing. Peter was convinced he could catch the thief. He used to hide out on the glass roof, looking down to catch the culprit.'

'Did he catch him?'

'The only thing he caught was a cold.'

She laughed at a sudden memory.

'There was a black cat, a stray I assume, just known as Library Cat and Peter loved him. Used to feed him his fish paste sandwiches.'

Billy laughed. 'I like the sound of Peter.'

'He was a character. He swore that books absorbed smells.'

Billy raised one eyebrow.

'Honest. Westerns always came back smelling of muscle rub and roll-ups.'

Billy laughed. 'And don't tell me, romance came back smelling of roses.'

'Nope. Cooking oil and Woodbines usually.'

'Figures.' He grinned. 'I can still see my mum standing over a stew pot, wooden spoon in one hand, an Ethel M. Dell in the other. Say, didn't this place used to be an asylum?'

'That's right. Follow me.'

Together they walked gingerly up an old staircase that led to the upstairs lecture rooms. The steps felt spongy and wet underfoot.

'Please be careful,' he whispered. 'Blackie and Darling would have a field day if they had to rescue us after trespassing on a bombsite.'

They crept down a waterlogged corridor and the air grew chill.

'Where we're standing now used to be the male block of the asylum,' she whispered, pausing by the lockers outside the upstairs reading room. 'Peter once told me about the cures they used.'

Her face clouded over. 'If you can call chaining people to their beds for days at a time a cure.'

'If they weren't mad before, they certainly would be after that treatment.'

Clara nodded. 'Such cruelty. Everyone used to say this corridor was haunted. We had a heating engineer who would never set foot up here.'

'I'm not sure whether I believe in ghosts, but two centuries worth of suffering has to leave a mark.'

'It did,' Clara said, pulling back what used to be her old locker, to reveal a patch of dark, distempered wall. There on the wall, scratched in a jagged hand were the words, *I have vanished from life.*

'My God,' breathed Billy. 'Is that what I think it is?'

Clara nodded. 'Nineteenth-century graffiti. Peter found it when they were doing some renovation work and he made the builders leave it. He used to say the library was a legacy, founded in order to obtain knowledge and sweep away the misery and poverty of the past. That we ought to leave it as a reminder of what the library was fighting so hard to eradicate.'

The silence in the chilly corridor seemed to expand, the only sound the drip-drip of water from somewhere up above. Here in the library, she felt his presence everywhere.

In that moment she knew exactly what advice Peter would have given her. *Tell him your story.*

'I lost my baby,' she blurted, surprised to hear the words leave her mouth.

'Oh, Clara,' he breathed. 'I'm so sorry.'

'No, no, it's all right, I should talk about it. I never do. My family, Duncan's family, they all blame me.'

'Why's it your fault?' he asked, incredulous.

'Because I was working late here, the Saturday afternoon the Blitz broke out. I should've given up work as soon as I found out I was expecting, evacuated to the countryside. But instead, I stayed on. Peter was so short-staffed; all the male librarians had been conscripted . . .' She shrugged. 'What else was I to do?

'So, I was here that Saturday helping Peter with some shelving, when the bombs began to drop. A week after Peter's death, we buried him, and right after the funeral, I started to bleed. Shock, the doctors said.'

'That's unbearably sad to lose a child,' Billy said gently. 'Especially as it was the last part of your husband. But it's *not* your fault, Clara.'

'Perhaps, but if I had only stayed at home.'

'Then you might well have been bombed there!' he exclaimed. 'War is devastating and meaningless, and to suggest that the loss of a child is your fault is downright cruel.'

'Maybe, but I still feel like I've failed. I look around the shelter and I see women with enormous families. I can't even manage one.'

'That's not the only marker of success though, is it?' he insisted. 'You've suffered unimaginable losses, Clara. Your husband, your mentor, your child . . . But you haven't let it define you. You are an astonishing woman who brightens the lives of everyone who walks through the library doors. I bet your Peter would be looking down on you now cheering you on.'

A breathless hush fell between them and Clara felt a

crumb of hope. Something warm and soft snaked round her ankles.

She leapt back.

'Oh, my God!' Her eyes fell on the small black cat with amazement and he leapt into her arms, nuzzling her cheeks with his face.

'It's Peter's Library Cat!' she exclaimed. 'I don't believe it. I assumed he'd been killed in the bombing.'

'Maybe your Peter is looking down on you after all,' Billy grinned, stroking the cat's ears, which caused a tractor-like purr to erupt from its body.

It seemed so silly but finding Library Cat was a moment of perfect happiness, proving that the war couldn't steal everything.

Before she could stop herself, she leaned in to kiss Billy, but he moved his head and so she ended up awkwardly kissing his ear.

'I'm so sorry,' she blurted. 'I . . . I don't know what came over me.'

He stared at her, blue eyes startled.

'Believe me, Clara, there's nothing I'd love more than to kiss you back, but . . .' He scrubbed at his face and Clara burned with humiliation. How had she misread the signs so spectacularly? She turned.

'Don't leave,' he pleaded.

'I'm sorry. That was clumsy of me.' Still clutching Library Cat, she turned and ran back in the direction of the only place she felt safe. The underground library.

★

Fortunately, Minksy Agombar and her sisters were singing harmonies in the shelter theatre, so the station platform was quiet. A tiny Tube mouse scampered in front of her path and slipped like a drop of ink into the crack between the platform and the boarded-over track. Clara wished she could follow.

She wandered into the reading room and Mr Pepper and the kids turned around in surprise. Mr Pepper had been reading from *The Country Child* with a magnifying glass. Everyone turned to stare and, at the sight of the cat, a chorus of squeals went up.

'Mr P, shall I take over?' Clara asked, handing Library Cat to Sparrow.

He handed her the book and she sat down heavily on the chair. Gripping the book, she began to read. Clara felt her heart rate calm. Thank God for books, whose pages she could hide in even when she had made a spectacular fool of herself. She read on, losing herself in the deep, ancient woods.

Her voice must have been soporific because the children had gone awfully quiet. She looked up. Billy was standing at the door to the reading room.

'Sorry to interrupt, children, but there's something I need to tell the librarian.'

Fifty sets of eager eyes swivelled from Billy to Clara. He crossed the room in three easy strides and gently pulled Clara to her feet.

'I'm a total chump. This is what I should've done in the library.'

Gently, he prised the book from her hand before cupping her face in his hands and kissing her.

As his lips met hers and their fingers entwined, she felt a scalding relief.

The room erupted. The girls giggled, wide-eyed with disbelief at the sight of the librarian being kissed in public. Sparrow affected nonchalance, crossing his arms, but later it would be discussed that he might have felt a tinge of jealousy. Ruby wandered in to see what all the commotion was about and leant against the doorframe, a delighted smile on her face.

'I'm so sorry I didn't kiss you back,' he whispered, as he drew away.

'That ain't no way to treat a lady, mister,' Tubby protested.

'Sorry?'

Tubby slapped an exasperated palm against his forehead.

'You gotta woo 'em! I'm a kid and even I know that.'

'Oh yes, sorry, Tubby, you're right,' said Billy, turning back to Clara with a luminous smile.

'Clara Button, I love the way you love this place. The way you fiddle with your hair when you're nervous but forget about it when you're fired up about something. The way you bend the rules because sometimes it's the right thing to do.' His speech was coming in shaky bursts now. 'I especially love your imperfections, your slightly chipped tooth, your toes – which are alas now covered up. But mostly, I think I just love you.'

Clara felt as if the library was spinning, with words, pages and stories spiralling giddily around her.

The cheers drowned out the Agombar sisters' harmonies in the theatre next door. And down in the little wartime library, in and among the chaos of war, a new love story was beginning.

12

Ruby

A library is more than its books, it's a place where women's lives have the potential to be transformed.
Magda Oldziejewska, Fundraising Coordinator, Feminist
Library

'And that,' said Clara, reluctantly closing the book, 'is the end of another wonderful story.'

It had taken them three weeks to get through Alison Uttley's *The Country Child*. The book was pure magic, spinning country folklore with vivid evocations of rural England.

Ruby listened in awe from behind the counter. No one could silence a crowd of kids like Clara. The storytime group was much diminished. Ronnie, Joannie and many more had been evacuated to the safety of the countryside, far out of reach of the doodlebugs. The battle-hardy little crew left behind had parents who couldn't countenance being parted from their kids. Ruby had to hand it to Clara. It was probably no coincidence she was reading a book set in England's green meadows and mysterious woods. If she couldn't transport them physically, she could at least take them there through the pages of a book.

'I'd love to spend the night in a dark forest,' Tubby mused.

'A bob says you'd never last an hour,' teased Sparrow. 'One hoot of an owl and you'd be out of there.'

'It's a wager,' Tubby retorted, spitting in his palm and reaching over to shake Sparrow's hand.

'Now, now, boys,' Ruby laughed, looking up to see her mum walk into the library for her Friday evening cleaning shift. 'Let's get this place tidied up.'

As the kids set about picking up cushions and books, she watched her mum set to work.

'No change?' Clara asked quietly, joining her behind the counter.

Ruby shook her head. 'Still refusing to join in book club or read that book you ordered her,' she said under her breath.

'I know, Mrs Caley decided to borrow it instead would you believe.'

'Good on her,' Ruby remarked. 'Mum can't see past that lousy swine's shadow.'

'Give her time.'

Ruby looked at the bruise mushrooming out from under her mum's headscarf, which Netty had blamed on a 'blackout tangle with a lamp post'.

'I'm not sure how much time she's got Cla. One of these days that bastard'll go too far.'

'Clara,' interrupted Tubby, tugging her arm.

'Tubby, can it wait please? I'm talking to Ruby.'

'Not really. Now, miss, I'm as broadminded as the next twelve-year-old, but do you really think the younger kids ought to be reading this?'

He held up a copy of *Birth Control for the Married Woman*.

'Where did you get this?' Clara asked, snatching it from him.

'It was on the shelf, right next to *Babar the Elephant*.'

Ruby and Clara looked at each other in astonishment.

'How did it end up there? That could be enough to get us shut down!'

'I swear I didn't put it there,' Ruby replied.

'It's all right,' she sighed, as she glanced over to the counter where Mr Pepper was painstakingly checking all the cardboard tickets in the tray with his magnifying glass.

'I think I know who did. I've been finding books turning up where they oughtn't to be. I've been letting it go, but I think this proves I need a chat with Mr P about his eyesight . . . You don't think . . .?' Clara trailed off.

'Don't think what?' Ruby asked.

'That it's Mr Pepper who's cutting out the racing pages from the newspapers? Even accidentally? I found another cut up yesterday.'

'No, 'course not,' Ruby replied swiftly, then with less certainty. 'Least I hope not. Come on. Let's set up for book club.'

But as she started to set out the chairs for the Friday night Bethnal Green Bookworm meeting, Ruby shuddered to think what would happen if one of the parents found out about the misplaced pamphlet.

Thirty minutes later, she slid out *The Art of Homemaking*, giddy with relief. The uncomfortable realisation dawned on her that she was looking forward to their evening tipple earlier and earlier these days. She thought back. When was the last time she'd had a night off the sauce? Well, the rockets hadn't helped of course. Then there was the worry over her mum. All right, she had little nip before she left the library to steady her nerves and help her get up those stairs without thinking of Bella. Then again before bed to stop the nightmares. *After the war's over, I'll stop,* she told herself unconvincingly.

She uncorked a bottle and while Clara was greeting Billy at the door, took a hasty gulp. The liquid hit the back of her throat and she closed her eyes in relief.

'Ready?' she asked, turning round with a painted-on smile.

'As I'll ever be,' Clara grinned, throwing open the library doors.

Queenie was first in, lowering herself into a chair with an exaggerated groan.

'Fix us one of them drinks, Ruby Red Lips,' she called. 'I'm so thirsty, I could spit sixpence.'

'Me and all, darlin',' said Irene, bustling in behind her. 'After the day I've had, I could drink stairs and passage water.'

'What's with the teacups, Rubes?' asked Dot. 'I can't face more splosh.'

'Don't worry, it's one of my specials. But seeing as how we ain't supposed to consume alcohol in the library, I'm serving it from a teapot, so if our boss should happen to poke his nose round the door, all he'll see is the Bethnal Green Bookworms having a nice cup of tea.'

'You are incorrigible, Ruby,' scolded Mrs Chumbley, stroking Library Cat, who had jumped up on her lap.

'I thought animals were barred from the shelter,' Dot exclaimed.

'She's making an exception,' Mr Pepper chuckled.

'Indeed I am. He's caught over twenty rats this week!' Mrs Chumbley exclaimed. 'He's doing more for the hygiene of the shelter than the whole of the borough's sanitation unit put together, which is just as well. I've just come from a tedious meeting at the Town Hall regarding the misuse of toilet paper. Seems shelterers are using more than their one allocated square.'

'So, I'm not the only one with a paper shortage,' Clara grinned.

'Clara, dear,' Mrs Chumbley said. 'I overheard a conversation between Mr Pinkerton-Smythe and the shelter manager in his office earlier. He was asking Mr Miller that, in the event of the shelter library being disbanded, what possible alternative use he could find for the premises.'

A cry went up from the book club.

'But he can't shut down the library, can he?' said Dot in alarm.

'Calm down everyone,' said Billy. 'Let Mrs Chumbley speak.'

'Thank you, Billy. It's important we stay calm. Anger won't serve our cause.'

'So, what will, Mrs Chumbley?' Clara asked. 'That man will not rest until he has closed this library down. You were a suffragette. Ought I chain myself to the library counter?'

A wry smile passed over the older woman's face.

'A common misconception. I wasn't part of the more militant arm. I was a member of the East London Federation of the Suffragettes. We believed in the power of a Women's Army to bring about change.'

'I don't understand,' Clara said.

'We knew breaking shop windows and ending up in prison wouldn't do working-class women any good. So, we opened social centres, a nursery and a cost-price canteen, and even a cooperative toy factory that paid women a living wage. We knew the only way to galvanise support for our cause was by helping people in ways that made a difference to their lives.'

Clara stared at her blankly.

'Pinkerton-Smythe can't very well close down a public facility that is clearly loved by the community.' She patted Clara on the arm. 'Defend this library by engaging a Reader's Army. Books are your weapons!'

'Perhaps we ought to play it safe for a while though,' Ruby interjected. 'Stop loaning out the birth control pamphlet, play by the rules for a bit.'

'NO, don't stop what you're doing in here.'

Everyone turned, surprised at the unexpectantly vociferous voice.

'This library's given me back my life.'

Mrs Caley shifted in her seat, uncomfortable with the scrutiny of the group.

'Go on,' Ruby urged.

'I've got nine nippers.' She traced the rim of her teacup. 'One for every year we've been married, my husband proudly tells it.' She looked up and her eyes radiated hope.

'But not this year. Clara leant me reading material that has helped me to understand my body better. I admit, I never thought I'd get through this though.'

The Tenant of Wildfell Hall sat on her lap.

'Thought it might be too, you know, wordy for me.'

'And?' said Clara, leaning forward.

'I'm leaving him.'

'How?' Netty blurted, looking up from the shelf she was dusting. 'Where'll you go with nine kids in tow?'

'To my sister's in Suffolk for a start.'

For the first time, the group noticed she had a tatty carpet bag under her chair.

'He's on a night shift. The older ones are down the tunnels as we speak getting the younger ones ready. I've saved enough to get us on a train out. We'll make it up as we go along, once we get out to the countryside.'

She drained her drink and stood up.

'But I wanted to come here and say thanks to you all. For reminding me about the sort of person I used to be.'

'What was it, Mrs Caley, about this book in particular which made you decide to leave?' asked Mrs Chumbley.

Mrs Caley cocked her head.

'I don't know. I found courage in its pages I suppose.'

She picked up her bag.

'Better go before I lose me nerve. Be lucky everyone and God bless you all.' When she reached the door, she turned. 'Ooh, nearly forgot.'

She placed her library ticket down on the counter.

Netty stared after her, astonished, as she walked out of the library in search of a new life. Ruby glanced at her mother, praying that by some strange osmosis some of that new-found courage would rub off on her. In that moment though, Netty looked so tiny, standing there clutching her duster like it was a white flag. Had she given up? Had Victor and his abuse entirely corroded her spirit? And it dawned on Ruby that this was the worst aspect of it. His coercion and control of her mother was slow and insidious, like a hidden dripping leak that suddenly causes a roof to collapse.

After that a strange feckless feeling seized the under-ground group, a kind of euphoria fuelled by Ruby's potent gin and Mrs Caley's liberation.

'Good luck to her, I say,' remarked Queenie. 'Her husband always was a wrong 'un.'

'Yeah, but keep quiet on this,' said Pat. 'A still tongue makes a wise head! Her old man won't like it one bit, and he'll come here looking for her.'

'Pat's right,' said Mrs Chumbley. 'If anyone asks, we did *not* see her this evening.'

'See who?' asked Irene, and all at once, everyone fell about.

'If I'd known a book club would be this much fun, I'd have joined myself,' said the shelter manager, Mr Miller, sticking his head round the door. 'Was that Mrs Caley I just saw leaving?'

'No, she hasn't been here this evening. Is there a problem, Mr Miller?' asked Mrs Chumbley casually.

'No problem. Just wanted to deliver this letter to Ruby.'

Everyone tried their hardest to look sober as he handed the letter over.

'Carry on,' he said waving as he pulled the library door

closed. 'If Hitler could see this reading group, he'd hang up the towel now. Cheerio.' His footsteps echoed up the platform.

'Wonder who's writing to me here?' puzzled Ruby, tearing open the envelope.

'I don't believe it,' she said, running her hand through her thick blonde hair. 'It's only that GI Eddie. You know the one . . .'

'Ooh, not many,' interrupted Dot. 'The one with the teeth, the muscles and the . . .'

'Yes, yes, thank you Dot, we get the picture,' said Mrs Chumbley. 'I thought he was over in France.'

'He was,' Ruby murmured, scanning the letter. 'He was injured and wrote this letter from a hospital troop ship on his way back to New York.'

She shook her head.

'He's enclosed an address in New York to write back . . . reckons he'll never forget the night we spent together. Apparently . . .' Her grin stretched further. 'The thought of our last night together is what kept him going and now he'd like to repay me by sending me over books from America. He's got a sister who works for Macmillan Publishing in Manhattan apparently.'

Her hands shook as she read on.

Sweetheart, I can't stop thinking about you. I hated leaving you alone in that hotel room, especially after . . .

Ruby folded the letter abruptly, aware of everyone's eyes on her. How could she admit she'd told Eddie about the disaster, spoken the unspeakable?

Instead, she tipped her head back and a throaty laugh poured out. 'What a load of old flannel.' Ruby knew she was hiding behind her caricature, but somehow it was easier this way.

She went to scrunch up the letter.

'Don't you dare!' screeched Irene, snatching it.

'The least you can do,' said Mrs Chumbley, taking out official Bethnal Green Borough Council headed paper from her bag, 'is write back.'

'Very well,' Ruby replied, taking the paper and a pen. She refilled her teacup and chucked it back in one gulp.

'Here, I was reading about some racy book they're publishing in America, *Forever Amber* or summit like that,' said Irene. 'Get him to send us a few copies of that.'

With the gin coursing through her veins, Ruby scrawled out a reply before stamping a full stop with a big red kiss.

Pat whipped it out of her hands and read out loud.

'If you're in the mood, write to me and I'll be in the nude.'

'Ruby! You never did!' Clara gasped.

'Don't worry, Cla. It'll never get past the censors.'

'You want to hope not, Ruby Red Lips,' said Pat, wiping her eyes. 'Else you'll have half the American army turning up here. You beat all, you do.'

A shadow fell over the door and Library Cat's ears went back.

'V-Victor!' Netty stammered. 'What you doing here, love?'

Just like that, Ruby sobered up.

'I've come to take it home.' He glared at Clara. 'It's not to work here no more.'

The laughter of moments earlier froze in the air.

'May I ask why?' Clara said.

Victor looked around the group suspiciously.

'I know what goes on here.'

'What the hell are you on about, Victor?' Ruby demanded.

'This library's the talk of my club,' he went on. 'Loaning out books written by Jerries. Pamphlets showing young unmarried women how not to have a baby. It's disgusting is what it is!'

Ruby's stomach clenched.

'And Clara's having it away with that conchie,' he sniffed, pointing to a stunned-looking Billy. 'And her husband not yet cold.'

'Oh, shut up, you ignorant fool!' Ruby exploded, leaping to her feet. 'Her husband's been dead four years now. You married Mum six months after your wife died.'

'And she dabbles in the occult,' he went on, ignoring Ruby.

Ruby laughed out loud.

'Now I know you're off your nut!'

'It's true. She can guess people's favourite books. In the old days, she'd have been lashed to a ducking stool.'

Billy stood up.

'You've said your piece. I think you better leave.'

'You going to make me, are you, conchie boy?' he taunted.

Mrs Chumbley stood up.

'I'm banning you from this shelter, Mr Walsh. Leave now.'

He smiled grotesquely. 'With pleasure.' He clicked his fingers like he was calling a dog to heel.

'Get here now.'

'Mum, don't go,' Ruby pleaded, but Netty was already out of the door.

Victor shook his head.

'This is what happens when you give women books.'

After he left, Clara put her head in her hands.

'Ignore him, darlin',' Pat soothed.

'Yeah, everyone knows he's full of drink,' Queenie agreed.

'Full of shit, more like,' Ruby muttered. How much more could she take from that man? She could already picture the scene when she got home. Broken crockery, broken teeth, more bruises to add to her collection?

What was the point of tricking the Old Bill into arresting him? They only released him as soon as he sobered up. Besides, 'flying plate night' wasn't just confined to her household. The police didn't care. They'd happily hunt down a lone rapist, but never mind the women who were getting beaten senseless night after night. That was all right, because the attacker was their husband.

Rage mushroomed through Ruby's chest, hot and toxic. If she had a knife, she honestly thought she could thrust it through Victor's guts. Instead, she reached for the teapot of gin, took a deep slug and felt it sluice through her veins.

Clara's hand rested on hers, cool and calming. She didn't need to say anything, Clara could tell when one of her episodes were brewing.

'I think we need to face facts,' Clara said to the group, without taking her hand from Ruby's, 'that people are talking. How's it got out that we're loaning out that pamphlet?'

'Search me, Cla,' Ruby said. 'I can't see Mrs Caley saying anything. Perhaps it was one of the factory girls?'

'I'm going to check he's really gone,' Mrs Chumbley said, squeezing Ruby's shoulder as she passed.

When she came back, she looked uneasy.

'Is he still out there?' Mr Pepper asked.

'No, it's not that.' She gripped the back of her chair. 'Did you not just feel that tremor?'

'Probably my stepdad's knuckles dragging along the platform,' Ruby joked lamely and the group laughed, grateful for the release of tension.

'No, hush everyone,' Mrs Chumbley ordered.

Shouts, followed by the pounding of feet.

Panic slammed down on all their heads.

'Rocket's come down in Russia Lane!' The shriek tore through the shelter.

Then another, 'The allotment's copped it!'

'The allotment!' Pat gasped, her teacup falling to the floor and smashing. 'That's where Sparrow and Tubby are!'

13

Clara

What we lacked in funds, we made up for with our imagina-
tions. Lots of love and a library ticket, that's all you need.
Claire Harris, retired children's librarian

Billy was on his feet in seconds, followed closely by the
rest of the book group.

As they emerged from the Underground, it felt like
they'd walked out into the thick of night. Footsteps slapped
on the pavement, ragged breaths, the clanging of ambulance bells, and all Clara could think was, *Please, God. Not*
again.

By the time she reached Russia Lane, Clara was sep-
arated from the group and, for a moment, she whirled
round, disorientated. Where was she? The allotment was
gone. Now there was nothing but a smoking hole in the
ground.

'Sparrow! Tubby!' she called, horror choking her voice.

'Out the way, love!' yelled a voice and Clara stepped
back as a stretcher transporting the crumpled remnants
of a human was carried past her.

The impact of the rocket was meteoric; the hole seemed
scorched into the earth, a black, bottomless pit. A cordon

had been placed around it and ten feet away, she saw Pat smash her way through it. It took the combined efforts of five rescue workers and Mrs Chumbley to hold her back as she fought against them. 'My boy! My boy!'

She stumbled towards Pat before tripping over something. She looked down. It was a child's foot, neatly cut off above the ankle.

Clara didn't remember getting home, other than one minute she was in the allotment, the next she was shaking violently on her doorstep. Billy put her to bed, wrapped extra blankets round her and insisted she try and sip some sweet tea, but she was in a state of deep and profound shock. He made a bed out of a bundle of blankets and slept on her floor.

Sometime around 3 a.m., she woke, and the shock wore off, to be replaced by a terrifying rage. In her despair, she lost control, sliding from the bed and pummelling her fists against the warped wooden floorboards. Agony and misery poured out of her. All she could see was Sparrow's face. She pictured him digging his allotment, elbow sticking out of his patched-up woolly. The quiet pride with which he had showed off his onion beds, the fizzing energy he put into everything he did. He was a good kid, a child of his time who had pitted his wits against a world that seemed determined not to let him succeed.

Her husband's death she had borne because he was a soldier. Sparrow was a boy. And Tubby . . . She didn't even think of him half the time as a child, he was that grown up. But he *was* a child. A twelve-year-old eviscerated by a scientist's rocket. What world was this? Grief cracked open her heart and a howl seeped from deep within.

'Clara, stop,' begged Billy, taking her in his arms. 'You'll hurt yourself.'

'They were kids, Billy. Just children. Why?'

Clara eventually fell asleep in Billy's arms, exhausted and hollowed out by grief sometime around 5 a.m. When a smoky dawn slid through the blackout blinds, she was up and getting dressed.

'Surely you're not going to work?' Billy asked as she buttoned up her slacks.

'What else am I to do? The library is about the only thing that makes sense to me right now.'

Billy nodded. 'I understand. At least let me make you tea first.'

He went to the kitchen to boil the kettle, watching as the steam fogged up the patches between the anti-blast tape. There was something so solid, so reassuringly normal, at the sight of him standing in her home, that on instinct she walked up behind him and snaked her arms around his waist.

'Thank you,' she murmured into the warmth of his back. 'For staying with me when I needed you.'

He turned slowly and pulled her tighter into his arms, stroking her hair, kissing her forehead, trying to touch the edges of her pain.

'I will always be here for you when you need me,' he whispered.

They drank their tea and forced down slices of stale bread with marge, pointedly ignoring the small bowl of dusky plums that Sparrow had picked two days ago from his allotment.

'I'm going back to the site. Digging's been going on all night and I have to help,' Billy said. 'They aren't expecting to find any more survivors though.'

She nodded, understanding. 'You leave first, and pull your hat down. People are already talking.'

'I don't care about tittle tattle,' he replied.

She looked up at his face and realised something had changed between them. This strange tug of war they'd been doing between expectation and desire had vanished. What he had or hadn't done in the past scarcely seemed to matter any longer. All that mattered was surviving each day.

'I love you Clara and I don't care who knows it. We've already wasted enough time.'

'I love you too,' she replied softly. 'But I have to think of the reputation of the library.'

Outside, an oily yellow fog clung to her face as she hurried to the Tube with a hankie clamped over her mouth. Her route took her past Russia Lane. Mrs Smart was already out, directing an army of housewives sweeping up glass and rubble from the rocket blast and leaving it in piles for the borough workmen.

A woman sat sobbing on her step, her tears mingling with the dust. Behind her, her home was sliced in two by the rocket's descent. Her bedroom was open for all to see. Her pink dressing gown was hanging on the back of the door, her bed smashed to pieces two floors below.

Clara knew it would be a bitter blow. The identities of the women of Bethnal Green were closely tied to their homes; the white starchiness of their nets, a gleaming front step, lovingly collected figurines. Things little afforded but long cherished, now wrenched violently from their pride of place.

On instinct Clara stopped and fished a sugar lump she'd been saving from her rations out of her handbag and handed it to the woman.

'Come by the library later, Mrs Cohen,' she said. 'I'll help you with the insurance forms.'

'Thank you dear,' she said shakily.

'And I'm sorry . . . about your home.'

She shrugged. 'What are you gonna do? I never did like the wallpaper.'

Underground, the tunnels were full to capacity, haggard faces staring out of the gloom as people read and knitted, too scared to go 'up there'.

The antiseptic from the previous night's fumigation stung her eyes but did little to cut through the marshy odour of the tunnels. Sometimes if felt as if there wasn't a breath of fresh air to be had anywhere.

She stopped at Pat's bunk, but she wasn't there. Further up the tunnel, she spotted Marie and Molly turning a skipping rope and chanting, their childish voices echoing through the Tube.

'Blackcurrant – redcurrant – raspberry tart,

Tell me the name of your sweetheart . . .'

Clara didn't know what she found more disturbing, the horrors up above, or the fact that for these kids, it was now normal that their childhoods were unfolding underground.

'Clara.'

A hesitant voice sounded behind.

'Beatty!' she exclaimed. She couldn't stop herself; just the sight of her suddenly felt so overwhelming she pulled her into her arms and hugged her fiercely.

'Are you all right?' she whispered in her ear.

Beatty nodded. 'We were in our bunks when it happened, but we felt the vibration.'

Clara felt a shudder run through her.

'Do you want me to walk with you to work?'

She pulled back and Clara saw how scared she was.

'Would you mind? Only Mum's, well . . .'

'I know. At work.'

They walked in silence to Rego's, but Clara could tell Beatty was glad of the company. With these rockets dropping day or night with little warning, even the simplest of journeys took on a nerve-wracking dimension.

They reached the factory and Beatty pulled out her clocking-on card.

'Thanks, Clara, for looking out for me and Marie. I'm pretty sure you've gone beyond the bounds of being a librarian.'

'Maybe,' she grinned, tucking a stray curl back under Beatty's turban. 'But only because I'm incredibly fond of you both.'

Clara could see she had something else on her mind.

'No word from the Red Cross?'

She shook her head. 'No. I have to face facts. It's been

over three months since the Allies landed in France. Jersey's been forgotten.' She picked at a patch of flaking paint on the factory door. 'I just have to hope he's alive.'

'Never stop hoping. I'm here for you as long as you need me.'

Beatty gave her a wobbly smile, trying so hard to be brave. 'Thank you.'

Clara watched her clatter up the factory steps and had to admit that Beatty was right. The Allies had bypassed the Channel Islands. Wherever her and Marie's father was looked set to remain a mystery until the war reached its bitter conclusion.

Back in the library, a stream of people came in all day to offer condolences. The community knew how close she was to the allotment kids. Even Pinkerton-Smythe came in, ostensibly to offer his sympathy. She bit back a retort about getting what he wanted to clear the shelter of kids. Sinking that low wouldn't change anything.

But it quickly became clear he had an agenda.

'In other news, I hear one of your regular library users has left,' he remarked casually.

She stared at him dully.

He consulted his beloved notebook.

'A Mrs Caley . . . She was a member of your Friday evening book club,' he continued.

'That's right.'

'So, you didn't see her last night? Only, there's been talk.'

'This is Bethnal Green, there's always talk.'

'Talk she has left her husband.'

'I don't see what her domestic arrangements have to do with me.'

'They do when her husband has made a complaint.'

'A complaint?'

'Yes. It seems her behaviour changed after she joined the Bethnal Green Bookworm club. She began to neglect her chief responsibilities to her husband and last night, she vanished, taking the children with her.'

She stared at his soft, bland face and wondered what it would feel like if her fist connected with it.

Just then her eye fell upon a bookmark poking out of the top of a book in the returns tray. It was Sparrow's ladder bookmark, which she had been using to chart his growing reading. He was one rung away from the top. She'd ordered in a copy of Jack London's *The Call of the Wild* from Stepney for book ten.

He'd romped through *Treasure Island*, unfortunately leaving a stain from the allotment on the front cover.

'So, do you know anything about her whereabouts?' Mr Pinkerton-Smythe added.

She met his gaze.

'No. But then, why would I? I'm just a children's librarian.'

He stared at her, and she could see the churn of his thoughts, wondering whether she was cheeking him.

'Very well, but you'll be sure to let me know if you hear anything. Morale is low enough in these times as it is without unhappy, neglected husbands to contend with.'

'Heaven forfend,' she murmured as he left.

'Cla, what do you want to do about storytime today?' Ruby asked softly. 'Ought we to postpone as a mark of respect?'

Clara picked up *Treasure Island* and, reaching into the drawer, she pulled out a soft cloth and began rubbing at the stain.

'I need blotting paper, I think, and some bicarbonate of soda to get rid of this,' she muttered. 'The spine needs restitching too. Sparrow, what did you do with this book? Use it as a shovel!' She was rubbing the cover, harder and harder.

A memory flashed through her mind. Sparrow in the allotment, the first time they'd talked. *He called me a dead-end kid.*

He didn't stand a chance.

The cover ripped clean off the spine.

'Damn it!' she screamed, throwing the book at the wall.

Silence draped the library.

'Sorry. I can't believe I just did that. We are so short of books and now I've ruined it . . . It's all ruined.'

Mr Pepper bent down awkwardly to retrieve the book and Ruby came and stood beside her, one hand over Clara's as her tears began to fall.

'I'm sorry . . .' Her voice trailed off. Shock knocked the breath from her body. She stared at the doorway, seeing but not believing. Every hair on her neck rose as if a feather had trailed down her spine.

'Clara . . . What it is? What's wrong?' Ruby turned to see what it was she was looking at and audibly inhaled.

It was Mr Pepper who spoke first.

'Sparrow, where have you been?'

He was covered in dirt, with a bundle of bedding slung over his back and a smug expression on his face.

'Go on there, where is he?' he grinned.

'Where's who?' Ruby gasped eventually, incredulous at the sight of him.

'Tubby, a'course. Little swine welched on our bet. I,' he said, jamming his thumb proudly against his chest, 'managed the whole night in Epping Forest, and he never even showed up. He owes me a bob.'

'W-what were you doing there?' Clara managed at last.

'We made a bet after listening to you read *The Country Child*, didn't we? Who could spend the whole night sleeping in a dark wood.' He registered the shock on all their faces.

'What's going on? Am I gonna catch it from Mum?'

It took less than five minutes for the sighting of Sparrow to reach Pat's ears and she ran full tilt into the library.

'I don't know whether to hug you or clump you!' she cried. She did both, clipping him round the ear before smashing his face against her bosom.

'Sorry, Mum,' he sniffed, his little face squashed against her chest. 'I didn't mean to worry you. We just wanted an adventure. Where's Tubby?'

Over his head, Pat looked hard at Clara and she realised it would fall to her to tell him.

'Sparrow. A rocket fell in the allotment yesterday. Tubby was seen there. I assume he must have been about to set off to meet you. He . . . He hasn't been found. . .' The words died on her lips.

'Is he gone?'

'It . . . It looks likely.'

Sparrow winced as if he'd been dashed with cold water. Then to everyone's dismay, he started to sob, big noisy gut-wrenching sobs. And then he kicked the library counter. Once, twice, before sinking to the floor.

'I'm so sorry, Sparrow,' Clara whispered, sinking down next to him.

He looked at her.

'What he wanna go and get himself killed for?'

'Come on now, Sparrow,' scolded Pat, looking embarrassed. 'Pull yourself together.'

Sparrow tried but he was still weeping as he was led from the library and Clara's heart broke a little more. *Pull yourself together.* She'd heard that a lot in the aftermath of Duncan's death.

That little boy had just lost his partner in crime and Clara knew that it would shape his entire life. He had lost his shadow.

It was a miracle that seemed to defy all the accepted laws of life, but the tragic fact remained; Sparrow had 'come back from the dead' as the *East London Advertiser* reported it, but Tubby was dead, swallowed into that hole along with dozens more. He had been late meeting Sparrow in Epping Forest because he had been helping his neighbour harvest her tomatoes.

His sudden death seemed like a disappearance, a sleight of hand rather than a permanent full stop. Clara half expected him to charge in any moment, pockets stuffed with half-sucked gobstoppers.

Tubby's parents returned his borrower's ticket, and Clara filed it in under 'deceased'.

'Thank you for all you did for him,' said his mother, her face scoured with grief.

'Me?'

'Yes. Coming here was the highlight of his life. He loved this library.' She hesitated. 'Don't give up on our kids.'

'I won't,' Clara promised.

As autumn sliced into a frozen winter, more of the new V2 rockets exploded out of the atmosphere, travelling faster than the speed of sound, leaving nothing but broken cloud and shuddering sky.

From that day forth, Sparrow never mentioned his vanished allotment or his best pal Tubby again. Not once. But Clara knew his grief was choking him. Pat had confided he was wetting his bed. Beatty pushed her pain down deep as well. At the realisation that she would not be returning home anytime soon, she had stopped talking about her beloved island. Her 'home' was now a Tube station, her hope fast slipping away.

What Clara would not do to give these wonderful, bright young people back the childhoods that war had stolen from them. She did the only thing she could.

Clara wrapped the shelter children in stories, lost them in fantastical tales of knights and buccaneers, mountains and mutineers, as if books alone could keep real life at bay.

It was Ruby who came up with the idea.

'It'll keep our minds off the rockets,' she pointed out.

Clara had thought her barmy. Building the *Titanic* out of lolly sticks and cotton reels wouldn't bring Tubby or Beatty's and Marie's father back. But it would keep them occupied. And as ridiculous as it seemed, that's what they built through those long winter nights, right there in the children's section of the library. It was silly. It was ambitious. *Tubby would have loved it.*

When it was finished, they huddled underneath its bow and read nautical stories, strange tales of giant whales, mermaids, and icebergs as tall as houses. And they read the Tube shelter library's last fragile copy of *Treasure Island*, repaired and the pages clinging together with string and paste. They all read it as if their lives depended on it. Sparrow finally got his gold star and stared at the award as if he couldn't quite believe it. Clara would have given a sky-full of stars if she could.

Each night after his shift, Billy came round after a day of digging bodies out of blast sites, so exhausted he couldn't even speak, before they fell asleep wrapped in each other's arms. Despite the raised eyebrows and 'the talk' of the relationship between the widowed librarian and the conchie ambulance driver, nothing untoward happened. It was too cold to even consider getting naked. Most of their nights were spent bundling on *more* clothes, Beauty and Library Cat gently snoring at their feet.

One wild winter night as rain beat the window, Billy turned to her.

'When the war is over, will you marry me?'

She smiled into the darkness and squeezed his gloved fingers.

'Why me?'

'Because I loved you from the very first moment I set eyes on you. That you now love me too is extraordinary to me.'

'Let's talk about it after the war,' she said sleepily. But as they surrendered to sleep, cosied together like two bookmarks in bobble hats, she knew she couldn't imagine a future without this gentle soul.

14

Ruby

Rene, who worked as Whitechapel's first female library caretaker, saw someone nick the clock off the wall. She must have been in her fifties, but she wasn't having that. She chased the thief all the way up Brick Lane and got it back. The thief might have thought twice if he knew he was taking on Rene. She used to live next door to the Krays. Libraries are anything but dull.
Denise Bangs, Idea Store Librarian,
Tower Hamlets, East London

'They look harmless enough.' Ruby picked up a copy of the plain green hardback and handed it to Clara.

'And it smells delicious,' Clara said, breathing in the alkaline tang of new paper. 'Nine hundred and seventy-two pages . . . It's long!'

'I'll have to have a read, see what all the fuss is about,' Ruby remarked.

'Not before I've catalogued them, you don't,' Clara said quickly.

'You must've left a big impression on him, Ruby my dear,' said Mr Pepper.

'S'pose I must've. I was gobsmacked when this lot arrived.'

They all had been when the delivery had turned up from New York yesterday, with all insurance and freight transport costs paid for. A dozen copies of the book taking America by storm: *Forever Amber*.

'I suppose this is what one might call a "bodice-ripper",' Mr Pepper said, picking up the innocuous-looking book as if were a hand grenade. 'I read in the *London Times* that fourteen US states have banned this book as pornography. The first was Massachusetts, whose Attorney General counted seventy references to sexual intercourse.'

'In which case, I'm definitely reading it,' Ruby said.

'Seems odd that a grown man should read a book simply to make a list of its sexual references,' Clara mused.

'Dirty bugger,' Ruby murmured under her breath.

'Even more reason why these books are definitely going to have to be kept under the counter,' Clara said. 'I don't mean to come over like an old goose, but we cannot afford any more talk after Mrs Caley's disappearance.'

'I understand, please let me apologise again,' said Mr Pepper.

Poor old Mr P. Ruby must've heard him apologise fifty times already for his accidental shelving of the birth control pamphlet in the children's library.

But now it seemed they had two inflammatory publications in their midst, so care needed to be taken. It was clear that someone had set about trying to blacken Clara's name, and it didn't take a genius to work out who. By spreading dissent among the husbands of Bethnal Green, Pinkerton-Smythe was making a scapegoat of Clara and the library. Ruby had hoped that bringing her mother here would give her a sense of her self-worth, but now that Victor had banned her from working here, his control over her was growing daily. Battle lines had been drawn. Ruby pushed down her anger. She detested Pinkerton-Smythe for giving her abusive stepfather the excuse he needed to isolate her mother further. How much more malign the patriarchy was when it joined forces.

While Clara set about carefully accessioning the new books, Ruby remembered Eddie's letter. She slipped it out of her pocket.

Well, you sure know how to keep a man's morale up. Ruby. She could almost hear the laughter in his voice.

I hope these books prove a big hit in the library. I had to sweet talk my big sister into giving me these copies hot off the press. They're like gold dust over here: 100,000 sold in the first week. I told her you folk are desperate for books. Now I have to shovel snow off her sidewalk every day until spring, but you're worth it, Ruby.

Every story has its point and here it is, yours truly (me) has fallen for you, Ruby. I know we only saw each other a handful of times. They were, and I'll say it again, the nicest times I had in England. I know you felt we ought to leave it as a glorious memory, well, hang it all, I can't, Ruby.

You're the smartest, most beautiful lady I have ever met. If you don't feel anything for me, well then, I'm a big boy, I can handle it, but if you do . . .

This is just about the craziest thing I've ever done, but, will you marry me? Come start a new life here with me in Brooklyn,

America, sweetheart. I can't promise you sunshine and a white picket fence, but I can promise you that I will put you on the pedestal you deserve to be on. We could make each other happy, and after everything we've both been through, isn't that the point of this strange life?

Your book angel signing off. Yours in hopeful anticipation of a reply.

Eddie xxx

P.S. Make sure you read p.134. It reminds me of my night with you.

Oh, Eddie. Beautiful Eddie with his warm, life-affirming words. She'd write back to say thank you. But marriage? Ruby Munroe, a GI bride? *Do me a favour.* Her life was here in Bethnal Green, protecting her mother, not chasing a fantasy. She folded the American dream and slid it back in the pocket of her skirt.

'What did he say?' Clara probed.

'Oh, you know, the sort of thing men say when they've had really good sex and they're not ready to let it go.'

'No, I don't know,' Clara replied. 'You forget that Duncan's the only man I've ever been with.'

'Then you don't know what you're missing,' Ruby replied teasingly.

'If what they say about this book is true,' Clara replied, 'then I'm about to find it. I still can't believe he sent you these.'

'You don't ask, you don't get.' Ruby shrugged.

'That's given me an idea. Rubes, would you mind

holding the fort for an hour? Mr P, I've got something I need your help on. I'll think we need to go somewhere quieter.'

'Of course, my dear,' he replied, anxious to make amends.

They left, and Ruby waited until she heard the faint tapping of Mr Pepper's stick on the platform grow fainter before she reached under the counter and pulled out *Forever Amber*. Couldn't hurt to have a quick peek.

By page 26, Ruby lifted one eyebrow. The plain cover hid its explosive contents. By page 50, she was in love. The protagonist, Amber St Clare, was a scheming, saucy strumpet.

Ruby had never read anything quite like it, and she was fairly certain it would be just the pick-me-up the women of Bethnal Green needed in these war-weary days. It wasn't just slightly spicy, it was the literary equivalent of an incendiary bomb! And Ruby had a feeling it would quickly light fires down the tunnels.

Transfixed, she read on, absorbed in the escapades of Amber, romping her way through Restoration London. 'Oh, Amber,' she murmured, turning the page, 'you are my kind of woman!'

A deep cough startled her.

Ricky Talbot was an imposing looking man. Standing at well over six foot two, his head almost grazed the roof of the library. He worked as a porter at Billingsgate Fish Market by day and, like most porters, boxed in his spare time.

'All right, Ricky, how's yourself?'

'Not too clever actually Ruby. The wife's left me.'

'No!'

Suddenly Ruby clocked who Ricky's wife was. Tuesday afternoon affair.

'Oh Ricky, I'm so sorry,' she said uneasily. 'Did she say why?'

'She's fallen in love with a dentist. Apparently, she met him in here. They used to meet here every week. Did you see them?

'I . . . Er . . .'

'So you did,' he said, looking so wretched that Ruby felt sorry for him.

'I'm sorry, Ricky. We never knew for sure and it's not really our job to go round spreading rumours. We see all sorts.'

He looked around the library.

'So, it seems it's true, what they say about this place.'

'What who say?' she asked warily.

'Down the markets and the pubs. They say that widow loans 'em books that put ideas in their heads.'

Ruby pushed down her annoyance. 'Well, Ricky, that's kind of the whole point of reading books.'

He looked unconvinced.

'Honestly Ricky, I doubt coming to this library was what made her do the double shuffle.' She wanted to suggest that if he'd spent less time down the pub and more time talking to his wife, she might not have found other diversions in the library.

'Well, there's something not right 'bout this place, if you ask me. I really loved her.'

'I'm so sorry, Ricky, but trust me, this library had nothing to do with your wife leaving you.'

'But it did nothing to stop it, did it?'

He left, ducking his head under the door as he disappeared up the platform, and Ruby breathed out deeply.

How could she tell Clara this? She'd already kept from her that three people had handed back their library borrowing tickets this week alone. Two had made see-through excuses, but Mrs Wandle who ran the WVS shelter nursery had come right out and said she 'no longer wished to be associated with Mrs Button or the sort of library she ran'.

Was it because Clara had taken up with Billy, the complaint from Joannie's mum, or Mrs Caley leaving her husband? Who knew, but once rumours started in the East End, they took hold like a Blitz fire in a woodyard. She wouldn't tell Clara. How could she? She was already delicate after losing Tubby. She'd worked so hard these past five years. The library was her life. Ruby was damned if she was going to let a few narrow-minded gossips pull her friend down.

After work, Ruby walked home across Barmy Park, oblivious to the cold because she had her nose buried in *Forever Amber*.

She stopped in her tracks when she came to page 134. Images of her last night with Eddie in that Soho hotel room blocked out her dreary surroundings. She remembered the heat, the feeling of reckless abandon as they peeled off each other's clothes . . .

The idea came to her and she almost laughed out loud at its simplicity and daring.

Amber's raison d'être was clear. She was firmly of the belief that a woman had no chance of succeeding in a man's world, unless she could turn their weaknesses to her advantages. Perhaps Ruby ought to be a little more Amber.

She would accept Eddie's proposal. With conditions.

It felt as if she'd been staring out at the world through a dirty window and now it was rubbed clean.

'Mum!' she called out, as she shrugged off her coat. 'Where is he?'

Netty was sitting at the kitchen table peeling potatoes. 'Down the pub.'

'Good, we need to talk. I've got an idea, and I know it'll seem barmy, but you must hear me out.'

'Go on,' she said warily.

'How do you fancy a fresh start?'

'Oh, love, I can't . . .'

'But you can, Mum,' she urged, taking the peeler out of her hand. 'I've had a proposal from Eddie, the American. If I can persuade him that we come as a package, you and me, then we can start over there.'

'Oh, yeah,' Netty laughed sourly. 'And what'll I do in America? I expect they're crying out for beaten-down char ladies.'

'Mum. They have cleaners in America, you know. Look, there's a lot to work out, but with your blessing, I'm going to accept his proposal. Think about it, Mum. We'll never get this chance again. *America! Imagine!*'

'I can't even think about it,' Netty whispered.

'Why?' Ruby blurted, her chest tight with frustration.

'Because I've fallen.'

Ruby stared at her mum in dismay.

'H-how could you let that happen? You're forty-five!'

'I didn't have much say in the matter.'

Netty picked up the peeler and carried on peeling pota-toes like an automaton.

'Are you telling me . . . ?'

'Ever since Mrs Caley done a moonlight flit, he's been forcing me. Expect he's worried I'll do the same, as if leaving your husband's contagious. He seems to have that library down as some sort of den of corruption.' She gave a hollow little laugh before picking up the pan of potatoes and walking to the stove.

Her back was to Ruby, so she couldn't see her face, but her words fell like rocks between them.

'America indeed. In about eight months, I won't even be able to make it out of this kitchen.'

And just like that, Ruby saw her dream fall away. She'd have more chance of making it across the Atlantic on her lolly-stick *Titanic*.

She walked up behind her mum and wrapped her arms around her as her tears fell, hot and heavy, over the stove top.

'It's all right, Mum. I'm not going anywhere. I'll never leave you.'

In the silence, a skipping rhyme she'd heard the Tube Rats chanting down the tunnels earlier came back to haunt her.

Apple tree, pear tree, plum tree pie,
How many children before I die?
One, two, three . . .

15

December 1944
Clara

In the 1970s, I applied for the position of library assistant at Tower Hamlets Council. I had no suitable shoes so I painted my pink shoes black with a tin of glossy black paint from Woolworths. The interview was a disaster as I dripped black paint on the parquet floor. The borough librarian who interviewed me was pompous. We ended up having a row when he told me it was pointless giving me the job as I'd only leave to go off and have babies.

Many years later I ended up with his job. I dragged the library system into the twenty-first century by rebranding East End libraries as Idea Stores. Not bad for a hippy with painted shoes.

Anne Cunningham, co-founder of Idea Stores and former Head of Libraries for Tower Hamlets

Clara staggered past the bedraggled Christmas tree at the bottom of the escalators, groaning under the weight of a box of books. A Salvation Army band was warming up, optimistically trying to get shelterers now entering their sixth Christmas at war into the festive spirit.

'Clara, can I talk to you?' Marie was waiting by the escalators.

'Hullo, sweetie, of course, but not now. Ruby's waiting outside in the bibliobus. We can talk after storytime, yes?'

Marie's face fell.

'But I can't come to the library this evening.'

'I'll come and find you after in your bunk then.'

Marie chewed her lip.

'Cheer up, poppet,' Clara replied. 'It's nearly Christmas!'

Distracted, she walked on, feeling the ache in her calves as she walked up the out-of-use escalator in heels.

'Clara Button in heels and a skirt, as I live and breathe,' Ruby teased as she heaved the books onto the back seat and slammed the doors.

'Ridiculous instruments of torture,' Clara muttered.

'You've got lipstick on too,' Ruby remarked suspiciously, gunning the engine as they bumped down Cambridge Heath Road.

'I've got a meeting with Pinkerton-Smythe after we've done the factory rounds and I need to get him on side.'

Ruby raised an eyebrow.

'I'll tell you later. And by the way, I think we'd better brace ourselves.'

'What for?'

'What I now call the Amber Effect.'

'Oh yes, that.'

'I take it you've finished it?'

Ruby nodded.

'I stayed up for three nights solid. It's quite the read.

It's been keeping my mind off what's happening at home, to be honest.'

Clara hardly dared ask.

'She's expecting,' Ruby said dully.

'Oh, Ruby, I don't know what to say.'

'There's nothing anyone can say. I just wish Mum had a bit of Amber's chutzpah.'

'A little more than chutzpah,' Clara snorted. 'She murdered her husband during the Great Fire of London with a riding whip.'

'Well, to be fair, he did try to poison her.'

'But only because she was sleeping with his son,' Clara pointed out.

They both shook their heads and laughed as the car bumped to a halt outside Rego's. It was an extraordinary book, and Clara was still grappling to get her head around whether she liked it or not.

They'd experienced many wildly popular wartime books, from *Gone with the Wind* to *Cold Comfort Farm*, but now there was a new contender. Clara couldn't put her finger on why, but it felt like the author, Kathleen Winsor, had given a voice to the many millions of frustrated and lonely women. A protagonist who manipulated, murdered and slept her way through the pox and fire of seventeeth-century London was hardly the most sympathetic of women, but maybe that wasn't the point. Wasn't she echoing what was happening in real life, albeit in a more sensational way?

In a world desperate for escape from rubble and rations, the escapades of Amber would prove irresistible.

'Well, I love that she's subversive,' Ruby said. 'It's gratifying to see a woman using her feminine wiles for survival. Besides,' she grinned, elbowing the factory door open, 'who can't love a protagonist who calls her enemies "stupid addle-pated boobies"?'

Three hours later, Clara arrived at the town hall for her meeting with Mr Pinkerton-Smythe, with a waiting list for *Forever Amber* as long as her arm. They'd only unpacked it seven days ago. How had so many women heard she'd got copies? Who was she kidding? It'd be easier to dam the Thames with matchsticks than stop gossip in Bethnal Green.

A secretary gestured for her to wait. Clara looked down in embarrassment. Her last good pair of black heels had finally given up the ghost and all she had left was a red pair, so last night she'd bought a pot of black gloss and painted them.

'Send Mrs Button in,' came his voice over the crackly intercom.

'Have you heard from Mrs Caley?' he demanded as soon as she entered the room. 'I've had her husband here again.'

'No, sorry.'

'And I've had another complaint.'

'From whom?' she asked wearily.

'Mr Talbot. Seems his wife has been conducting an affair in your library and now she too has left him.'

Clara wilted. Why did he seem to hold her personally responsible for the morals of all the women who passed through her library doors?

'That is unfortunate, but I don't know anything about that.'

'It is peculiar, isn't it though, how many women seem to get a library ticket then get silly ideas in their heads? When you give these people inflammatory books, it leads to all sorts of trouble.'

These people?

'I've spoken to you in the past about providing more edifying fare and now I hear the library is in possession of a scandalous American book.'

'*Forever Amber*?' Clara asked.

'Yes, that's right. Have you read it?' he demanded.

'Yes, I read every book before I decide whether to put it out on loan.'

'And you consider this suitable?'

She shifted slightly. 'Well, it's not without its critics, but frankly, you'd hear worse down the Camel on a Friday night. Women need something to offset the dreariness of the blackout hours.'

'Women are driven by emotion, not reason. We've seen it with Mrs Caley, now Mr Talbot's wife. They will do things that they shouldn't do because they don't know any better.'

'I scarcely think the women of Bethnal Green will be reading *Forever Amber* for tips. Most women's husbands are serving away.'

'Nevertheless, these vulgarising books are undermining our national culture.'

'With respect, Mr Pinkerton-Smythe, British life *has*

changed, whether you or I like it, from how it was before the war.'

He steepled his fingers together.

'Look here. I'm far too busy to indulge in a discourse on British society. Why are you here?'

'Well . . . it's about an idea I had.'

He flicked a look at his watch. 'Go on.'

'We desperately need classic children's literature. There's a waiting list now for every decent children's book we have.'

'We all need things, Mrs Button. Don't you know there's a war on?'

She curled her fingers into loose fists, her fingernails digging into her palms.

'Yes, I'm aware of that. But there's no reason not to reach out to countries who are in a position to help, surely? With your permission, I thought I might write to the Canadian Library Association with a request for children's books.'

'But there are salvage drives for that sort of thing, surely?'

'Yes, but with respect, sir, no one round here has the books to give. I've made a list of fifty classic children's books.'

'Such as?'

'*Alice in Wonderland, Little Women, The Jungle Book.* We're down to our last *Treasure Island,* so that had to go on, various Enid Blytons . . .'

'Enid Blyton? Why's she on there? She's appallingly formulaic.'

'She's one of the library's most popular authors,' Clara protested. 'One of our patrons, little Babs Clark, must have read *The Faraway Tree* at least a dozen times.'

'Poor child,' he said witheringly. 'Should you not be encouraging her to read another book?'

'Children who reread books have a far wider vocabulary and . . .' she trailed off when she saw he wasn't remotely interested. 'Look, I can leave you the list. The point is these are the books on which lasting reading habits are founded—'

She stopped. He was staring at her feet.

'What's wrong with your shoes? They appear to be melting onto my floor.'

'Bother, sorry. I painted them black, but it's not really taken.'

'How peculiar. Look here, I really am very busy. Go ahead and write but you're wasting your time.'

He pressed his intercom. 'Mrs Clutterbuck, see Mrs Button out.'

Back in the library, it took one of Ruby's gins to calm her down.

'That man!' she fumed, taking off her ridiculous painted shoes and tossing them behind the counter. 'He's a . . . a . . .'

'Stupid addle-pated booby?' Ruby suggested.

'Don't be disheartened,' said Mr Pepper, 'I'll do the children's storytime. Go and write your letter.'

Clara paused, pen in hand. What would Amber St Clare, arch manipulator, write?

Dear Sirs,

I am writing from Britain's only underground library, in the heart of London's Blitz-battered East End.

It was at a house in Bethnal Green that Samuel Pepys lodged his famous diary during the Great Fire of London. Once more, we have been ravaged by fire and lost a great deal of our precious children's books.

A whole generation of children are growing up without access to great books of the past. This is an urgent appeal for children's classics.

All imports of books are now stopped unless it's a charitable donation. If you have any surplus of the books on this list then we here in Bethnal Green would be grateful.

We have lost so very much, but we have not lost heart nor hope. Books help to keep us human in an inhumane world. Don't you agree?

She paused and nibbled the end of her pen. More flattery required.

I know Canadians to be warm-hearted and enlightened.
Yours sincerely,
A fellow librarian, Clara Button.

She thought of dear Tubby. It was too late for him, but it wasn't too late for Sparrow, Marie, Beatty and all the rest of the Tube Rats.

She labelled the letter, *Chief Librarian, Public Library, Toronto.*

'I'm heading to the post office,' Clara called to Ruby.

'Before you go . . .' Ruby held up a newspaper with a big chunk cut out from the middle, her face grimacing through the hole. 'Just found it cut up in the reading room.'

'Racing pages again?'

Ruby nodded.

'And an article on *Beauty is your Duty*!'

'Oh for pity's sake! What can our phantom paper snipper have against women making the best of themselves? We need to keep a closer eye on the reading room.'

A few minutes later, she strode past the café. For once, Dot didn't look up and wave. She was frying liver, spatula in one hand, *that book* in the other. The last thing she saw as she emerged into the frosty December air was Mrs Chumbley in the shelter office cubbyhole, where Clara could see the corner of a green book poking out from behind *War Wounds and Fractures.*

What had she unleashed on the women of Bethnal Green?

'It celebrates the extremes of femininity. Amber's pushing boundaries, like so many wartime women,' Mrs Chumbley declared later that evening in book club.

'And there was me thinking she was merrily bonking her way round old London town,' sniffed Pat. 'Good luck to her. Wish I was twenty-one again with pert breasts and an eighteen-inch waist.' The women of the group hooted.

Irene sighed. 'After another day worrying about whether my boys will ever come home, this book,' she hugged it to her chest, 'made me the happiest I've felt in a long time.'

'I agree,' said Dot. 'It took me out of myself.'

Everyone nodded.

'What do you think, Billy and Mr P, as male readers?' Clara asked.

'This might surprise you, but I enjoyed it,' said Mr Pepper. 'Stories from the past are the threads that weave us into a bigger picture.'

'You're right,' Billy agreed excitedly and Clara smiled to see him so animated. 'Stories are how we make sense of the chaos of this war.'

'You didn't think it a little too scandalous?' she probed. 'They're burning it on the streets in Boston, you know.'

'War's reconfigured the literary landscape,' said Mr Pepper. 'The speed of change in women's lives is astonishing. I suspect your patrons are more than ready for this.'

'Precisely! Don't you dare deprive the women of Bethnal Green a little harmless fantasy,' implored Ruby.

'I reckon you should sneak a copy to your mum,' Pat said. 'Poor Net, she could probably use a bit of fun in her life right now.'

'You're not wrong there. Cla, do you mind if I pass mine on?'

''Course, if you think she's time to read it,' she replied.

'Hang about Ruby Red Lips, weren't you planning on writing a saucy book?' Irene asked.

'Was I?' Ruby said.

'Yeah, you told us so yourself at Rego's remember? "Jam-packed full of sex", you said. I'm holding you to that.'

'Oh yeah, cause I can just see a publisher wanting anything from the likes of me,' she scoffed. 'I ain't just dropped my aitches. They've rolled under the floorboards.'

'There's plenty of working-class writers, Ruby,' Mr Pepper ventured. 'Take Walter Greenwood, *Love on the Dole*, for example.'

'Ooh I loved that book,' said Clara.

'And how many of these working-class writers are women, Mr P?' Ruby asked.

'But the fact that we're discussing this book, written by a woman about a woman, a *bold*, *enfranchised* woman at that, means there's progress surely?' Clara countered.

'Yes, but she's American,' Ruby replied, reaching for her glass. 'It's different over there. Let's face facts shall we. The only publication about sex that we stock in this library by a British writer is *Birth Control for the Married Woman*.' She took a slug of her drink and laughed sourly. 'And that's probably written by a man. I'm no author, I'm just a library assistant.'

'Never *just* a library assistant,' Clara insisted, wishing Ruby could see her own potential. 'I couldn't run this place without you.'

'Thanks Cla.' She smiled sadly. 'So, come on Irene, what's your favourite bit? I know there's a reason you've stuck a bookmark in there you dirty mare.'

'Funny you should say that,' Irene laughed, opening a well-thumbed page. Have a listen to this.' Irene read an impressively detailed extract on the physical attributes of Amber's swarthy love interest.

She looked up from the page and jokingly fanned her

face. 'Lord, if you're listening, please send Bruce Carlton into my life.'

'Hello,' said a deep lilting voice.

Everyone in the group started and looked to the door, where a tall man with a mop of dark curly hair and penetrating green eyes stood nervously.

'Blimey, Irene,' murmured Pat, 'you must have a direct line.'

'Hello. I'm Clara, the branch librarian,' Clara said, jumping to her feet.

'Erm, I'm Roger, sorry to disturb your group.'

'Welcome m'lord,' Ruby purred, 'I know of a wench who has a mind to lay with you.'

Pat looked like she might fall off her chair from laughing. 'Saucy mare!'

'Ignore them,' said Clara. 'How can I help?'

'You're that man who escaped from Jersey in a rowing boat, ain'cha?' remarked Dot.

'That's right. I've just finished a talk in the theatre. Someone suggested I come to the library to find out some information on a family I used to know in Jersey.'

'Do come in,' said Clara. 'We'll try and help.'

'Please let me shake your hand,' said Mr Pepper. 'Escaping from Nazi-occupied territory is a terrifically brave thing to do.'

They shook hands and Roger shrugged.

'I'm not so sure about that. I think I owe more to good tides than courage. But listen, I wonder if you might help me track down two girls called Marie and Beatty Kolsky.'

'Marie and Beatty!' Ruby exclaimed.

'Oh, you know them,' he replied. 'That's a stroke of luck. I assumed they'd be in a children's home.'

Mrs Chumbley leant forward. 'Why do you think they should be in a children's home?'

'Well, after the death of their mother,' he replied, looking puzzled.

'Wait!' snapped Ruby. 'The death of their mother?'

'Why yes,' said Roger. 'We heard word via the Red Cross she was killed during the first week of the Blitz. And given the girls' ages, we assumed they'd be under local authority care.'

'Their ages?' said Clara.

'Yes. Marie is eight, and Beatty would be, let me see, twelve by now.'

Clara closed her eyes and tried to gather her thoughts.

'I knew something was wrong,' Ruby gibbered, white with shock. 'I knew Beatty was covering up something.'

'Y-you *did* know their mother had died?' Roger asked.

'No,' said Clara. 'No, Beatty told us her mother worked nights. She told us she was sixteen. She's been holding down a job at a local factory.'

'But Beatty's a child! How could you not see that?'

'It was chaos here in the months after the bombing,' Ruby said defensively. 'It would be easy enough for a person determined enough to hide a secret.'

'Of course, I apologise,' Roger said.

'No, the failure for this lies squarely with me,' said Mrs Chumbley, who'd been sitting in stunned silence. 'The occupants of this shelter are my responsibility. I've failed in my duties. Tomorrow I'll inform the authorities, then hand in my notice. This is a grievous dereliction of care.'

A clamour ran over the group.

'Look, there's time enough for recriminations,' said Clara. 'I must also take some of the blame. We had our suspicions about the mother.'

'My God,' Ruby breathed. 'I thought she was on the game, that's why she was working nights.'

'But I don't get it,' said Queenie. 'Why would they go to such trouble to lie?'

'Knowing Beatty, she'd do anything to stop her and her sister being taken into care and split up,' said Ruby.

Another thought came to her. 'Their father. Beatty's been writing letters to him every week. What news?'

Roger's eyes darkened.

'I'm afraid the States of Jersey have much to answer for when it comes to the handling of our Jewish population,' he said bitterly. 'Most Jews in the Channel Islands left for England before the invasion. Those remaining found themselves subject to laws enacted at the requirement of the Germans. Jersey's Chief Aliens Officer handed the Commandant a list of every Jewish person on the island. Those that didn't go into hiding were shipped to the continent. One wonders if they will be seen again. You hear rumours . . .'

'Rumours?' Ruby questioned.

'There's an island in the Channel Islands closest to the northern tip of France called Alderney, which contains a work camp where they send Russian and Ukrainian prisoners of war, French Jews, Spanish Republicans and more.'

He lowered his voice. 'In Jersey, we heard tell of atrocities on this island, but no one knows for sure. Yet.'

A hush fell over the group.

'Beatty and Marie's father hasn't been seen since 1942. With luck, he's in hiding.'

He shook his head.

'I have seen the Huns' brutal treatment of their Russian slaves close up. To them, they and the Jewish are *Untermenschen*, subhuman.'

'Where one burns books, one will, in the end, burn people,' murmured Mr Pepper. 'It was Heinrich Heine, a poet, who said that many years ago.'

Billy's face crumpled. A look of pure hatred flickered over his usually placid features.

But Clara didn't have long to dwell upon it, for all of a sudden, a memory from that morning flashed through her mind.

I can't come to the library this evening.

'Marie wanted to talk to me this morning. I was too busy. Has anyone seen them today?'

'They didn't come to storytime,' said Mr Pepper.

'Did they know I was coming to the shelter?' Roger asked.

'Yes, it was widely advertised,' said Ruby.

'They've gone!' Clara cried.

As one, the group stood up and made for the door, copies of *Forever Amber* tumbling to the floor.

'We'll terrify them if we all charge up en masse,' said Billy. 'Clara and Ruby. You go.'

By the time they reached the Kolsky girls' bunk, their

worst fears were realised. The bunks had been stripped of bedding.

'No!' Clara cried, gripping the metal edge of the top bunk.

All that remained were their library tickets, neatly placed side by side.

16

Ruby

Library workers are frontline staff. I've had so many people
come in to tell me their problems. We're a bit like counsellors.
Michele Jewell, former library assistant from Kent

Two weeks later and with just days to go until Christmas, there was still no trace of the missing Kolsky sisters.

It was the coldest winter that Ruby could ever remember, yet despite this, the end of the war was so close, she could virtually touch it. Dim-out instead of blackout meant the faint glimmer of home lights shone through the Christmas fog. Every evening, shelterers gathered round the tree at the bottom of the escalators and sang carols by candlelight. Hope was fragile, but it knitted the shelter together like a soft blanket.

Running in parallel to this, in spite of the freezing grip of winter, or perhaps because of it, *Forever Amber* fever had caught fire.

Rumours about 'that mucky book' swept through the shelter. Factory girls sat huddled in stairwells reading extracts out loud, housewives neglected their steps, secretaries kept it in their desk drawers for sneak peeks. Even her mother who, by her own admittance 'wasn't one for the books', had taken to reading it when Victor was out.

'What is it about this book, Cla?' Ruby mused, as she added Belle Schaffer from bunk 854 to the waiting list.

'Cla?' Ruby touched her arm and she jumped.

'Sorry,' she sighed, breaking off from shelving. 'I just can't stop thinking about the girls. They're not safe, not with these rockets and they still haven't caught that rapist!'

She shuddered. 'I can't bear to think about it. Now we know about their mother, I feel like I have to take responsibility.'

'They'll turn up, Cla,' Ruby insisted.

'How can you be so sure?'

'You've got Billy and his brigade looking. The *East London Advertiser* ran a front-page article on them. Even the Tube Rats have got search parties going.'

Ruby looked around the library. It was nearly closing time on a Saturday. Apart from a couple of loiterers and an odd-looking bloke huddled over the *Daily Mail* in the reading room, it was quiet.

'The theatre've got a Yuletide party on for the shelter kids tonight. Everyone'll be in there,' she mused. 'Why don't you get off home and get some rest? I can finish up here.'

'Thanks. Billy finishes his shift in an hour, and he's promised me he'll come out looking. There's a café owner over at Mile End who told him two girls matching Beatty and Marie's description come in most evenings. I want to be there. Just in case.'

'Is there any danger whatsoever of being attended to?' interrupted a voice.

'Sorry,' said Ruby. 'How may I help?'

'I loathe books,' snapped the man who had just appeared at the desk, removing his bowler hat, 'which is to say novels, chiefly.'

'Well, we have a reasonable stock of non-fiction,' Clara said.

'I doubt you'll have anything of the calibre I like to read. I'll just take *The Times* into your reading room.'

'As you wish,' Ruby said, raising one eyebrow as he settled himself next door.

'Queer fish,' she mouthed to Clara. 'Go on, you get off.'

By 7 p.m. Ruby decided to close early. By the sound of the noise from the theatre next door, the children's Christmas party was warming up.

'Library's closing. Time to finish up now please, folks.'

She walked through into the reading room and stopped in her tracks. The abrupt gentleman was still absorbed in his copy of *The Times*, but the other man was engrossed in something entirely different.

He was pretending to read his newspaper, but both his hands were under the table, his right arm moving vigorously up and down.

'Unbelievable,' Ruby murmured. Calmly, she returned to the counter and picked up the sturdiest hardback she could find before returning.

'Any harder and you'll yank it off.' The man looked up, not at all fazed at being caught masturbating in the library. Instead, he leant back in his chair and pulled his coat

open. He smiled and waited for the ensuing shock, but
instead . . .

'I've seen bigger,' Ruby remarked and, raising *Forever
Amber* up in the air, she brought it down with a crack on
the top of his manhood. He crumpled like a paper concer-
tina.

His face registered the pain as he bent double on the
floor of the library. Ruby grabbed him by the scruff of
the neck. Fortunately, he wasn't a big man in any sense
of the word, so she was able to drag him from the library.

Mrs Chumbley was just escorting Father Christmas into
the theatre to surprise the kids as Ruby wrestled the man
out onto the platform.

'Mrs Chumbley, just the woman,' she puffed. 'Would
you help me eject this man from the shelter? I caught him
playing with himself in the library.'

'Perfect nuisance,' she retorted, shooing Father
Christmas into the theatre before any kids saw.

Mrs Chumbley didn't need telling twice and rolled up
her sleeves. It was a terrific shame his knees cracked so
many escalator stairs on the way up, and that he landed
face down in a stagnant puddle outside the Tube.

'Don't want that kind of member in the library,' Ruby
sniffed.

Ruby and Mrs Chumbley were still laughing as they
clattered back down the stairs to the Underground.

'We've earned ourselves a quick sharpener, what say
you, Mrs C?' Ruby asked as they walked into the library.

'What did you hit him with?' Mrs Chumbley asked, as
Ruby poured them both a slug of brandy.

'*Forever Amber.*'

They dissolved into laughter once more, Mrs Chumbley laughing so much she had to sit down and wipe her eyes with her sleeve.

'Hang about,' said Ruby, scanning the counter, 'I left the copy here.' She placed a hand on the counter where she'd left the hardback before grappling the man out of the library.

'Right here.' She raced through into the reading room, in case in the chaos she'd maybe left it there. But it was gone, and so too was the bowler-hatted gentleman.

'Oh, God. Clara will go spare. It's been stolen.'

'Don't panic, my dear, it's not the end of the world,' soothed Mrs Chumbley, her voice nearly drowned out by the rising crescendo of noise from the Punch and Judy show next door.

But Ruby felt an irrational annoyance. Over the course of the war, surprisingly few books had been stolen, and she liked to feel it was a reflection of the high esteem in which the shelter held them.

'It had to be that queer bloke I left here reading the paper,' Ruby mused.

'Ought we go and look for him?' Mrs Chumbley asked.

'No point, he'll be long gone by now,' she sighed. A movement by the door made them both start.

'Netty!' Mrs Chumbley exclaimed.

Standing at the door to the library, dressed only in her nightie, was Ruby's mum. Her spindly arms and chest were covered with an embroidery of bruises.

Mrs Chumbley took off her warden's coat and wrapped it around Netty.

'Quickly now, dear, you'll catch your death.'

Netty didn't even seem to register the coat, she was trembling so violently.

'Pour your mum a brandy,' Mrs Chumbley ordered.

Ruby did as she was told and pressed the glass to her mum's lips.

'That bastard has gone too far this time,' Ruby seethed, not knowing where to even start in patching her mum up.

'I'm going to my office to get the first-aid kit,' said Mrs Chumbley. 'I'll be as quick as I can.'

Netty started to talk, her words tumbling out. 'H-he caught me reading *Forever Amber*. I thought he'd be out for the night, but he come home.' Her voice was so quiet against the noise of the Christmas party, that Ruby had to strain to hear her.

'He said I deserved a hiding I wouldn't forget . . .' She stared straight through Ruby, to an unknown place of horror in her head. 'He was out of his mind from the drink . . . He kicked me over and over. Told me I was the devil . . .'

She gripped Ruby's hand.

'I thought he was going to kill the baby.'

Ruby was filled with an impotent rage. The abuse was inexorable and terrifyingly inescapable.

'I waited until he passed out and then I ran for it. I couldn't think of anything else but getting out of there.' She stared at her daughter wild-eyed. 'I've left him. I've finally done it.'

'Why now, Mum? Why this time?'

'I've already lost one child,' she whispered and both their thoughts went to Bella. 'I won't lose another.

'Oh, God! What'll happen when he wakes up and finds me gone? There'll be blood on the moon.'

Ruby felt a cold rinse of fear. And where would be the first place he'd come looking?

She looked at the door and jumped in shock. Mrs Chumbley was back, but with no first-aid kit.

'He's coming. I spotted him at the top of the escalators.'

Netty crumpled and Ruby had to hold her up. 'He'll kill me.'

Ruby thought her heart might explode with fear.

'The keys!' screamed Mrs Chumbley. 'Ruby, get the keys, lock the library.'

Her mind turned to soup. Where had she put her keys?

'On second thoughts forget it, there's no time,' Mrs Chumbley said. 'He'll be here any moment. By the look on his face, he's capable of kicking the door in.'

'What'll we do?' Ruby cried. 'The ventilation chute in the tunnels, can we get Mum out there?'

'No time. Help me move the table,' Mrs Chumbley ordered, running to the reading room. 'We'll barricade ourselves in.'

Together, they heaved a trestle table across the library and Mrs Chumbley began to shout.

'Help! Help! We need help in the library!'

But even her deep voice couldn't compete with the excitable shouts from the theatre as the Punch and Judy show reached its climax.

'Mum, get behind the counter,' Ruby ordered as they wedged the table in front of the door.

Netty stood paralysed in shock.

'For God's sake, Mum, you have to hide.'

Ruby half-dragged her mum's rigid body behind the counter.

In a trance-like state, Ruby took her place next to Mrs Chumbley behind the table.

The library door seemed to jump as Victor's foot made impact.

'Sssh,' Mrs Chumbley mouthed, raising her finger to her lips. 'Don't move.'

'Where is she?' Victor's voice was thick with drink. 'She's the devil! I've come to kill her!'

An almighty smash crashed the door, and splinters of wood skidded across the library. The door was only made of cheap plywood; it wouldn't hold out much longer against Victor's rage.

Thud! Thud! Thud! His heavy boot pummelled at the door until Ruby could make out the tip of his foot.

'Oh, God,' she whimpered. 'He's nearly in.'

'Keep holding!' Mrs Chumbley ordered, using her body to block the table against the door.

With one enormous grunt, the door smashed in, sending the trestle table and Ruby flying across the floor.

'Where is she?' he roared, flailing around, his body lurching drunkenly.

Ruby struggled to get up, but books were raining down on her on head as Victor swept them off the shelves. He seemed gigantic in his rage.

'I won't have my wife reading books, you hear me!' he bellowed, flecks of spittle flying from his mouth. 'You're all wicked, the whole flamin' lot of you. Filling women's heads with nonsense.'

'Victor, you must calm down,' said Mrs Chumbley.

He ignored her and, dragging Ruby off the floor, he pinned her to the bookshelf.

'Where is she?'

Ruby tried her hardest not to let him see her fear, but it was there, leaping like flames in her throat.

'She ain't here,' she said, looking him square in the eye. 'Even if I did know where she was, I wouldn't tell you.'

'Liar!'

His fingers squeezed harder, pressing the pale flesh around her jugular as if he could wring the truth from her.

'Tell me or I'll kill you.'

His face was twisted with rage and paranoia and, for the first time, Ruby could see the full extent of his sickness. He clapped one hand over her mouth and struck her with a hard, stinging slap.

Her head cracked off the bookshelf. Strange, nebulous shapes drifted at the edge of her vision. Behind him, she saw her mum rise from behind the counter.

'I'm here, Victor.'

Ruby tried to talk, to say the words to stop her mum, but breath wouldn't come. And then she was being thrown from the library.

Her back hit the curved tiled wall, just under the red-and-blue-tiled Bethnal Green Underground sign. She slid down onto the platform floor, pain bursting behind her eyes.

17

Clara

As a child our local bagwash in Peckham, South London, had long shelves on the wall which were packed with paperbacks for customers. You could donate and borrow, all free of charge. Everyone was so honest and considerate in returning the books, so that others could enjoy them too. The lady who owned the shop would welcome us, discuss the books and pass on other customers recommendations, in between taking in bags of washing and it was so informal, friendly and perfectly normal. Quite amusing really when you consider it was nothing to do with laundry. The Little Peckham Bagwash Library triggered a love of reading which has lasted all my life.

Ida Brown, from the London Borough of Bexley

They'd reached the bottom of the escalator when Billy caught hold of Clara's hand.

'Please let's leave the library. Just for one evening, Clara. You look wretched.'

'Oh thanks,' she laughed.

'You know what I mean. It was a long walk to Mile

End and back. Why don't I take you to the Salmon and Ball and buy you a stiff drink? Ruby can lock up can't she?'

Clara stared at the group gathered round the Christmas tree, their faces bathed in the light of the candles they were holding. 'Silent Night' washed over her, and she felt overcome with weariness.

'That does sound tempting. But can you just give me five minutes? I accidentally picked up Ruby's keys earlier and I need to drop them back.'

He kissed the top of her head.

'Very well, but let's not spend too long in the library. We need the rest of the night to celebrate . . . hopefully.'

'Celebrate what?'

But Billy wasn't listening. He was sinking down onto one knee.

'Billy,' she muttered, looking nervously at the carol singers. 'What are you doing?'

'Something I should have done properly months ago,' he replied, taking her hand. 'Clara, will you marry me? I can't wait until the end of the war. I don't want to waste another minute.'

The singers tailed off and turned to stare, smiling expectantly.

'B-but why now?'

'Because when we find the girls, I want them to have a proper family home. If that's what they should like. And you and I together, as man and wife, can provide that.'

He smiled.

'And also, I'm madly in love with you.'

'I-I don't know what to say!'

'Try yes,' urged a woman in the Salvation Army band.

Clara looked from the faces of the hushed crowd, back to Billy. What she saw staring back was the purest love she had ever seen. Why had she been so intransigent since her husband's death, giving 100 per cent of herself to the library? She couldn't make a mausoleum of her heart forever.

Billy's love was teaching her that life was rich and big and full of possibility, even in wartime. The simple joys of existence that grief had rubbed out. Being with him had felt like discovering doors in her library she hadn't noticed.

'You would do that? When we find the girls, you'll help me take care of them?'

'I would do *anything* that you ask of me, Clara.'

'Even if they never returned to Jersey and stayed with us for life?'

'For life.'

'Then my answer is yes.' She began to laugh and shake. 'Yes, I will marry you, Billy Clark.'

Billy leapt to his feet in a great rush of energy and picked her off her feet.

'Billy,' she laughed, holding on to her hat as he swung her round. The crowd burst into applause and started cheering. The mood in the station became electric as the crowd surged forward to pump Billy's hand and kiss Clara's cheek.

Ten minutes later they managed to extricate themselves and the band serenaded them with 'O Holy Night'.

They watched the singers in silence, Clara luxuriating in the feel of being nestled in Billy's arms, still not quite able to believe her brave new beginning. The girls were still missing, the library still in jeopardy, life was fragile, but hope had spun a net around her heart.

'Shall we go and get that drink now?' he whispered.

'Yes. Just as soon as I've dropped those keys back. Also, I really want Ruby to be the first person I tell.'

He laughed. 'I guess I'm going to have to get used to saying yes once we'd married.'

'Too right you are,' she grinned, until a sudden disturbing thought occurred to her.

'Will you want me to leave the library, only—'

He placed one finger gently on her mouth.

'Clara. I would never, *never* ask you to choose between being my wife and being a librarian. It's who you are.'

Relief melted through her.

'Come on.' She tugged his hand in the direction of the library.

As they walked a high-pitched scream sounded from somewhere deep up the westbound tunnel.

'Sounds like Santa's going down a storm in the theatre,' Billy remarked.

'Of course, it's the children's Christmas party this evening,' Clara replied.

They turned left and hurried down the platform, but as they got nearer, the screams grew louder, reverberating off the tunnel walls.

'That's not coming from the theatre,' Clara said. 'It's coming from the library.'

'Is that Ruby?' Billy asked, straining his eyes against the dim light. At the furthest end of the platform, at the entrance to the library stood two figures, yelling and hammering on the door of the library.

'Oh my God, it is Ruby,' Clara cried. 'What's happened?'

Billy dropped her hand and began sprinting, his long legs easily outpacing Clara's. By the time she reached him, she couldn't work out what had happened.

'Rubes. What's going on?'

'It's Victor!' cried Mrs Chumbley. 'He broke in in a fearful rage. He threw me and Ruby out and he's got Netty in there.'

'Run, Mrs Chumbley,' Billy ordered. 'Call the police.'

'There's no time, don't you see?' Ruby turned on them, helpless with terror. 'He's going to kill her.'

A thud and a muffled cry sounded from inside.

She gripped Billy's arm.

'Do something. He's used a table to block the door.'

A noise, so awful it didn't even sound human, halfway between a sob and scream, rang out.

'He's killing her!' Ruby screamed, covering her ears. 'Oh God, he's killing her!' Billy's whole face blanched. Turning around, he began to run.

'Billy, stop, wait,' Mrs Chumbley called after him.

Clara stared after him in disbelief.

'Looks like it's up to us,' Mrs Chumbley said and, raising her foot, she kicked once, twice. 'Come on!' she urged.

Together, Ruby, Clara and Mrs Chumbley kicked again and again, but their combined force couldn't break through whatever was holding the door fast.

'Listen,' Ruby ordered. They stopped, their breath coming hot and heavy. The silence was ominous. Clara thought Ruby might implode as she threw herself at the door again and again, wild with fury. Clara closed her eyes against the horror, the helplessness of this situation. On the other side of that door, a woman was being beaten to a pulp.

She opened her eyes and there was Billy, armed with a metal shovel.

'Move out of the way,' he ordered. Using the heavy shovel like a battering ram, he bashed it against the door, once, twice. Finally, the heavy impact of steel on wood pushed the stack of tables Victor had wedged under the door handle enough for Billy to force his way in.

The scene that greeted them was beyond anything Clara could imagine. Books were scattered everywhere, and sprawled on top, pinned down among the pages was Netty. Her husband's hands were clamped around her neck, the force turning his knuckles white.

In one fluid movement, Billy wrenched him off Netty and Victor sprawled breathless on the floor. In that moment, Clara prayed he'd come to his senses, sober up and, after a few curses, storm from the library.

Instead, he rose with surprising speed for a drunk man and launched himself at Billy, headbutting him with a hollow crack. Clara screamed. She hated herself for her total inability to do anything but scream, even as the men careered crazily back and forth around the library, like they were taking part in some grotesque dance. Victor wasn't tall, but he was a solid man. Billy barely recovered from being headbutted before Victor landed the next punch in his guts.

Billy doubled over, but Victor dragged him up by his collar until their faces were inches apart.

'This is for getting in my way before, conchie boy,' Victor taunted, plunging his fist like a hammer into his solar plexus.

The blow sent Billy skidding on his back across the library and he hit the counter with an inhalation of pain.

Billy's stunned gaze was so wide you could see all the whites of his eyes, at first Clara thought in pain, but then she realised, in shock.

'You . . .' he spluttered, clutching his chest but with recognition dawning behind his eyes. 'It was you who attacked Clara!'

Clara whipped round and stared in horrified disbelief at Victor.

'Yeah and when I'm finished with you, I'll finally sort out that bitch,' he grunted, drawing back his fist.

Clara closed her eyes, unable to watch. She heard the solid knock of bone against wood, the skid of paper then a hollow, wet-sounding crack. It could have been ten seconds, but it felt like hours.

When she opened her eyes again, she realised Billy and Victor had crashed their way out of the library, onto the platform outside.

Images came to her in snapshots. Mrs Chumbley was running up the platform, scattering the assembled crowds, calling for someone, anyone to call an ambulance. Ruby cradled her mother in her arms, the pair of them looking the other way.

Victor lay face down on the platform, a red bloom spreading up the concrete. And standing over him, holding the shovel in his hand stood Billy.

Clara's throat muscles were so stiff with horror that at first she couldn't speak, until finally a mournful sob broke from her.

'B-Billy, what happened?'

Billy gazed at the prone figure vacantly, then at the shovel in his hand. The incredulity on his face shifted at last to a kind of horror at what he had just done. He stared at his hands in disbelief.

'I've killed him,' he breathed, reaching out to the tiled wall to steady himself. 'Oh God Clara, I've killed a man.'

3rd January, 1945

The New Year slithered in on a cloud of freezing fog. News broke that the Red Army was barely 160 miles from Berlin, but Clara barely noticed global events. The news that had unravelled on their own doorstep was explosive and deeply shocking.

At the police's insistence, the underground library had closed for two weeks to allow the febrile atmosphere to settle and the blood stains on the platform to be scrubbed clean. The summons to the town hall to see Mr Pinkerton-Smythe came daily, but every day since the death of Victor Walsh, Clara had spent with Billy, coaxing him to open

up. Apart from trips to the police station to give a statement and walk Beauty, he'd refused to leave his flat in
Stepney, and he'd taken leave from his beloved ambulance
station.

'It's been ten days now, Billy,' she implored, when she
went round one drizzly Wednesday morning with fresh
beigels from Rinkoffs. 'If you don't want to talk, at the
very least, you must eat.'

He refused to take a warm beigel, just kept staring out
of the taped-up windows of his self-imposed prison. Food
wasn't the only thing he was refusing. The bruises round
his eyes from where Victor had headbutted him had faded
to a yellowy mustard colour, but he wasn't remotely interested in letting Clara smooth on anything that might help
him to heal.

'Billy,' she repeated softly.

Beauty looked up from her sleeping spot on the bed
and thumped her tail on the eiderdown.

'You heard what the police said,' Clara persisted, putting
down the beigels and sitting next to him on the bed.
'They're not charging you. They've taken enough state-
ments from witnesses who saw what happened when the
fight spilled out of the library.'

'Oh yes, and what did happen, according to them?' he
said dully.

'You know,' she replied, confused. 'Mrs Chumbley, the
Salvation Army choir, the theatre manager . . . They all
say that you were only embroiled in the fight to help
defend Netty, and that Victor was attacking you. He had
you against the wall and was strangling you when you

struck him with the shovel. The police seem satisfied it was self-defence. You'll have to give evidence at the inquest, of course, but there's no suggestion at this stage that you'll face charges or a trial.'

Billy kept on staring blankly out the window at a small group of children pushing a pram filled with scavenged firewood up the narrow street. The pram wheels had stuck on a cobblestone.

'You've overloaded it,' he murmured. 'Lighten the load.'

'Billy please listen,' she persisted. 'If it wasn't for you, I shudder to think what that man would have done to me outside my home last year. Think how many other women he attacked! We'll probably never know the full extent.'

She reached out and stroked his neck, but he batted her arm away. Pushing down her hurt, she gently persisted.

'It was just a dreadful accident, Billy.'

'No, it wasn't. I deliberately struck Victor with a shovel. If I hadn't done that, he wouldn't have fallen back and cracked his head open.'

He scrubbed his face, his voice freighted with agony.

'He wouldn't be dead now.'

'But if that's the case, and he was still alive, we'd almost certainly be burying Netty now. If you hadn't intervened and got us in the library, he'd have strangled her.'

She took Billy's face in her hands.

'Look at me, Billy,' she said softly. 'My refusal to mourn that man goes deeper than the attack on me. I never told you this as Ruby forbade me, but he's been beating Netty for years. It's got worse since she found out she was expecting his baby. You saved not just her life, but that of her unborn child. You're the hero here, not the villain.'

He jumped to his feet so fast, Clara nearly toppled off the bed and Beauty sat up and barked.

'Don't be so trite, Clara!' he snapped, scrubbing his fingers through his hair. 'There are no heroes to be found here. This isn't a story from one of your library paperbacks. I killed a man! A man is dead because of me!'

She stared at him in shock as he started pacing the room.

'I know he was a brutal man, but at the end of the day, his life wasn't mine to take. The best place for men like Victor is prison. I'm a pacifist, or have you forgotten that?'

'No . . . of course not.'

'This . . . This isn't me. I barely recognise myself. I'm an ambulance man. I only became one to mitigate all the death and destruction and yet now *I'm* the killer.'

'But Ruby and Netty don't blame you.' She shook her head, trying to find a way to articulate the humiliation, the reign of fear, rape and brutality that Netty and goodness knows how many other women had been subjected to. She would never say it out loud, but she knew Ruby was pleased her stepfather was dead.

'Netty lived in fear. You can't imagine the things he did to her and, now as we can see, to plenty more women. He was a monster.'

His adrenaline vanished and Billy sank back onto the bed.

'They may not blame me, but others do, plus plenty more who will say I killed him in revenge.'

Sadly, that part at least was true. Victor's death had divided the shelter, with some convinced of his innocence. Death seemed to lend people dignity and, suddenly, he was talked about in hushed tones. No matter that he beat his wife, tried to attack Clara and regularly disturbed the peace of the buildings with his drunken outbursts, suddenly Victor had gone from 'that bloody man' to 'that poor man'. Billy had many supporters, but there were some, led by Ricky Talbot and Mr Caley, who were demanding the immediate closure of the library, claiming it was a hotbed of vice and sin.

'The most important thing is we ride this out,' Clara insisted. 'I'm going to see Pinkerton-Smythe, I can't keep putting it off, and then next week, we'll reopen the library. I think you should go back to work too, to take your mind off things.'

He stared at her, his eyes wide.

'Take my mind off things?' he repeated.

'Look, Billy. I love you so much. What happened was horrifying, but thanks to you, Netty is still alive and women are safe on the streets. I just want things to go back to the way they were before. We need to concentrate our efforts on finding the girls, and then . . .' She sighed, swallowing back her mounting panic. 'Then maybe we can get married, like we planned?'

He shook his head.

'I'm sorry, Clara, but things can't ever go back to the way they were before. Not now. You and me . . .' he broke off and looked down, scuffing a patch of torn lino. 'It's a bad idea.'

The pain rose inside her, questions jamming her throat.

'I-I don't believe what I'm hearing,' she stammered. 'Ten days ago, you were pledging your love to me on bended knee. Now you're cutting me off. I don't understand.'

'I can't explain,' he said miserably.

'This is about what happened at Dunkirk isn't it!' she exclaimed and Billy looked down. 'For pity's sake Billy, just tell me,' she begged. 'Whatever you did out there, I promise I won't judge. I know you're a good man.'

He shook his head, dripping in shame.

'I'm not. I'm a coward.'

'That medal you hide at the back of your wardrobe says otherwise!'

'Just please believe me, Clara. You're better off without me.'

'So a-are you saying we're over?'

He walked back to the window, unable to look her in the eye. The children had vanished. 'I think you ought to go now.'

She stood, picked up the bag of beigels that had fallen to the floor, put them on the bed and walked to the door with as much composure as she could muster.

At the door, she turned.

'I know I won't be better without you.'

Outside, Clara started to run in the direction of the library, a solid knot of anxiety pressing down on her chest, and a question mark as big as the moon. All this time she had brushed off questions and concerns over Billy's past, but it seemed that whatever had happened in France was still haunting him and Victor's death had only inflamed it. It occurred to Clara as she ran: she didn't really know Billy at all.

Underground, she found a clear-up team of Mr Pepper, Mrs Chumbley and Ruby shelving books and attempting to restore order to the library before they reopened.

'He's thrown me over,' Clara managed.

'Oh, sweetheart,' Ruby said. 'Why?'

'I don't know.'

'He's in shock, dear,' said Mr Pepper. 'He'll change his mind, you'll see.'

'I don't know much about matters of the heart,' admitted Mrs Chumbley, 'but it's as plain as day he's deeply in love with you.'

'Clearly not because he doesn't want to be with me anymore.'

Clara made a heroic attempt to push back her tears and opened the hatch in the counter. She felt everyone staring at her. 'Please, can we change the subject?'

'Where's your mum? Is she all right?' she asked Ruby.

'Fine. She had a midwife appointment and now she's having a lie-down.'

'The baby?'

'Absolutely fine, must be a tough little thing.' Ruby smiled and, for the first time in years, Clara saw a lightness behind her eyes.

'Like you,' Ruby added. 'You're strong, Clara, strong as a soldier in fact. We'll all get through this.'

Ruby hugged her tightly.

'I'm so sorry for what he tried to do to you, Cla,' she whispered. 'I can't bear the thought of him touching you.'

'Thanks to Billy, I never had to experience it. I shudder to think what your mum went through.'

'I know, but it's over now. She's safe at last.'

'There you are, Mrs Button.' The reedy voice split the air between them.

Clara froze, then mentally steeled herself for the encounter that lay ahead.

'Mr Pinkerton-Smythe and –' Her eyes ran over the well-built man accompanying him.

'This is my associate from the town hall. He's here to ensure there's no trouble.'

'Trouble? We're librarians, not gangland bosses!' Ruby flashed back.

Mr Pinkerton-Smythe raised one eyebrow, and Clara knew that whatever was about to unfold, a part of him would enjoy it.

'I've sent numerous messages for you to come and see me, but as you've ignored them, you've left me little choice but to come here. Where can we talk privately?'

'I'm sorry, it's been a difficult time. I-I was going to come and see you this afternoon.'

'Well now, I've saved you the bother.'

Ruby squeezed her hand as she walked past her and into the reading room.

'I'll get straight to the point, shall I?' said her boss once he was seated.

'Bethnal Green Borough Council can no longer tolerate

the continuing scandals that this underground library seems to elicit. Under your tenure, we've had complaints from irate mothers, of women abandoning the family home and now this, the death of a man.'

'Technically, that last one didn't actually happen in the library.'

'You're splitting hairs. The way I heard it, Netty Walsh began reading *Forever Amber* and took it into her silly head to leave her husband . . .'

'Because he was beating her within an inch of her life.'

'Good God, woman, stop interrupting me,' he exploded, banging his fist down on the table. Clara winced.

'Understandably, he took umbrage to this and pursued his wife to the library, with the intention of persuading her to come home. He ended up dead on the platform!'

'With respect, sir, he was extremely drunk and, moments before, had been attacking his wife.' She kept Victor's attack on her to herself. She doubted it would change her boss's mindset.

'Can you blame him for being angry?' he persisted.

'It was a dreadful accident,' Clara said, trying desperately to keep her cool.

'In which a man died, and it was a member of your book club who is at the heart of this latest affair. It tarnishes the entire reputation of the library service.'

'I'm sorry for that.'

'I warned you. Didn't I say what happens when you get women overexcited through fiction? You plant a book like *Forever Amber* in a woman's hands and of course she will be dissatisfied with her domestic life.'

'She was dissatisfied because he once beat her so savagely, she ended up in the London Hospital for a fortnight being fed through a straw,' Clara said coolly, feeling something flick inside her. 'I'm deeply sorry for the scandal it caused and his death, but I can't mourn his passing any more than I regret encouraging her to read books.'

Clara saw herself on the edge of a big precipice that she was about to step off. The drama of Victor's death, and her bruising encounter with Billy earlier . . . They had sloughed away the last of her restraint.

'Netty Walsh has a right to live in safety,' she insisted, jutting her chin out. 'Mrs Caley has the right to leave her controlling husband. Ricky Talbot's wife has the right to happiness.'

She leaned forward in her seat, blood pounding in her ears. 'This might genuinely surprise you, but women aren't chattels! If the books I've loaned them give them the strength to act on their convictions, then good. I'm pleased.'

Mr Pinkerton-Smythe's mouth was so thin, it reminded Clara of the blade of a knife.

'And while I'm at it. You might not like this, but the fact remains that every child who is a resident of Bethnal Green from the age of eight upwards has the indisputable right to join the ranks of registered readers. And yes, even vagrants and dossers are allowed in here. *All* society is allowed in here because guess what? They own this library, not you or I, or any other stuffed shirt at the town hall.'

Mr Pinkerton-Smythe leaned back in his chair and allowed himself a girlish chuckle.

'Well, well . . . There we have it.'

He stood up, a fly circling his bald head.

'I expect your resignation on my desk in the morning.'

'And if it's not there?'

'Then you will be escorted from the library. This library *will* be reopening next week as planned, but you are no longer its branch librarian, Mrs Button. Good day.'

He swept from the library and Clara wondered how it was that in the space of one day she had lost two of the most precious things in her life.

18

March 1945
Ruby

Quiet in libraries? I don't think so! Anybody can walk in through the doors, and we have to be ready to listen and help.
Michelle Russell, Library Manager at Romford Library
in the London Borough of Havering

The library had lost its heart and soul. That was the general consensus eleven weeks on from Clara's abrupt departure. The cold winter had thawed into an uncertain spring. Hitler's Third Reich had entered its final death throes. It seemed as though, at last, the war would soon be over.

Ruby glanced over at Mr Pinkerton-Smythe. The top of his bald head was gleaming, pink and sweaty as he eagerly unpacked the book consignment, humming a little tune to himself.

When he had forced Clara out on that awful overcast January day, her mother's screams still resonating in the library, Ruby had come so close to handing in her notice, but something had stopped her. A plan had formed in her mind, cloudy to begin with, but sharpening in focus over the following weeks. What use would she be on the outside? Double agents could be far more devastating. God knows it had been difficult to resist the temptation to tell him where to shove his new agenda. Even more difficult as she watched him dismantle everything Clara had worked so hard to set up.

The library cutbacks had been swift and brutal. First, he'd reduced opening hours to between 1 p.m. and 5 p.m., closing completely on weekends, meaning that no factory workers could come in and change their books. Next, he'd restricted children's access to just thirty minutes a day at 3 p.m. and suspended the bibliobus service and children's storytime too.

The homeless had been discouraged from using the library. The Major was no longer welcome.

Library services to the people who needed them most hadn't just been scaled back, they'd been cauterised. The final insult had come when he'd blacklisted *Forever Amber*, tearing up the waiting list with a triumphant flourish. A unanimous motion was passed for the confiscation of racy books from the library and he scaled back their stock of romantic and light fiction.

The members of the Bethnal Green Bookworm – Pat, Queenie, Irene, Dot and their kind – gradually stopped coming. Even Library Cat flicked his tail in disgust and left. Nowadays, the only people who ventured in were the odd middle- to highbrow patrons. The place was as quiet as the grave. Clara's worst fear of libraries preaching to the converted had been realised.

But tonight was different. The library was staying open late for a special event and a select group of children, hand-picked by Pinkerton-Smythe, had been invited.

Ruby felt her stomach churn at the thought of what she planned to do.

'Can I help, Mr Pinkerton-Smythe?' she asked sweetly.

'Yes, you can make a display out of these books on the counter. Make them look pretty. Sort of thing girls like doing.'

'Certainly, sir.'

As she began unpacking the books, Mr Pepper emerged from the reading room and, without saying a word, began to help.

'Such a terrific idea of yours to write to the Canadian Library Association,' she said to Mr Pinkerton-Smythe, flattering him with her brightest smile. 'First class.'

He stared back at her, a little suspiciously at first, but seeing no trace of sarcasm, puffed his chest out.

'Thank you, my dear. We have a duty of care to our young patrons, do we not?'

'Does this mean we can bring back children's storytime?' Ruby asked.

'Absolutely not. It is desirable to keep the juveniles and the adult readers apart. Right, well, now that's all in order, I'm off out. I have some last-minute details to attend to at the town hall, but I'll be back in plenty of time to meet and greet the Minister and press.'

'What time are they arriving, sir?'

'Six sharp.'

'Terrific! Don't be nervous; bet you're a smashing orator.'

He fiddled with his cufflinks.

'One tries.'

When he left, Mr Pepper turned to her.

'I really don't know about this, Ruby. He won't like this one bit.'

'I certainly hope so. You haven't told Mrs Chumbley, have you?'

'Course not, I wouldn't want to compromise her position as deputy shelter manager.'

'Or as your fiancée?' she grinned, tugging his tie. Mr Pepper's face softened as he shook his head.

'Gracious, if you'd have told me this time last year, that in a week's time, I would be getting married to Mrs Chumbley, I'd have said you were quite barmy.'

'So, what changed, Mr P?'

He ran his hand over the brand-new copy of *Treasure Island* and smiled.

'She's a wonderful woman and I'll admit, I misjudged her.'

'Well, she does have a formidable reputation in the shelter.'

'Yes, but that's just one side of her. A side she's had to cultivate. I think when she lost her fiancé in the first show, she developed a thick skin in order to survive, but underneath that is an extraordinary well of kindness.'

He shook his head again.

'It's no surprise to you or Clara, of course, but my eyesight's not what it was. I know I regularly make mistakes in shelving and you and Clara have had to rectify those mistakes many times.'

'Not that many . . .' she lied.

'Please, my dear,' he said. 'There's no need to make excuses for me. My eyesight is rapidly degenerating. I'll be lucky to be able to see at all in six months' time, or so my doctor tells me.'

'Oh, Mr P,' Ruby said, 'I'm so sorry to hear that.'

'Come now, my dear. No need for sympathy. I'll miss reading my books, but I've a lot to feel grateful for. Mrs Chumbley and I are lucky enough to have secured three wonderful rooms over Whitechapel Library. She's been offered the job as caretaker there, so we'll be moving after the wedding and she's promised to read to me. More than I deserve.'

He smiled wistfully and to Ruby, he looked like a little owl, blinking from behind his spectacles.

'She's a remarkable woman to want to take on a blind old man.'

'Oh, Mr P, I'll miss you both so much.' Mr Pepper was a part of the fixtures and fittings of this library, and the tunnels wouldn't be the same without Mrs Chumbley's booming voice echoing up them.

First Clara, now this. Even her own mother, who had been so dependent on her, was gradually growing in confidence now she was out from Victor's shadow. She had come home from work yesterday to find her sitting outside in the courtyard with all the women of the buildings, setting the world to rights, hand placed proudly over her swelling tummy. After years of having the life pummelled out of her, she was on the road to a better life, to freedom.

The world was changing. The post-war world beckoned, but the question remained: what place was there in it for a twenty-six-year-old library assistant who'd notched up more wartime flings than stamps in an Agatha Christie library book?

'You and Clara will be there, won't you? The red church on Bethnal Green Road next Tuesday?' Mr Pepper persisted.

'Are you telling me this in case I'm blacklisted from the shelter by tomorrow?'

'Well . . .'

She winked. 'It's all right. I'll be there. Wouldn't miss it for the world.' She straightened his tie.

'For what it's worth, I think Mrs Chumbley's the lucky one to have such a handsome, erudite man.'

'Hush now,' he chuckled. 'We're both very lucky. I only hope you and Clara find the happiness that we have.'

'I don't need a man complicating my life, thank you very much, Mr P. But Clara . . .'

'Still not reconciled with Billy?'

'Worse than that, she hasn't heard a peep from him. He never answers his door or replies to her letters. He's completely cut her out of his life. It's as if he blames himself for the whole thing and now it's driven them apart.'

'It was a deeply traumatic experience,' he pointed out.

'I just know that Clara and he were so perfect for one another. They both deserve to be happy,' she mused.

'Trust in love,' Mr Pepper replied. 'It always finds a way back.'

'I hope so Mr P. Now, come on, these books won't unpack themselves.'

As they went back to work, a tall man walked in and caught Ruby's eye.

'Say, honey, do you have Jack the Ripper's birth certificate here,' said the American, army personnel by the looks of him.

'Sorry,' said Ruby. 'You'll have to go to Whitechapel Library for that. Think they might have a photo of him.'

'Wow, thanks I will. I just love your British history.' He gave her a lingering look, then left. Mr Pepper raised one eyebrow at Ruby.

'What?' she said with an impish grin.

'I almost feel sorry for Mr Pinkerton-Smythe,' Mr Pepper replied.

By 6.15 p.m. that evening, the library was heaving.

'Gracious, has it really been a year since I was here last?' said Minister Rupert Montague, Director of Home Publicity at the Ministry of Information, over the rumble of voices. Since the Minister had arrived, Pinkerton-Smythe had stayed glued to his side, obsequiously guiding him around the room, introducing him to journalists. Ruby took a deep breath and engineered herself into his path.

'Now, you, I do remember,' he purred. 'But where's that terrific young librarian, Mrs Button, our library poster girl?'

'I'm afraid she resigned, Minister,' Mr Pinkerton-Smythe replied quickly. 'Shall we press on?'

'What a great shame,' the Minister replied. 'She had such energy and vision, didn't seem like the sort of woman to throw in the towel.'

'No. She didn't, did she?' Ruby replied caustically.

'Minister, you have another engagement in forty-five minutes,' said his aide.

'Righto.' He turned to face the members of the press and clapped his hands briskly. The room fell silent.

'We are gathered here today to celebrate something of a coup by Bethnal Green's Underground shelter library.'

'Mr Pinkerton-Smythe, chair of the Library Committee at Bethnal Green Borough Council, came up with the ingenious idea of writing to the Canadian Library Association, appealing for donations of children's books.

'His appeal was not only sent to sixteen Toronto branch libraries, but also read out on the wireless over there on the Canadian Broadcasting Corporation and published in the Toronto *Globe and Mail*.

'Mr Pinkerton-Smythe, perhaps you'd like to tell us the response?'

He held up both hands, blushing as all eyes in the library turned to him.

'Far be it for me to blow my own trumpet . . .'

'I know where I'd like to shove that trumpet,' Ruby muttered under her breath. Mr Pepper laid a hand on hers.

'But the appeal was rather successful.'

'Come now, don't be so modest,' said the Minister. 'The donations flooded in from every part of the dominion, from Prince Edward Island at one end to British Columbia at the other, from mining districts up north to farms on the prairies. Girl Guide groups even acted as collectors.'

He strode to the counter and gestured to Ruby's display.

'Look! Fifty copies of *The Secret Garden* from Vancouver, ten copies of *Treasure Island* from a high school, thirty-three copies of *Little Women* from the Girl Guides in Charlotte-town. The Women's Canadian Club in Toronto had a book shower, which obviously turned into a deluge as they sent one hundred and forty books!'

'What's a book shower?' asked a man from the BBC.

'Apparently, it's customary over the pond for people to shower gifts on expectant mothers and brides-to-be to set them up, and they had the bright idea to have a book shower.'

An audible murmur ran round the crowd.

'What was in the box of one hundred and forty?' called a reporter from the *Daily Herald*.

'Too many treasures to name, but I can tell you there're forty-four copies of *Water Babies*.'

He picked up a copy of *Ivanhoe*.

'Many have come with inscriptions, like this one. *May the boys and girls of Bethnal Green enjoy reading Ivanhoe as much as I did sixty-three years ago.*

'That one comes from an eighty-year-old farmer from Alberta who many years ago taught in the Nichol Street Ragged School.'

The Minister turned to the crowd.

'Canada have opened their arms to us and expressed their love through literature. Questions, please.'

Mr Pinkerton-Smythe was deluged by the press pack and Ruby felt Mr Pepper's eyes on her. A voice in her head urged her on.

Now! Do it now!

But suddenly, in this busy room full of men, her jaw turned to lead.

'Well, if that's all, I think we should have a photo of the Minister in front of the books.'

'No!' Ruby blurted. 'I've something to say.'

Mr Pinkerton-Smythe began hustling the Minister towards the library counter and the crowd started to talk all at once. But Ruby had waited too long for this moment for her voice to be swallowed up. Kicking off her heels, she nimbly hopped onto the library counter and stood up.

'I said, if you don't mind, I've something to say.'

Sensing an element of anarchy, the crowd stopped and strained their necks to look up.

A perfect silence settled in the library. Ruby felt her head spin as she realised the press were taking photos of her. Journalists, sensing a juicy story, had their pens hovering over their notebooks.

'Go on,' mouthed Mr Pepper, smiling encouragingly.

'People don't just come to the library for something to read.'

'They don't?' said the Minister, a hint of amusement in his voice.

'No. Actually, in lots of cases, people come for someone to talk to because they're lonely, or scared, or both. Often, a librarian might be the only person they've spoken to all day.'

Her gaze settled on Mr Pinkerton-Smythe, who looked ready to implode.

'My friend, Clara Button, who is the *true* branch librarian of this place, understood that. She taught me that we ain't just here to assist in the borrowing of books. We're a listening ear. In fact,' she flashed the crowd an irreverent smile, 'librarians should be paid twice what they're earning as they're doing the job of social reformer, agony aunt, teacher and community worker. Stick that in your paper.'

The assembled press men laughed, not quite knowing who the sparky blonde was, but knowing it would make good copy. Ruby relaxed, enjoying herself now.

'My pal Clara understood that books offer the promise of transformation and escape, taking you away from this dreary war, to worlds you never dreamt of visiting.'

She thumped a folded fist into her palm. 'Borrow, stamp, read, return. Bosh! You've travelled the world without leaving Bethnal Green. How bleedin' clever is that?' More laughter. The Minister's aide was plucking at his sleeve, urging him to leave, but he shrugged him off and smiled, spellbound, at Ruby.

'Clara believes passionately that all members of society should have access to free library books – *especially children*! So, while it's terrific that we have all these new children's books – books, I hasten to add, which Clara, not Mr Pinkerton-Smythe, came up with the idea to request – it's a bit like a chocolate fireguard. Pointless!'

'Why's that?' asked a journalist from the *Daily Mirror*.

'Because the current library rules stipulate that children are only allowed in for thirty minutes a day and storytime's been abolished by Mr Pinkerton-Smythe,' she flashed back.

'Kids are the lifeblood of this library, but they aren't welcome no more so they're staying away. It's quieter than a flea's hiccup in here.'

'Is this true?' the Minister demanded, turning to Mr

Pinkerton-Smythe. 'Was this whole thing Mrs Button's idea?'

'I . . . I forget who first came up with it, but it was me who rubber-stamped it,' he stammered. 'I've always been a staunch advocate of childhood reading and literacy.'

'So why are they now allowed in for only thirty minutes a day?' the Minister questioned.

'Well, I have been forced to make certain cutbacks,' he said defensively.

'So, we have a petition that we'd like to present the Minister with,' Ruby added. She looked to the library door, where a sudden swell of noise rose.

'Come on in kids!' Ruby yelled.

The crowd parted and a noisy procession of Tube Rats, headed by Sparrow, marched in holding up hand-painted placards.

Don't stop our stories! Books over bombs!

In they surged like bobbing corks – a burbling bunch of excitable kids, and behind them came the old library regulars Ruby hadn't seen since the previous December.

Rita Rawlins and her potty-mouthed parrot, Pat Doggan, Queenie, Irene, Dot and Alice from the café, the Major, the couple who borrowed the sex manual, the factory girls who'd read the print off the birth control pamphlet . . . Library borrowers from the shelter stood shoulder-to-shoulder, protesting that the light at the heart of their library had been extinguished.

'Mrs Chumbley, have these protestors removed immediately,' Mr Pinkerton-Smythe ordered.

'Oh, do it yourself man!' she boomed cheerfully, folding her arms and leaning back against the door.

'There's over five thousand signatures on that petition requesting the reinstatement of Clara Button as branch librarian,' said Ruby, hopping down off the counter and handing the pages to the Minister.

'Thank you for this, Miss Munroe, I shall give it my full attention, you have my word,' said the Minister.

He turned to Sparrow, who was clutching his placard, and crouched down to his eye level.

'Hello, young chap. What's your name?'

'Sparrow, sir.'

'As in cockney sparrow?'

'Somefink like that.'

'I've always wondered, what's the definition of a true cockney?' the Minister asked. 'Does one have to be born within the sound of the Bow Bells?'

'Nah! You have to be able to say, "forty thousand feathers on the thrush's throat."'

'Gracious, I'd never manage that tongue-twister,' he said, laughing uproariously.

'So, what does this library mean to you, young man?'

'Everyfing, sir. Me mum don't have time to read to me cause there's so bleedin' many of us, leastwise that's what she says. Sorry, Mum. And she's shocking busy in war work. Clara used to read to us every night. She also . . .'

He faltered and looked to his Mum. Pat nodded encouragingly.

'Well, she taught me to read as well. And after my mate Tubby died, I was sad. Coming here made me feel better.'

The Minister looked crushed.

'I'm so sorry about your pal, Sparrow. How did Tubby die?'

'Flying bomb.' He shrugged, biting down hard on his lip.

'So, what was Clara reading you, before she left?'

'*Moby Dick*, sir.'

The Minister smiled nostalgically.

'Oh, I adored that book; every child deserves to be read that story. But I must ask, can't you read at home?'

'We got bombed out, sir. We live down here now. It's great and all, but a bit too dark to read down the tunnels.'

The Minister shook his hand and stood up.

'I think you're an exceptionally brave and fine young fellow. It's been an honour to meet you, Sparrow.'

'Fanks, you an' all.'

'We'll see to it that Mrs Button returns to read you that book.'

He turned to the crowd.

'And now, I really must go before my poor aide has a coronary. Enjoy your new books everyone.'

Ruby was close enough to hear the Minister pull Mr Pinkerton-Smythe to one side as he left.

'You'd better have a damned good reason for letting Mrs Button go. You've a mess on your hands here. Clean it up, man!'

Later that evening, Ruby nearly hammered the door down until Clara opened it.

'We did it Cla!' she yelled. 'Oh, you ought to have seen

old Pinkerton's face. It was covered in egg – scrambled, fried and poached!'

Clara stepped aside to let a breathless Ruby, Mrs Chumbley and Mr Pepper in.

'Did what?' she asked, pulling her dressing gown about her. 'What are you all doing here?'

'Sorry for the late intrusion, my dear,' said Mr Pepper, as Mrs Chumbley helped him into Clara's small living room.

Ruby was ready to burst but looking at her friend nearly toppled her. She looked shocking. There was barely any weight to lose but she was no further through than a coat hanger. But the thing that really set alarm bells ringing was the absence of any books in the room.

'Can someone please tell me what's going on?' Clara asked.

'Your appeal to Canada paid off and, oh Clara, you ought to see the books that have turned up!' Ruby gushed. 'Hundreds! All the books you and Mr Pepper requested, and crate loads more besides. So many have inscriptions too. Listen.' She pulled *The Adventures of Huckleberry Finn* from her bag and turned to the inside page.

'*To the boys and girls of Bethnal Green, in gratitude for your sacrifices for freedom.*'

Clara covered her mouth with her hands, her eyes wide with amazement.

'That's incredible.'

'Isn't it!' Ruby enthused, relieved to see the good news shake her out of her despondency.

'The story of our little wartime library has touched so

many people and that's down to you, Cla,' Ruby insisted. 'Best of all, we set the Minister straight about whose idea it really was and we presented him with a petition.'

'A petition? What for?' murmured Clara.

'To get you reinstated, of course!' said Mrs Chumbley. 'So many people have boycotted the library since you left, because of all the cutbacks, so it wasn't hard to persuade them to sign. Do you remember what I told you all those months ago?'

Clara's face paled. 'No . . . ?'

'I told you to defend the library by engaging a Reader's Army. What I hadn't banked on was the Reader's Army coming to your defence.'

'Bloody brilliant, isn't it?' grinned Ruby, barely able to stand still. 'So now the powers that be know it's your idea, and all the shelter coming out in your defence, old Pinkerton don't have a leg to stand on.'

'She's right, Clara, my dear,' Mr Pepper said softly. 'I have a feeling that if you go and see Mr Pinkerton-Smythe tomorrow, you'll have some excellent leverage with which to reclaim your position.'

Clara stood in silence.

'B-but I resigned.'

'Well, technically, yes, but only 'cause he forced your hand,' said Ruby.

'But what's the point?'

'What's the point?' she echoed in astonishment.

'Yes, I mean, I'm only a placeholder, until the male librarians come back from war and that shan't be all that long now if we're to believe the news.'

'I can't believe I'm hearing this, Clara!' Ruby snapped. 'Where's your fight gone?'

Ruby stared at her friend, pale and defeated in her dressing gown and wanted to shake her.

'I think we ought to give Clara some time,' said Mr Pepper diplomatically. 'It must come as quite a shock, us all bursting in here.'

'I don't need any more time Mr Pepper. I shan't be asking for my job back.'

'But why?' Ruby exclaimed. 'You *are* the library!'

'Because I'm moving.'

'Where to?' Ruby demanded. 'You didn't discuss this with me! Have you a job in another library?'

'No. I don't have another job. I'm sorry, Ruby. I've been steeling myself to tell you.' Her fingers wrung the edge of her dressing gown.

'I'm moving in with my mother-in-law.'

'You're moving to Boring Wood!' Ruby gaped. 'What the hell for? To dust that old crone's aspidistras?'

At Ruby's cutting words, a tear broke and slid down Clara's cheek.

'How could you do this to us, to the shelter kids?' Ruby yelled angrily. 'What'll they do without you? What'll *I* do without you?'

'Let's leave Clara in peace to digest what we've told her,' said Mr Pepper. 'But I beg you, my dear, to reconsider.' He took her hands in his. 'Ruby's right. The library needs you. You told me your love of people is as, *if not more*, important than a love of books.'

'But that's just it, Mr Pepper. I always believed that

librarians could help to make a fairer, better society, but I was wrong.'

'What are you talking about, Cla?' Ruby asked, exasperated.

'I was stupid to think books can transform lives . . . No book stopped that flying bomb killing Tubby. No story stopped Beatty and Marie from running away. No happy ending stopped their father from being persecuted by the Nazis!'

Her tears were unstoppable now as months of grief and heartache shook free.

'A man died in my library because I was stupid . . .' She gripped her head in her hands. '*Stupid* enough to put an incendiary book in his wife's hands and now Billy hates me. Don't you see?' she cried. 'Books are a nice diversion, but life, real life, marches on regardless.'

She showed them to the door and opened it, her face bathed in shadows. 'I won't change my mind.'

Ruby went to follow Mr Pepper and Mrs Chumbley, but at the last minute turned back to face her friend.

'Five thousand people want to see you back in that library,' she whispered. 'But I need you back, Cla . . . As my friend.'

'I'm sorry, Rubes. I'll always be your friend. But I have to find a life outside of the library now.' She closed the door softly. Ruby had never felt so alone.

19

Clara

As a librarian, people trust you. They let down their barriers.
We are a social worker, a listening ear, a confidante.
Maggie Lusher, Manager of Kesgrave Library
in Suffolk

One week later, the day of Mr Pepper and Mrs Chumbley's wedding dawned. Clara dressed quickly. A pale blue frock and a slick of Tangee lipstick seemed as good a rig-out as any for a wartime wedding. She looked in the mirror and shuddered. Ruby could carry bright red lips off. She on the other hand looked like a painted clown.

Once she'd wiped it off, she picked up her copy of *The Secret Garden* and let the pages drift open.

To my friend Sparrow. You have so many doors still to open.
Please keep reading. Love, Clara.

She lit a cigarette, something she hadn't done in years. Smoking helped to anaesthetise the pain over not being able to read. For the first time in her life, Clara couldn't follow a sentence; the words floated off the page, disconnected and meaningless.

The despair over losing the girls had merged with the pain of being thrown over by Billy and only served to intensify her grief over Duncan. When it came to relationships, she seemed to have the Midas touch, but in reverse. Everything that was gold tarnished under her touch.

After Ruby, Mrs Chumbley and Mr Pepper's visit she had taken to her bed, marinating in despair. She should have stayed there too. Her mind trailed mortifyingly to yesterday. In her attempt to get through to Billy, she'd visited Station 98. Blackie had told her that he'd had a transfer to Brentford.

'Or wasn't it Hendon?' Darling had chipped in.

They knew exactly where he was. They had closed ranks on her to protect him.

As she'd left, she could have sworn she'd heard Beauty barking.

Had he been there? Hiding from her? The thought made her buckle in shame.

None of it made any sense.

I will always be here for you when you need me.

That's what Billy had told her in the aftermath of Tubby's death. That vow had seemed so genuine and heartfelt at the time and yet, where was he now?

The sooner she was out of the East End the better. She mashed out her cigarette and picked up her suitcase.

'Well goodbye then.' Her voice seemed to die in the empty room.

Outside, Clara cut through Barmy Park. A spring mist gilded the trees. The ruins of the old library seemed to float through the mist. She turned away and glanced at her watch: 6 a.m. It must be gone that by now. She shook her wrist. Every day for the past five days now, her watch had stopped at precisely six, always accompanied by the howl of next door's dog.

She had hoped to get past the entrance to the Tube unnoticed but no such luck.

'Clara,' called Mrs Chumbley, and reluctantly she stopped.

'You are coming to the wedding, aren't you? Ceremony starts at nine a.m. sharp.'

'Wouldn't miss it for the world. Say, would you do me a tremendous favour?'

She dug around in her bag and handed Mrs Chumbley *The Secret Garden*. 'Would you give this to Sparrow?'

'You don't want to give it to him yourself? He's still in his bunk.'

She looked down the steps that led to the Underground. 'I . . . I can't. Sorry!'

She turned quickly and continued down Bethnal Green Road.

A boy clipped the latest front page of the *East London Advertiser* into its stand.

FROM CANADA TO BETHNAL GREEN . . .
CHILDREN'S BOOKS FOR THE OLD COUNTRY.

She turned away, unable to look at the smug expression on the front-page photo of Pinkerton-Smythe.

'Clara . . . wait . . .'

She turned and Sparrow was tearing towards her, clutching *The Secret Garden.*

'Mrs Chumbley just give me this,' he said, out of breath.

'Oh yes . . .' She swallowed hard. 'It's a leaving gift.'

'W . . . what! But I thought you was coming back? We did a petition and everyfing!'

She shook her head.

'I'm sorry, Sparrow. It's complicated.'

'Adults always say that. Was it something I did?'

'Oh God no. *No, no, no.* Reading to you has been the biggest privilege.' Tears filled her eyes. 'I'm so very fond of you Sparrow.'

'Not that fond, else you'd have come and said a proper goodbye.'

She winced.

'First Tubby,' he breathed in disbelief. 'Now you. How could you?' He stared down at the book. 'I trusted you.'

'I'm sorry,' she cried, 'I'm leaving the East End, not you.'

He slammed the book into her hands, shimmering with anger.

'Same difference. I don't need you anyhow. You're a coward, is all.'

'Sparrow . . . Please don't be like that,' she called after him, but he had gone, his footsteps echoing like gunshots.

Bethnal Green Road greeted her like a potty-mouthed auntie. Shrieks of laughter. Wiry costers, calling out in an indecipherable patter.

As she listened to their voices, so pungent and lyrical, telling their own stories, she felt ripped in two. Sparrow was right. She was a coward.

She turned left down Vallance Road, where a small army of women were emerging to wash down their doorsteps with great steaming buckets, the smell at once clean and rotten, like bleach in a butcher's shop.

An older man stuck his head out of number 48, with a shaving cup of water, foam still covering half his face.

'Clara, you've gotta go back to the library,' he pleaded. 'Her indoors has stopped going since you left and now she's giving me verbal every night. Only bit of peace I get is when she's got her head in a book.'

'Sorry Fred.'

At least a half-dozen women ran out with little wedding gifts for Clara to pass on to Mrs Chumbley. She hadn't realised quite how much she loved these strong and loyal women. In the end, they valued kindness above all else.

She was turning her back on Bethnal Green in favour of what? Serving drinks at Maureen's whist drives?

'Clara! You better not bleedin' go without saying goodbye.'

The voice tore up the long street.

Ruby was running towards her, wearing an unfeasibly tight, hot-pink dress, matching headscarf and pink-framed sunglasses.

'As if I'd dare,' she laughed. 'Besides, we've a wedding to go to.'

Ruby slipped her arm through Clara's.

'Too right, which still gives me plenty of time to change your mind.'

'Can you actually walk in that dress?' Clara asked.

'Who needs to walk when you can wiggle?'

'You are incorrigible, Ruby Munroe.'

'Go on, I know you're dying to say it.'

'What?'

'That I'm Bethnal Green's answer to Betty Grable.'

Clara was about to reply with a lame joke when something odd happened. A vivid flash lit up the street. She stared down at her legs. How did she end up on the pavement? There was no pain, but a bloom of red unfurled like a poppy over the blue of her dress. Ruby was sprawled a few yards away, her headscarf glittering with silver.

Clara staggered to her feet, shards of glass dropping from her. She helped Ruby up and the pair of them stared in horror as a solid wall of black smoke mushroomed towards them.

'A flying bomb!' yelled a disembodied voice. 'Hughes Mansions caught it.'

And suddenly the street came alive. People ran headlong into the cloud of smoke.

'Come on, Clara,' Ruby urged.

Vallance Road was a long one. The same doorsteps Clara had just passed moments before were now completely shrouded in smoke. Doors were blown off their hinges and windows shattered. Terraced houses had been wrenched open by the blast, vomiting their contents onto the road, so that several times, Clara and Ruby had to clamber over rubble. Bricks and concrete sliced painfully into Clara's feet and it was then that she realised. Her shoes had gone.

As they plunged deeper into the cloud, her senses began to cut out. For a second, she lost Ruby. Panic exploded.

'Rubes!' she screamed, running her fingers through her hair. She looked down, her fingers were smeared with blood and she realised her hair was full of tiny shards of glass.

A hand reached out and grabbed her. 'Don't let go,' Ruby yelled.

There was no mistaking where the rocket had buried itself.

Hughes Mansions at the Whitechapel end of Vallance Road were familiar to Clara. Many of her library patrons, a lot of them Jewish, lived there. Three identical five-storey blocks stood side by side. Except the middle block was missing, nothing but a giant crater where people had once lived. Traumatised and hysterical people crawled over the rubble, flinging bricks aside, hunting with their bare hands for loved ones.

'Get down!' yelled a rescue worker as he frantically tried to erect a rope cordon around the crater.

A man staggered past, soaked in blood and carrying his baby son, calling for his wife. A soldier stood silently weeping over the body of a woman, her legs just visible in the rubble. The tattered remains of a *Welcome Home* sign lay nearby.

It was the very image of hell. Clara looked down at her cracked watch. Why it felt important to know the time she didn't know, other than to try and root herself in the midst of this chaos. 7.21 a.m. So many people would have been eating breakfast, getting ready for work or the Passover holiday. The scale of the loss of life was incomprehensible.

'We can't just stand here,' she cried, turning to Ruby.

Coming through the crowds that were rapidly gathering around the cordon, she recognised Miss Miriam Moses, founder of the Brady Girls' Club. She visited the library with the girls and boys of the Brady Boys' Club frequently. Clara was always struck and inspired by the energy of the social reformer. This would be her greatest test yet.

'Miss Moses! What can we do to help?'

Miriam turned to Clara, her face pale.

'We're using the Brady Club as HQ for the heavy rescue squad. Go.'

She left, off to hunt for the young members of her club.

'Cla, you go to the club,' said Ruby breathlessly. 'I'm going to go and find Mrs Chumbley and Mr Pepper, tell them what's happened. I'll be back as soon as I can. And I'll bring shoes for you.'

The two women embraced, hearts shattering at the sights unfolding around them.

Ten hours passed in the blink of an eye and, with every passing moment, Clara felt her soul shrivel. She barely drew breath as she helped other volunteers to transform the club into a makeshift canteen. Ruby returned with slacks, a clean shirt and shoes.

'I found this too,' she said, tucking *The Secret Garden* into her bag, 'where you dropped it.'

They buttered bread and beigels and brewed up huge urns of tea and Bovril. Making tea and sandwiches seemed such an inconsequential thing to do in light of what the teams of workers were doing outside. But Clara had the powerful feeling that she needed to be here, to be doing something to help, however mundane. Outside, they heard the clank of machinery as a mobile crane was brought on the site to remove huge chunks of masonry and allow rescue workers to reach those that were trapped. Screams and moans seemed to soak into the fabric of the building. She couldn't imagine how many people were entombed in the nooks and crannies of the crater, so close to where she was standing.

As the afternoon light softened and the smoke began to clear, the sense of disbelief turned to raw anger and bewilderment. In the club, the WVS had also set up a help centre, including a list of the confirmed dead.

The trickle of people coming into the club to find news of their loved ones soon turned to a flood. No sooner had one person left the queue than another joined, faces etched with raw anguish.

The room reverberated with the sounds of, 'Have you seen . . .' Some got good news, if you could call it that, that their loved ones had been dug out and taken to the London Hospital, others walked away, still none the wiser. But for some poor souls, it was the end of the road. The list of the dead quickly ran into double digits.

Before long, the Club was deluged, and the exhausted rescue men who filed in couldn't get past the crowds of desperate people who came back again and again to demand answers. It was bedlam. Clara and Ruby helped the WVS women to take down names and addresses from hundreds of distraught relatives. At the back of her mind, one thought persisted. Should she have fought for her position at the library? She could have formed an information bureau there and alleviated the strain here. The sense of suffering was overwhelming. Despite the atrocities she was witnessing, a guilty feeling sneaked through her that at least Sparrow and the rest of the Tube Rats were safe in the shelter.

Clara recognised the soldier she'd seen earlier, slumped against the wall at the edge of the room.

'Drink this,' she said, pressing a cup of tea with as much sugar as she could heap into it, in his hands. He barely seemed to notice the hot cup as he looked up at her.

'I've been in Burma for the last year,' he murmured. 'I'm only home for forty-eight hours. We was supposed to be having a family party this evening.'

'I'm so sorry for your loss,' she said. 'Was that your wife?'

He looked at her.

'No, my mum. And it turns out, my three sisters.'

'Oh, my love,' she said softly, and laid her hand on his wrist. At her touch he seemed to crumble. The tea slid from his fingers and his head fell into his hands as his body convulsed with sobs.

'That's my whole family gone,' he wept. 'What'll I do?'

Clara held him tightly, like you would a child, and shared in his grief.

By the time she managed to find him some warm clothes and an ambulance man who could take him to hospital, she was bone weary and sick of heart.

'Some homecoming. Poor sod,' said Ruby, shaking her head.

Nearby, the news broke that the bodies of two children, home a few days after three years of evacuation, had been pulled dead from the rubble. Their mother folded onto the floor, her body heaving with silent sobs. 'I don't think I can bear much more of this,' Clara said quietly.

'Have this,' Ruby said, putting a cigarette in her hands, 'and take a moment outside.'

Tears blinding her eyes, she stumbled out of the Brady Club. Immediately, she was blinded by the powerful beam of a white arc light, erected to help the rescuers keep hunting through the crater as darkness fell.

As Clara stepped forward, the breath was knocked from her chest as a body thumped straight into her.

'Look where you're going, won't you . . . ?' His voice tailed off.

'Clara!' In a moment, the ambulance man was holding her, steadying her arms. It took a moment for her brain to register.

'Billy!' Relief, love, and then hurt flooded through her.

'I thought you were in Barnet, or Hendon, or somewhere,' she said.

'I . . .' he began. 'It's complicated. What are you doing here? Are you hurt?'

'No, I'm fine, well apart from a few minor cuts.' She gestured to the club. 'I'm helping out.'

'I don't think this is the right place for you, Clara. Why don't you go back to the library?'

His words were laced with tenderness, but Clara felt aggrieved. What right had he to show concern? He'd absolved himself of that right the day he'd ordered her from his flat. Clara wanted to scream at him. Tell him she hated him, that he was pathetic for running away when she'd needed him most. But the painful truth was inescapable. Despite her best efforts not to, she loved him.

'Please Clara, go to the shelter, you'll be safe there.'

'I don't work in the library anymore. I resigned after you left me.'

'What?' His face was a picture of astonishment.

They stared at each other, their bodies illuminated in the light.

'That's a travesty,' he said at last.

'That's what Ruby and the others said. But I'm leaving the East End. I was supposed to be going today.'

'Don't go,' he said, pushing back his tin hat in despair.

'But why do you care?' she cried in frustration. 'You left me.'

'Clarkie, hurry up. We need those blankets.' A woman's voice called out. Blackie and Darling were working on the lip of the crater, transferring a broken body onto a stretcher.

'Look. I've got to go,' he said. 'But we need to talk. There's things I must explain. But not now.' He turned to go, then stopped.

'I love you, Clara. I always have.'

20

Ruby

There's no such thing as a child who doesn't like reading, just a child who hasn't found the right book.
Nicola 'Ninja Librarian' Pollard, school librarian for St John Fisher Catholic High School in Harrogate

The search for the missing was now in its third day. Ruby had never seen anything like it. Rescuers worked around the clock, day and night, the sense of urgency growing with every passing hour. They'd even drafted in specially trained dogs to locate people trapped in the rubble. The death toll was now well over a hundred and rising. But in and among the despair, there were fragments of hope. Only yesterday, a boy heard his brother and sister talking under the debris and guided rescuers to them. They were brought out alive after twenty-four hours buried under the ruins.

Organisation at the Brady Club was now much smoother, especially since Mrs Chumbley had set up a rest centre for relatives of the missing and those made homeless by the bombing in nearby Deal Street.

Ruby and Clara were just on their way there with a heap of donated clothes when Ruby glanced up.

'Is that who I think it is?' she asked, squinting.

It was extraordinary, the impact of the blast. In the centre was the crater that had swallowed up the middle block of flats, but the front block of flats, facing the street, was more or less intact. On the open-air landing that ran along the length of the building was Mr Pinkerton-Smythe, on the third floor, leaning over the balcony railing. He stared out over the crater beneath before turning and going back inside.

'I had no idea he lived here,' Clara exclaimed.

'Me neither.'

'We ought to go and check he's not concussed or in shock.'

'Oh leave him Cla, he's a total shit and besides, we're the last people he wants to see.'

Clara turned to her, her expression full of reproach. 'Maybe, but he's still a human being.'

Ruby wasn't so sure about that, but she wasn't going to let Clara go on her own and she was already heading for the buildings.

'I must need my head examining,' she muttered as she ran after her.

They knocked and the door was answered by an older man.

'Yes?'

'We're helping in the rest centre downstairs,' said Clara. 'We just wanted to check everyone's all right. We have plenty of warm clothes if you're in need.'

He looked down witheringly at the bundle of old clothes in Clara's arms.

'I rather think not. You'd better come in I suppose.'

He gestured for them to come into the small flat.

'Gerald,' he called into the hallway. 'Visitors for us.'

As he called through, Ruby stared at him, her mind swirling. Where had she seen him before? He was so familiar, she just couldn't place him.

Mr Pinkerton-Smythe walked into the room and, at that precise moment, she remembered.

'What are you two doing here?' he asked coldly.

'My God, it's you!' Ruby exclaimed, staring at the man who answered the door. 'You were in the library the night I had to run out . . . The night *Forever Amber* was stolen.' He was the bowler-hatted man who had dismissed their stock before taking *The Times* through to the reading room.

For a moment, both men stood perfectly still and Ruby looked around the flat. It was similar to most flats in this area, except for the fact that it was stuffed with books. Most households barely contained more than a handful; this was positively overflowing with what looked like expensive hardbacks stacked in tall bookcases. One stood out, green as an apple, nestling like a jewel on the bookcase.

Quick as a flash, Ruby pulled it out and opened the cover. It still had the reserve ticket in the inside pocket.

'Clara, look! This is the stolen copy!'

'What?' she gasped, dropping the jumble of clothes and taking the book. She ran her fingers over the Bethnal Green Library stamp.

'You're right, Rubes. It is . . . .' she said looking up in disbelief.

'Don't be so absurd!' Mr Pinkerton-Smythe snapped, but fear lurked at the back of his eyes.

Ruby began scanning other titles and suddenly she saw with perfect clarity.

'You're hoarding these books to sell when the war's over, aren't you?'

Clara's eyes roved over the bookcase.

'There are some valuable books in here!'

She took one at random – *Pride and Prejudice*.

'Poplar Library! Another library book!'

Ruby looked at Clara's face and could not remember the last time she had seen her so angry. She was actually shaking with rage.

'O-of all the treacherous and perfidious acts,' she stammered. 'To steal books from libraries, especially those frequented by people who treasure and need them most.'

Then Ruby spotted them, stacked on the edge of a bookcase, a neat pile of newspaper cuttings, the top of which showed a young woman jitterbugging in the arms of an American. Underneath that were the racing pages.

'And that was you as well, the person cutting up the newspapers!' Ruby exclaimed. 'You or him,' she said gesturing to the other man. 'Why?'

'Well, someone needs to act as guardian of the library's morals because Mrs Button here clearly wasn't up to the job!'

'My God,' Clara breathed. 'You actually want to censor people's leisure time, as well as their reading. And to think, I suspected poor Mr Pepper!' She laughed at the absurdity of it. 'You're a snake!'

'And you are a bleeding-heart liberal wasting your time on dead-end kids,' said Mr Pinkerton-Smythe, rounding on Clara. 'And Miss Munroe here is nothing but a cheap painted tart.'

Ruby leapt at him with a howl but Clara pulled her back.

'No Ruby,' she said breathlessly. 'Don't sink to his level.'

Ruby's heart was thundering in her chest and as much as she wanted to gouge his eyes out, she knew Clara was right.

'Well, I'm calling the police then. Let's see how this goes down at the town hall.'

'Wait!' said the other man, grabbing her arm as she passed.

'Get your hands off me!'

He dropped her arm.

'I'm sure we can come to some sort of agreement. There's no need to get the authorities involved.'

'Who are you?' she demanded.

'I'm Gerald's brother. What'll it take to keep quiet about this?' He pulled out his wallet.

'If you don't step aside and let us out, you'll need a surgeon to extract that wallet,' Ruby snapped.

'Wait Ruby,' Clara interrupted. 'I think we can come to some sort of agreement.'

Ruby turned round in astonishment.

'Clara . . . you can't mean . . . ?' But as she stared at her friend's face, she could see something extraordinary happening. Her anger had tempered into something else and for the first time in such a long time, Ruby caught a glimmer of the old Clara. Resolute. Strong and perfectly in control.

'First, you will step down as chair of the Library Committee,' she said calmly.

'Don't be ridiculous!' Mr Pinkerton-Smythe laughed.

She shrugged. 'Bye then.'

'Stop,' said the man, glaring at Mr Pinkerton-Smythe. 'Gerald. We'll never survive the scandal of being arrested. I have my job in the civil service to think of.'

'Your brother's right,' said Ruby. 'Imagine the headlines! *Library Boss Filches Bodice-ripper*. Or how about this, *Corrupt Council Boss Steals Strumpet?* You'll be a laughing-stock when that comes to court.'

As Mr Pinkerton-Smythe thought through the ramifications, he grew pale.

'But what'll I tell them?'

'Tell them you're traumatised from the flying bomb and you're looking to be relocated, away from Bethnal Green,' said Clara. 'At least you get to leave with your dignity intact.'

Mr Pinkerton-Smythe sank into a chair.

'Is that all?'

'No. Before you resign, you'll announce your replacement.'

'Who might that be?' he asked warily.

'Mrs Chumbley. She'll make an excellent Chair, subject to you getting enough support for her appointment, but I can't see that being a problem after all she's done at the shelter.'

'And the branch librarian?' Ruby asked and Clara smiled.

'Why, me of course,' she replied. 'But only until the men come back, then I should like to resume my old position of children's librarian.'

'Really Clara?' Ruby cautioned. 'I thought you hated being seen as a placeholder.'

'Not *just* the children's librarian,' she said, eyeballing Pinkerton-Smythe. 'But *the* children's librarian. I'll have input into the refurbishment of the library and my position will be seen as holding equal status to the adult department.'

Clara held up *Forever Amber*. 'I'll keep this as insurance, shall I? Just to make sure you carry out my wishes. Do I make myself clear?'

He nodded, almost incandescent with fury.

'Get out!' he managed at last.

'With pleasure,' Clara replied. 'Come on, Ruby.'

From the balcony they spotted Miss Moses below, rushing over to the Brady Club, looking absolutely shattered. It had already been confirmed that twenty-two Jewish children from the club had died in the explosion.

'Actually,' Clara said, turning back. 'One last thing to buy my silence. Sell as many of those books as you can and make a substantial donation to the Brady Club, so that when this nightmare is over, Miss Moses has some money to take the survivors on a holiday.'

Mr Pinkerton-Smythe's brother laughed.

'I do believe you're mad.'

Ruby turned to the balcony railing, put two fingers in her mouth and whistled. A policeman manning the cordon looked up.

'Very well, we shall.'

'Good. Make the donation in the name of Amber and when you're done, leak it the local rag so I know it's happened. Oh, and all those copies of *Forever Amber* I know you've got under lock and key at the town hall, make sure those go back to the library so that they are available to borrow immediately.'

And with that, Clara and Ruby swept from the flat leaving the shattered men behind them.

21

Clara

Growing up poor in a council flat with no money to do anything, meant the library was my escape. I devoured books. Libraries changed my life and now I'm a librarian. I want a big neon sign to say 'We are here for everyone'.

Charlotte Begg, Supervisor at Freshwater Library,
Isle of Wight

As they walked back to Deal Street, Ruby was beside herself.

'Cla! What the hell just happened?'

'I don't really know,' she laughed, disbelievingly. 'You don't think I went too far, do you?'

'No bloody way! He deserved everything he got. My God, girl. You played a blinder! Even Amber St Clare would be proud of you.'

She squeezed her hand and Clara suddenly felt her legs might go from under her. How she'd kept so calm was anyone's guess, her heart was galloping so hard.

'But where did that come from?' Ruby asked. 'A couple of days ago you were all ready to leave.'

'It's when he told me I was wasting my time on dead-end kids. It reminded me of that promise I made to Tubby's mum in the library, to never give up on their kids. I let her down.'

She remembered the look of hurt on Sparrow's face the last time she saw him.

'And more importantly, I've let the kids down.'

She'd allowed her trauma over Victor's death and her heartache over Billy to cloud her judgement, but now the way ahead was clear. Sparrow. Ronnie. Molly. Maggie May. Joannie. *All* the kids in that underground library needed someone on their side.

'No more behaving as others expect me to or living in the past either,' she vowed. 'This is my life and I need to be back in my library.'

'With or without Billy?' Ruby asked.

'With or without. I love Billy and he says he loves me too, but whatever is going on with him can't define me any longer.'

Sparrow's harrowing experiences, Tubby's death, the Jersey girls' upheaval from the island they loved . . . she couldn't shield the children from this war, but she could make it more bearable.

'Those kids deserve more. I've got to get them back in the library.'

'That's my girl,' said Ruby, playfully punching her on the arm. 'It's good to have you back! What about Pinkerton-Smythe heh? Or should I say, Gerald! I always knew he was an absolute toe rag!' Ruby cocked her little finger. '*Miss Munroe here is nothing but a cheap painted tart!*'

Clara was still laughing at her uncannily accurate

impression of Pinkerton-Smythe as they pushed open the doors to the rest centre.

'The clothes!' she exclaimed, suddenly remembering she'd left them in Pinkerton-Smythe's flat. 'I'm so sorry Mrs Chumbley, but we forgot them.'

'Never mind that,' she said, her tone grim. 'There's news. You'd better sit down.'

Clara knew before she'd even opened her mouth it concerned Beatty and Marie.

'Apparently, they've found a Union Jack scarf in the rubble. Someone remembered a girl wearing one similar in the underground library. Can you think who that might be?'

'Beatty!' Clara murmured. 'It's Beatty's, I know it is.'

'It could belong to anyone though,' Mrs Chumbley reasoned.

'But they're looking, yes?'

'Of course they are,' said Mrs Chumbley. 'But it's been three days now . . .' She left the sentence hanging in the air.

'All the more reason why they can't waste any more time.'

'Look after this Mrs Chumbley,' Clara said. She thrust *Forever Amber* at her and ran out of the rest centre. Dimly she could hear Ruby calling after her but she didn't stop running until she reached the buildings.

The police were in the process of sealing off the site and every single man and woman who had toiled there for the past three days looked sick and shattered.

'Please, I need to see Billy Clark!' Clara cried, clutching the arm of a policeman.

He hesitated.

'Miss, they're winding down the rescue effort. They don't believe there's much chance of finding anyone still alive.'

'I don't care! Get Billy Clark if you can, he's station chief at Station 98.'

'Very well. Wait there.'

Ruby caught up with her. Breath heaving, she bent over, hands on her knees.

'Cla, please don't get your hopes up,' she begged, but Clara wasn't listening for she had spotted Billy walking towards the cordon.

'Clara,' he gasped, 'what's wrong?'

Wearing protective gear, a thick rubber all-in-one, with his face covered in a ghostly veil of dust, they barely recognised him.

'B-Billy please hear me out. I know you've found Beatty's scarf.'

'We're not sure who it belongs to yet, Clara. The dogs are trying to pick up a scent. Please, go and wait at Deal Street and we'll update you with news . . .'

'But . . .'

'No arguments.'

'Let's do as Billy says, shall we?' Ruby said, gently leading Clara back to the rest centre.

The atmosphere at Deal Street was tense as they waited.

'Clara, please try to calm down. Sit and have a cup of tea,' Mrs Chumbley begged, but Clara ignored her, just pacing up and down the room, biting at a flap of skin by her thumb. Her vow earlier of never to give up on the library kids felt even more poignant in light of this. Were Beatty and Marie trapped in an underground tomb, frightened and alone, injured or worse?

As she looked around the rest centre, she realised she wasn't the only one waiting in dread. East Enders had lost so much in this war, but none as much as their Jewish friends. With the news emerging from parts of liberated Europe of giant death camps containing the emaciated bodies of men, women and children, of walking skeletons, the horrors were just stacking up.

The death toll at Hughes Mansions was now running at 134 lives lost, 120 of whom were Jewish. This rocket was Hitler's last roll of the dice, and it had fired right into the heart of an already grieving community.

An hour or more passed before word came back that, out of all the dogs, it had been Beauty who had detected a scent. Clara was out of the door like a whirlwind, Ruby close behind.

Beauty was scrabbling like crazy at a patch of rubble in the furthest corner of the bombsite and the tail end of the rocket was lodged ominously nearby. Pieces of timber were propping up what looked like a dangerously precarious piece of rubble, with the slenderest of openings just visible beneath. The arc lamp had been positioned over the hole.

'Billy! What's happening?' Clara cried over the cordon, and he came over.

'We think we've heard something. The building caretaker thinks it's the site of the door to the basement.'

'Exactly the sort of place you could hide away in!' Clara exclaimed.

'Please don't get your hopes up.'

'But you are going to try?'

'Of course. Where there's hope, we will always try.'

Clara looked at the tiny opening that plunged down into a dense pile of shattered brick and concrete and felt the skin on her back shrink. It looked like a trapdoor to hell.

'Who's going down?' she asked, feeling short of breath.

She knew the answer before Billy had even replied.

'Oh no, Billy, no,' Clara said tremulously. 'Why does it have to be you?'

'It's a simple case of physiology. I'm the skinniest.'

Clara looked at the other burly heavy rescue men and couldn't argue with that.

'Besides,' he said, 'I volunteered. If they are down there, they'll be dangerously dehydrated and terrified. I know them, so I'll have a better chance of coaxing them out.'

Clara closed her eyes, resigned to what was about to happen.

'Thank you,' she whispered.

'It's my job, Clara.'

'We're ready for you now, Billy,' called one of the rescue workers.

'Coming,' he called back.

A heavy silence fell between them and she could see Billy mentally brace himself.

'Go inside and put the kettle on, would you Clara?' he said. 'I'll be back before you know it. Then we'll sit down, have that chat.'

He was gone before Clara had time to respond.

Clara felt like she might pass out with fear.

'Come on, I don't think we should watch this,' said Ruby.

'I'm not going anywhere,' she said fiercely. She turned to face Ruby, her breath like smoke in the fading light.

'He did something similar during the Blitz, you know. How much luck can one man reasonably expect to have?'

When they turned back, Billy was already gone, slipping down into the bowels of the shattered earth.

Time took on a strange quality. The minutes felt warped and never-ending, the atmosphere one of agony and suspense. One of the rescuers brought Beauty over for Clara to look after as she kept whining and trying to follow her master down the hole.

As the gloaming descended, a fog began to creep in over the bombsite, and the tension was palpable. The struts holding up the entrance to the hole seemed to Clara's mind as slender as two matchsticks when you looked at the weight of the rubble they were carrying. The ground beneath their feet seemed to tick and groan as the temperature cooled.

Clara could see the worried looks the rescue team kept exchanging.

Just then, one of them crouched down, and then he was reaching an arm into the hole. A cry sounded and suddenly the atmosphere became electric.

A child's hand came out first, and the ambulance girls leapt into life, preparing the stretchers. It was a girl, her long dark hair matted against her head, her face a mask of plaster dust.

'Who is it?' Clara asked. 'Is it them?'

'I don't know, I can't see, it could be,' Ruby babbled. 'Wait! It is! Yes, I think it's Beatty. No, wait, it's Marie.'

The girl was lifted out whole, and hoisted into the arms of an ambulance man, her crumpled body loose in his arms as he picked his way carefully towards the stretcher.

Clara felt like she'd swallowed the moon as they drew closer. 'Yes, it's definitely Marie, and wait! There's some activity. They're lifting someone else out . . .' She covered her face and began to cry, overwhelmed at the miracle she was witnessing.

The assembled crowd inhaled as Beatty, nothing more than a blackened scrap, was lifted safely from the hole.

'Come on, Billy, come on . . . Where are you?' Ruby urged. Clara glanced at her watch and began to shake her wrist in agitation.

'It's stopped again at six.'

Suddenly, Beauty lifted her head to the heavens and howled.

The tunnel collapsed.

22

Ruby

I feel like a bartender because people who get to know you will stop and talk about their lives. I should have a glass, a rag and a range of booze bottles behind me sometimes.
Anna Karras, Librarian at Collier County Public
Library in Naples, Florida

'Please, doctor, there must be something you can tell us?' Clara begged.

'I'm sorry, but there's nothing more I can say at this stage. His condition is critical and we are doing all we can. I suggest you go home,' the doctor replied abruptly before turning on his heel, his shoes squeaking on the tiled corridor as he marched off.

Clara slumped down on a wooden bench and scrubbed exhausted at her face.

'Cla,' Ruby said gently, crouching down and taking her hands. 'You heard the doctor. It's 4 a.m. We should go home and get some rest.'

Clara looked up, hollowed out with pain. 'How can I leave him? What if he dies in the night?'

Ruby didn't like to say anything, but from what they had witnessed after the tunnel collapsed, that looked like a distinct possibility. It had been indescribable. In the chaos and confusion, she had pulled Clara back as the team of rescue workers frantically dug to free Billy from the debris. Clara's screams had mingled with Beauty's howls and seemed to penetrate every last corner of that shattered hell hole.

They'd found him just as darkness fell. It had taken every last drop of Ruby's strength to restrain Clara from beating down the doors of the ambulance as they shut them and drove him as fast as they dared to the London Hospital.

'He's in good hands, Cla. I should really like to get you home now to rest. We can return again first thing in the morning.'

Clara shook her head.

'You go if you like but I'm not moving from here.'

'Very well, budge up then.'

Clara looked up wearily.

'Where you go, I go,' said Ruby. 'So come on. Shift up.'

Ruby peeled off her sweater and gently curled it into a pillow and put it on her lap.

'Rest your head there.'

Gratefully Clara kicked off her shoes and lay horizontally on the bench, with her head on Ruby's lap.

'Thanks. But I won't sleep, just in case the doctor comes back.'

'Sssh now, just rest,' Ruby whispered, stroking her hair.

'Rubes . . .'

'Yes . . . ?'

'What will I do if he dies?'

'Go to sleep sweetheart,' she replied, bending down and softly kissing her head. It was going to be a long night.

By 7 a.m. the night shift nurses clocked off and Ruby still hadn't slept a wink. She rubbed her neck gently so as not to wake Clara. Her legs had gone completely numb but she didn't dare move. Clara needed all the rest she could get if she were to face the trials ahead. Ruby thought back to the tunnel he'd been buried alive in. How could any human survive that?

The matron came out and pulled down the blackout blinds from the high windows in the corridor and light streamed in. Clara stirred groggily.

From the far end of the corridor came a familiar pair of figures.

'What's happening?' Mrs Chumbley's voice boomed.

'Mrs Chumbley. Mr P?' Clara said, sitting up and yawning.

'Thought we'd find you here,' Mrs Chumbley said. 'Any news?'

'No,' Ruby replied.

'Why don't you both go outside for some fresh air and take this,' she said, handing Ruby a thermos and two enamel mugs.

'You look like you could use a cup of tea my dears,' said Mr Pepper, pulling out a paper bag. 'I've a couple of bacon rolls here from Dot. Everyone at the shelter sends their love. They're praying for Billy.'

'I'm off to get some answers,' said Mrs Chumbley, stomping flat-footedly down the corridor.

'Come on Cla,' Ruby said, feeling like someone had

chucked sand in her eyes. 'I'm gasping for a tickler and a cup of rosie.'

Clara shook her head.

'You're a stubborn sod at times, Clara Button. What news from the shelter Mr Pepper?'

'Well, the most peculiar thing. It's the talk of the tunnels. Mr Pinkerton-Smythe has tendered his notice.'

'Is that right?' Ruby murmured, shooting a glance at Clara.

'Yes. Apparently he's been offered a new job with the government, terribly hush hush. But here's the really strange thing. He's recommended to the committee that Mrs Chumbley take over as chair and Clara be reinstated as branch librarian.

'He's also found a terrific pot of money to put towards the renovation of the central library so we can move the underground library up there as soon as the work is completed.'

He shook his head in disbelief.

'And he brought back the library stock of *Forever Amber* this very morning. I've never seen such a volte-face.'

'Maybe he does have a heart after all,' Ruby remarked caustically. 'Eh, Cla?'

But Clara wasn't listening, for Mrs Chumbley had returned, with a doctor.

'This is Mr Clark's fiancée, Clara,' said Mrs Chumbley, shooting Clara a look that brooked no argument.

Clara looked like she might pass out and grabbed Ruby's hand.

'What news, doctor?' Ruby asked.

'He's alive,' said the doctor and Ruby felt Clara's body sag in relief.

'If I might speak plainly?'

'Please do,' Mrs Chumbley urged. 'We have all witnessed more than enough in this war to be little shocked by anything.'

'He has suffered massive internal bleeding and a broken hip. We have managed to stabilise him but he's in a coma. I'm also afraid we had to remove one of his eyes which was badly damaged as a result of the tunnel collapse.'

Clara shot to her feet. She clamped her hand to her mouth and ran up the corridor.

'Oh Billy,' Ruby cried.

'To be blunt, the eye is the least of his worries,' said the doctor gravely. 'I think it's fair to warn his fiancée that his condition is critical. I like to offer hope where I can, but he has the slenderest of chances of recovering from this. From what I understand, he's an immensely brave man.'

He stopped short of offering his condolences.

Clara returned, wiping her mouth and Ruby wrapped her arms around her. There was nothing she could say to assuage the sense of hopelessness.

'Can we see him?' Clara asked.

The doctor nodded. 'Very briefly.'

Inside his room, Ruby expected Clara to break down, but she remained remarkably composed. In fact, it was Mrs Chumbley who wept openly at the sight of him.

Everything in that room was scrupulously clean, even the nurse seemed as crisp as a starched napkin. Which just made the sight of Billy even more incongruous. His face was covered with lacerations. Some had been treated with iodine solution, others had been stitched.

Ruby couldn't stop herself from staring at his right eye, which was no longer spherical but flat. So many questions churned round her mind.

Would he die, would he live, and if he did, how would he cope with being blind in one eye? Would he be able to work or read again? Would he have brain damage? Would he remember Clara?

He looked so vulnerable, nothing more than paper-thin skin and broken bones.

Clara's composure abruptly ended. Tears slid down her face, dripping off her cheeks and onto the bed linen.

'Billy. You have to live. I need you. The girls and I need you.' She held his cold hand to her cheek, let the salty wetness of her tears stain his skin.

'Clara Button?' The matron had slipped discreetly into the room. 'There are two girls asking to see you.'

Two floors down Ruby and Clara clung to Beatty and Marie, hugging them and kissing them over and over.

'You girls gave us quite a fright,' Ruby said.

'Sorry,' said Beatty sheepishly. 'I suppose you know the truth?' She looked every inch the twelve-year-old girl she actually was and now that Ruby knew her real age she found herself wondering how on earth she hadn't guessed.

'We do,' said Clara. 'And it's we who are sorry. Sorry that we didn't look after you better.'

'It's not your fault,' said Beatty miserably. 'I was just so terrified that if the authorities found out they'd split us up and we would be sent to children's homes. I promised my dad before we left Jersey that no matter what, I'd never let that happen.'

She looked at them, her eyes wide with fright.

'Except I expect that's exactly what will happen now?'

Clara shook her head.

'No. When you're discharged the only place you're going is back to my home. I'll look after you until we hear from your father. You have my word.'

'No more working at the factory either,' said Ruby. 'You can come and help us at the library instead.'

Marie smiled in relief.

'Me too?'

'Especially you, pip squeak,' Ruby replied, hugging her tightly. 'I want you where I can see you. No more horror room escapades.'

'Ooh ouch,' Marie said. 'That's sore.'

'Sorry sweetie,' Ruby said, pulling back.

Marie had three cracked ribs and Beatty a ruptured spleen, but apart from that and some nasty bruising and dehydration, remarkably they seemed physically unscathed from their ordeal. Ruby had a feeling their mental scars would take longer to heal. Neither of them could remember a thing about being trapped underground, but the doctor had assured them that was the brain's way of processing such a traumatic event.

'How's Billy?' Beatty asked. 'I'd like to see him and say thank you for rescuing us.'

Ruby looked to Clara and hoped she wouldn't soft soap the truth too much. After all these girls had been through, honesty was the only way forward.

'He's not in great shape,' Clara said softly. 'They're deliberately keeping him sedated until he can recover from his injuries. All we can do is pray.'

Beatty burst into tears.

'If he dies it will be my stupid fault,' she sobbed. 'I'm sorry we ran away, Clara.'

'Hush now, don't be daft,' Ruby said, giving her the biggest hug she dared.

'The main thing is you're back with us, your library family, and we will never stop loving you, no matter what happens.'

Ruby and Clara exchanged glances over the sisters' heads as they hugged them gently. They were back in the library. The girls were safe. The war was on the brink of ending, but the future had never looked so uncertain.

23

Clara

It took me fifty-three years but I'm finally working in the library I used to visit as a child. I feel like I've arrived in life. It's the best job in the world.

Michelle Mason, Library Information Worker,
Tilbury Library

Clara's reading rut had ended. It had been five weeks since Billy had been stretchered into the hospital clinging to life, and books had been her backbone, holding her together while he remained in a coma.

Every day she sat with Billy during visiting hours and read. She read on the bus from the library to the hospital. She read in the newly resurrected storytime session and to Beatty and Marie when she tucked them in last thing at night. She read because right now it was the only thing that made any sense.

She pulled out the *East London Advertiser* and noticed with interest that finally they were reporting the rocket attack at Hughes Mansions by name, after weeks of vague references to a large block of flats being bombed 'somewhere in the South of England'.

'You'll hate this, Billy, but you're being hailed as a hero,' she said. 'They're talking about your gallant service in rescuing the runaway girls.'

There was a picture of him on the front page, next to one of Beatty and Marie.

She scanned the paper for nuggets of good news to read out. On the next page was a story about Sparrow. She had been deeply saddened to learn that he had been caught with a knife trying to break into a Prisoner of War camp for captured German soldiers. The article reported him as saying he wanted revenge for his friend Tubby's death. Her heart squeezed knowing that if she had been at the library at the time, she could have coaxed him to express himself in another way. She pictured Sparrow's accusatory face the last time she'd seen him. *I don't need you.*

Without the allotment or the library, what focus did this grieving boy have? She had to find a way to get him back where he belonged.

Sighing, she turned the page.

'Oh Billy, look. Turns out a mysterious benefactor known only as Amber has donated a large sum of money to Miss Moses at the Brady Club. She plans to use it to replace sports equipment and to take survivors away to the countryside.'

She smiled in satisfaction. Pinkerton-Smythe had gone and she didn't feel one ounce of regret. Mrs Chumbley had turned down the job at Whitechapel Library and was settling in well into her new role as chair of the Library Committee. They'd even found ground-floor lodgings near Vicky Park, with a postage-stamp backyard where Mr

Pepper could sit under the shade of a mulberry tree and listen to the birdsong.

Between Mrs Chumbley and Ruby, the underground library was well covered while Clara visited Billy and the girls in hospital. It was a juggle, but one she supposed she had better get used to, especially if her application to foster the girls was approved.

'Visiting time's over,' said the nurse. 'No point asking whether you'll be back tomorrow?'

Clara nodded.

'I've noticed you reading a lot. Why don't you read books out loud to Billy? I have a theory it all goes in.'

'Good idea. I'll do that.'

'Who's his favourite author?'

'I don't know,' she admitted, realising she never did guess. There was still so much left unsaid between them, so much she still didn't know about Billy. A shaft of dusty sunlight spilled into the room, swirling between them in the shape of a secret. Billy lay lost in darkness, his story under lock and key. She turned quickly.

By the time she reached her doorstep, Ruby was waiting for her, one foot resting on the wall, smoking a fag.

'It's like a bleedin' Red Cross food drop round here. Mind you, you need it. I've seen more meat on a sparrow's kneecap.'

She pinched her arm teasingly.

'Mum's made bread and butter pudding, Pat's made something which I'd hazard a guess is corned beef hash, and Queenie and Irene have sent twenty Players.'

'I've stopped the smokes.'

'Good, never suited you. Come on, let's go inside. How's a cup of tea and foot rub sound?'

'Like heaven on earth,' she replied.

Ruby laughed throatily and mashed out her cigarette on the kerb.

'Any change with Billy?' she asked, as Clara pushed open the door.

'No. But the girls are being discharged next week hopefully. The matron has agreed to let them come home with me until the foster proceedings are underway.'

'Clara, that's wonderful news!' she declared as they walked straight into the living room.

'What's wonderful news?'

Ruby jumped and clutched Clara's arm.

'Mrs Button, you scared the life out of me!' she exclaimed.

'And me,' Clara breathed.

Clara stared, stupefied, at the vision of her mother and mother-in-law sitting like two bookends either side of the fireplace.

She hadn't seen her mother for over a year and shock stole her voice.

'H-how did you get in?' she stammered eventually.

'I do have a key,' Maureen said icily. 'My son gave it to me. This was his home, you know.'

'Of course,' Clara said, pushing down her anger. 'Hello Mum.'

'Hello dear,' she replied tersely.

'We were expecting you some weeks ago,' Maureen went on.

'I'm sorry, I did write to explain. So much has happened. The flying bomb, then the Jersey girls turned up.'

'So you said,' she replied. 'So, you're to be these girls' . . . substitute mother?'

'Yes, that's right. They need someone to protect them until their father's located. I'm the closest they've got to a family right now.'

Maureen raised one eyebrow.

'Shame you couldn't manage to protect your own unborn child.'

Clara felt like she'd been struck, the shame vibrating from deep within.

'You really know how to stick the knife in don'cha, you nasty old cow!' Ruby yelled.

'Leave it Ruby, please,' Clara begged.

'Honestly though, Clara. What kind of way is this to honour my son's memory?'

'The best way,' she insisted hotly. 'Duncan would have loved those girls as much as I do. He had a heart as big as the moon!'

'Clara, can't you see how insulting this is to Duncan's family?' Her mother spoke at last, reaching over to put a supportive hand on Maureen's.

Clara wanted to scream out. Why can't you support me, your own daughter? Why can't you love me unconditionally? But she knew with sadness that since Duncan's death something had broken between them – perhaps it had only really been him acting as a bridge?

Her mind flickered back uncomfortably to her childhood. Clara hiding from her mother under her bed with a book. Clara feeling like the odd one out. In pursuing a job in the library instead of being a full-time wife, she had breached an unspoken code of conduct. She realised with immense sadness that she had only ever really found true acceptance with Peter at the library.

'I'm sorry Mum. I don't mean to insult any of you, but I can't change who I am or how I feel.'

Her mother rolled her eyes.

'I told you Maureen. It's a waste of time.'

Mrs Button stood up, searching her brain for some way to remain. Clara knew it wasn't about love, but control.

'So are you saying you'd choose two Jewish girls over your own flesh and blood?' she demanded. 'It's their lot what brought the war here you know!'

How interesting that when backed into a corner all of her mother-in-law's innate prejudices showed their ugly face.

'I shan't dignify that with a response,' Clara replied quietly.

Maureen tossed the key onto the mantelpiece, her mouth a razor-sharp line.

'Then I wash my hands of you. Seems your mother was right all along, you've obviously chosen that library over your real family.'

The two women walked out, the air behind them scented with sweet perfume and mothballs. Clara searched herself for regret, but realised that actually all she really felt was relief.

Ruby hugged her long and hard after they left.

'You all right ducks?' she asked at last and Clara nodded.

'I suppose in a way I have chosen the library.'

'Your library family,' Ruby added. 'Who love the bones of you.' She kissed her forehead, leaving a big red lipstick stamp behind. 'I'll make that tea.'

That night Clara slept more deeply than she could remember in a long while. Her mother and mother-in-law's judgement of her, their condemnation and the lies had been exhausting. Billy had been right. Losing the baby hadn't been her fault. She could no more have prevented that miscarriage than she could the trajectory of the bomb which triggered it. She had been shrouded in blame and guilt for too long.

The next afternoon, feeling lighter, she returned to the hospital clutching a library book, hopeful that maybe today would be different, that Billy would be conscious. But nothing had changed. He lay, not dead, but seemingly not alive either. Trapped in some strange, dark, cavernous hinterland.

She gazed at his eyes, the skin around them dark and bruised, like a crushed petal. He looked so fragile, as if death was simply a footstep away.

She picked up the book.

'*Love on the Dole* by Walter Greenwood.'

They'd read this in book club and Billy had loved it, likening the language to crunching on a crisp lettuce. He'd also declared it the most moving book he'd ever read.

Set in the working-class district of Salford during the Depression, it chronicled the poverty and squalor of the past.

'Do you remember, Billy, what a strong reaction this

book provoked?' she said. 'You said it was a book that spoke its truths loudly. I'd never seen you so animated.'

The younger members of the book club couldn't remember the Depression all that clearly, but Mr Pepper and Mrs Chumbley had, as had Pat, Irene and Queenie.

Queenie had told them all how her father had sat elbow-to-elbow in the library with hundreds of other men scouring the jobs pages, and Irene shared her father's despair of ever finding work and how he took that out on her mother with his fists.

'This book opened us all up from the inside out, didn't it, Billy?' she mused. 'It drew out our own stories.'

And suddenly, she realised. Renovations on the over-ground library were coming on a pace. Soon their little wartime library would be consigned to the past. Being cocooned underground with friends and Billy had been the very best days of her life. Already, they were crystal-lising into memories. The smell of old and battered books, glue in their spines, faded dust jackets. Candlelight. Laughter. Gin.

She began to read, and as she tumbled into the pages, she hoped the words she threw out were reaching him. That somehow, somewhere, those spoken truths were stir-ring him. The end of the war was achingly close, an announcement expected any day. Would Billy be alive to see the kind of world he had always dreamt of? A world at peace?

Word spread that Clara was back in the library and that she was reading to Billy to try to raise him from his coma.

With the doctor's permission, a reading rota was arranged, with all the members of the Bethnal Green Bookworm coming in once a day to read to him, enabling Clara to begin work at the library and prepare the house for the girls' discharge from hospital.

Over the course of the next four days, no man could have heard more stories. Mrs Chumbley read from Georgette Heyer's *Friday's Child* on the basis that as he wasn't all that keen on Regency romance, it might sufficiently annoy him to rouse him.

Mr Pepper read him poetry with the aid of his magnifying glass. Wordsworth, Keats and Tennyson. Even some of the nursing staff stopped by to listen to his calming voice wash over the room.

Pat brought Ernest Hemingway and news that Hitler had topped himself. Queenie abandoned her usual thrillers and read extracts from Graham Greene's *The Power and the Glory*.

Only Irene couldn't be parted from her usual fare and read out extracts of Denise Robins' *Desert Rapture* with gusto.

But it didn't seem to matter what the genre, there wasn't so much a flicker of life from Billy. It felt to Clara like he was floating somewhere at the bottom of the deepest, darkest ocean, a place where stories couldn't penetrate. A sense of nervous exhaustion fell like a blanket over her as they waited.

The doctor spoke to her and his family. The sweet sister who had donated her Beatrix Potter collection appeared and spoke to Clara with such kindness that she could have wept with gratitude. But it didn't soften the bitter reality. Every day that passed meant any recuperation looked less likely.

Words like 'testing for brain activity . . . persistent vegetative state . . .' flowed over and around her, and yet . . . and yet. What was it Billy had said before he'd climbed down into that tunnel from which he'd never really emerged? *Where there's hope, we will always try.*

Finally, on the Tuesday, the waiting ended.

Clara heard a tremendous noise from outside the hospital. She ran to the window. The whole of Whitechapel High Street was exploding with joy.

Heart hammering, she ran out of the room and into the corridor, but for once, there were no nurses on duty. They were all in the matron's room at the end of the ward, gathered round a wireless as a familiar gravelly voice spoke to the nation.

God bless you all, this is your victory . . . In all our long history, we have never seen a greater day than this. A moment's silence then a thunderous roar of applause seemed to rise from outside.

She watched the nurses abandon their customary professionalism to hug and kiss. She walked back to Billy's room, took his hand and pressed it to her face.

'It's over.'

She lowered her lips to his ear.

'The war is over, Billy.'

Nothing. He lay as if entombed in a marble sarcophagus.

As the afternoon inched on, the scenes outside the hospital window grew more astonishing. Crowds decked in red, white and blue surged up Whitechapel High Street. An enormous bonfire grew, waiting for darkness and the stroke of a match. Buildings that had been drenched in darkness for years were now floodlit, and silver ribbons of light were beamed into the sky in the shape of a V.

The light felt blinding to Clara.

She turned away from it. Inside the hospital room all was cool, sterile restraint.

The door clicked softly.

'Thought I'd find you here.'

Her presence filled the room, a sunbeam muscling out from behind a cloud.

'Rubes! What are you doing here? There's the party of a lifetime going on out there.'

'Tell me about it,' she laughed. 'You ought to see the buildings. Mrs Chumbley's in charge of the kiddies' games. Pat's so drunk, she's leading a conga line up Russia Lane. Minksy Agombar and her sisters are doing harmonies on top of a milk float, and Mrs Smart knocked out slippery Stan with a dustbin lid for feeling up Mary O'Shaughnessy.'

Clara raised one eyebrow.

'I think I'm safer off in here.'

She turned back to Billy.

'Oh, and Sparrow, Ronnie and his crew have made an unnervingly realistic Hitler to put on the bonfire,' Ruby laughed, peeling off her gloves.

At Sparrow's name, Clara looked up sharply.

'I read what happened in the paper.'

'He got the hiding of a lifetime from Pat for that.'

'Poor Sparrow. He's never really been allowed to mourn

Tubby. Is it any wonder he's angry? I'm afraid I've ruined his trust by trying to sneak off without saying goodbye. He probably hates me, and with good reason.'

'Rubbish,' Ruby scoffed. 'He'd get the top brick off a chimney if you asked.'

Clara laughed in spite of herself.

'Honest, Cla. He misses you. All the Tube Rats do . . . Billy would want you to be out there with them.'

Clara shook her head.

'I can't leave him.'

'Thought you'd say that.' Ruby shrugged off her coat and pulled a stack of books from her bag.

'I raided the library. Which one'll I start with? *Grapes of Wrath* or *Pride and Prejudice*?'

'Rubes, you don't have—'

She held up a hand.

'Shut up, you ninny. We went through the whole war together. As if I'm going to leave you now.'

'But your mum,' she protested. 'She needs you too.'

'Mum is going to be fine,' she said adamantly. 'She has her bad days still, but she has the baby to think of now.' She ran her hands up the spines of the books. 'As much as that seemed like a curse when Victor was alive, now in a funny sort of way, it's what's holding her together.'

She fixed those ice blue eyes on Clara. 'It's you we need to hold together, just till this fellow comes round.'

'Your lips to God's ear,' she replied, wearily.

Ruby held up the books.

'New American or old English classic?'

'Old English classic.'

Ruby picked up the book and began to read. Clara rested her head against her shoulder. Jane Austen's prose washed over her, as soothing as a lullaby. She closed her eyes.

24

Ruby

Libraries and love both take their own time to develop. I met my partner for the first time when we worked together as young librarians just before the new millennium. We didn't come together romantically until nearly twenty years later. We each had a lot of thinking, growing, and – yes – reading, to do first.

Anne Welsh, Beginning Cataloguing

'God almighty, can anyone hear themselves think with that flamin' racket?' Ruby yelled out from the library door and up the echoey platform.

In the three days since Victory in Europe Day, the theatre had gone. So too had the nursery and the doctor's quarters. The banging was the sound of a team of workmen taking down the metal bunks from the tunnels.

Ruby turned back to face the library. She wondered what would happen first. The dismantling of the library or its total collapse? The wooden floor was now so worn through that every day she wondered whether the weight of the library books would finally prove too much, and they would all find themselves in a heap on the tracks of the westbound tunnel.

They'd finally been served their eviction notice. London

Passenger Transport Board was reclaiming its station. Central Line Tube trains were to run down the tunnels, not children. The hiss and rattle of carriages, instead of laughter and shrieks. The war was over, and they'd been given until the end of the summer to pack up all the books and get out. Council workmen were even now repairing the bomb-damaged library in Barmy Park so the books of Bethnal Green wouldn't find themselves homeless.

Ruby felt cast adrift. Who was she to be now, up there on the surface in civilian life? Everywhere she looked, people were hoisting up *Welcome Home Son* banners, and the streets were already filling with men in their demob suits. Peace had brought a desperate desire for normality, and although Ruby would never admit it out loud, she'd miss the foreign voices, the potential for reckless behaviour, clattering down the escalator steps after a night on the sauce. The whirl of wartime life would be a hard aphrodisiac to kick.

'Not sure librarians are allowed to disturb the peace, are they?'

Ruby spun round.

'Thank f . . .' She tailed off when Clara widened her eyes and jerked a thumb behind her.

'Girls!' she exclaimed when she spotted Marie and Beatty standing shyly behind Clara. 'Ooh, come here, I ain't half missed you.' She grabbed them both in a big bear hug that made them laugh.

Marie giggled so much she started to cough.

'Come on, cough it up, could be a gold watch,' Ruby teased.

'Rubes,' Clara scolded. 'She's getting over broken ribs.'

'You worry too much,' Ruby replied. 'Tough as old boots these two.'

But for once her friend didn't laugh. In fact, Clara looked worn to a thread.

'We just met the King and Queen,' Marie announced, hopping on one leg.

'You never did!' Ruby breathed.

'The King and Queen *and* Princesses Elizabeth and Margaret visited Hughes Mansions this morning,' Clara said. 'At the last minute, I got a message saying they wanted to meet the girls who were rescued.'

'My God!' Ruby breathed.

'I know, that's what I thought. I wasn't sure whether it'd be a good idea, to go back there. They've only just been discharged after all, but I thought I'd let the girls decide.'

'And we decided yes,' said Beatty firmly.

'The Queen was ever so nice and Princess Elizabeth was so pretty,' Marie gushed. 'They all told me how brave I was.'

'It was emotional,' Clara said thoughtfully. 'There was a huge crowd that broke through the cordon and got the wind up their security men, but they surged round them and sang, "There'll Always Be An England".'

'Astonishing,' Ruby said.

'It was. They'd been terribly well-briefed, even asked me how Billy was.'

'And?'

'No change,' Clara replied.

'Do you think we ought to be allowed to visit him, Ruby?' Beatty demanded.

'I, er . . .' She looked to Clara.

'I've told the girls that I'll think about it. I'm not sure it's the best idea right now.'

'I think we're old enough to make our own decisions,' Beatty announced, those dark eyes flashing defiantly.

She stomped off to the children's section and Ruby raised her eyebrows at Clara.

'What did the doctor say when they were discharged?'

'He told me to expect some challenging behaviour. Marie's her usual self, but it seems Beatty's guilt over Billy has turned to anger. Oh Rubes. I can't bear to talk about it any longer. Let me help with packing.'

Two hours later, the Tube Rats spilled into the library after word had spread that storytime was back. None of them were sleeping down the tunnels anymore, but some wartime rituals couldn't be parted with.

Molly and Maggie May charged headlong into the reading room. Clara had put Marie and Beatty in charge of giving out paper and pencils to the kids as they came in. The library was filling up fast and Ruby spotted faces she hadn't seen in months.

'Joannie!' Clara exclaimed. 'You're back!'

The red-headed tomboy over whom they had got in trouble for loaning *Emil and the Detectives* grinned.

'Yeah, me mum says I can come while we wait for my school to reopen.'

'And Ronnie, look at you!' Ruby exclaimed. 'They plant you out in compost?'

He'd only been evacuated for six months, but he'd shot up.

'Nah,' he said, grinning shyly. 'They have a lot of food out in the countryside.'

'Where's your sidekick?' Clara asked, scanning the door anxiously for Sparrow.

He shrugged.

'Sorry, I ain't seen him since I got back.'

Somehow, they all squeezed in, sharing the room with stacks of boxes.

'Great news,' said Clara, clapping her hands to get their attention. 'In those boxes are hundreds of new children's books waiting to be unpacked when we move to the proper library once it's ready. All for you to read!'

There was a perfect silence as all the kids stared at the tower of boxes.

'Blimey,' breathed Maggie May, 'that's a LOT of books.'

An eight-year-old girl called Dolly, who had only just joined, burst into tears.

'I'll never be able to read all of them,' she cried.

Fortunately, the general consensus was one of great excitement that their new library was to have lots of shiny new books, just for them.

'A lot of them were donated by boys and girls from Canada, so I thought it would be fun to have a competition to see who could write the best letter of thanks,' Clara announced.

Competition was fierce and soon all the kids were absorbed in their letters. The library was filled with the sound of pencils scratching over paper.

There was a movement at the door and Ruby nudged Clara.

'Sparrow!' Clara exclaimed. The sight of him had completely caught her off guard, and a knot of emotion lodged in her throat. 'You're back!'

'So are you.'

They stared at each other across the library. Ruby knew what this child meant to Clara. You weren't supposed to have favourites, but she adored this clever, misunderstood boy.

'Are you stopping?' she asked.

He walked in, trailing mud on the floor, and handed Clara a lumpy parcel covered in dirt.

'For you,' he sniffed, wiping his nose on his sleeve.

'Gooseberries!' she exclaimed, unwrapping the parcel.

'Thought you could make a pie or summit.'

'Where did you get these?'

'I didn't steal 'em,' he said defensively.

Clara reached out and touched his arm.

'I know you'd never do that.'

'Only that thing with the Prisoner of War camp, I weren't going to hurt 'em. I just wanted to scare 'em, make them feel frightened. The way Tubby must have felt . . .'

'I believe you,' Clara replied. 'So, what did the police say?'

'To keep my nose clean. So, I've dug meself a new allotment down by the railway. I've got fruit trees and all sorts . . .' he trailed off, embarrassed.

'I'm so pleased you're here because I've something to ask you.' She put the gooseberries down.

'When we move to the permanent library, I should like you to come and work for me, as a full-time library assistant in the children's department.'

'Like a library boy?'

'More of an apprentice. I can't offer you much money I'm afraid, but it's a start.'

'But I ain't educated.'

'You're library educated and that makes you even more suitable.'

'How would I learn?'

'Sitting next to Nelly initially . . .' she replied, then seeing his confusion. 'You know, by shadowing me. Then in time we'll find a way to get you your library diploma. If that's what you should want.'

Ruby could see him turning the prospect over in his agile mind.

'Me mum would have to approve it.'

'Of course. I'll ask her myself. This isn't charity. I really do need someone like you, Sparrow, to help kids round here understand what reading can do.'

He nodded slowly.

'I'm going to introduce comics into the library,' Clara continued, 'and I'd need you to choose a good selection.'

His face came alive.

'Why didn't you say? In that case . . . When do I start?'

'Oh, terrific, I'm so happy!'

'And I'm sorry too, miss.'

'Whatever for?'

'For calling you a coward.'

'You were right.'

She went to hug him, then clearly thought better of it.

'Would you take that copy of *The Secret Garden*?' she asked hopefully. 'I still have it.'

'I reckon.'

'Good, I'll drop it by yours later. Why don't you come on in? There's a brand-new copy of *Treasure Island* that's been donated by a girl called Dawn from Toronto. I saved it especially for you. I thought you could write back?'

He hesitated. Ruby knew he wasn't as confident with his writing as he was with his reading.

'I'll read over it afterwards if you like?' Clara offered and he nodded, took a pencil and flopped down next to his pal Ronnie. Without further ceremony, Sparrow was back in the fold.

Storytime galloped by. Tubby's favourite *The Family from One End Street* was dusted down, and a chapter entitled 'The Gang of the Black Hand' received a raucous reception.

Ruby watched Clara in admiration as she hammed it up for all she was worth. As she recounted the adventures of little Jim Ruggles stowing away in a drainpipe on board a barge, you could almost see the hatching of plans in Ronnie and Sparrow's mind.

Little Dolly was so overcome with excitement when it was revealed he'd only gone and ended up in France, she was sick on the floor, which seemed like a timely place to stop.

'Fanks Clara!' chorused fifty or so voices.

'Who wants to visit the horror room, one last time?' yelled Ronnie, and suddenly there was a mass exodus from the library.

'You didn't hear that, did you?' Sparrow asked as he turned to follow.

'Didn't hear what?' Clara replied with a wink.

'You're all right, you are,' he grinned, turning and running in search of one last underground adventure.

'Hi, Jimmy Nacko, one, two, three . . . Obobe, Obebe-all-y-over!'

Sparrow hollered the old rhyme before he leapt onto Ronnie's back and they dive-bombed up the platform, arms outstretched like Spitfires.

Ruby and Clara watched them machine gunning their way back down the platform, their rat-a-tat-tats reverberating up the tunnel. Ruby knew the memories of living underground would linger long for these children. The games of kiss chase, the tantalising fear of the horror room, tap dancing in the theatre, stories in the library . . . All would stamp a deep and lasting impression on them.

Ruby caught a strange waft of something marshy, mingled with carbolic and sick.

'Tell you what though, I won't miss the stink down here.'

They were still laughing when Mr Pepper and Mrs Chumbley made an appearance, flushed with excitement from exchanging their wedding vows.

'Please don't be cross,' said Mrs Chumbley, 'but it didn't feel right to make a big hullabaloo.'

'Yes, it seemed more respectful to Billy to just sneak off and do it quietly,' Mr Pepper said.

At the mention of Billy, Clara's smile slipped.

'We're just off now to visit him and do a little reading,' Mr Pepper added.

'That's kind, thank you. I'm going tomorrow.'

'With us,' said Marie, appearing at the counter.

'Yes, Clara is refusing to let us see Billy,' Beatty chipped in. 'She's treating me like a silly child, which I am not!'

Clara looked to Mr Pepper despairingly.

'Mr Pepper, help me out here. Please tell the girls it's not appropriate for them to see Billy just yet. They've been through such a lot.'

'Clara, my dear. Children are more robust than we give them credit for.'

'See, told you!' Beatty said.

Ruby saw Clara wrestling with conflicting emotions and realised she had probably only shared a fraction of the challenges she was having with Beatty.

'I still don't know,' Clara continued. 'The doctor said we really need to avoid any difficult situations.'

Beatty slammed her library book down on the counter, making them all jump.

'For pity's sake. We fled our home, my mother was killed, my father's missing and Marie and I were buried alive.'

She stared at Clara, her eyes burning with rage. 'How can you say something as ludicrous as that?'

'I didn't mean that, Beatty. I just want to protect you both,' Clara said, reaching out to touch her arm. Beatty shook her off angrily.

'We don't need protecting by you, you're not our mother.'

She ran from the library.

'I'm afraid that until we know the fate of the girls' father, you will face some difficult times,' Mr Pepper said quietly.

Miss Moses from the Brady Club popped her head round the door, interrupting the conversation.

'There you are Clara,' she said, bustling in and unpinning her hat.

'I'm glad you came in Miss Moses,' Clara replied. 'I was going to come and see you about enrolling the girls in the Brady Club.'

'That will have to wait,' the older lady said, her face grave. 'I have news. We need to talk alone urgently.'

'We'll leave you to it,' said Mrs Chumbley discreetly. 'We ought to be pushing off if we're to make visiting hours.'

'I'll make myself scarce too,' said Ruby.

'No,' said Clara, gripping her hand. 'Please stay. I need you here.'

Without a word, Miss Moses motioned to them to sit in the reading room.

'It's their father isn't it,' Clara blurted. 'He's dead isn't he. Good grief. How will I break this news on top of Billy?'

'Calm down my dear,' Miss Moses replied. 'The news does concern their father, but he's alive, Clara.'

'He's been found!' she exclaimed.

Miss Moses slid a letter across the table.

'This arrived at the Brady Club. It's from a Mrs Moisan in Jersey.'

Clara and Ruby stared at the sliver of paper like it was a hand grenade.

'Apparently, she's been desperately searching for her nieces via the Red Cross. Then she picked up the *Evening Post* and could she believe her eyes, but there they were on the front page, an article talking about the heroic rescue of two girls evacuated from Jersey. She wrote to the club. It was mentioned within the article, you see, and she hoped we might know of their whereabouts. She only knew they had been evacuated to Bethnal Green, but since the Blitz and the death of her sister, she'd lost all trace of the girls' whereabouts.'

Ruby's heart grew leaden as she looked at Clara's face. She had turned white with shock.

'What else does it say?' asked Ruby.

'She's been out of her mind with worry and would like the girls to come home immediately. Their father was liberated from Belsen camp.'

Miss Moses paused, to let her words sink in.

'He is being repatriated to St Helier. Next month.'

'Well that is news indeed,' Clara said, breathing out slowly.

So there it was then. And just like that, Ruby saw her plaster on the ubiquitous 'stoic' smile.

'I had better go and find the girls and tell them the news. They'll be beside themselves.'

'I'll come too,' Ruby said but Clara shook her head.

'No. I had better do this on my own.'

Ruby watched her and Miss Moses leave the library together and knew her best friend's heart was gently breaking as her dream of motherhood imploded once more.

Change was everywhere that first Friday in peacetime. No sooner had Clara left than Ruby heard a tapping up the tunnels. She knew it was her mum before she even stuck her head round the door. Even her footsteps sounded more confident these days.

'Hello, love. We've all been invited down to Mrs Smart's for a bit of a knees-up. You fancy it?'

'Not really, Mum. I'm done in. You go on and have fun though.'

'Thanks love, I will. There's a chop under a tea towel on the range. Don't wait up. Ta-ra.'

She turned back.

'Ooh, love, I meant to say. Mr Rosenberg, the foreman down at Rego's, has offered me piece work on the machines. It'll mean regular wages and, best of all, I won't be on my hands and knees all day.'

'That's wonderful news, Mum!'

'Isn't it. Especially now this little one's making herself felt.'

She patted her tummy.

'How do you know it's a girl?'

'Trust me, it's a girl. I'm thinking of calling her Amber Bella.'

'That's pretty, Mum.'

'Do you think your big sister would approve?'

Ruby leant over and kissed her mum's cheek.

'She'd be tickled pink.'

'I miss her.'

'Me too . . . Now go on, shoo!'

Netty hurried off, the air around her just that bit lighter. She had suffered for years, never knowing when or where the next fist or boot would come from, but Ruby knew the mental abuse had left a far more profound indent. Her mother's peace had been hard won.

Without thinking, she pulled out a bottle of gin from behind *The Art of Homemaking*.

Tucked away inside were Beatty's letters to her father,

written in hope and before the knowledge of the camps. Ruby had queued along with so many others to get into the Troxy to watch the Pathé news footage of British troops entering Bergen-Belsen. It was snatches of an unimaginable hell.

What unspeakable horrors had Mr Kolsky endured?

Ruby took a sharp swig of her gin, and suddenly felt the same burning rage that had led Sparrow to pick up a knife and seek out a German. She thought of the families pulled from the crater at Hughes Mansions. The papers had finally published their names. Good Jewish families, many of whom had been library regulars.

She put the glass down, her hand trembling. The road ahead was complex and impossibly tangled. Ruby had to remain clear-headed, not pickling in toxic rage. The problem was, drink was the only thing that softened the edges, her little treat. With a Herculean effort, she forced herself to tip the gin back into the bottle.

She walked around the library, straightening chairs and clearing away newspapers, when she heard a noise outside. Heavy footsteps moving with purpose up the platform.

'Mum, that you?' she called, even though she knew it wasn't.

The Underground was pretty much deserted by this hour, apart from the council security men employed to patrol the tunnels and stop looters.

She picked up the gin bottle and crept to the door, her heart drumming as she remembered the night Victor broke in.

'Hello?' Her voice echoed into the void of darkness. The

tracks where the theatre had stood were solid tunnels of black. Dust kicked up from the removals shrouded the air.

A tall figure seemed to loom out of nowhere and Ruby gasped, raising the bottle over her head.

'One more step, pal, and you'll be wearing this.'

'Ruby, it's me!' The man took a sudden step back, his arms held up in surrender.

Ruby's pulse was galloping.

'Eddie!'

Carefully, he took the gin bottle from her.

He grinned. 'Is that any way to greet a man who's crossed the Atlantic to see you?'

'W-what in the hell are you doing here?' she stammered.

'Pour me a glass and I'll tell you.'

Ten minutes later, Ruby had just about recovered her composure, but she couldn't keep her eyes off the man sitting opposite her in the library.

He was still the same old handsome Eddie she'd last seen tumbling naked out of bed in a Soho hotel room, but there was a weariness around his eyes. A man who perhaps had seen too much. He certainly didn't look twenty-one anymore.

'So, how are you?' she asked in disbelief.

'I won't be running any races anytime soon, but I can't complain. So, did you get the books I sent.'

'Oh my God, Eddie! I'm so sorry, I meant to write and thank you for those, but well, it's been . . .'

She stared at the patched-up library door and tapped the side of her glass.

'My stepfather died.'

'I'm so sorry.'

'Don't be. He was a grade-A shit.'

'Oh . . .'

'Oh Eddie, that's no excuse though, I'm sorry. It was so kind of you to send all those books.'

She grinned.

'You made a lot of women very happy.'

'It's not the books I care about actually. It was the question I asked you in the letter.'

'The question?'

He smiled at her so tenderly, something inside her seemed to fold.

'I asked you to marry me.'

She felt like she couldn't breathe.

'Oh Eddie, why do you want to marry me, really? I'm flattered and all, but well . . .' she trailed off, thinking of the tiny thorns that had embedded in her heart.

My big sister crushed and tangled on a damp stairwell. My mother's broken teeth. That smoking crater. And let's be honest here Ruby, your drinking.

'I'm not GI bride material,' she insisted, searching for the right adjective and failing. 'I'm tired.'

'I'm not surprised,' he said softly. 'Strikes me you've spent the last two years punishing yourself for something that wasn't your fault . . .'

He pulled his chair closer to hers and curled his fingers round the soft skin at the nape of her neck. Then he leaned over, his leather jacket creaking slightly as he pressed his lips softly against hers. He smelt of expensive cologne, of places that whispered fresh air and sea salt.

'You remember what I told you then,' she whispered into the charged space between them.

'How could I forget? I've thought about it most days since.' She felt his body tense. 'I *hated* leaving you alone in that hotel room. I promised myself that if I survived the war I would come back and tell you how astonishingly brave and strong I think you are. Some soldiers haven't experienced half of what you have.'

She closed her eyes. He just didn't get it.

'I'm not strong. I'm bloody shattered.'

'Hell, we're all tired, aren't we Ruby? The whole goddamn world.' He took her face, kissed her forehead, then trailed kisses down her cheek until he found her mouth. She felt her resolve falling away like petals from a flower.

'But I refuse to spend my life in regret.' He searched her face. 'I think our survival, the fact that we are here, when millions no longer are, means that we have a moral duty to live our lives.'

She thought of her aching heart and its hundreds of little lacerations. One more thorn and she might bleed to death.

'You can't stay down here forever in this underground library, Ruby,' he said astutely. 'Sooner or later, you're going to have to step up there, into this new world.'

'But . . . But this is madness! Where would we live?'

'Details.' He shrugged. 'Bethnal Green. Brooklyn. I don't care.'

'And what would I do in America? I'm too mouthy, I talk too loud and I'm too opinionated.'

'You'll fit right in!'

'But . . . But I'm a library assistant.'

He started to laugh.

'We have libraries in America, Ruby, lots of them.'

She crossed her arms.

'Very well. I'm totally unsuitable. In fact, I ought to be put in a museum display cabinet, labelled, *Fallen wartime woman*!'

He shrugged.

'Who wants to marry a suitable woman?'

'I smoke and swear too much.'

'Me too.'

'When I get drunk, I tell really filthy jokes.'

'I look forward to hearing them.'

Her mind scrambled for anything that might put him off.

'I carry a bleedin' knuckle-duster in my handbag for goodness' sake.'

Here he did look a little surprised. 'I'm sure you've got your reasons.'

She uncrossed her arms and threw them in the air.

'Why me?'

'Because, Ruby Munroe, I've never met anyone quite as smart or beautiful as you. And you make me laugh. After you, anyone else would be half measures.' He smiled and it seemed to take up his whole face. 'And because the heart wants what it wants.'

And finally, Ruby ran out of questions.

'So, come on then,' he asked. 'What's your answer?'

She automatically reached for her glass but stopped herself. She wouldn't find the answer there.

'Can you give me until the morning?'

'Take as long as you need,' he said, leaning back with a smile. 'But I ought to warn you, I'm not sailing back without you.'

'Cocky sod, ain't you?'

He drained his glass and stood up.

'Nope. Just head over heels in love with you, Ruby Munroe. I'll never meet anyone like you as long as I live and I don't intend to waste my time trying.'

He took her chin and gently tilted it up until she was forced to look into his eyes.

'I love you Ruby.'

He stroked her cheek, his fingers warm and soft on her flesh.

'I know you're scared, even though you pretend not to be, but I promise you this. You'll *never* have to pretend with me.'

He kissed her slowly and drew back, his lips stained red.

'I'm staying at Rainbow Corner in Piccadilly. Come find me there.'

And then he was gone, his footsteps echoing up the deserted platform.

Ruby locked up and walked up the escalators slowly. When she reached the stairway out of the Tube, she trod on each of the nineteen steps up, counting the reasons why she couldn't leave with every breath. *Clara needs me. Mum needs me.* Then a nastier thought. *You don't deserve him.*

Fear trailed down her spine like a bony finger. It was

happening again, the unbearable pressure on her chest, the racing heart. The darkness seemed to press in on her, as thick and hot as soup. She saw bodies tumbling all around her, a flash of red tangled hair, waxy crushed limbs.

'STOP! GO BACK!' she screamed as her legs buckled under her. She held onto the rough concrete step, gasping for breath. She fumbled in the darkness until her hand found the central stair rail that would have saved Bella's life.

She forced herself to sit very still, holding in the scream that she felt might burst out of her like a phantom, until it occurred to her. She had never really exhaled properly or allowed herself to acknowledge the gaping hole her brilliant sister had left in her life. She'd had no choice but to swallow her pain, paint on a red patriotic smile and drown her feelings with jam jars of gin. But the war was over, and her grief felt like a fall with no end. And now here was this beautiful man offering her a chance of happiness and the trouble was, she didn't know if she could do it. Ruby cried helplessly, her sobs tearing through the darkness.

'Rubes? Is that you?'

'Cla,' she whispered. 'What are you doing here?'

'I told the girls the news.' She frowned and sat down next to her on the step. 'They're ecstatic and terrified. Marie's asleep now but Beatty's totally pushed me away. She wants to be on her own. I feel like I've lost her already . . .' She broke off, touching her hand to Ruby's tear-stained face.

'Rubes. Are you're crying? What's happened?'

Ruby told her everything between sobs. Eddie's sudden reappearance, his marriage proposal, her fears of stagnating in the East End and turning out a bitter drunken train wreck like Victor.

'But I won't leave you, Cla, I promise. I'll be here every step of the way with you.'

Clara drew back, a funny smile on her face.

'Oh sweetheart. All this time you've been focused on looking after everyone else around you. Me, your mum, that we haven't stopped to see what it is that *you* really need.'

'And what's that?'

'Love,' Clara replied. 'Sounds to me like you've got a shot at happiness with a man who adores you. For goodness' sake Rubes, he's travelled from America to see you!'

'But what about Mum, the baby and Bella?'

'Your mum has a small army of women to help her when the baby comes! Besides, she's stronger than you think . . . you have that same strength running in your own veins.' Her voice softened. 'And Bella has gone. You can take your memories of her with you wherever you go.'

'But *you* need me,' she worried, picking at a bit of flaking polish on her nail. 'Especially with the girls going and Billy still so sick.'

'Oh sweetheart, I have to face some uncomfortable facts. Billy's been in a coma for six weeks now. The doctors aren't sure if he'll ever come round and if he does, how much of the man he was before will be left . . .' she broke off, breathed out deeply.

'You can't put your life on hold for us. Me and your mum'll be just fine. It's time to see who the real Ruby Munroe is.' She grinned and nudged her shoulder. 'God help us!'

Ruby smiled at last and realised with an ache how much she had come to depend on her friend. Hadn't her strength always come from the solidity of their friendship?

Clara hesitated. 'I think it's time to let Bella rest in peace, don't you?'

Involuntarily, Ruby held her breath again as she pondered the question. They both stared down into the inky depths of the dark staircase. And then something so extraordinary happened, that had Clara not been there to see it too, Ruby would have sworn it was a trick of her imagination. A whisper of black curled its way up the steps like smoke and coiled its way around their ankles, purring seductively. Ruby jumped.

'Library Cat!' Clara exclaimed.

'As I live and breathe, he's back again,' Ruby murmured.

They hadn't seen the black cat for months, not since he'd vanished in disgust after Pinkerton-Smythe took over the library.

'I'm not really one for portents,' Clara said. 'But this little cat seems to turn up just when we need him most.'

He leapt into Ruby's lap and she buried her face in his fur, drawing comfort from his delicious warmth.

'Where have you been boy?' she murmured.

In the darkness she caught the intoxicating scent of lavender from his fur, Bella's favourite, and Ruby felt her sister's warm presence as powerfully as if she was standing

right behind her on the steps. Clara was right. She couldn't
stay incarcerated in the past. What had happened on this
staircase was unspeakably horrific but she had to keep
moving forward, to live alongside her grief. Otherwise,
what? She thought of prickly Maud, drinking herself
into a sodden stupor in the Salmon and Ball every night
and poor Sarah, rumoured to be in an asylum receiving
'treatment'.

She reached out and hugged Clara as tight as she could
and their tears mingled together, Library Cat a small
warm bundle of fur nestled between them. Ruby felt
Clara's deep well of compassion and strength ripple
through her. Her friend was extraordinary, perhaps she
could be too?

Ruby pulled back and gently handed the cat to Clara.

'Where are you going?' Clara asked.

'I'm going to see Eddie before I change my mind.'

Two bus rides later, Ruby jumped off at Piccadilly Circus
and started running in the direction of the American Red
Cross club, her heart beating a tattoo in her chest. It began
to rain heavily. Soon her blouse was clinging to her and
her headscarf was soaked through.

'Oh bugger,' she muttered as the rain turned into a
deluge. Why hadn't she thought this through, or brought
an umbrella?

The wet pavements shimmered with neon lights. Couples
dashed past, shrieking with laughter, shielding themselves
from the sudden outburst under newspapers.

Ruby's feet slid around in her wet high heels, so much

so that as she flew across the roundabout she nearly fell out of them.

'Oh buggery bugger.' Taking off her shoes she ran in her stockinged feet through the wet Soho streets. With her head down she barely noticed him until she flew into him with a sodden thump.

'Ruby . . .'

'Eddie . . .'

'What on earth are you doing?' he asked, eyes full of laughter. 'You're soaking. And where are your shoes?'

'I didn't want to keep you hanging about,' she shivered, rain drumming on her head.

'Well I sure appreciate that, but come on, I think we better get you inside into the dry.'

'No, no I have to talk now,' she babbled. 'If I don't tell you now, I'll lose my nerve. My answer is yes.'

His eyes widened. 'Are you serious?'

Ruby nodded. 'Yes. I want to marry you and live in America.'

She caught a glance of herself in the window of a Lyons tea house. Her lipstick had smudged off and her blonde curls were plastered to her face. 'That's if you still want me. Hell's teeth. I've got a face that'd stop a clock!'

Eddie started to laugh and pulled his coat round her. His delicious scent surrounded her and she felt safe, cocooned in the warmth and strength of him.

'You've never looked so beautiful,' he whispered, his voice soft in her ear as he interlocked his fingers at the small of her back. He went to kiss her, but she pulled back.

'And I won't be rushed,' she added. 'I have to go to the Channel Islands with Clara and spend some time with my mum. My terms.'

'I'll wait for as long as it takes,' he promised. 'You're the boss, baby!'

'Are you sure you want to marry me?'

'Yes, now will you shut up and let me kiss you?'

And on that wet spring evening of 1945, Eddie bent down and kissed her so tenderly that her shoes slipped from her hands onto the pavement. In that instant, Ruby forgot the rain. In fact, she forgot everything.

25

Clara

During the war, my predecessor was the grandly named Arscott Sabine Harvey Dickinson, who had the unenviable position of chief librarian of St Helier Library during the occupation of Jersey. There was little else for anxious, hungry islanders to do in the blackout hours but read.

Edward Jewell, Chief Librarian of Jersey Library

It was one of those dreamy summer days as the old mail boat slid away from Weymouth Harbour and into the cool waters of the channel. The salt air had a luminous golden feel yet was so crisp you could have taken a bite out of it.

The cobalt sea was dazzling, the sky a brilliant, billowing blue. After years underground it was sensory overload.

'Marie, that's your dinner,' Clara scolded, blinking, as the girl tossed pieces of her cheese sandwich to a noisy scrawl of seagulls.

'I'm too excited to eat,' she replied.

Beatty said nothing, her face an inscrutable mask as she fixed those dark eyes on the bright blue line of the horizon. From the moment Miss Moses had brought round the letter telling them the girls' father was still alive, none of this had felt real to anyone in the little wartime library. Beatty's guilt that had ignited into anger had now given way to an unnerving silence.

In the event, it had taken five weeks before Mr Kolsky had arrived back in St Helier, via a New Zealand troop transport ship. They still knew so little, other than the girls' maternal aunt had requested they be chaperoned home immediately.

The mail boat was just settling into a comfortable chug, when Beatty leapt to her feet.

'The letters! I forgot them!'

'What letters?' Clara asked.

'The ones I wrote and gave to you, Ruby, for safe-keeping.'

'Oh yes,' Ruby said, her face squinting up against the bright sun. 'Never mind, you'll get to see him in person soon enough and tell him how much you've missed him.'

'That's not the point, is it? I wanted to show them to him, to prove that we never forgot him.'

She turned and ran up the boat, scattering passengers who tutted.

'Leave her,' Ruby urged, gripping Clara's hand as she went to follow.

'Can you imagine how she's feeling? She's about to see her home and her family for the first time in five years.'

Clara sighed and settled back on the slatted wooden bench.

'No . . .' she admitted. 'I can't imagine. Added to which

she's coming home without her mother, and we still don't know whether her father knows that.'

The whole world was a question mark right now. The war had tossed millions of people up in the air, like so many pieces of a jigsaw. Now they all had to work out where they slotted back in.

'I don't think I'm sure of anything anymore,' Clara sighed. The complexity of the days that lay ahead seemed to have tied her up in ribbons.

'Everything feels so messy. I feel guilty when I'm not with Billy and when I am with him, I feel guilty for not being with the girls.'

'Well you ain't alone there,' Ruby remarked. 'Women have the monopoly on guilt. Well, bugger guilt I say,' she said loudly over the squabbling seagulls.

'Sssh,' Clara said, 'People are looking.'

'I couldn't give a monkey's. Let 'em stare.'

Finally, Clara laughed.

'That's better,' Ruby grinned.

Clara looked at Ruby's face and a long moment unravelled between them.

After Ruby had accepted his proposal, Eddie had spent every spare moment in the library, arriving each day with armfuls of flowers, or escorting a delighted Netty out for tea and cake. She had never seen her friend so content. She was still the same old Ruby mind you, lacquered to within an inch of her life, with a laugh as dirty as a drain, but there was a softness there, a light perforating the darkness. She would never be 'fixed' or forget what happened on that stairwell, just as Clara would never forget

Duncan and her baby. The war had broken them all, but it was time to piece the jagged edges back together.

'To think,' Ruby said. 'The next time I'll be on a boat trip will be to America!'

'I'm going to miss you so much,' Clara groaned. 'I still can't believe you're actually going.'

'Nor can I,' Ruby said, as she fished out a Black Cat cigarette and lit up. 'Do you think the ravens'll leave the Tower when I leave London?'

'Probably. I'm so proud of you though for taking a chance.'

'I've thought of little else, Cla,' she replied, her headscarf fluttering in the ocean breeze.

She breathed in and sighed out tobacco smoke. 'But you're right. I owe it to Bella. I have to live a life big enough for the both of us.'

'Does this mean you've forgiven yourself for what happened that day?' Clara asked.

'No, but I'm ready to try and that's a start, ain't it?'

'Guilt is a cold and twisted knot,' Clara said softly. 'I ought to know. It takes a long time to unravel, but you'll get there.'

Ruby sighed and lifted her face up to the sun. A lock of her blonde hair slipped free from her headscarf and shone like liquid gold.

'Let's hope so. Being somewhere where no one knows what happened will be good for me I think.'

Clara nodded. 'That makes sense.'

'I've even decided to have a go at that novel when I get to Brooklyn, in the spirit of nothing ventured and all that.'

'Oh Rubes. That's incredible.'

She shrugged. 'Who knows if I can even write a salacious paperback.'

Clara nudged her shoulder. 'Well you've certainly got enough research material.'

'Saucy cow!' Ruby's market jewellery glittered in the sun and that deep, throaty laugh poured out. 'You're right though.' She looked to the horizon. 'God I love him, Cla. I really do. Eddie just gets me. And the queerest thing is, he genuinely seems to love me too, just the way I am.'

The relief Clara felt that her friend had actually met a man who seemingly didn't want to change her was indescribable. She didn't think she could let her go under any other circumstance. After so many years underground, Ruby had earned the right to big skies, she needed a country as bold and bright as she was.

'Who'd have thought it, Ruby Munroe, finally ready to be a wife.'

'The question is though, is America ready for you?' Clara asked.

Ruby threaded her arms around her and they hugged each other tightly. Clara breathed in the scent of her, of tobacco and Phul-Nana. All that was warm and familiar was being torn from her grasp.

'Thanks for coming with me today,' she whispered.

'There's no way I'd let you do this on your own. We've always faced everything together. It's who we are,' Ruby murmured.

Clara saw Ruby's eyes drawn to something over her shoulder and she turned slowly.

The imposing granite cliffs of the north coast of Jersey rose steeply ahead of them, scratching into the cerulean blue of the sky. It was time.

At the harbour, the crowds jostled as they picked their way down the gangplank and onto the quayside. Every so often, someone would dart from the crowd and fly into the arms of a disembarking passenger. The evacuees were still returning to the island they had fled that dark summer's day in 1940.

Scenes of immense emotion played out around them and as Clara felt Marie's hand slip through hers, she felt overwhelmed.

'What does your auntie look like?' she asked.

'So pretty,' Marie replied. 'Lots of very dark wavy hair, and lots of her to cuddle.' She frowned suddenly. 'From what I remember.'

She scanned the crowds, nibbling her bottom lip.

'She'll be with our cousin Rosemary, I expect,' Beatty said, her first proper sentence since they'd left London.

'Beatty! Marie!'

A husky voice sounded behind them and they turned.

'Auntie?' Beatty said. The note of disbelief in her voice wasn't lost on Clara.

'Haven't you both grown?' she exclaimed. 'I swore I wouldn't say that.'

She opened her arms and the girls stepped into them.

As they hugged, Clara studied her curiously. This was not the woman Marie had just described. She was tissue thin and her hair was a silver grey, scooped up high on her head like a meringue.

'So lovely to meet you, Clara,' Mrs Moisan said, over the tops of the girls' heads. 'And you must be Ruby. You must be exhausted and hungry. Come, let's go home.'

They followed the crowds leaving the quayside. After the bustle of London, the narrow cobbled streets around the harbour felt sleepy and still.

'I'm afraid we shall have to go shanks' pony, as your Churchill would say. It's not far from here to Havre des Pas where I live.'

'Where's your car, Auntie?' Beatty asked.

She turned to Ruby and Clara with a note of pride. 'Auntie was the first woman on the island to drive a brand-new Austin 10.'

'The Germans took it,' she said, with an air of finality.

'And where's Rosemary. Is she at home?' Marie asked, scurrying to keep up with the smart pace her aunt was setting as they took the road that led east.

And here the woman stopped abruptly and dipped her head. 'The Germans took her as well.'

Twenty minutes later, they reached her home, a pretty Victorian seaside villa painted in cream, which sat over a fine sweep of golden sand, like something out of a post-card. The handsome houses and hotels that hugged the bay looked like little frosted cakes.

At the door, Mrs Moisan turned.

'Once I have shown you to your rooms and you've had the chance to wash and change, we'll have tea in the parlour. And then I must share my news. There is so much to tell.'

She touched first Marie's face and then Beatty's, pain swimming in her eyes.

'I know you have been so brave these past five years *m's anges*, but you must promise me to be brave a bit longer.'

She slid her key in the lock, and Ruby and Clara exchanged a look.

Thirty minutes later they gathered in what Clara guessed was her best room. Two brocade-covered mahogany chairs sat by a marble fireplace. The room was long, and the far end had tall picture windows which looked out over the bay. The last of the sun lit up the horizon, a blazing stripe of burnished orange.

The dying rays illuminated a darker patch of carpet.

'That is where the rest of my furniture used to be,' said Mrs Moisan. 'But we had to burn it for firewood last winter.

'And so, girls, I'm afraid you must sit on the floor,' she said and, wordlessly, Beatty and Marie sat cross-legged in front of the small fire. She gestured to Clara and Ruby to take the only seats.

'I'll stand by the fireside.'

'Please no, I'll stand,' protested Clara.

'I wouldn't hear of it,' she said curtly. 'You are my guests.'

She turned to poke some life in the fire and as she did so, Clara could make out the angular blades of her shoulders poking through a thin cream blouse.

'I apologise for the state you find us in. I can assure you we did not dress nor look like this before the war.

'Us islanders are proud people and we have been reduced in all ways imaginable by our . . .' her lips thinned, 'our uninvited guests.'

On the mantel was a framed photo and Clara felt a bolt of recognition. There were three girls standing knee-high in foamy water, in matching polka-dot bathing suits. Mrs Moisan caught her staring.

'This was my sister's favourite photo. Rosemary was a dear child. You could never get her out of that pool, could you girls?'

'Auntie,' Beatty blurted. Long hours of travelling had tired her and she looked close to breaking point. 'Please tell us. What happened to Rosemary, where did the Germans take her and where is our father? And where is Uncle Tim?'

Clara leaned over and placed a hand on her shoulder.

'Give your aunt some time.'

'Please no, it's all right. They deserve to know the whole truth about their family, or what's left of it. I'm so sorry, but Rosemary died . . .' She ran her hand up the mantel-piece and reached for the photograph.

'And I'm afraid I received word that so too has her father, my husband.' A heavy silence pressed down on their heads.

'How?' Beatty asked, her voice so tiny and afraid.

'I'll start at the beginning.'

Clara rose to her feet and gently took hold of Mrs Moisan's arm. She led her to the chair and this time she did not object, sitting down, still clutching the photo in her hand. Clara sat cross-legged on the floor. Instinctively, Marie curled into her lap, wrapping Clara's arms around her like a blanket. Mrs Moisan watched, her gaze missing nothing. She tightened her fingers on the armrest as she began her story.

'When the war broke out, there was little difference in our lives. My husband Tim and I ran this place as a guest house. My sister, the girls' mother, used to come in and help me cook the breakfasts, while their father ran his jewellery business in St Helier.

'But then France was invaded and everything changed.

Your British government decided not to defend us in the event of a German invasion.'

'But why?' Clara asked, ashamed that she knew so little about the fate of the Channel Islands.

'There was no strategic value to defending us and so we were abandoned. At least, that's how it felt to us.'

'So why were the girls and their mother evacuated and yet your family and Mr Kolsky stayed put?' Clara asked.

'Aah,' she sighed, a wry smile on her lips. 'To stay or to go. The question that everyone on this island wrestled with.'

She shrugged. 'For my sister, it was easy. She said from the very beginning that if the Germans got too close, she would take the girls and go to England. We had an auntie in Whitechapel and she felt they'd be safer there.'

'And look how that turned out,' Beatty said, her voice bitter with regret. 'Our auntie had evacuated herself by the time we got there and Mum was killed on the first night of the Blitz. We'd have been better off here.'

'No, you wouldn't,' Mrs Moisan said so sharply, Beatty flinched.

'If I could turn back the clock, Rosemary and I would have run onboard that evacuation boat with you.'

'So, what made you stay?' Ruby asked.

'My husband came from one of the oldest families in Jersey. His roots were too firmly planted.'

She sighed.

'Life is full of choices. Most of them mundane and then one comes along, a choice so devastating, you scarcely know which way to turn. In the finish, I left the decision to my husband.'

She looked down at the photo and ran her thumb gently over her daughter's face.

'Not a day passes when I don't regret it. As for your father, girls, he respected your mother's wish to go, but he sided with Tim. He saw the other men who were taunted as they boarded the evacuation boats, called rats and deserters. He had his pride.'

She shuddered and started to worry at a stray thread on the arm of her chair. 'And yet, as a Jewish man, he was in the very gravest danger of all . . .'

Clara was bursting with questions, but this was Mrs Moisan's story to tell and she could not be rushed.

'At first, the privations were nothing more than irritations.' She waved her hand dismissively. 'The time was changed to be in line with Berlin, and we were issued with identity cards.

'The Germans were courteous. Rosemary couldn't walk down the street without a pat on the head. With her blonde hair, she reminded them of the daughters they'd left behind. But gradually, the veneer slipped.'

She twisted her wedding ring round and round.

'Curfews, blackouts, rationing . . . Our world became smaller and darker.

'This whole area became a military zone. Can you imagine? We risked being shot simply for being on the wrong side of the line after nine p.m. And my God, the neighbours . . .'

She grimaced and Clara couldn't tell if she was about to laugh or cry.

'The whole of the Havre des Pas was a rats' nest of Germans. Directly next door at number 1, Silvertide, was the *Geheime Feldpolizei*, the secret military police.'

'Like the Gestapo, you mean?' Ruby asked.

'Not technically, but the second-in-command at Silvertide was notorious on the island. Heinz Carl Wölfle. Even he called himself "Wolf of the Gestapo" so I'm not sure the distinction was all that clear to anyone. Least of all to my husband and your father, girls, whose arrests he ordered.'

'But why?' Beatty asked.

'1942,' Mrs Moisan announced, ignoring Beatty's question. 'That was the year that everything changed. In the March of that year, the restrictions on Jews were tightened. It was Tim who came up with the idea.'

She gripped the chair.

'He was sitting in this chair when he told me we had no choice but to hide the girls' father here. If he stayed living above his business, it would be only a matter of time before they came knocking.'

'But you were living next door to the secret police!' Ruby exclaimed.

'I know. We reasoned that hidden in plain sight might be so daring as to actually work. It was audacious, but also, in truth, we had little choice. We hid him in the basement and covered the trapdoor with a rag rug. He only came out after dark when the blackout blinds went up, and we talked in whispers.

'Any Jews left on the island by this stage were in hiding, but an empty belly can make informers of people you once counted as friends. We became an island of secrets and spies.

'Who could you trust? Who was resisting, who was collaborating?'

Her delivery was cold, as if the occupation had sterilised her emotions.

'The Germans made political prisoners of everyone. There was a steady stream of people marching next door for "a little chat with the Wolf".'

Mrs Moisan closed her eyes. 'It was a Saturday in June. I'd been to the market and I ended up in a fight with Barbara Vibert, my old hairdresser. I got the last stinking cabbage at the market and she was so cross. My coat was ripped in the struggle.'

'Over a cabbage?' Ruby asked.

Her eyes snapped open. 'Have you ever gone a day without food?'

'Sorry,' Ruby mumbled.

'I could see how angry Barbara was. After we fought, she turned to walk away, but at the last minute, she stopped.

'"I haven't seen your brother-in-law Mr Kolsky for some time," she told me. That was all, but the warning was implicit.'

In the darkness of the room, the tension was almost unbearable.

'They came just before dawn the next morning. Wolf of the Gestapo with two of his men. It didn't take them long to find the door to the basement. They arrested Michael and my husband.'

She paused, lost in the moment.

'It's funny, you know. There was no violence. Wolf was smartly dressed; you might have mistaken him for an insurance salesman.'

'But weren't you terrified?' Ruby asked.

'Oh yes. I was under no illusions that, in time, they would return for us. I had helped to hide a Jew under their noses, there was no way that would pass.'

'So, what did you do?' Clara asked, feeling her insides tighten.

'I had to think fast. I ran to the only person I trusted. Dr Noel McKinstry. I'd heard he helped people in trouble.'

'But how did you know you could trust him?' Ruby asked.

'I'd got to know him well over the course of the war. Rosemary had diabetes, you see, and he always went to great lengths to ensure she had insulin supplies. Straight away, he wrote a letter to the German authorities, informing them that Rosemary and I had tuberculosis. He even switched medical samples.

'The exemption letter did the job. The Germans were terrified of TB, you see, so we were left alone.'

'But it was too late for your husband and Mr Kolsky?' Clara asked and Mrs Moisan nodded.

'Michael was shipped out to the continent two days

later. My husband was deported a few weeks after that as part of a group of twenty Jersey political prisoners. Two from my family went and only one came home.'

'H-how?' Clara asked shakily.

'The girls' father was liberated from Belsen. I must warn you, girls, he is very sick and in the sanitorium in St Helier. But he is alive.'

Beatty was weeping openly and Clara wanted to scoop her into her arms and shield her from this pain.

'My husband was moved about to various French prisons, but the Allied advance meant he eventually ended up pushed further east to Auschwitz-Birkenau concentration camp.'

Finally, she closed her fingers into a fist and pressed it to her mouth. Her expression hollowed Clara out.

'I suppose his death from typhus would have felt like a release, but still I wonder, how did my husband, such a gentle man, end up dying in that place?'

'And Rosemary?' Clara ventured. 'I don't understand, if you escaped arrest, how did she die?'

For a long time, Mrs Moisan stared at the floor as if searching for something.

'She may not have died in a concentration camp,' she said eventually, 'but believe me, she was every bit as much a victim of the Third Reich as her father.

'By the winter of 1944, all insulin supplies had run out and she was gravely ill. There was great relief when Dr McKinstry heard of a consignment from France and he himself rushed down to the port. But when he got there, the container was empty.'

She swallowed and reached for a glass of water by her foot, taking a shaky sip.

'Insulin reached a high price on the black market. Rosemary slipped into a diabetic coma and died. She never lived to hear of her father's death and, for that at least, I am grateful.'

Her eyes were horrifyingly blank.

'Why did I not go to England when I had the chance? I'm a foolish woman and I've paid the very highest price imaginable. They say the heart breaks, but mine . . .' She touched her chest lightly. 'Mine keeps on stubbornly beating.'

Marie slipped off Clara's lap and went to her aunt, wordlessly threading her arms around her neck. At her touch, Mrs Moisan shuddered, as if she'd forgotten what it felt like to be hugged by a child and began to weep.

For a long time, they sat there, digesting the complicated strands of this devastating story.

'Beatty, please fetch me something from the top drawer of the sideboard over there,' Mrs Moisan said at last.

Beatty rose shakily and pulled out a bundle of Red Cross messages.

'When Wolf and his men were searching the top of the house, Rosemary slipped down to the basement and your father gave her these.'

'What are they?' Clara asked.

'Our messages to our father,' said Beatty, staring at them in disbelief.

'He kept every single one. He clung to the knowledge that you were safe.'

She smiled and a flicker of light returned to her eyes.

'He was so proud that his girls had joined an underground library. "My clever little bookworms", he used to say.

'Rosemary managed to hide them under her chess set. He was terrified that if they got into Nazi hands, they would know where you were.'

'Your daughter was incredibly courageous,' Ruby said.

Mrs Moisan nodded. 'She was.' She kissed the top of Marie's head. 'Now girls, I think you need to rest, for tomorrow we will visit your father.'

The next morning when Clara came downstairs Mrs Moisan was back to her usual brisk efficiency, her emotion of the previous evening bolted back in place.

She was reading a copy of the *Evening Post* while Beatty and Marie tucked into bread and jam.

'Do sit down. I must say, this is my small joy reading a paper that is no longer censored.' She lifted the teapot and began to pour.

'This might be of interest to you, Clara, being a librarian. Himmler's private library, filled with books stolen from all over Europe, has been found in a village. Near the library they found a special book crematorium to burn books that were unwanted in Germany.'

A book crematorium?

'Let's hope they can salvage some,' she said, gratefully accepting the tea. Clara had a sudden image in her mind, of a colossal ash cloud hovering over Europe. She blinked as the steam from the tea rose into her eyes and she felt tears gathering.

'I apologise if I spoke too frankly to you last night. This has been my reality for so long that I forget it's hard to swallow.'

Clara rested her hand over the older woman's. 'Please, you must never apologise to me. I'm here to support the girls and how can I do that if you sugar-coat the past?'

She nodded. 'Thank you. Now tell me about you. What was your wartime library like?'

'Oh, Auntie, it was the best little library,' said Beatty and they both turned in surprise.

'It's been a sanctuary to me and Marie. I don't know what we would've done without it. And Clara is the best librarian in the whole world.'

'That's absolutely not true,' Clara blustered, 'but thank you, Beatty, for the glowing endorsement.'

She was astonished. This was the most Beatty had spoken to her in weeks. There was a softness in her eyes and Clara knew this was her way of apologising. She could have wept with relief.

'It's true, Auntie,' Beatty insisted. 'When we went missing, she never stopped looking for us, not until she found us and Billy rescued us . . .'

She trailed off when she saw her aunt's expression.

'Gracious, she's been rather more than a librarian to you.'

Clara looked down at her tea and felt uncomfortable. Had she overstepped the mark? In her desperation to be a mother, had she allowed herself to get too close to the girls?

Ruby came into the kitchen, and Clara was grateful for the interruption.

After more tea and bread smeared with something spicy and delicious made from apples and cinnamon called black butter, it was time to leave.

Everyone's nervous chatter dried up as they bundled on coats.

'Your father is at the hospital in St Helier and they are rather strict about visiting times,' Mrs Moisan announced at the door. 'I've arranged to borrow some bikes.'

As she talked, Clara was dimly aware that their appearance was causing a stir. A few neighbours had come out of their homes and were gazing curiously at the girls.

All of a sudden, Mrs Moisan's face froze. An inoffensive-looking woman in her fifties clutching a wicker basket was walking up the road towards them.

'Been to the shops, have we?' Mrs Moisan taunted as she drew level. The woman picked up her pace, refusing to make eye contact. 'I hope you choke on your food, you disgusting bitch!' She spat hard at the woman's feet.

Clara and Ruby exchanged stunned looks.

'May you never know a moment's peace for what you did.' She pointed to the girls, who both looked terrified.

'These are Mr Kolsky's children. Look at them . . .'

The woman started to run.

'Look at their faces, then see if you can live with what you did!' she screamed. The woman turned the corner and vanished from sight.

Clara gently touched Mrs Moisan's back.

'That was her, wasn't it? The woman who informed on you?'

Mrs Moisan nodded, her face a mask of fury.

'I can't believe there haven't been repercussions,' Clara said.

'Apparently, there's no law that provides an appropriate penalty for those who informed on fellow islanders. It was felt the ends of justice would be best served if it was left to the people to ostracise those who were guilty of collaboration.'

Clara's mouth fell open. The whole thing had more than a whiff of the Wild West about it to her.

'And so I am simply supposed to move on, like she has.'

Mrs Moisan kicked off her bike stand and began to cycle up the blustery seafront, her back rigid.

The dreadful encounter hung like a dark cloud over them as they pedalled through St Helier. The streets were busier today, shops were filled with meat and vegetables and Clara even spotted a sweet shop doing a roaring trade.

'Your British Force 135 are doing a wonderful job of clearing up the German's mess and getting our economy back on its feet,' Mrs Moisan remarked as they looked at the queues of chattering housewives.

It wasn't until they paused at traffic lights that Clara saw a visible sign that the Nazis had left their mark: a large black Swastika painted on the side of a house in tar.

'Jerrybag,' Mrs Moisan sniffed. 'When a woman was caught fraternising with a German, her home was marked.'

Ruby, Clara and the girls stared, intrigued, at the branding.

'Please do not stare,' Mrs Moisan said. 'Believe me when I say, there were a great many more acts of resistance on this island than collaboration.'

Her eyes shone defiantly in the bright morning sunshine.

'Those who lay down with the enemy are outnumbered by those who subverted them.'

The traffic moved on and she cycled off smartly.

Ten minutes later they pulled up outside a forbidding Victorian building, rising behind a solid granite wall.

'Here we are,' Mrs Moisan said.

As they stepped inside the hospital, Clara's head was still mired in the murky pool of retribution and anger that clearly still washed over the beleaguered islanders and the impossible situations they had faced and continued to face.

A doctor and a nurse were sent to greet them.

'Good morning, Beatty and Marie.' The doctor spoke warmly to the girls. 'Before we go and see your father, I must speak with your family.'

Clara's heart thumped as she followed Mrs Moisan and the doctor down a long corridor into his office.

Once seated, he pulled out a file.

'Mr Kolsky is an extremely sick man. He is severely malnourished and suffered with septicaemia, possibly from food poisoning or dirty water . . .'

He trailed off and tapped his pen against his thumb.

'All the physical ailments are being treated and we are seeing an improvement in those conditions.'

'But?' said Mrs Moisan warily.

'It's his mind I fear for. The septicaemia, or his experiences, or both, have led to a perturbing unbalance that will require at least another six months of convalescence here and intense psychiatric treatment.'

Clara's heart was beating so fast, she was surprised no one else could hear it.

'What were his experiences?' said Mrs Moisan. 'Speak plainly.'

'Well, there will be a report gathered in the fullness of time, the horrors are still unravelling. But I understand that in Mr Kolsky's case, it wasn't so much the length of time he spent at Belsen, but rather the intensity of the experience, which has led to this unbalance . . .' he wavered. 'How could I put this to ladies?'

'For pity's sake,' Mrs Moisan snapped, 'the war was many things, but it was not discriminatory. It meted out its brutality to both sexes. We are women. We can take the truth.'

'Very well. By the time Mr Kolsky arrived, the camp authorities were trying to conceal all evidence of their crimes before the advancing Allied Armies arrived.

'Many prisoners were forced to leave, marched to their deaths. But Mr Kolsky remained. It was his job, I understand, alongside many others, to dispose of the dead. For the three days prior to the liberation of Belsen, he was forced to drag the dead into burial pits. He was whipped and beaten until he had dragged many thousands into ghastly mass graves.'

'Go on,' Mrs Moisan ordered calmly. A vein flickered in her temple.

'I'll leave to your imagination how unspeakable it must have been to wade through corpses, some of whom had suffered cannibalism.'

A raw silence as they digested this news.

'What does that do to a man?' Clara breathed.

'He appears to be suffering a complete loss of memory of his pre-war life. We are hopeful that seeing his daughters may help to trigger some of those memories.'

Mrs Moisan turned to Clara.

'This will be so hard for the girls. This is why I wanted you to come here today. They need someone whom they have come to trust.'

Clara wanted to run from this small room with its cloying smell of carbolic, but Mrs Moisan was right. The girls needed their father back, and he needed them.

She nodded as the doctor rose to his feet.

'Shall we?'

By the time they reached the girls, who were sitting by the nurses' station, Clara's insides were tightly coiled.

'Now, girls,' said the doctor gently, crouching down to speak to them, 'your father is convalescing in his own room. The last time you saw him, he was forty-four years old, but I must warn you, he looks much older now. This is because of what he experienced in the camps. He will not look or act like the father you remembered back in 1940.

'Seeing you both will be an important step in his recovery, but if you don't feel ready, or you need more time . . .'

'We're ready,' Beatty insisted.

'Very well,' said the doctor. 'But please, it's very important you don't mention the camp at all.'

As they made their way along a maze of corridors, Clara held both the girls' hands, felt their apprehension snake up her arms and into her heart.

A door opened and suddenly they were in a bright white

room. At the centre of the room, propped up in bed with pillows, lay a very old man.

Clara felt her breath catch in her throat. He was a skeleton with skin draped over it. He looked closer to eighty than forty.

His hair was white and stood up in tufts like clumps of dandelions, and his skin had an odd yellow tone.

'Mr Kolsky,' said the doctor, softly. 'I have some special visitors for you. It's your daughters, Marie and Beatrice. They have been in England and now they have come home.'

It took him a while to adjust his gaze as slowly he turned to stare at them. His eyes were so rheumy, he struggled to focus. Clara released her grip on the girls' hands, but Marie refused to let go.

A slow light of recognition dawned on Mr Kolsky's face. His fingers inched slowly along the bedsheet as Beatty took a tentative step towards her father.

She was the first to speak, her expression so full of love.

'Papa, it's me . . .' Gently she took his hand in hers. 'It's me. Oh, Papa.'

'Come into the light where I can see you,' he whispered.

She moved forward again, and he lifted her hand to his cheek. All at once, he seemed to shudder, a spasm passing over his face.

'Rose . . . My darling Rose, where have you been?'

Beatty's eyes snapped wide open.

'No Papa, it's not Mama, it's me. Beatty, your daughter.'

He shook his head and tightened his grip on her hand.

A storm of emotions passed over his face. Confusion. Anger. Fear.

'Where are our girls?' he trembled. 'What have they done with them?'

He started to shake. 'They must not take them, Rose. You hear me, you must not allow them to take our girls.'

Beatty pulled her hand away and choked back a sob.

He struggled to sit up as she stumbled back.

'Please Rose, you must hide the girls for their safety.'

He was trembling now, trying to get out of the bed, but he was so weak, he could scarcely lift the bedsheet.

The doctor rushed forward and Beatty flung herself into Clara's side.

'I think you had better leave now,' the doctor urged.

As they left the room, they heard Mr Kolsky's fragile voice echo up the corridor.

'Where is my wife? Where are you taking her?'

The nurses guided them to a private room where, for twenty minutes solid, Beatty cried uncontrollably in Clara's arms and Marie sat folded into her side. The door opened softly and the doctor entered.

'As you can see, your father is a very ill man,' the doctor said.

'How can you help him?' Mrs Moisan asked.

'There are no clear answers,' the doctor replied wearily. 'We have never encountered anything like this before.

'Your father's brain is trying to protect him from witnessing such horror.'

'Like a fuse box that's blown, you mean?' Beatty asked.

The doctor smiled sadly. 'That's exactly right. You're a clever girl. But I promise you, my dear, we will do everything in our power to care for your father here, until he can find a way back to himself.'

They left the hospital irrevocably altered by their experiences. The image of his emaciated body would forever remain scorched into Clara's brain.

'I think we need a walk and some fresh air,' Mrs Moisan announced.

'Yes, good idea,' Clara agreed.

'Sorry, I meant just me and the girls,' said Mrs Moisan.

Clara felt as if she'd been struck. 'Oh. Of course. Absolutely. I'll see you back at the house.'

She got on her bike and pedalled as fast as she could, so the girls couldn't see the tears stream down her face. She cycled fast out of St Helier, grateful for the stiff island breezes that dried her tears the moment they fell.

Ruby didn't say a word, just cycled after her, as they headed west, skirting St Aubin's Bay and onto St Brelade's Bay. Fields and beaches scarred with ugly fortifications flashed past, giant concrete monstrosities as impenetrable as Mr Kolsky's mind. Clara had never felt battered by such a maelstrom of emotion.

Finally, exhausted, she stopped when the land ran out at the southwest corner of the island. Clara inhaled at the dramatic beauty of the landscape. The tide was out, and a causeway flanked by black rocks led to a majestic white lighthouse. In the distance she heard a tremendous boom as the ocean battered the land.

'Looks like we've reached the end of the road,' Clara

murmured, dismounting from her bike. 'Feels like an appropriate metaphor.'

Her headscarf had shaken loose and her dark hair whipped around her face. She shivered as the wind picked up, scudding huge silver clouds across the headland.

'I've lost them, haven't I?'

'Oh, Cla,' Ruby sighed, 'do you really think that they were yours to lose, sweetheart?'

'No, I suppose not. I can't stop thinking about Mr Kolsky and Mrs Moisan.'

'Listen, can you do without me?' Ruby asked suddenly. 'I'll meet you back at the house.'

'Where are you going?'

'I promised Stan from the buildings that I'd meet with his uncle who runs a pub down by the docks.'

Clara raised one eyebrow.

'Ruby Munroe. Don't get involved in the black market.'

'No, it's nothing dodgy, he ain't a fence. I just need to pass on a message.'

She leant over and kissed Clara on the cheek.

'See you later.'

Clara wasn't ready to return to the town just yet and she sat down, closed her eyes and listened to the roar of the ocean. She and Ruby were due on the first boat back tomorrow.

She lay back against the cool grass on the clifftop. The wind seemed to whisper stories, the ocean an endless shush. The pounding of jack boots would always be a haunting echo and she wondered how the girls would find their place on this war-torn island, and more importantly, how they would cope with the fragility of their father's mind. She would have to accept that they would need to do it without her.

She stayed there for so long, she must have dozed off because when she looked up, someone had painted the sky.

The sunset was spectacular. Blood orange slipped into indigo. She cycled back slowly, marvelling as the night sky formed a glittering canopy over the low hills, the blackness above salted with stars.

Clara pushed her bicycle along the Havre des Pas and was surprised to find Mrs Moisan waiting on the doorstep for her.

'There you are. I worried you'd got lost. We need to talk.'

Something in her demeanor had changed.

'Come.'

She gripped Clara's elbow. 'Leave the bike here.'

They walked along the promenade, past the grand hotels that bordered the front, until at last she stopped and sat on a bench. She gestured to Clara to sit.

'I've been watching you with the girls. You're the closest thing they have to a mother. I see that now. This morning you asked for total honesty and so . . .'

She looked out to sea.

'I'd like the girls to go home with you. I'm an old woman now, too lost in my grief to give them what they need.'

'But what about their father?' Clara asked.

'They can return on their holidays to see him. He will recover, I hope, and they can be a part of his recovery, but in the short term, the best place is by your side.'

She smiled. It was a beautiful smile and they'd seen so little of it.

'They need your stories, Clara, your books and your library. But mostly your love.'

'What do the girls want?' she asked breathlessly.

'That's why I took them off for a walk. They are trying not to be disloyal, but they want to return with you.'

'Are you sure?'

She nodded.

Clara breathed out slowly.

'I will take such great care of them, and I'll bring them home on every holiday. I love it here. It's such a beautiful island.'

'It was and it will be again. It too needs to recover.'

'You are so resilient.'

A wry smiled flickered at the corner of her mouth.

'So I'm told. But I don't want to be resilient anymore. I'm tired. I just want to live in peace, with my memories.'

The girls and Ruby were waiting for her at the house. One look at their faces told Clara that Mrs Moisan was right.

'Can we come back with you to London?' Beatty asked, scanning her face nervously.

'Of course you can,' she said, laughing and crying all at once as she touched their faces.

They clung to each other for a long time before Beatty pulled back.

'I was so scared you'd say no because I've been beastly to you. I've been so angry about Billy you see, blaming myself and I took it out on the wrong person.'

Clara smiled and kissed her forehead.

'From the little I understand about motherhood, that's part of the job.' She looked from Beatty to Marie. 'I'll be here as long as you both need me. And even when you don't.'

The next morning at the docks, the bright summer sunshine was crystalline, bouncing off the waters as the crowds made their way up the quayside.

Mrs Moisan looked as if an enormous weight had been lifted from her shoulders.

'Come here,' she grinned, pulling the girls into her embrace.

'*J'vos aime bein, èrvénez bétôt,*' she whispered.

As they hugged, it hit Clara the sacrifices she was making for her nieces' happiness. In letting them go back to Bethnal Green, she was giving them a safer way to return.

Over their heads, Clara saw a familiar face.

'That's her,' she whispered, digging Ruby in the ribs.

'Who?'

'Barbara Vibert. The woman who denounced Mrs Moisan.'

She was laden down with luggage as she attempted to haul two suitcases up the gangplank.

Ruby lit a cigarette and regarded her shrewdly through the smoke.

'So she is. At least she won't be around to disturb Mrs Moisan.'

'Ruby,' Clara said, slowly. 'Do you know anything about this?'

She smiled archly, her red lips curling at the corners.

'Search me. Maybe she just fancied a change?'

'Rubes . . . how did you . . . ?' Clara began. 'Actually, do you know what, no, don't tell me.'

Ruby clamped her cigarette between her teeth and began to gather up their bags.

'Come on,' she muttered, 'let's get home. I miss the big smoke.'

Once onboard, the boat engines started up noisily and the air filled with the nervous excitement of new voyages, heavy with the scent of salt and oil.

Up on the deck, the girls waved furiously at their aunt as the boat creaked and slid away from the dock. Soon, they were slicing through the waters towards England. Some stories, Clara reflected as she glanced over at the hunched over figure of Barbara Vibert sitting alone with her back to Jersey's departing shoreline, would always remain too raw and dark. The wounds too deeply sliced. The unfiltered gush of human experience would soon scar over, and wartime survivors would either heal or bury their stories deep.

As the coastline of England hove into view, Beatty rested her head on Clara's shoulder.

'Don't ever give up on your father,' Clara urged.

'I don't intend to,' Beatty replied. 'As long as you don't give up on Billy.'

Beatty stared at her, daring her to look away.

'Very well. We can go and see him, but please don't get your hopes up.'

For a while they sat in silence and Clara grappled with

what to say. How could this girl cope with the uncertainty and complexities of Billy on top of her father? How much trauma could one child reasonably be expected to face?

The gangplank hit the quay with a jolt.

'It's my fault he's in that hospital bed,' Beatty said quietly as she stood up. 'I've already lost one father, I'm not about to lose another.'

26

Ruby

Libraries are still some of the safest and free institutions we have. They are still a statutory service, and local authorities are still required to provide a free public library.

Kathleen Walker, retired librarian

As soon as Ruby opened her eyes, she knew they'd overslept. They hadn't got back from Jersey until late the night before and so as not to disturb her mum, she'd stayed at Clara's. Clara had given her bed to the girls while she waited for a place with two rooms to become available, and so she and Ruby had talked long into the night before falling asleep, curled up in two easy chairs by the fireplace.

Ruby yawned and ran her hand through her rumpled hair. The room was filled with church bells and sunshine.

'Morning sleepy-head,' said Marie, busy stirring a pan of milk over the stove. 'Cocoa?' Beauty sat patiently at her feet, waiting hopefully for any stray morsels to come her way.

'Yes please. How lovely to hear church bells ring again. Where's Beatty?' she asked. 'Is she in the yard?' Ruby gestured to the outdoor lav.

'Oh no. She's gone to see Billy at the hospital,' Marie replied cheerfully.

'Pardon me?' said Ruby.

'She left about an hour ago. Said not to wake you or Clara.'

Instantly, Ruby was wide-awake.

'Cla!' she cried, shaking her awake.

Clara peeled one eye open and sat up stiffly.

'Did someone say tea?'

'No time for that. It's Beatty. She's gone to see Billy at the hospital.'

'Oh my goodness. No, no, no. She can't possibly go on her own. It's not supposed to be this way! I haven't prepared her for the sight of him,' she gibbered. 'But wait, she's only twelve, surely they wouldn't let her visit on her own?'

'This is Beatty we're talking about, Cla.'

Clara sprang out of her chair and forced her feet into a pair of pumps.

'You're right. She's the most determined girl I've ever come across. Come on, we have to go.'

'Cla, sweetheart. Don't you wanna get dressed?' Ruby asked. 'You're still in pyjamas.'

'No time. Come on. And you, Marie, turn that pan off the heat. We have to leave. Now!'

'Why are we running, Clara?' Marie asked as they tore through Barmy Park and past the library, with Beauty running after them yapping in excitement.

'She can't visit Billy on her own.'

Bemused locals on the way to church stopped to stare

at the sight of the librarian pelting through Bethnal Green in a pair of pyjamas, with Ruby, Marie and a small Jack Russell in tow.

'Please God say she's not in there,' Clara panted, her breath ragged as finally they took the hospital steps two at a time, then stopped.

'Beauty!'

Ruby and Clara looked at one another.

'They won't spot her,' Marie said, bundling her under her coat.

At the nurses' station, the matron looked up in alarm.

'Mrs Button, we were about to contact you.'

Clara held up her arms, then pressed a fist into her side to stop a growing stitch.

'I know. I know. I'm so sorry. She's only twelve, I know she seems older and she's had a fearful time lately,' she said between breaths.

'His older daughter's in there with him now if that's who you referring to?'

Ruby's heart plummeted. How could Beatty be so irresponsible and wilful to lie about her age again?

'Oh for goodness sake . . .' Clara snapped.

' . . . Mrs Button, you must listen to what—'

But there was no time to stop and listen. Frantically, Clara pushed open the door to Billy's room, then stopped so abruptly Ruby cannoned into the back of her.

It was too much to take in. Doctors in white coats, and nurses, so many of them, were crowded round his bed Ruby couldn't even see and her heart froze. Had he died?

Clara cried out.

'Beatty. Come away this instant. You mustn't be here, not now.'

The emotion of the past week released like a cork from a bottle and the tears swamped her friend.

'Please, Billy wouldn't want you to see him like this.'

'Clara's right, please come with us sweetheart,' Ruby entreated.

'Billy can speak for himself,' she replied.

The doctors turned to stare and suddenly it was Ruby who was seeing. Really seeing.

'Billy?' she gasped, turning to Clara.

Clara stood rooted to the spot, both hands covering her mouth.

Billy's eye was open, his hands laced through Beatty's. A book lay open on the sheets between them.

'He woke up when I was reading to him,' Beatty said calmly.

'I . . . I just . . . I don't believe it . . .' Clara stammered at last.

Billy looked at her, his weary face full of love.

'Clara. Why are you wearing my pyjamas?' he whispered.

Suddenly the door burst open behind them. Marie and Beauty ran in, the little dog leaping up onto the bed.

'Hello old girl,' he whispered as the dog plastered him with wet kisses.

'This is most unorthodox,' said the matron, bustling in behind them. 'This room needs to be cleared immediately.'

'Leave them,' said the doctor in charge, a tired-looking

medic who had clearly seen too much during the war to be shocked by this. 'This chap's lost enough time.'

And then Clara and the girls were hugging and kissing him as gently as they could, drinking in the miracle of Billy's return. Ruby smiled and then backed silently out of the room, leaving the unconventional little family to their privacy.

She walked home slowly, processing the emotion of the past few days, but there was simply no way to absorb everything she had seen and experienced. Ruby felt as if she'd witnessed the best and worst of humanity, the emotion brimming out of her so overwhelming it felt like she'd swallowed the sun.

Billy had come back to them. The Jersey girls were home and safe. There was only one person with whom Ruby wanted to share all that with, but that would have to wait. First she needed a wash and a strong coffee. A sudden thought occurred to her and it made her mind stumble. Usually in the past, whenever anything happened, be it good or bad, her first thoughts had always turned to drink. She used to mark all milestones with a tipple. The desire was still there, but since Eddie's arrival it was more muted.

She cut through Barmy Park. All around her, summer sun lapped the dusty park, kissing it with a warm syrupy feel. Among the leftover detritus of war, a border of hopeful flowers had pushed their way out under a scrawl of rusted wire and embroidered the grass with bright yellow blooms.

On impulse, she picked a yellow flower and ran to the entrance of Bethnal Green Tube. She placed it on the top stair.

'Love you sis,' she whispered. Clara was right. Her sister was no longer there. She would have to look for her spirit in other places. In the sacrifices of women like Mrs Moisan, Eddie's unquestioning love, in the wonder of Billy's recovery and the sight of sunlight glittering off the new panes of glass in the old bombed library.

'Ruby. You're back!' She turned to see Mrs Chumbley heaving a box of books up the steps from the Tube.

'Miss me?' she grinned. 'Come on, I'll give you a hand.'

'Ruby,' she said gravely. 'Your mum was expecting you last night.'

'Yes, sorry it took us an absolute age to get back from Jersey. You won't believe what's . . .'

'Never mind all that,' she interrupted. 'You have to go home immediately.'

Something about Mrs Chumbley's expression sent a thrust of fear through her. Ruby turned and began to run. She rounded the corner to Russia Lane and pelted into Quinn's Square. The square was still filled with bunting left over from VE day and it fluttered in the morning breeze. She took the steps two at a time and burst in through the door.

Mrs Smart, in fact most of the women on the landing, seemed to be assembled in her tiny kitchen, all busily engaged in various jobs. Incongruously, Eddie was sitting at the table, smoking a cigar. A huge pan of water simmered on the stove.

'Oh Ruby. You're back,' said Mrs Smart in relief. 'Your mother's been blessed.'

Her mind scrambled. Blessed? What did she mean? And

why were so many people gathered in her flat? Usually that only happened when there'd been a death in the buildings.

Ruby felt faint and crashed to her knees. Eddie leapt up.

'No sweetheart,' he soothed, pulling her up. 'You don't understand. Your mother's been blessed with a baby.'

Her mouth opened and then shut.

'Not like you to be lost for words,' Mrs Smart chuckled, turning to Eddie. 'Our Rubes here is the only woman who can go on holiday and come back with a sunburnt tongue.'

'B-but the baby wasn't expected for at least another month,' she managed.

'Well, babies have their own sweet way of doing things,' she replied. 'They come when they're good and ready, not on our timetable. Now less of the dramatics missy. Go on in and meet your little brother.' Mrs Smart gave her a gentle shove in the direction of her mother's bedroom.

The door creaked open and Ruby inhaled. Her mother was propped up in bed. In her arms was a little scrap of a baby, no bigger than a skinned rabbit, swaddled in blankets.

'Hello love. Meet the little 'un. He's tiny, but the midwife's been and she reckons he's healthy.'

'Oh Mum,' Ruby gasped, sinking down on the bed next to her. 'I'm so sorry I wasn't here.'

'S'right love.' Her mum smiled wearily, unable to tear her eyes off the baby's face.

'It all happened so fast. Your Eddie came to take me shopping yesterday. Halfway down Petticoat Lane my waters went.'

Ruby's eyes widened.

'I know. You couldn't write it! Eddie hailed a taxi. First time I'd been in a taxi. It was like something out of the movies. Back home, he ran for the midwife, but it was too late. By the time he came back with one, Mrs Smart had already delivered him on the kitchen floor!'

'Oh Mum, I can't believe it.'

'Nor can I love. Your Eddie's a good 'un and no mistake. If it weren't for his quick thinking, this one would have showed up in the middle of the bleedin' market.'

Finally, Ruby started to laugh.

'I know,' Netty grinned, shaking her head. 'Can you imagine? According to Mrs Smart, Eddie's the hero of the hour. Half of Bethnal Green's already heard the story.'

'He's beautiful, Mum,' Ruby breathed, running her finger down her brother's velvet soft cheek. 'What'll you call him?'

'I think James, after my father. It's funny. I was so set on the baby being a girl, but now I can't imagine why I ever thought that.'

'Things have a habit of not turning out how we expect,' Ruby murmured, realising that she was as transfixed on the baby's face as her mum was.

'You're right there. It felt like a curse when I discovered I was expecting. Now I can't imagine my life without him.'

The baby stirred, his mouth forming a perfect O.

'He's probably after a feed,' Netty said. 'Help us sit up would you love?'

''Course Mum. I'm so sorry I wasn't here. But I won't leave you again. I'll be here all the time to help.'

For the first time, Netty turned her gaze away from the baby.

'You'll do no such thing. There's a fine young man out there who's offering you a good life. Me and this one are in safe hands.'

'But Mum . . .'

'No. I mean it. I'm not saying I won't miss you every single day, but the way I see it is that there's been too much lost, too many lives wasted. You're going to America my girl and that's that.'

Ruby smiled as she helped her mum sit up and plumped the cushions behind her.

'If you're really sure Mum.'

She nodded. 'I'm free now, and I want you to be too.'

And as the sunlight shone through the window on the three of them, the future stretched ahead of them, vast and luminous.

27

Clara

A love of reading and writing shouldn't just be the preserve of the privileged, it's for everybody.

Lisa Roullier and Lena Smith,
Barking and Dagenham Libraries

It was another two weeks before Billy was deemed strong enough for Clara to take him out of the hospital in a wheelchair for a little fresh air. The doctor had warned her to go gently. He had suffered a tremendous trauma and, though the early signs were good, they didn't want to risk anything that could send him into a relapse.

No one knew what had brought him back to them. Time? Or had Beatty's voice reached him in a way that they could never fathom?

It had been at least five days before he could speak in more than one weak sentence, but from the moment he had come back to consciousness, Clara hadn't needed words to know that he knew exactly who she was. She saw it in his expression, in the way he clung to her hand, even when the nurses were changing his dressings or administering medication.

But what he seemed to enjoy most was visits from the

girls, his eyes lighting up as they clattered into the room. His amusement was evident as Beatty scolded Marie for being too rumbustious. He adored those girls, and the promise he'd made to raise them made his recovery seem more logical. Beatty had been right. She shouldn't have underestimated either of them. How much she had to learn about motherhood! Surely if working in the library had taught her anything, it was to expect the unexpected.

She pushed Billy to a little baker's nearby and bought apple strudel before heading to Swedenborg Square. They found a bench facing a small patch of green, lined with rows of handsome eighteenth-century townhouses.

Clara fussed round him, tucking in blankets.

'I know I'm an invalid, but I won't get stronger if you do everything for me.'

'Sorry,' she said, flustered.

In the bright daylight she saw his sandy blond hair was now streaked with grey, his cheekbones gaunt.

'Is it queer?' she asked. 'You left in war and have come out the other side into a world at peace.'

'It was a shock when I discovered they'd disbanded Station 98,' he admitted.

Blackie and Darling had visited yesterday and explained it had already been shut by London County Council and was being turned back to a school again.

'I feel a bit redundant.'

She hesitated, crumbling pastry between her fingers and letting the flakes drift to the floor. The clouds drifted and a sudden burst of sunlight illuminated them. Time seemed to slow.

Be brave, Clara, tell him how you feel.

'Every day that you were in that hospital bed, I swore that if you woke up, I would tell you this,' she blurted. 'I still love you.'

She took his hands in hers, felt the bones of his cold, fragile fingers.

'Outside the Brady Club, you told me you loved me too. Do you remember?'

'Of course I remember,' he replied, squeezing her fingers. 'I've always loved you. I think I loved you before I even met you.'

Clara laughed in relief.

'I think that might be stretching believability.'

'Is it?' He turned to face her, his body moving slowly and painfully. 'The way Duncan described you, so beautiful, so elegant. "Punching above my weight" were his exact words.'

She stared at him. Her eyes wide as her mind stumbled.

'S-sorry, did you just say Duncan?'

He nodded, his gaze holding hers with such intensity.

'You knew my husband?'

'Yes, I knew Duncan,' he confessed. 'The last time I saw him, I made a promise to him that I would watch out for you, make sure you were safe.' Clara saw shame cloud his eyes. 'I think I might well have over-delivered on that promise.'

Clara's mind spun off in a hundred different directions.

'I hadn't intended on falling in love with you, you see, Clara. At first, I just kept an eye on you from a distance, like I'd promised Duncan. It wasn't hard. You were in all the papers for setting up the shelter library.

'But then came the night you were attacked by Victor and I was forced to come out of the shadows, literally. Before he grabbed you, I'd watched you sitting alone in the park after the memorial and I came so close to introducing myself. You looked so lost and alone.'

'My God,' she breathed, remembering the barking of a dog.

'You were in the park with Beauty?'

He nodded.

'I followed you to check you got home safely in the blackout, and that's when I saw Victor.'

Shock stole her voice.

'I don't suppose I would ever had introduced myself were it not for that,' he continued, 'and then every time I came into the library, I fell that bit more in love with you.'

'But . . . But why didn't you just say you knew him?' she managed.

'You told me your husband had been killed in combat . . .' He trailed off. 'I didn't want to put you in a difficult position, or compromise your story, so it seemed easier to say nothing, and then the more time that passed, and the deeper I fell in love with you . . . ' He exhaled. 'The harder it became to admit that I'd known him.'

'Where did you meet?' she asked, feeling a creeping sickness.

'Initially Dunkirk. Then back in England in a field hospital on the south coast.'

'So, you know . . .' She broke off, and suddenly it felt as if someone was stomping on her heart with boots. She felt hot and cold all at once as her whole world tilted.

'That he killed himself? Yes.'

She pressed herself back against the bench and squeezed her fingers around the edge.

'Why didn't you say?' she asked. Her voice sounded distant.

'Because you didn't, and I know how shameful society finds suicide. I felt you come close to telling me that time in the old library, but you held back.'

'I did,' she remembered. 'But I made a promise to my mother-in-law that I'd never reveal the truth of his death. She came up with the story and, by God, she made sure I stuck to it. It sounded so much braver than . . .' The word alone clogged her throat.

'Suicide,' Billy whispered.

'It was hardly the war hero narrative my mother-in-law put about. She felt—' Clara broke off, hardly believing that she was voicing these words out loud. 'She felt the stigma would mean we would all be ostracised.'

Billy nodded.

'It might all have been easier, of course, had I not been expecting his baby. I conceived on his last leave trip before Dunkirk. I always felt that had he known that, things might have turned out differently.'

Billy shook his head.

'I doubt it, Clara. He was not a well man. On the times we sat and talked, I could see that he was suffering deeply.'

And suddenly, it hit Clara that he'd *known* Duncan, had sat and talked with him in his hospital bed before he'd taken the overdose.

'Tell me please, Billy,' she pleaded. 'I want to know everything. The unvarnished truth.'

He scrubbed wearily at his face and the doctor's words came back to her.

'Sorry Billy. This is too soon. I can wait.'

'No. You deserve to know the truth.'

He cleared his throat and suddenly, she felt afraid.

'I was working as a volunteer ambulance driver for the Red Cross in France when we were called to assist during the evacuation of the British Expeditionary Forces in Dunkirk. It was undiluted hell. We were under constant bombardment. It was a case of tending only to those who had a fighting chance and those we could stretcher onto the ships.'

Clara sat frozen on the bench, unable to move, even when the blanket slipped from his lap.

'On the fifth day, we were called to assist a battery on the outskirts of the town. They were under orders to evacuate to the beaches before the advancing German troops arrived.

'But before they could move out, thirty dive-bombers swooped down. We filled our ambulance with the wounded in no time at all.

'But then, out of that abyss I spotted a young soldier carrying a man over his back.

'It was his Commanding Officer, the soldier explained. He had shrapnel in his skull. I could see the man was already dying. I told him there was no room left in the ambulance, but he begged until I agreed.'

'The soldier was Duncan, wasn't it?' she said, heavy with resignation and Billy nodded.

'We'd just squeezed him in when we were dive-bombed again. The red cross on the white circle should have made us off limits, but to my mind it was more of an invitation to attack,' he said bitterly.

He turned to her. 'Your husband threw me into a ditch and shielded me with his body.'

'And people would call him a coward today,' she murmured.

Billy nodded. 'Quite.'

'What happened next?'

'When the bombers passed over, we scrambled out of the ditch.'

He lost his thread and seemed to drift off and Clara felt her heart clench. This was too much, she ought to stop questioning him and yet . . .

After an agonising moment he began again. 'The ambulance was burning. Everyone inside was on fire. All lost. We had no choice but to leave them and make our way to the beaches where we managed to board one of the final boats out.'

Clara closed her eyes against the image.

'Your husband was a hero that day,' Billy explained. 'He tried his hardest to save his CO's life and almost certainly saved mine. But back in Portsmouth, when I went to visit him in hospital where he was receiving treatment for a broken collarbone, he didn't see it that way. He blamed himself for the death of his CO. He said that if only he hadn't insisted he be put in that ambulance, he would still be alive.

'God knows, I tried to explain the odds were already

stacked against him, but he refused to believe me. Kept saying how he had faced the first test of his war and had failed.'

'If only I'd known,' Clara breathed. 'He was a kind, conscientious man. He would do anything for anyone, so it stands to reason I suppose he would see this as a failure.'

'I could tell his mind had snapped,' Billy confessed, 'so I visited him as often as I could.

'On my last visit, before he was discharged to rejoin his unit, he seemed resigned to his own failure. He'd been visited by some army official, been told to pull himself together.'

That phrase again.

'I was being reassigned to East London as the threat of invasion was high. He told me his beautiful wife worked in Bethnal Green as a children's librarian.'

Billy looked at her, hollowed out from the retelling of the story.

'Told me to be a pal and keep an eye out for you. Even showed me a photo of you both on your wedding day, which somehow he'd kept with him all through France.'

Billy smiled weakly.

'I told him he was lucky to have such a knockout wife.' His smile vanished. 'He told me he didn't deserve you.'

'And when did he . . .'

'Two days later. One of the nursing staff told me in secret that he'd broken into the stores, taken some pills. I was crushed. I guessed his trauma had got the better of him.'

Clara sat in silence with the news.

'There's no shame in suicide, Clara,' he said. 'He had the courage of twenty men.'

'I know. I never felt ashamed of him, not once,' she insisted, 'but as the months wore on, it was felt that we ought not to tell anyone how he really died.'

'Does anyone know?' he asked.

She shook her head. 'Apart from my mother and his. Oh, and Ruby of course, I could never keep anything from her.'

Something pricked at her consciousness.

'That day outside the Ambulance Station, my mother-in-law recognised you, didn't she! She had met you.'

Billy exhaled deeply.

'Yes. I met her briefly when she came to visit Duncan, shortly before he took his life.'

'She never told me she went to see him!' Clara exclaimed. 'She must have known how sick he was.' Clara started to shake with the betrayal. 'How . . . how could she have kept it from me? I would have gone too. I could have . . .'

'Clara,' he interrupted her gently. 'No good can come of blaming her. Grief is a complex thing. I suspect layered over the top of hers is misplaced guilt and shame. I can understand that.'

'Y-you?' she stammered. 'What have you to feel ashamed about? Wait! Is this the secret you've been keeping all along, the shame you talked of?'

He nodded.

'I've betrayed your husband and I'm not proud of that. He trusted me to keep an eye out for you, not fall in love with you.'

'Is that why you held back when I kissed you in the library?'

'Trust me, Clara. I had imagined what it would be like to kiss you a thousand times before that. I won't blame you in the slightest if you walked away right now.'

Clara bent down and picked up the blanket and tucked it around his legs. 'And what good would that do?' She took his face in hers and kissed him softly on the lips. 'For then surely we would both be miserable.'

He stared at her, astonished.

'But it's such a complicated mess.'

'No, it's not,' she insisted. 'Actually, for the first time in a long time, it's never felt clearer to me. I see no shame in Duncan's suicide, and I see no shame in loving you either.'

She placed a hand over his heart.

'Don't you see? There are no secrets between us any longer. I need to love you, it's the only way to make meaning of Duncan's death.

'He entrusted you to look out for my future happiness. He saw something in you that made him trust you. And this, *you*, *us*, makes me happy.'

'You truly believe that?' he replied. 'That the concept of us would make him happy?'

'Honestly, I do. The past five years, all that pain and loss, have been excruciating. I need to let go of the past. It's exhausting.'

She held his gaze.

'Aren't you just exhausted by it all?'

He nodded, starting to cry as he let go of the secret he had carried for so long.

They sat that way for some while, Billy silently weeping, until finally he drew in a shaky breath.

'Enough. Clara, will you marry me?'

'I will. On one condition.'

'Anything.'

'You tell me what your favourite book is.'

'Aaah,' he said, smiling through his tears. 'In that regard, it seems Beatty knows me best of all. She was reading it to me when I came round.'

'Beatrix Potter?'

He nodded.

'Talking animals?'

'What can I say? I confess, I find the idea of animals leading secret lives quite compelling,' he joked. 'You sure you still want to marry me?'

'Yes,' she said, laughing. 'Yes, yes, yes!'

The bomb-shattered square in a scruffy corner of London seemed barely big enough to contain all the emotion lodged in Clara's heart.

It was late afternoon by the time she took Billy back to hospital. She began her walk back to Bethnal Green. For the first time in all those long years, houses glowed back, showing off their interiors, families sitting round tables, some with their loved ones, others with only their photographs. Whatever the future held with Beatty and Marie, all the difficulties that undoubtably lay ahead, at least now she could face it with Billy by her side.

Clara paused in Barmy Park and looked at the handsome red brick library, its newly repaired glass dome roof shimmering in the late afternoon sunshine. It stood like a beacon of hope. She was about to go home when she saw smoke drifting through the shadows. A woman with the reddest lips and a fur trimmed scarlet swagger coat strutted her way through the park.

'Ruby Munroe, where do you think you're going?'

'Bleedin' hell Clara, you gave me a fright.'

'Sorry,' she laughed. 'But you do look a bit furtive. What you up to?'

Ruby grinned, composure regained.

'Mrs Chumbley gave me these.' She dangled a set of keys from her fingers. 'The Tube library's getting demolished tomorrow now that all the books have been moved. Fancy a last look?'

'I ought to be getting home to the girls . . . but ten minutes can't hurt.'

They clattered down the escalators, the only sound their footsteps bouncing off the walls as they plunged further into the cylinder of darkness.

'It's so quiet,' Clara whispered when they reached the bottom. They stopped and listened. With the bunks and the theatre, the nursery, and the doctor's quarters dismantled, it was hollow and echoey, the only sound the scurrying of rats up the tunnels and the distant rattle of Tube trains. For the first time ever to Clara, it looked like a half-finished Tube station.

'Doesn't feel the same does it,' Ruby whispered. 'It was the people who made it.'

Clara nodded. 'All life was here,' she mused. 'Remember the weddings in the theatre where anyone was invited, the grand piano, the impromptu sing alongs—'

'Endless tatty carpet bags, the snorers, shelter throat . . .' Ruby interrupted.

'The stench!' they both said at the same time and burst into laughter.

'God, I'll miss it,' Ruby blurted, her milk-coloured skin luminous in the darkness. 'You don't think we've become institutionalised do you? We've lived deep for too long?'

'No,' Clara said, slipping her arm through Ruby's. 'Sometimes you need to come underground into the darkness in order to be able to see.'

'It saved lives too didn't it,' Ruby remarked.

'Thousands.'

They walked arm-in-arm one last time up the westbound platform and Ruby pushed the key into the lock.

'Don't know why Mrs Chumbley bothered to lock it,' she laughed, flicking on the light. 'There's nothing in here.'

It was true. Clara looked around at the empty library. Every last book had been removed, the shelving and stacks taken down, the wooden counter unscrewed. The reading room revealed itself to be an empty plywood shell. She shuddered. Stripped of its books the library looked naked and forlorn. The magic had gone.

'It's a bloody wonder we never ended up on the tracks,' Ruby laughed. 'Especially when the Tube Rats all charged in at storytime. Look how thin the floorboards are! I can see the pits below through the cracks.'

But Clara wasn't listening, she had her arm pushed into the cavity in the tunnel wall.

She pulled out *The Art of Homemaking* and a dusty bottle of gin.

'Mrs Chumbley must have forgotten these. Do you want the gin, Rubes?'

She shook her head.

'No, ta.'

'You sure?'

'I've given up drinking.'

'Blimey, this Eddie is having an effect on you. You might want this then?' She passed her the book.

'Behave! I'll be too busy writing my own book to read that.'

Clara laughed. 'That's my Ruby Red Lips. When are you going?'

'End of this month, all being well. We'll need to get married first. Nothing fancy, just a quick registry office do.'

'Mind if me and Billy share it with you?' Clara ventured.

'You're getting married?'

Clara nodded. 'He proposed – again – this afternoon when I took him out of hospital for a walk. Your face,' she laughed.

'Oh Cla,' Ruby cried, picking her up in a bear hug. 'I can't tell you how happy that makes me.' She drew back. 'It is what you want isn't it? You're not just doing it for the girls I mean?'

'I won't lie. It will make adopting the girls that much easier, but truly it's what I want, more than anything.' She held back the story about Billy knowing Duncan. That story was his alone to tell.

Ruby suddenly frowned. 'You won't have to give up work at the library, will you?'

'I'll speak to Mrs Chumbley. Because of Billy's health he won't be able to work for a while, so he's agreed to stay at home and be there for when the girls get back from school. We'll need my income now.'

'Good,' Ruby said. 'You've worked too hard to turn your back on Bethnal Green Library now.'

'True,' Clara agreed, casting her eye round the dusty little library. 'It was the best of times, wasn't it.'

'Bloody hard work,' Ruby said.

'Yes. But worth it. I mean, they won't be pinning any medals on our chest, but we did our bit didn't we?'

'You did Cla, you're a pioneer!' Ruby insisted. 'It was a social revolution this little underground library. When people couldn't go to the books, you brought books to the people. Helped a fair few of them fall in love with reading too.'

'I hope so,' Clara said thoughtfully. 'I just wanted to help people escape the war, if only for a few chapters.'

'You should write about it. You know, document it for future generations.'

'A memoir you mean?'

Ruby nodded. 'Or a legacy.'

'Sounds a bit narcissistic if you ask me,' Clara replied. 'Besides, no one would believe we ran a library in a Tube tunnel.'

'Perhaps you're right. Come on,' Ruby said. 'Let's get out of here.'

Ruby breezed out of the door and Clara followed, but she couldn't resist one last look at the scene of the Second World War's greatest resistance story. A landmark of love. Keeper of all their secrets. She blew a kiss to the empty room and turned the sign on the door. *The Library is Now Closed.*

28

Clara

Want to see the world? Don't join the army, become a librarian.
Denise Bangs, Idea Store Libraries,
Tower Hamlets, East London

East London Advertiser

HAPPY EVER AFTER FOR POPULAR
BETHNAL GREEN LIBRARIANS

On a glorious July day last Saturday, St John on Bethnal Green saw a tremendous turnout for the nuptials of two of its best-loved librarians.

Librarians from the surrounding boroughs of Stepney, Whitechapel, Poplar and Bow turned out to form a book 'guard of honour' under which the newlyweds stepped.

Looking radiant in cream lace, Clara Button exchanged vows with former ambulance man Billy Clark. Clara is best known as the librarian who helped to set up and run Britain's only underground library, as well as persuading Canadians to donate hundreds of children's books to replenish the newly opened over-ground library once damaged by enemy action. She and her new husband have fostered two evacuees from the Channel Islands.

The second bride, Ruby Munroe, bamboozled guests as she walked up the aisle on her mother's arm in a white Max Cohen suit. She and her husband, former GI Eddie O'Riley, set sail to America the day after the wedding, where the bride is believed to have secured a job at a library in Brooklyn. She is also rumoured to be planning a career as a novelist.

Spring 1946

Clara looked out of the window at the spring afternoon. The sky was a biscuity brown, the colour of an old page as the sun finally muscled through the smoke from a nearby brewery.

She and Billy had been married nine months now. The hastily planned double wedding had culminated in a wedding bash that was still being talked about. Ruby hadn't so much left the East End as gone out in a blaze of glory.

Now, life had settled into a gentler rhythm. Their prefab had a small garden, not much, but just enough room for a little allotment for Billy to grow some veg and keep some hens. It was a lazy Sunday afternoon. Library Cat, who they had adopted, or he had adopted them, had been renamed Peter and was stretched out and basking in a patch of dust.

The rasp of a lawnmower drifted over the fence. Marie was making a grotto out of shells she'd brought back from Jersey. Beatty was reading to Billy, and he sat very still listening, Beauty curled up on his lap.

He still tired easily and hated not being able to work. Beatty reading to him was a perfect distraction and the bond between them strengthened with every chapter. He wasn't their father, they had one already, but until Mr Kolsky's mind was strong enough to deal with the atrocities of the past, Billy was in place.

Just as she was. Their love was unconditional. She knew the girls could decide to return to Jersey to live at any point they liked. She had already taken them back for a week last Christmas.

The return visit had been emotional. No longer living under the shadow of her informer, the girl's aunt had seemed a great deal stronger. Beatty had been thrilled to learn that Mrs Moisan had started a swimming club at an old Victorian bathing pool in her daughter Rosemary's name, which was well attended on the weekends. Clara hadn't been brave enough to join them for the club's inaugural December dip, but she had stood on the bridge and cheered all the Jersey kids on as they dive-bombed into the pool amidst shrieks of adrenaline-filled laughter. A new story was being written.

Mr Kolsky was stronger in his body, though still very unwell. They had visited him every day. He no longer thought that Beatty was his wife, but he was confused and agitated. On their third visit, he was so overwhelmed with emotion that he clung to Marie and wept. She had been so tender and patient with him – both of them had – and Clara was immensely proud, but not surprised by their bravery.

As their stay had worn on, the apprehension had gone from the visits and, on the last day, the girls were even allowed to push him down to the beach in a wheelchair wrapped up in warm blankets, Marie chatting away ten to the dozen. Clara had kept a discreet distance. Watching them all together, sitting on a bench overlooking the ocean eating fish and chips, was humbling. The girls were growing into fine young women and Mr Kolsky had enjoyed being with them. It occurred to Clara as she watched Beatty tuck her frail father up under blankets and read to him that, in many ways, she was more like a parent to him now. The doctor had been impressed with their mature attitude and urged them to bring back more books on their next visit so that they might read to him again.

He even told them all that reading to their father could play an important part in his recovery, but of course, they already knew that.

There was more than one way to be a father, or a mother. Her job was simply to love the girls, until they were ready to leave. But Clara reasoned that wasn't so different to the position many women found themselves in with their own blood. Children didn't belong to you, they were to be enjoyed, for as long as they wanted.

Back in the East End, the Brady Club kept the girls busy, and Miss Moses and Beatty had formed a close friendship. She was even teaching Beatty Yiddish and had encouraged her to join Whitechapel Library to access their enormous section of Jewish literature. She hoped that reading to him in his mother tongue might open up some of the frozen pathways in her father's brain. There was much to be hopeful for.

The wireless crackled from the open kitchen window. She had a chicken roasting and some nice spring cabbage from the garden to go with it. Life was good.

Clara smiled to herself as she set about buttering slices of yesterday's bread to make bread and butter pudding. The library was progressing beautifully. Now the building works were complete, she was starting to fill the handsome room with moveable green baize screens covered in pictures from around the world, of plants, mountains and wild animals. There were round tables filled with flowers, low bookcases, rag rugs on the parquet flooring and cherry-red curtains at the window. She had even set her sights on a mini theatre. Her dream of making the children's library a bright, inviting space to inspire young minds was coming to fruition.

Sparrow was proving to be an enthusiastic guardian of all their beautiful new books from Canada. Recently, he had started a comic club to encourage more boys into the library and a pen pal club so the boys and girls of Bethnal Green could write to the Canadian children who had donated a book.

'Why should the library just be about books?' he'd argued. He was right. As long as the activity led to learning, who was she to argue? Though she had a sneaking suspicion the pen pal club might have something to do with a pretty redhead called Dawn from Toronto who had replied to his thank you letter with her own and a photo.

He wasn't the only one with grand plans. Clara smiled as she sprinkled mixed spice over the pudding and glanced up at the pin-board on the kitchen wall. A cutting from *The New York Times*.

DEBUT AUTHOR REACHES NEW HEIGHTS.

Underneath the headline was a publicity photo of Ruby posing at the top of the Empire State Building, all tall hair, teeth and a tight sweater.

She had done it! Not that there had ever been any doubt in Clara's mind. She cast her mind back to the sweaty garment factory and Ruby's vow.

One of these days, I'm going to write a bodice-ripper, jam-packed full of sex.

'I started *Behind the Blackout* on the journey over to the States,' she'd told the reporter. 'My protagonist, Bella, finds sexual liberation during the Blitz. She makes Amber St Clare look like a convent girl.'

She was being touted as the next Kathleen Winsor and the manuscript had launched a frenzied six-way bidding war among New York publishers.

Ruby had reached for her big horizons. Her ultimate scheme had paid off and Clara couldn't have been happier for her. The ache of missing her was only superseded by the joy at seeing her best friend fulfil her potential.

Clara blew her a kiss as she put the tray of bread and butter pudding in the range.

She'd been thinking about the future a lot recently, ever since Ruby had suggested she write about their little wartime library, but it had taken a while for the right idea to settle. She pulled out a piece of paper and reached for a pen. She wanted to set down her story, document the library's life underground, for future librarians. Like a time capsule, she thought, to be opened by the branch librarian of Bethnal Green on its one hundredth anniversary. She worked out that would be 2022. How far off that sounded.

If she was still alive, she'd be 103. She laughed to herself at the ridiculous notion.

You may be interested to know of my challenges and joys in your office. I am writing this in the spring of 1946. It is easy to reflect in peacetime, to look forward and imagine a future, but I assure you, when the bombs began to fall, that future was far from certain.

You might also be amused to know we ran the library from a temporary 'branch library' over the tracks of the Central Line during the war. We loved that creaky little library. It saved our lives in so many ways. I expect you find that hard to believe now. Do people still travel on the Underground? My foster daughter has a fancy that people will all travel on machines that hover above the ground or in aeroplanes in the sky.

With the smell of cinnamon scenting the air around her, Clara wrote of the joys of Underground life, the challenges of finding new books, the rationing of paper, something of the bombs, but more about the camaraderie of storytime. She touched on her tangles with Mr Pinkerton-Smythe, but she kept the tone of the letter optimistic, firmly focused on the books they read, the way stories had nourished them in wartime.

The back door banged open. 'I'm starving, when's dinner ready?' bellowed Marie, and Clara decided to wind it up.

And so I wonder, what is life like in the library for you in 2022? What challenges do you face, how has the library endured and modernised? Do you still refer to the park as Barmy Park? I wish I could sit and trade stories with you but, of course, I can't. Congratulations on one hundred years of the library.

The future belongs to you, my friend. I hope my words resonate and you find something enlightening in the story of our little wartime library.

May Bethnal Green Library of 2022 be as cherished and used as it is today. What are we, after all, without libraries?

EPILOGUE

September 7th 2020

Time slips by in a library. It's one of the few public social spaces where you can go to feel safe and warm, to escape, explore and enrich your life. In a conspiracy theory age, being able to access trustworthy information makes libraries more relevant than ever.
        Professor Shelley Trower and Dr Sarah Pyke, *Living Libraries*

'Oh Mum . . .' Rosemary says at last, breaking the silence. 'That is just astonishing. We had no idea what you went through in the war.'

Beatty nods, exhausted. She is hollowed out from the retelling of those dark events. 'I know, love, and I'm sorry I didn't tell you it all before now. It's difficult to explain, but I suppose ultimately the need to share overcame the desire to forget.'

When the girls were growing up, she had told them the bones of the story. That they had been forced to flee Jersey, her mother's death in the bombings, her father's brutal experiences in the camps and that Clara and Billy had ultimately saved her and Marie with their love. She had never hidden her adoption or her painful past from them.

But the details, *the flesh and the blood and the guts* that turn a story from dry bones into human, lived experience, now that was harder to voice.

For so many years, no one ever really talked about the war. It wasn't the done thing, was it? Who wanted to be the old dear in the corner, stewing in the past? Not her. She had always had one eye on the future. Her work as a primary-school teacher, getting the girls through university . . . until suddenly one morning she had woken up and discovered she was old.

The pandemic had shattered their expectations of a safe and secure life. No one's tomorrow felt certain now. The discovery of her letters had felt as if her childhood library was calling to her, tempting her to open the story of her life. Her colourful, beautiful life.

'It's we who should be apologising, Mum,' says Miranda. 'We never really asked you much about the war, or what you went through. We didn't want to upset you by talking about Grandad Michael.'

'And if we're honest, Mum, it felt a little disloyal to Grandad Billy to talk about him,' Rosemary adds.

Beatty nods. 'I understand. You were young when he died, too young to take you to the funeral in Jersey. And Billy and Clara were the only grandparents you knew.'

Rosemary smiles nostalgically. 'I can see him now, sitting in his allotment, feeding Granny Clara's seedcake to the birds. He was there that much, it always came as a surprise to see he had feet and not roots.'

Miranda shakes her head.

'So that's why he wore an eyepatch!'

'He told me he had an accident with a pitchfork and the pitchfork won,' Rosemary laughs.

'Always a good storyteller your grandfather. It would never occur to him to blow his own trumpet and talk about how he really lost the sight in that eye.'

'Saving you and Auntie Marie from that bombsite.'

Questions crackle like currents up the Tube rail, each new realisation sparking another question.

'Did Granny Clara and Grandad Billy not want children of their own?' Rosemary asks.

'Later in life, Mum admitted that they tried, but it wasn't to be. She, rather *they*, felt that me and Marie were enough.'

'Funny,' Miranda says. 'I had no idea she created an underground library from scratch. She was a pioneer! What a coup getting all those books from Canada. I thought she was just a librarian.'

'If you've learnt nothing else from hearing my story, it's that is there's no such thing as *just* a librarian. She was a facilitator of joy, as you youngsters might say!'

'And you knew Ruby Munroe,' Miranda breathes, shaking her head in astonishment. 'She's a legend, I have all her books at home; I always imagined she was American.'

Beatty chuckles, and if she closes her eyes she can hear the jangling of Ruby's market jewellery, catch a whiff of her black-market perfume.

'She may have lost the accent, but trust me, she was a Bethnal Green girl all right. Oh boy, was she a lifeforce. You had to hand it to her, she was a born survivor.'

Beatty looks at her beautiful daughters and she can almost hear the tick of their thoughts. She knows what she has told them will force them to recalibrate everything they know about her.

Beatty thinks of the nineteen steps it had taken them an age to negotiate on the way down to the Underground. She thinks too of the beautiful teak inverted staircase memorial erected at the top in Barmy Park, which a hardy little group of survivors and their relatives had raised the money to erect in order to remember the dead. She was heartened to see the victims' names carved into the wood, relieved that not all wartime stories are buried and forgotten. Not that Ruby ever forgot. She etched her sister's name not on wood, but paper. Why else were all her thirty novels dedicated '*to the memory of Bella*'?

Only now, with the benefit of hindsight, can Beatty see how utterly traumatic it must have been for Ruby to walk over her sister's grave every single day, the heavy burden of loss and shame that she and everyone else in Bethnal Green carried.

'They never lost touch you know, Ruby and your grand-mother. Right up until Ruby died in the seventies she wrote to Clara.'

'Why did Granny Clara never visit her in New York?' Rosemary asks.

'People didn't travel in those days, and there was no Zoomy, or whatever you lot use today.'

She smiles, picturing the suitcase of letters she found under Clara's bed after her death.

'They turned writing into an art form. You could fill a book just with their letters alone.'

Commuters pass on by oblivious and it suddenly strikes her what an odd little sight they must make, this huddle of women on the westbound platform, on a journey into the past.

'Being buried underground like that. It must have been traumatic, Mum,' Miranda says. 'Is that why you can't be in crowded spaces?'

'And always have to sit near the door?' Rosemary asks.

'I thought I'd managed to hide that from you,' she replies sadly. 'Believe you me, my suffering wasn't unique.'

'Ooh and what happened to Sparrow?' Rosemary asks and Beatty shakes her head.

'You'll never believe it. Last week, I opened *The Times*, to read the obituaries. Imagine my surprise, there's Sparrow. He died last month.'

'Well, he would have been quite an age, Mum,' Rosemary replies.

'No, what made it remarkable was that he was an OBE. He'd amassed a fortune as some sort of global entrepreneur and he left it all to Save the Children. It amounted to millions, apparently.'

'Never!' Rosemary gasps.

'Honest. We lost touch but seems he moved to Canada and married his pen pal Dawn, set up a business there. Not bad for a boy whose education was in a little wartime library.'

'And our grandfather, our biological grandfather that is? Tell us more about him. I barely remember him.'

'I wish I could tell you there was a happy ending, but he never recovered, how could he after all he witnessed?'

Beatty traces a circle on the dusty platform floor with her
stick, then crosses it out.

'The human soul can only withstand so much. He didn't
make old bones, but I know he drew comfort from being
with me and Marie at the end. He didn't know who we
were, but he knew we loved him as much as a human
heart can love.'

She turns now to face her daughters, flooded with relief
at having shared a story that has pressed heavy on her
heart for nearly eighty years.

'Isn't that all that really matters? Love.'

She closes her eyes and sees. History isn't about dates
and battlefields, leaders and royalty. It's about ordinary
people getting on with the business of living in spite of
such unforgiving odds. And somehow in the process always
managing to hold hard to hope. It was such a simple truth.

Her eyes snap open and she stares at the empty track,
not seeing a grimy tunnel, but a higgledy-piggledy room
filled with books. A sanctuary. An escape. An asylum from
the madness of the world above their heads. Her gaze is
clear now.

'Thank you for indulging an old woman by bringing
me here.'

'It was obviously a very special place, Mum,' Rosemary
says, and Beatty smiles, remembering the anticipation and
the anarchic female energy that crackled from the shelves.

'A library ticket and a lot of love. Turns out that's all
we needed.' She grips the handle of her stick. 'Now we
can go and get that coffee.'

'No, Mum,' Miranda says, reaching out for her hand.

'Let's go and look at the memorial and find Ruby's sister's name.'

'Really? Haven't you had enough of me rattling on about the war?'

'No,' she insists. 'I want to hear all about her. In fact, I want to listen to every war story you have. Let's not waste any more time.' Ever so gently she takes her mother's yellowed wartime letters, worn tissue thin with age, hidden all these years in this time-capsule tunnel. 'Let's start in the library.'

Author's Note

It's not about the book. People come into the library in search of something. I can tell what people need before they even speak. Knowledge. Escape. Safety. Guidance. Enrichment. Magic. It's a privilege to be a part of that search. After all, are we not put on this earth to help one another?
                            Alka Lathigra, Stoke Newington Library

There's an assumption – an unfair one – that if you work in a library, you are a cardigan-wearing introvert. Bethnal Green Library, where my novel is set, is one hundred years old this year, so I set myself the goal of interviewing one hundred library workers. From post-war librarians, to feminist and activist librarians, school librarians to Britain's oldest library reading volunteer (can we all say hello to the inimitable Nanny Maureen) qualified and unqualified, all share one thing in common, a passionate belief in the power of books and reading to change lives. I've started each chapter with some of my favourite quotes. These interviews make for lively, eye-opening reading, so please do take a look at the article I've written for the paperback edition of this book, 'Save Our Libraries'.

As a child, in the 1970s and '80s, I loved visiting my

local library. Coming from a noisy household, I embraced the feeling of solitude and order. As soon as I caught the intoxicating scent of old paper and polish and heard that satisfying *thunk* of the librarian's stamp, I relaxed. It was no red brick, or arts and crafts architectural beauty, more of a concrete civic-centre box, with scratchy grey carpets and spider plants behind the desk, but that didn't matter. It was a destination, and I can still vividly remember the feeling of calm and freedom that came over me as I walked through the door. It was my haven.

First came the ritual of choosing the book, then I'd take it to the furthest end of the library, rather like a dog scurrying off with a juicy bone, sit on a small green plastic chair and fall into a story, while my mum stood at the counter and gossiped (in a theatrical whisper) with smiley Jacky the librarian, who always let her off the late fines. I vividly remember thinking as a small child, *how interesting, so rules can be broken*!

What did your childhood library look, feel and smell like? Bet you can remember!

Like most, when it came to Enid Blyton, I virtually read the print off the page. *Malory Towers* gave me the keys to a boarding school experience I'd never have. *Black Beauty*, the opportunity to own the horse I so desperately wanted, *The Secret Garden*, the delicious possibility of finding undiscovered doors.

It unlocked my imagination in a way that always made me feel safe. Without weekly trips to my local library, I'm fairly certain I wouldn't be a writer today and I'm forever grateful to my mum for taking me.

Libraries have changed from quiet, hushed repositories of books to vibrant cultural community hubs, and I can confidently say that the people who work in libraries are among the nicest and most hard-working on earth. I have a hunch they do a lot of unpaid work.

BC (before Corona) I did a lot of library talks and experienced the behind-the-scenes planning that goes into these events. The homemade cakes, the posters, the social media and the setting up and clearing away of these evening and weekend events, I'm fairly certain isn't reflected in their pay.

They are frontline workers used to dealing with the mentally ill, the disenfranchised, homeless, the lonely, and vulnerable, while navigating the complexities of whatever is thrown their way. One librarian I interviewed told me she never knows what each day might bring and that only the previous week she dealt with an overdose in the foyer.

A librarian is often the only person someone might talk to all day. What's more, they have the emotional intelligence to deal with whoever walks in through the door, which to my mind, makes them more than someone who loans out books. They are part counsellor, social worker, listening ear, facilitator and friend. They regularly go above and beyond.

When I started my interviews, the COVID-19 pandemic began, and I saw first-hand how many librarians changed roles almost overnight to helping out with supporting the elderly and those in need, by dropping off food parcels, delivering books on bikes, collecting medication and checking that those people who could so easily slip between the cracks in society did not go ignored.

During the Second World War, at the time this book is set, libraries were in peril from bombs, rockets and paper rationing. Today, our much-loved but beleaguered public libraries are under threat once more from something more stealthy. Cuts and closures. After years of austerity and now COVID, they are under strain to deliver more services than ever before, while council leaders, under pressure to make cuts, sharpen their knives.

They are, as Chief Librarian John Pateman told me, 'easy targets. There is hardly any money saved by closing libraries, but when you close a library bad things start to happen in the neighbourhood where the library used to be. It is difficult to prove the positive value of a library, but it is easy to prove once it has been taken away. The library is the glue that holds a community together and you only miss it after it has gone unfortunately'.

Another librarian told me that after the closure of the local children's centre, babies are now weighed in her library! Don't hard-working communities deserve more?

The importance of libraries was recognised by the Public Libraries Act 1850. Since a further Act in 1964, there has been a statutory requirement for the provision of a free local library service. The surge in reading throughout the pandemic and the flexibility and skill of library staff in dealing with the outbreak, proves how relevant and import-ant libraries are within the community. They are our birth right and our inheritance.

A library is the only place you can go – from cradle to grave – that is free, safe, democratic and no one will try to flog you anything. You don't have to part with a penny to travel the world. It's the heartbeat of a community, offering precious resources to people in need. It's a place just to be, to dream and to escape – *with books*. And what's more precious than that? So, here's to all library workers. We need you.

The True Story of Bethnal Green Library and the Fight to Save It

Never has history felt so blisteringly relevant. As I began researching and writing this novel, based on the astonishing true story of Bethnal Green Library in wartime, eighty years on, it was in peril.

When the pandemic began, the library closed, before reopening as a COVID-19 Vaccine Trial Centre. Then, nasty rumours started to circulate that it was under threat of cuts or closure. I joined a campaign to save the library and played my part by highlighting its history, a history you've just read.

As council leaders made plans to reduce this symbol of resistance to a shadow of its former self, I wondered how much any of them knew about the remarkable history of the building and those within it, who ensured that, even in the darkest of times, working-class East Enders had access to books.

As the fallout from the pandemic put pressure on councils to slash their budgets, I suggested they looked back to find imaginative ways to tackle the funding crisis and draw inspiration from their wartime predecessors.

★

A large crowd assembled on a crisp October morning in 1922, when Bethnal Green's first permanent public library opened its doors in a handsome red brick building in Barmy Park (There had been a small temporary one in Old Ford Road since 1919). The philanthropy of Scottish businessman Andrew Carnegie provided £20,000, and the remaining £16,000 was raised by the local authority.

Crowds of children gather outside their new public library. Photo reproduced with kind permission of Tower Hamlets Local History Library and Archives.

'The council was handing down to future generations a legacy which would enable them to obtain knowledge and sweep away misery and poverty,' said the Mayor in his opening speech. This was a thinly veiled reference to the fact that only two years previously, an asylum stood on that site.

Bethnal 'madhouse' operated for 120 years in Bethnal Green, East London, and was notorious for its cruel treatment. Even today, most East Enders still refer to the grounds around the library as Barmy Park. Shockingly, the asylum only closed in 1920.

Two years later, the library opened in what had been the male block. The disturbingly cruel incarceration of the mentally ill, replaced with learning and literacy. What a message of hope that must have sent to the community.

It was described by the *Daily Herald* on its opening as 'one of the finest libraries in the metropolis'. From the outset, Bethnal Green Library established itself as the cultural centre of the borough and by June 1924, the number of books issued had passed the million mark. The Carnegie United Kingdom Trustees expressed themselves as 'delighted'.

The father of a blind girl who, only a year after the library opened, obtained a first-class honours degree from London University, attributed her success to the assistance of the new library.

But trials loomed ahead.

Eighteen years after the library opened, in September 1940, a bomb crashed through the roof of the adult lending library at 5.55 p.m. on what would later be known as 'Black Saturday', the start of the Blitz. What had been an orderly and well-equipped library became in a split second a scene of destruction.

No. 18   Central Public Library
Taken after crater had been filled in and roof repaired.
Incident, Sept. 7, 1940

Thousands of books were destroyed when the bomb hit Bethnal Green Public Library on the first night of the Blitz in 1940. Photo reproduced with kind permission of Tower Hamlets Local History Library and Archives.

And here the story takes a surprising twist. Rather than simply hurrying for the nearest shelter, the borough librarian, George F. Vale and his deputy, Stanley Snaith, calmly pulled a tarpaulin over the shattered glass dome roof and set about planning a pioneering social experiment that would transform the lives of wartime Londoners.

Bethnal Green Underground was a half-completed stop on the Central Line when war broke out. Builders were working on connecting it to Liverpool Street, but from 1939 it had been locked up and left to the rats. One week after the Blitz began, East Enders defied Churchill's orders not to shelter in Tube stations and claimed their right to safety. At seventy-eight feet below ground, it was one of the few really safe places to shelter in Bethnal Green and was referred to by locals as an 'Iron Lung'.

Over the course of the next twelve months, it was transformed into a fully-functioning subterranean community with an astonishing array of facilities. Metal triple bunks sleeping up to 5,000 stretched three-quarters of a mile up the eastbound tunnel. A shelter ticket reserved you a bunk.

There was a three-hundred-seat shelter theatre with a stage and spotlights, which hosted opera and ballet, a café, doctor's quarters and a wartime nursery, which enabled newly enfranchised women to go out to work. But here's the best part – there was a library!

I love surprises in history and finding out about George and Stanley's secret underground library, built over the boarded-up tracks of the westbound tunnel, felt like nothing short of magic. In fact, it sparked this whole novel.

Triplet metal bunks didn't offer much in the way of comfort, but sleeping deep underground saved lives. Photo reproduced with kind permission of Tower Hamlets Local History Library and Archives.

I first discovered its existence when I sat down with inimitable East Ender Pat Spicer, ninety-two.

'I used to borrow *Milly-Molly-Mandy* from the underground library. I didn't worry about the bombs when I had my head buried in a book,' she told me.

'A library underground?' I queried.

'Yes, dear,' she replied patiently.

Never doubt a nonagenarian cockney. A trip to Tower Hamlets Local History Library and Archives revealed Pat's memory to be razor sharp.

There was a photograph of a librarian, calmly stamping books, alongside copious written memories.

'Libraries in converted shops, in village halls, in mobile vans, are common enough. But libraries in Tube shelters

George and Stanley's pioneering underground library. Photo reproduced with kind permission of Tower Hamlets Local History Library and Archives.

are something new under the sun,' George's deputy Stanley wrote gushingly in *Library Review* in 1942. 'When Londoners, undergoing the heaviest bombardment in history, defied all laws and rules by taking possession of the Tube platforms and stairs, it was quickly evident that a new social situation was in being. People spending from eight to fourteen hours a night on a station far below ground had to have food, sleeping facilities, medical attention and recreation, both physical and mental. A new organisation had to be created, and created it was, partly by central planning and partly – it is our English way – by brilliant improvisation.'

The wheels of bureaucracy clearly moved fast in wartime, and a grant of £50 was approved by the council.

'The Borough Surveyor was quickly on the job,' wrote Stanley. 'All last summer, the caverns echoed to the din of hammers and saws. The result was a triumph.'

The library, which had a captive audience during a raid when the doors were locked, was open from 5.30 p.m. to 8 p.m. every evening and loaned out 4,000 volumes of consciously chosen stock. Romance sat alongside literary classics, children's books, poetry and plays.

I have used some creative licence by making my fictional library run by Clara and Ruby a little larger and with longer opening hours, but everything else about the underground shelter and its amazing community and facilities, from the theatre to the nursery, the children playing kiss chase up the tunnels and even the horror room, is all true. There was even a real Mrs Chumbley, a heroic air-raid warden who saved the lives of children during the Tube disaster. I have used her name as a way of honouring her wartime work, but my character is purely fictional.

When it came to Underground Tube station shelters, Bethnal Green was a cut above.

'Throughout the war, I must have slept on every platform on the Central Line, from Liverpool Street Station right up to Oxford Circus,' ninety-year-old Gladys confided. 'Bethnal Green was the best though.'

My ninety-year-old friend Babs Clark is not quite so sure about that. 'It was cold and smelly, Kate, and we had to do our business in a bucket. But the community down there was rock solid. Sleeping down the Tube eventually felt quite normal, all things considered.'

Can you imagine growing up in a Tube station, your childhood unfolding next to the tracks, all your rites of passage taking place in the booking hall, on the platforms, down the Underground?

Patsy Thompson (née Crawley), eighty-four, doesn't have to. The first six years of her life were spent mostly down Bethnal Green Tube shelter. 'It sounds ever so funny now, but back then it was just normal. I knew no other life,' she laughs.

'My mum Ginnie volunteered at the Tube shelter café. She was such a lovely, smiley lady, always bustling round a million miles an hour in her apron. Everyone just knew her as Auntie Ginnie.

'When she was working, I'd knock about with my six male cousins. We had such fun running up and down the tunnels like little tube rats. We used to dare each to go in the "room of horrors" as we called the ventilation shoot. It was strictly forbidden but being adventurous kids, we climbed up.

'During the war, the facilities were amazing down the Tube; it had everything you needed. There was even a mobile hairdresser, who used to come down the tunnels doing people's hair out in rags before bed so they woke up with nice curly hair. Terrific!

'When war was over, I missed life underground, and even now when I go to Bethnal Green and see the Tube sign, I feel a warmth spread over my chest. To others, it's a transport network; to me, it was my home.'

Heartbreakingly that 'home' was tinged with horror one dark, wet night in March 1943. As I described through Ruby and Bella's story, 173 people *were* crushed to death on the steps going down to the shelter when, with the sirens wailing, a mother carrying a baby tripped.

The sights that night were unimaginable. ARP wardens

worked alongside housewives and Boy Scouts to save the injured. Bodies were piled into anything with wheels and rushed to hospital. When word came back the hospital had no more room and the dead were being laid out in the corridor, bodies were taken to the crypts of nearby churches, or laid out by the railings near to the library.

It took more than sixty police, rescue workers and volunteers to pull the corpses and injured people from the top of the staircase. The darkness, the pressure and the angle of the bodies made extricating people from the crush slow and difficult. Horrifyingly, dead and alive were pressed together in a tangled mess of such complexity that it was three hours before the last casualty was pulled out.

Authorities moved quickly, washing down the steps and ordering those that witnessed it to say nothing.

The fearful noise people reported hadn't even been enemy aircraft, but the government testing new anti-aircraft missiles from a recently installed Z Battery in nearby Victoria Park. Due to reporting restrictions, they were unable to tell local residents. One of the Second World War's biggest civilian disasters was quickly hushed up under the Official Secrets Act by a wartime government desperate to avoid news of the scandal falling into enemy hands. It was deemed bad for morale.

The enforced silence just compounded the survivors' feelings of guilt. Rescuers' hair turned grey overnight, whole families were torn apart at the loss of all those children. Women who I described in the story, like poor

Maud who drank to obliterate the pain of losing her two young daughters, are real people. Ruby's suffering is based on their suffering, a pain which never faded but festered.

I can't think about that crush without feeling breathless. Ruby's panic attacks and flashbacks are based on the fact that with no opportunity to share stories, no counselling, no acknowledgement of what we now call post-traumatic stress disorder, survivors and witnesses were forced to internalise their suffering. Just because something happened a long time ago, doesn't mean it's ever too late to start talking about it.

Over the years, I have interviewed many survivors, including the impressive young female doctor who was on duty that night when the trickle of corpses coming into hospital soon turned into a flood. Six months before her death aged 102, heroic Dr Joan Martin, MBE, confided, 'I was haunted by vivid nightmares of people being trampled to death every single night for seventy-three years.'

Babs Clark was just twelve when her big sister wrenched her free from the crush, saving her life. As they walked home later, she asked her mum Bobby why there were so many people lying on the pavement. 'They're having a little sleep, Babsey,' she replied. The truth was revealed the next day when she went to school and discovered half her classmates missing, suffocated to death.

Perhaps that's why the library staff felt such a fierce loyalty towards their patrons.

Stanley Snaith wrote movingly of East Enders like Pat,

Babs, Patsy and Ginnie. 'Each dusk sees the first contingent making its way down to the bowels of the earth. The well and the ill, the old and the young, they come trooping down, carrying carpet bags, parcels, bedding in sheets or drab sacking – here a chokered docker, there an undersized lad with an Atlas load improbably poised on his head, playing preux chevalier to a crippled mother – rough people, nice people, typical East Enders.

'In the Library, the youngsters are vocally busy with their book-selection, but why should they not chatter to their hearts' content? Cheery young imps, they have little enough brightness in their lives, and this is no time for repression.'

These 'youngsters' are now in their nineties, and memories of the little library are embedded in their hearts.

'It was a sanctuary to me,' Pat told me. 'By 1943, I was fourteen and there had been so much horror, the Blitz, the Tube disaster. You can't imagine what that library represented to me as a place of escape and learning. It had a profound effect on my life.'

And I suspect not just on Pat's.

Library patron, Pat Spicer.

'We can look back upon this subterranean library with mixed feelings of pride in a task well done, and heartfelt hope that it will never have to be done again,' concluded George Vale.

I wondered how George and Stanley would feel at the plans to sweep aside a hundred years of history? Proposals on the table included slashing Bethnal Green's opening hours from fifty to just fifteen, or closing it altogether, cuts to opening hours of other libraries in the borough, and the complete closure of Cubitt Town on the Isle of Dogs. How many jobs would be lost? How many librarians left out of work after toiling heroically through the pandemic to support their users?

I grew angry. When you become emotionally involved in the history of such a valued public institution, you become invested in its future. Did history count for nothing?

How was it, I wondered, that during a climate of fear, deprivation and economic instability, their wartime predecessors had found the imagination and means to extend library opening hours and open new branches?

Kate Thompson in the tunnel where the
long-lost library used to be.

The Blitz and COVID are very different beasts, but the effect on reading has been the same. Never have we read so voraciously or needed and valued our libraries more.

'Reading became, for many, the supreme relaxation,' wrote George of his wartime patrons.

Sound familiar?

Libraries are vital to the future of communities, now more than ever. COVID reminded us that not all children have access to remote learning and the internet. That was compounded in Tower Hamlets, where hundreds of children live in cramped, overcrowded homes. Many rely on the borough's precious libraries as a sanctuary and an extension of their living room.

But thanks to the tireless campaigning of so many in the borough, of which I'm proud to say I was a very small part, the library was saved at the eleventh hour! Deep joy.

'WE SAVED OUR LIBRARIES!' wrote campaign leader, Glyn Robbins. 'I'm delighted to tell you all that, under pressure of our campaign, Tower Hamlets Council has thought again. At its Cabinet meeting, a new proposal was put forward, as an alternative to cutting and closing libraries. As a result, Cubitt Town Library will not be sold, but along with Bethnal Green library and Watney Street Idea Store, will now have more, not fewer, opening hours. This is a fantastic victory. Thank you. There are still lots of cuts to vital public services being made and the decision on our libraries will be reviewed in 18 months, so our celebrations will be muted. But celebrate we should! It shows, once again, that when people get angry and organised, we can win.'

I write this in September 2021, relieved to hear that

finally the library is about to reopen to the public once more and is no longer a COVID-19 Vaccine Trial Centre. Who knows, I may even be lucky enough to launch this book in Bethnal Green Library as part of a series of events to celebrate its centenary. Pat and Patsy, along with a host of other East Enders will, of course, be guests of honour!

Because a hundred years of providing people with access to free books is worthy of great celebration.

It is a story worth telling.

Read for Victory!

The library at Holland House in Kensington, London, damaged by a Molotov 'Breadbasket' fire-bomb, in October 1940. Image licensed with permission from Central Press/Hulton Archive/Getty Images.

The year is 1940 and Bethnal Green is on fire. The streets are bathed in an orange glow as German planes roar overhead, dropping yet more bombs into the fiery furnace.

But one little girl is oblivious. Pat Spicer wanders up the long gloomy tunnel, scarcely noticing the ripe stench of so many unwashed bodies or the distant crump of bombs, for *Milly-Molly-Mandy* has her enthralled. The eleven-year-old has fallen into a book she loves, with characters she cares for, and real life can wait. Just as well, because right now real life is terrifying. Seventy-eight feet above the underground tunnel which Pat now calls home, streets and buildings are pulverised and lives destroyed.

The Blitz is like nothing anyone has ever experienced. It's the first time women and children have found themselves on the frontline. Few people dare attend the dance halls and picture houses in the early days of the bombardment. There's knitting and crosswords of course, but they don't drown out the noise of the bombs and ack-ack guns. A thumping good read is the only medicine to smooth balm on fractured nerves. Reading offers precious respite, allowing Pat Spicer and countless others to escape the lonely churn of their thoughts.

At the outset of the Second World War, the President of the Library Association, Arundell Esdaile, wrote: 'Patriotism is not enough. The right reading of books is one of the chief ways of maintaining and even enlarging the culture of the mind which knows no frontiers. And, after all, is it not on behalf of that culture that we are fighting to destroy the new barbarism?'

The rhetoric was clear. Books were to be a key weapon in the fight for morale.

The newly formed Ministry of Information was quick to cotton on to this and enlisted the help of public libraries. Every library in the land was urged to set up an Information Bureau, to embed themselves firmly in the life of the community, as well as open their doors to evacuees and soldiers from local battalions.

Professor John Hilton, Director of Home Publicity, wrote to put fire in librarians' bellies:

'Books in war time can be a refuge into which we make our way to escape the slings and arrows of outrageous conflict . . . Books can be a storehouse from which to draw sure knowledge and rich emotion to clarify our minds and strengthen our souls for the tasks to which we have set our hand.'

Stirring stuff, but despite this in the first months of the so called 'phoney war', library use was sluggish, and dwindling issues were further reduced with male librarians called into service and early closing with the advent of darker, blacked-out evenings. But then came the Blitz, and everything changed. More leisure time was devoted to reading than ever before. Borrowing rates soared to never before seen levels, because as little Pat Spicer found, a good book can help you forget the atrocities of real life.

By 1942, Manchester Public Libraries had a record-breaking issue of over five million volumes – there were a further one million in Portsmouth – and areas like Barnes and Swindon, which had no public library service at all prior to the war, rapidly opened branches.

In London's Bethnal Green, East Ham, Shoreditch, Tottenham and Westminster, despite falling populations, issue rates rose to the highest ever recorded. Between them, these five heavily bombed boroughs, issued in 1942-3 a total of 3,585,732 volumes, proving that bad times are good for books.

The Mass Observation organisation, that great barometer of public opinion, studied the reading habits of over 10,000 people in the spring of 1942 for their Books and the Public Project. And when I say studied, I really mean it. On occasion, their volunteers would follow unsuspecting people into libraries and bookshops, into cafés and on buses and observe them reading, while secretly scribbling in a notebook.

'Female. Medium height, slim built, intelligent face. Wearing dark fawn tweed coat, green felt hat. Carried "Daily Telegraph". Went straight to section marked "Poetry". Observer followed', is one of many slightly farcical observations of the book reading public in wartime.

The Mass Observation Surveys are fascinating, because they offer a snapshot into working-class culture and feature the innermost thoughts of women whose voices would ordinarily be lost to history.

But the success of the public municipal library is the untold story here. Libraries boomed in wartime as book sales dipped. Four out of ten people borrowed books from a library in wartime and it transformed lives. And best of all, unlike a Boots subscription library or a tuppeny library, it was *free*.

The survey found that many people, especially young working-class women, developed a passion for reading that their parents never had the time for and joined the library for the first time. Some began reading during the Blitz to keep their minds off the bombs and kept it up. Twice as many women as men used the library and they preferred fiction.

Fiction readers typically devoured their books in just four days, while non-fiction readers took three times as long. In moments of severe conflict like the evacuation of Dunkirk, the Battle of Britain, the Blitz and then the V1 and V2 rocket attacks, women gravitated to romance, historical fiction and thrillers for escape.

With the war seemingly unrelenting, women wanted escapism with a strong conquering heroine. This would explain the success of the first ever bodice-ripper. It wasn't published in the United Kingdom until shortly after the war, but when *Forever Amber* by Kathleen Winsor came out in America in 1944, it was a publishing sensation.

Set in the 17th century during the bubonic plague and the Great Fire of London, its heroine Amber ruthlessly uses her sexuality to scheme and manipulate her way through Restoration London. Fourteen US states banned the book as pornography, with one attorney general citing seventy references to sexual intercourse, thirty-nine illegitimate pregnancies, seven abortions, and ten descriptions of women undressing in front of men. Needless to say it flew off the bookshelves selling over one hundred thousand copies in its first week of release and going on to sell over three million copies. It's pretty mild by today's standards, but as subversive, irrepressible protagonists go, Amber is right up there.

The chapters set during the plague are absolutely riveting, especially when you find yourself reading it mid-lockdown during another global pandemic. The sound of the dead cart rattling over the cobblestones and the chiming of the bell, entreating people to, 'Bring out your dead', makes for chilling, but page-turning reading. And it made me think. Did women reading about pox and fire in the seventeenth century, in the ruins of a post-war twentieth-century landscape, draw reassurance from its pages?

Is that why historical fiction was so popular during the Second World War? Our small island had survived wars, fire, threat of invasion and disease before. And so this too shall pass?

These are generalisations of course, not *all* women wanted epic historical bodice-rippers. Here's a list of some of the most borrowed library books in 1942. How many do you recognise?

Gone with the Wind; For Whom the Bell Tolls; How Green Was My Valley; Pride and Prejudice; Scum of the Earth; Herries Chronicles; Three Musketeers; Finnegans Wake; The Stars Looked Down; All This and Heaven Too; When the Rains Came; My America; Rebecca; Berlin Diary; This Above All; Hatter's Castle; Seven Pillars of Wisdom; The Power and the Glory; Love on the Dole; Northbridge Rectory; Shall our Children Live or Die; Knife in the Dark; Evil Under the Sun; Heart of a Child.

It's worth noting how many of the books in this list provide a commentary on society and the war and how many were turned into popular Hollywood films.

Ultimately though it appears the true function of wartime reading for women was escapism. Books were time machines, whisking women away from the crash and the horror of the war.

'Reading is like a drug to me, I read much more than in peacetime,' said one wartime woman in the Mass Observation survey. 'No war books for me thank you. I can read all that boasting and piffle in the papers. I want a book to escape from it all for a few hours,' said another.

And they needed it because in most cases the surroundings were cramped, smelly and dingy. Women read on buses, their windows covered in anti-splinter nets, in dusty tunnels, over powdered egg dinners and squeezed into Anderson shelters. As was the case with Bethnal Green

Tube Shelter Library, libraries popped up in unusual places like troop ships and hospitals. In Edmonton, Canada, seats were even stripped from one of their trams and replaced with two thousand books, tapping into a new reading public.

Midway through the Blitz, St Pancras Borough Council launched London's first Travelling Library van, which carried two thousand books on polished mahogany shelves and drove round to shelters, rest centres and Balloon Barrage and Home Guard units. This self-contained miniature lending library promised 'A Library to your Door'.

'People without books are like houses without windows,' remarked the Mayor at the ceremony that launched the van. The press flocked to report on this wartime innovation and even American newscasters reported on the social welfare activities of London under the Blitz.

'If they won't come to the library, we will take the library to them,' remarked the travelling librarian. What could be more gratifying than the thought of these librarians dodging bombs and racing through London's cratered streets to deliver books?

'Librarians are alive to the conditions and adapting themselves to the exigencies of the moment,' said the Library Association four months into the Blitz.

They had to, because above ground libraries were as much a casualty of war as munitions factories and other military targets. Bethnal Green Central Library lost the roof of its adult lending library five minutes before closing on the first night of the Blitz and a total of 4,283 books burnt to ash, but it still came off well in comparison to many others.

Beautiful Exeter Library, once described as one of the most palatial libraries in the country, was bombed on 4 May 1942 and lost all of its books, bar one – *English Men of Letters* – which remains in their library archives today.

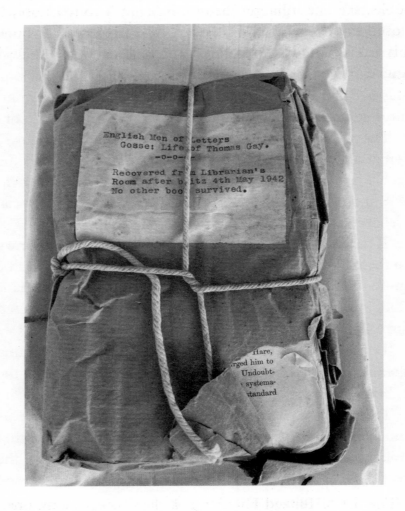

I went to view 'the Blitz Book' as the library calls it. Am I the only person strange enough to travel 185 miles to sniff a book? I'm so glad I did though. Eighty years on from the end of the Blitz this book still wears its perfume from that dramatic night, a curiously evocative odour of mildew and bonfires. I love the smell of old books. It's like inhaling history. Raising it to my nose, I closed my eyes and tried to unpick the mystery of how this book out of thousands survived with only a few singed pages.

The list of Blitzed libraries is a depressingly long one. An estimated 750,000 library books were destroyed during the bombardment.

Liverpool's William Brown Library was entirely destroyed, as was Plymouth Central Library and great damage was caused to Bristol, London's National Central Library, Edinburgh, Coventry and many more.

Librarians once more were there in the thick of it, helping to salvage books as well as rehousing the homeless by tactful handling, born of long experience in dealing with the public.

Libraries adapted to wartime conditions, opening for record hours. For the first time ever, many branches opened on Sundays to allow factory workers to change their books.

Who better to deal with these emergencies with compassion and empathy than female librarians? With so many male librarians conscripted it was left to women, often junior or children's librarians, to step up and fill the roles left behind. Female librarians working in public library service were not subject to withdrawals and though many were there merely as 'placeholders' and would no doubt have been reminded of that, it was a good opportunity for many to show their skill, creativity and resourcefulness.

'A ray of light has crept into Whitehall,' said a circular from the Board of Education.

Women were reading more than ever before, but what they were reading increasingly began to be of concern.

Writing in the Library Association Record in 1942, Hilda McGill from Manchester Public Library wrote of the surge of housewives who, finding themselves with more time on their hands as their husbands were away serving, ended up in the public library. 'At 18 she probably read the light novels of the day,' Hilda wrote. 'As literacy has increased, so has the standard of light reading depressed itself to something approaching the nadir of imbecility . . .'

But she concedes 'it is better to read a light novel, than skim the pages of an illustrated paper' on the basis that 'even the most foolish book is a kind of leaky boat on a sea of wisdom: some of the wisdom will get in anyhow'.

Condescending attitudes, especially towards women and romance prevailed.

Dr Robert James is Senior Lecturer in History at the University of Portsmouth.

'The first public library opened in Manchester in 1852 and was driven by the lofty aim of encouraging the population to use its leisure time more wisely. Libraries were there so that people, particularly Britain's working classes, could learn how to become "good citizens",' Robert told me. 'In light of this, library authorities started to advocate the purchasing of "good" books to improve society's reading habits. This meant stocking the classics, like Austen, Dickens, and Hardy, not what one Peterborough librarian described as the "mere butterflies of fiction", written by the likes of the then hugely popular, but now largely forgotten, romantic novelists Ruby M. Ayres and Ethel M. Dell.

'Even during the Second World War, a period in which the boundaries between the social classes were supposedly blurring, class was still central to people's understanding.'

Robert told me about a war of words that erupted in the library world in the interwar years about working-class reading habits.

'One contributor to the discussion, Frederick J. Cowles,

Chief Librarian of Swinton and Pendlebury public library service, had been a highly vocal supporter of the inclusion of fiction in public libraries for some time and was lambasted for it.

'One male librarian even went so far as to say: "If [women] have not enough energy left to read anything but trash, we should be doing them a real service if we could prevent them from reading at all".'

It would be fair to say that the character of Pinkerton-Smythe was inspired by the attitudes of this (and many other) snooty librarians of that time.

Frederick took the opportunity afforded to him by the wartime softening of attitudes to promote his beliefs again, observing one month after war was declared:

'It is not easy to assess exactly what the public shall want,' he wrote. 'The only thing we can be sure of is that quantities of cheap fiction will be required . . . The soldier will carry a book in his kitbag, the civilian will keep books for his fireside, the child will learn the delights of literature. We are a nation of readers, and the war is only going to increase the demand for books.'

'By the war years there was a shift in attitudes as the authorities began to realise the morale boosting properties of romance in literature and the cinema,' says Robert. 'The government realised that if morale is high, people support the war effort and are more productive.'

Alistair Black, Professor Emeritus at the University of Illinois and author of *The Public Library in Britain, 1914-2000*, which I found really useful for research, told me:

'In America librarians had for decades been much more

relaxed about giving people what they wanted. In Britain it was not until the Second World War that the trend towards accepting the lending of fiction as a legitimate function of the public library quickened. This more "democratic" attitude was connected to the cultural contribution public libraries made during the war to plans for reconstruction and the formation of an embryonic welfare state. In this respect, it is no coincidence that the watershed report on the future of public libraries – the McColvin Report, named after its author Lionel McColvin, the twentieth century's most famous public librarian – was issued in the autumn of 1942, just a few weeks before the publication of the seminal Beveridge Report, which laid the foundations of the post-war welfare state.'

It might have taken the Second World War to trigger it but thanks to the Mass Observation diaries and the democratisation of libraries, the innermost thoughts, views and wishes of women were beginning to be acknowledged and catered for. And we as modern female readers, writers and book lovers have benefitted from it ever since.

Sources:

I accessed the *Library Association Record*, covering the war years (1939-1945) held at the British Library.

Interview with Robert James, Senior Lecturer in History at the University of Portsmouth and author of *Read for Victory: Public Libraries and Book Reading in a British Naval Port City During the Second World War*.

Interview with Alistair Black, Professor Emeritus at the University of Illinois and author of *The Public Library in Britain, 1914–2000* (2000).

I read *Forever Amber*, by Kathleen Winsor, reissued by Penguin in 2002, originally published in 1944.

Select Bibliography

The Library Book by Susan Orlean (Atlantic Books, 2019). This is a book lover's dream, a superb and colourful history of public libraries. I borrowed the idea for Clara writing to the future librarian of Bethnal Green to be opened on its 100th anniversary from a true story Susan unearthed of the innovative librarian Althea Warren writing a letter to the future City Librarian of Los Angeles to be opened on their 100th anniversary. It struck me as absolutely visionary. Thank you, Susan, for writing such a beautiful love letter to libraries and their custodians.

The Librarian by Salley Vickers (Penguin Books, 2018). A novel set in a post-war library that poses important questions about childhood reading and the power of books to change our lives.

The Librarian: A Memoir by Allie Morgan (Ebury Press, 2021). Everyone who uses a library should read this, and especially those that don't, because Allie makes you realise that libraries are the very last thing communities can do without. Packed full of strange, weird, wonderful, eye-watering and life-affirming stories.

Broken Pieces: A Library Life, 1941 to 1978 by Michael Gorman (American Library Association, 2011). Michael writes so beautifully about the rhythms, variety and complexity of library life.

An Illustrated History of Mobile Library Services in the United Kingdom by G.I.J Orton (Branch and Mobile Libraries Group, 1980). Oh, how I loved this little gem of a book. It made me want to buy a bus and start up my own travelling library service.

Public Library and Other Stories by Ali Smith (Penguin Random House, 2016). A joyous outpouring of love for public libraries.

The Public Library in Britain 1914–2000 by Alistair Black (The British Library, 2002). A complete social history of the public library and its relationship within communities. Chapter Four, 'Bombs and Blueprints, 1939–1945' in particular made me realise the reach, relevance and the democratisation of public libraries in war. Social history gold.

The Library Association Record (1939 to 1945), held at the British Library, gave me such a useful insight into the roles and activities of libraries and their workers in the war years.

The Forgotten Service: Auxiliary Ambulance Station 39 by Angela Raby (Battle of Britain International Ltd., 1999).

Really helpful for seeing how Billy would have slotted into wartime life in the ambulance service.

Leisure in Britain, 1780–1939 by John K.Walton and James Walvin (Manchester University Press, 1983). Great section on reading in the working-class home.

A Library Service in a Bombed Area by George F. Vale (Bethnal Green Public Libraries Local Collection, 1947), held at Tower Hamlets Local History Library and Archives. I was so pleased to have found this. Pat Spicer's recollections of using this little underground library first sparked the idea, but finding this beautifully written, engaging paper which George wrote to read at the post-war Library Association Conference at the Pavilion, Brighton, put flesh on the bones. How proud George sounds of his pioneering social experiment! How I'd love to have met him!

A Tube Shelter Lending Library by Stanley Snaith (Library Review), held at Tower Hamlets Local History Library and Archives. George Vale's Deputy, Stanley was apparently a poet as well as a librarian and you can tell as he talks with love – and a note of amazement – about how he and George created a new reading public out of the chaos of the Blitz. 'It is by the aid of such fortuitous survivals that man puts together the shattered image of his past,' Stanley concludes.

I read the 200-page 'Mass Observation Report on Books & The Public' – Report 1332 (1942) held by the Mass-

Observation Archive, University of Sussex. (http://www. massobs.org.uk). It acted as a time machine whisking me back to 1942 and to the innermost thoughts of ordinary women and what reading did for them.

The Children's Library: A Practical Manual for Public, School and Home Libraries by W.C. Berwick Sayers (George Routledge & Sons Limited, 1911). A great insight into children's librarianship in the twentieth century and it would have been a bible to Clara.

The East End: My Birthright by Albert Turpin (Francis Boutle Publishers, 2017). Fascinating memoir by a man who fought for the rights of working people and confronted unimaginable horrors during the Second World War as a firefighter.

London's East End Survivors: Voices of the Blitz Generation by Andrew Bissell (Centenar, 2010). I love this book because the author conducted hundreds of interviews with wartime East End survivors to amplify the voices of ordinary but extraordinary men and women and provide the tiny domestic details of life under fire.

The Fishing Cats of Fort D'Auvergne (And Other Tales) by David Cabeldu, (2019). A wonderful peek at a childhood spent growing up in Jersey. Huge thanks to David for allowing me to use his childhood antics, spent building rafts, fishing and getting into scrapes and mischief, as young boys do, as inspiration for Beatty and Marie's childhood.

A Boy Remembers by Leo Harris (Apache Guides Ltd, 2000). Leo lived through the occupation of Jersey and remembers the terrifying moment his brother was arrested by the Secret Police. His generosity in sharing his memories with me provided the information I needed to write about Beatty and Marie's father's and uncle's arrest. His memoir provides a chilling insight into life under the Nazi jackboot.

The Family from One End Street by Eve Garnett *(Puffin Books,* 1937*)*. This book was recommended to me by a librarian and I loved it. The antics of the working-class Ruggles family sum of the spirit of the Tube Rats.

Forever Amber by Kathleen Winsor (first published in America in 1944 by Macmillan and in England in August 1945 by Macdonald & Co, republished by Penguin, 2002). I read this trying to feel my way into the skin of a wartime woman, surrounded by bombsites and rationing. In its time this book was explosive, decadent, scandalous and utterly absorbing. 78 years on it still is.

Acknowledgements

I spent much of the COVID-19 pandemic, when I researched and wrote this book, speaking with elderly cockneys and librarians and I can't think of two better groups of people to while away those uncertain days with.

This book really owes its existence to the generosity and kindness of so many wonderful librarians, working and retired, private and public sector, university and children's, volunteers, qualified and unqualified, assistants and managers – the whole range – who shared their precious thoughts, memories and most importantly, their stories with me. I'm afraid the list is too copious to publish here, but to each and every person I interviewed, thank you from the bottom of my heart. Why not read my article, 'Save Our Libraries', in the paperback edition of this book, for a fuller flavour of some of those interviews. Enormous thanks to my friend Sarah Richards for transcribing most of these interviews.

I'm indebted to the generosity, kindness, hospitality and warmth of wartime East Enders, many of whom I am privileged to call friends.

East Enders are just walking books, crammed with stories. To Ray, Pat, Patsy, Beatty, Marie, Babs, Sally, Gladys, Minksy and her daughters Lesley, Linda and Lorraine, Alf and Phoebe, everyone at the Brenner Centre at Stepney Jewish Community Centre, The Geezers of Bow, Joe Ellis and all on Bethnal Green & East London Facebook site.

Sincere thanks to Robert James, Senior Lecturer in History at the University of Portsmouth and author of *Read for Victory: Public Libraries and Book Reading in a British Naval Port City During the Second World War.* Robert was so generous with his time, not only allowing me to pick his brain about the concept of reading for victory and reading a first draft of this book, but also for sending me the Mass Observation Survey, which in a time of total lockdown I would not have been able to access and would have found it very difficult to write this book without. I am so indebted to you.

I am exceptionally grateful to Alistair Black, Professor Emeritus at the University of Illinois and author of *The Public Library in Britain, 1914–2000* (2000) who also allowed me to interview him, proofread a first draft and shared his library contacts with me. No one knows more about the history of public libraries than he does.

Huge thanks to Liz and Alex Ditton, Alison Wheeler, Anne Welsh of Beginning Cataloguing, Helen Allsop, Charmaine Bourton, Mark Lamerton, Dave Cabeldu, Lor Bingham, Gloria Spielman, Vince Quinlivan for being early readers, sounding boards and for sharing their expertise.

Much appreciation to Paul Corney, President of CILIP and everyone at CILIP, the Library and Information Association, who have really engaged with this book and for that I am so grateful. A special thanks must go to Gemma Wood and Natalie Jones at CILIP, whose enthusiasm, contacts and passion for libraries knows no bounds.

I really enjoyed speaking with Dr Sarah Pyke and Professor Shelley Trower, who put together an absolutely fascinating oral history project called Living Libraries, documenting public libraries in the words of people who use, work and run them. Do check out: https://www.livinglibraries.uk

All the staff at Tower Hamlets Local History Library and Archives. I was the first person in through the doors when they reopened after the first lockdown. The records that the real librarians of the war years, George F. Vale and Stanley Snaith left were so evocative and such a source of joy and courage. I would have struggled to write this book based on a true story without the fantastic local history libraries and their staff, who act as co-pilots, helping me to navigate my way into the past.

Enormous thanks as always to Sandra Scotting from Stairway to Heaven, for being such a support to me. For more information on the Bethnal Green Tube Disaster please visit www.stairwaytoheavenmemorial.org

Thanks Glyn Robbins and Louise Raw for orchestrating the campaign to save the library and for being so supportive of this book.

I would like to thank everyone whom I interviewed during my various trips to Jersey, especially Ann Dunne, all the staff at Jersey Archives, Age UK, Eric Blakeley, Jenny Lecoat, Edward Jewell Chief Librarian of St Helier Library, Howard Baker, The Channel Islands Occupation Society (CIOS), writer and resident Gwyn Garfield-Bennett and Deborah Carr. And especially to all the occupation survivors who shared those dark days with me – Bob Le

Sueur, Leo Harris, Maggie Moisan, Audrey Anquetil, Don Dolbel – my profound thanks and admiration. My interest in the story was sparked on a visit to Jersey for the Jersey Literary Festival. This is truly an island simmering with stories. I have amassed more material than could ever be condensed into the last chapter of this book.

So much gratitude to my writer friends, whom I love dearly. Always there with warmth, wisdom and wine!

And finally to my irrepressible editor Kimberley Atkins and Kate Burke my agent – *the dream team*! I have so much respect and admiration for these women and everyone at Hodder & Stoughton who helped bring this book to life.

_____ This book was created by _____
Hodder & Stoughton

Founded in 1868 by two young men who saw that the rise in literacy would break cultural barriers, the Hodder story is one of visionary publishing and globe-trotting talent-spotting, campaigning journalism and popular understanding, men of influence and pioneering women.

For over 150 years, we have been publishing household names and undiscovered gems, and today we continue to give our readers books that sweep you away or leave you looking at the world with new eyes.

Follow us on our adventures in books . . .
🐦 @HodderBooks 👍/HodderBooks 📷 @HodderBooks

HODDER &
STOUGHTON